The Separation

By the same author:

The Separation

Christopher Priest

Old Earth Books
Baltimore † 2005

THE SEPARATION

Published by Old Earth Books
Post Office Box 19951
Baltimore, Maryland 21211
www.oldearthbooks.com

Book Design by Robert T. Garcia
Garcia Publishing Services
919 Tappan Street, Woodstock, Illinois 60098
www.gpsdesign.net

10 9 8 7 6 5 4 3 2

ISBN: 1-882968-33-6

To Paul Kincaid

PART ONE
1999

1

The rain was falling steadily on Buxton that Thursday afternoon in March, the town veiled by drifting low clouds, grey and discouraging. Stuart Gratton was sitting at a small table in the brightly lit bookshop window with his back to the street, but from time to time he turned to look outside at the slow-moving cars and trucks, the pedestrians splashing along with their faces averted, umbrellas low over their shoulders.

On the table before him was a glass of wine which he had almost finished drinking and next to it a half-empty half-bottle of hock. Beside the wine glass was a narrow-necked flute, with a single red rose standing upright in the water. On the table to his right was a pile of unsold copies of his most recent hardcover book, **The Exhausted Rage**, an oral history of the experiences of some of the men who took part in Operation Barbarossa, the German invasion of the Soviet Union in 1941. To his left, on the edge of the table, were two smaller piles of unsold copies of his books, both paperback editions reissued to coincide with the new hardcover. One of the titles was **The Last Day of War**, the book published in 1981 which had established his reputation and which had been in print more or less ever since. The other was called **The Silver Dragons**, another oral history, this one recounted by some of the soldiers and airmen who took part in the Sino-American war in the mid-1940s.

His ballpoint pen lay on the table next to his hand.

The manager of the bookshop, an attentive and clearly embarrassed man whose name Gratton remembered only as Rayner, was standing beside him when the signing session had begun, half an hour earlier, but he had been called away to attend to other business a few minutes before. Now Gratton could see him on the far side of the shop, apparently involved in some problem with the till or PC. The area manager from his publishers, who was supposed to come along to support Gratton at the signing, had called on his mobile to say there had been a traffic accident on the M1 and that he was going to be late. The bookshop, situated in a side street but close to the main department- and chain-stores in the centre of Buxton, was not busy. People came in from the rain from time to time, looked curiously at him and at the poster on the wall beside him announcing his signing, but none of them seemed interested in buying any of his books. One or two of them even shied away when they realized why he was sitting there.

It had not been like this when the signing began: two or three people had been waiting for him, including a friend of his, Doug Robinson, who had magnanimously driven over from his home in Sheffield to give moral support. Doug even bought one of the paperbacks, saying he needed to replace his old, worn-out copy. Gratton gratefully signed that, as well as the copies requested by the other customers, but now all of them were gone. By arrangement, Doug would be waiting for him in the bar of The Thistle, two doors down from the bookshop. Rayner, the manager, had asked him to sign some extra copies, a few 'for stock,' and three or four more for mail-order customers who had ordered the books in advance, but in effect that was that. Somewhere, somehow, people must be buying his books because his work attracted consistently good sales and in his field Gratton was considered a leading author. However, few of his readers appeared to be in Buxton during that afternoon of dismal rain.

Gratton was regretting having agreed once again to a signing session. He had undertaken similar stints in the past, so he should have known what was likely to happen. What made this one worse was the fact that he had cut short a research trip abroad to be home in time for the appointment. He was jet-lagged from the long flight across the Atlantic, he was also tired from lack of sleep overnight and he was feeling oppressed by the backlog of work which had accumulated while he was away. In his introspective mood he suddenly remembered his wife Wendy, who had died two years before. Wendy liked this shop and used to buy most of her books here. He had hardly been back since her death. There had been obvious changes in the meantime: new shelving and cabinets, brighter lighting, a few tables and chairs where customers could sit and read.

Still with more than twenty minutes to go before the signing session was officially at an end, Gratton saw a woman coming into the shop from the street, a large padded envelope under her arm. She looked quickly around the shop, spotted him sitting at his table and walked across to him. For a moment they stared at each other. Her hair and coat, and the padded envelope, were rain-damp. There was a fleeting illusory sense that he had seen her before, that they had met somewhere.

'I'd like to buy one of these, please,' she said, reaching forward to select a paperback of **The Last Day of War**. Droplets of water fell on the table. 'Do I pay for it here?'

'No, you have to take it to the till,' Gratton said, pleasantly surprised to be doing something at last. 'Would you like me to sign it for you?'

'Yes, please. You are Stuart Gratton, aren't you?'

'I am,' he said, opening the cover and beginning to inscribe the title page.

'My father was one of your most avid readers before he died,' she said in a rush, while he was still signing. 'He thought you were doing important work, recording those experiences.'

'Would you like me to dedicate the book to you? With your name?'

'No . . . just sign it, please.' She turned her head to see what he was writing, then said, 'It was about my father, actually. Coming here to see you.' She nodded towards the poster on the wall next to him. 'I was in this shop the other day and I found out you'd be here. I only live in Bakewell, so it was too good an opportunity to miss.'

Gratton finished inscribing the book by writing in the date. He handed the copy back to the woman. 'Many thanks,' he said.

'Dad was in the war too,' she said, still speaking quickly. 'He wrote down his experiences in notebooks and I wondered if you might be interested . . .?' She indicated the padded envelope she was carrying.

'I wouldn't be able to get them published for you,' Gratton said.

'It's not that. I thought you might be interested to read them. I saw your advertisement.'

'Where was that?'

'An old wartime colleague of Dad's sent it to me. He'd spotted it in a magazine called *RAF Flypast*.'

'Your father wasn't called Sawyer, was he?'

'Yes, he was. I'm a Sawyer. That's my maiden name. I saw your ad and I thought that Dad's notebooks might be what you're looking for.'

'And he was in Bomber Command during the war?'

'Yes, that's the point.' She pushed the large envelope towards him. 'Look, I have to tell you that I haven't read Dad's notebooks myself. I've never been able to decipher his handwriting. He didn't say much about them but he spent hours in his room, writing away. He retired ages ago, lived on his own for years, but towards the end he moved in with me and my husband. He was with us for the last two and half years of his life. He was always scribbling away in his notebooks. I never really paid much attention, because it was keeping him out of my hair. Maybe you've had a similar experience . . .?'

'No. Nothing like that. Both my parents died some years ago.'

'Well, Dad told me once that he'd put down everything in writing, his whole life, his time in the air force, everything he did. That's the other problem for me. Most of what he wrote about is the war, which I've never found interesting. But then I was sent your ad — so, well, here I am.'

Gratton regarded the damp padded envelope lying on the tabletop.

'These are the originals?' he said.

'No, the originals are a couple of dozen ordinary exercise books. They're lying around in his old bedroom, gathering dust. I can let you have the originals if you need them, but what I'm giving you are photocopies. I thought if the material turned out to be no use you could have the pages recycled.'

'Well, thank you . . . er . . .?'

'Angela Chipperton, Mrs Angela Chipperton. Do you suppose Dad is the man you're interested in?'

'It's impossible to say until I've read what he wrote. I'm curious about something I came across. Sawyer's not an unusual name, as you no doubt realize. I've already received ten or twelve responses to the advertisement, but I've been away and I haven't been able to get around to any of them yet. I'll read your father's memoir as soon as I can. Have you left an address where I can contact you?'

'There's a covering letter with my address.'

'I'm really grateful to you, Mrs Chipperton,' Gratton said. He stood up.

'I hate to ask you,' she said, while they were still shaking hands. 'But is there likely to be . . . I mean, if the material turns out to be suitable for publication and there was the possibility of payment, would I —?'

'I'll do what I can and let you know what I think. But in practice, war memoirs don't have a general market these days, unless they're by someone famous.'

'You see, when I saw your ad I wondered if that might be it. To me he was just Dad, but I thought perhaps he'd been involved in something important during the war.'

'I don't think so. I've never seen references to anyone called Sawyer in the standard works on the war. I think he must have been just an ordinary airman. That's why I've been advertising for information, to see what I can turn up. There might be nothing in it. And of course, your father might not be the man I'm looking for. But if anything comes along I'll certainly let you know.'

She left soon after that and Gratton resumed his vigil in the bookshop window.

2

The next day Gratton found that Mrs Chipperton's padded envelope contained more than three hundred unnumbered pages, photocopied, as she said, from ruled exercise books. The ruled lines of the pages had come out of the copier with almost equal density to the words themselves, promising hours of eyestrain ahead, the occupational hazard of researchers of popular histories. The handwriting was small and some of it at least was regular and clear, but there were several long passages where the writing became wilder and less legible. Other parts of it appeared to have been drafted in pencil, because they had photocopied badly. Gratton glanced through a few of the pages, then placed them back inside their padded envelope. He took out the covering letter and put it in his correspondence file. She lived in Bakewell, a small Derbyshire town on the other side of Buxton, on the road to Chesterfield.

So far he had learned of the existence of about a dozen officers and men called Sawyer who flew operationally against German targets in RAF Bomber Command during the 1940s. Nearly all of them were dead now, and few of them had left little more than letters or photographs as records of their experiences. Gratton had already been able to eliminate most of them. The rest would need more detailed investigation. Mrs Chipperton's late father looked promising, but the sheer size of his text was daunting.

Gratton put the padded envelope on top of the pile next to his desk. He would have to get around to reading everything later. Much of the material sent in response to the Sawyer enquiry was waiting for him on his return from abroad, an additional workload he should have anticipated. His trip this time had been a long and circular one, taking in several interviews and a great deal of archival research. Much travelling had been necessary: first to Cologne, Frankfurt and Leipzig, then from Germany across to Belarus and Ukraine — Brest, Kiev and Odessa — then north to Sweden; finally ten edgy days in the USA, visiting Washington DC, Chicago, St Louis, beset by suspicious officials every time he boarded one of the great transcontinental trains or, the one time he took a short internal flight, when he passed through an airport. It was increasingly difficult for foreign visitors to travel about in the USA, partly because of the currency restrictions but mainly because of a general distrust of anyone from Europe. Another occupational hazard was what Gratton considered this to be, but the long delays created by US Customs & Immigration when entering or leaving the US were becoming a substantial nuisance. Beyond the aggravations of travel his researches involved the usual itinerary of old men and, increasingly often these days, of their widows or grown-up children.

It was gratifying, though, to keep being reminded how much in demand his work still was. In addition to the mountain of letters and packages lying in the hallway for him on his return, there were several hundred e-mails stored on his server in-box, and a score or more messages were waiting on the answering machine. Most of the recorded messages sounded vexed because they hadn't been able to get through to him on his mobile number: it was a plus or a minus, depending on your point of view, that European cellphones were still unusable in the US while deregulation was being fought over.

Gratton worked for two days on his backlog, glad to be home and free to work once more. He labelled and indexed his most recent tapes, then parcelled them up to be sent to the transcription agency. While he was doing so, he again noticed the huge Sawyer manuscript. He was tempted by the detail he glimpsed in certain passages. It would save time in the long run if he had it transcribed professionally — the agency he used had someone there who specialized in deciphering holograph manuscripts. Once he had thought of doing it there was no going back. He wrote to Mrs Chipperton and asked her to send him the originals of the notebooks. He enclosed a formal copyright release note that would allow him to have the transcription made and later let him quote from the manuscript if he needed to.

All this made him think again about the Sawyer problem. On his fourth morning at home he sat down at his computer and carefully composed a letter to one of his earlier interview subjects.

3

Captain Samuel D. Levy Ret'd
P.O. Box 273
Antananarivo
Republic of Masada

Dear Captain Levy,

I hope you will remember me: I came to interview you in Antananarivo some eight years ago, about your experiences flying with the USAAF in the Chinese and Manchurian campaigns in 1942-43. You were kind enough to give me several hours of your time. From these conversations I extracted some excellent material about the fire-bomb missions in which you took part: the raids on the Japanese strongholds at Nanking and Ichang. I used most of that in my history of the campaign called **The Silver Dragons: the 9th US Army Air Force**

in China. I recall that at the time I asked my publishers to send you a complimentary copy of the book. I realize that I never heard from you afterwards, so in case you did not receive the earlier copy I am enclosing one from the recently reissued paperback edition. As in the earlier editions, your interview features prominently in the first few chapters.

Let me get to the point of this letter.

I have recently become interested in the life and career of a man who was involved in the war, whose name was Flight Lieutenant Sawyer. (I don't know his first name, or even his initials.) A certain mystery attends Mr Sawyer. I found out about it through Winston Churchill. I came across a brief description of the puzzle in the second volume of Churchill's wartime memoirs, **The German War: Volume II, Their Finest Hour**. I am enclosing a photocopy of the relevant extract. It is from Appendix B of that volume, which consists of Churchill's prime ministerial minutes and memoranda from the period. This minute, sent to various members of his war cabinet, is dated April 30, 1941. Churchill describes Sawyer as a conscientious objector who was also an operational RAF bomber pilot. He found it intriguing and so did I. What also interested me about the passage was that I had never come across any mention of Mr Sawyer in my other researches. Churchill himself never refers to the mystery anywhere else.

From Churchill, I can work out that Sawyer was a serving officer in the RAF in 1941 — probably before then, possibly after. This information rang a distant bell, which made me scour through the interview material with ex-RAF members I have on file. Sure enough, on one of your own tapes I came across a passing reference to a man called Sawyer. You were talking about your background, before you went to the USA to join the Commonwealth Wing of the USAAF for the American invasion of the Japanese islands. That must have been in the summer of 1941, which was when most ex-RAF men signed on with the Americans.

It therefore seems likely to me that you were still serving in the RAF in April, which is a coincidence I can't ignore. From the context of the tape, it sounds as if the Sawyer you knew in Britain was an officer, perhaps a pilot, but it is not clear whether he was in your own crew. I should love to find out if the Sawyer you knew was the one Churchill was briefly interested in. If so, did you by any chance know Sawyer well and what memories do you have of him?

I'm sure you have a busy life and therefore I do not expect you to reply to this letter at great length. If there's enough in the Sawyer story, I would hope to get a contract out of my publisher for a book about him. If that comes to pass and you would prefer it, I would be able to make a special trip to Madagascar to visit you again and record your memories on tape in the same way as we did before.

I have only just begun to research Mr Sawyer, so there will be many other avenues to explore. Your possible connection with him is a long shot. There must have been many chaps in the RAF with that name. I have advertised fairly widely in the usual specialist and veterans' magazines. The main responses, twelve so far, have come from former RAF members or their families. However, it does seem there was rather more to the man than his time in the RAF, so I shall be fascinated to learn anything you are able to pass on to me.

I hope this letter finds you well and active and that you are continuing to enjoy your retirement in that beautiful house I was privileged to visit last time. I look forward with intense interest to hearing from you.

Yours sincerely,
Stuart Gratton

4

Stuart Gratton was born during the late evening of May 10, 1941. He was about three weeks premature, but otherwise his birth was normal. He grew up in the post-war years, a time of great social and political change in Britain, but because he was a boy at school for most of those crucial years, he was hardly aware of what was going on in the wider world.

For him, the war against Germany was an event that affected his parents' generation, something that bonded people of that age in a way that he never really understood while a child. The most interesting and obvious legacy of the war, from his point of view, was the immense amount of physical damage that had been caused to most of the major towns and cities in Britain by the German bombing. Throughout his childhood he was aware of public rebuilding and restoration programmes — but, even so, hundreds of acres of the city of Manchester, close to where Gratton was brought up, remained unrepaired for many years. Even in the strategically unimportant village where he was living, traces of the war remained for a long time. A quarter of a mile from the family home there was an area of derelict land where he and his friends regularly played. They knew of it as the 'gun base,' a huge zone of concrete aprons and underground shelters, all now in ruins, which for the period of the war had been an anti-aircraft gun emplacement.

Only later, as Gratton's adult awareness began to dawn, did his interest in the events of the war start to grow. The beginning was the historical accident of his birth date. To many historians, May 10, 1941 was the culminating date of the war, the day that hostilities ended, even though the treaty itself was not signed until a few days later. His mother certainly treated his birthday as significant, always talking about her memories of the war each year as the date came around.

Gratton became a history teacher after he left school and university, working with a growing enthusiasm for the subject, but as the years went by his interest in a teaching career diminished. He was married in 1969 and for a few years he and his wife Wendy, another teacher, lived in a series of rented flats close to their respective schools. During the 1970s two sons were born. Trying to help make ends meet, Gratton began writing books of popular or oral history, concentrating at first on local people's memories of the Blitz. What fascinated him about the war period was the stoic nature of the British as they suffered the news of military setbacks and the terrible experience of the bombing of civilians, still glumly relishing their traumatic memories years after the war. By the seventies, life for most ordinary people in Britain had been transformed by the post-war boom, yet the survivors of those dark days still seemed to think of them as a defining experience.

Although his early books did sell reasonably well, especially in the localities where they were based, they never provided more than a minor supplement to the family income. Gratton tried broadening his interests, and in the seventies he wrote a straightforward history of the Sino-American War and the way in which the sequence of apparent military successes against Mao, after the invasion of Japan, had led to the economic and social stagnation of the USA. The deep American recession had been a problem when he wrote the book, as it still was today. That book received respectful views and was stocked on the reference shelves of most libraries in the UK, but again did little to change the Gratton family finances.

In 1981, Gratton's adoptive father Harry died, leaving Gratton the house where he still lived, a large stone-built cottage in a village on the outskirts of Macclesfield. In the same year, Gratton published the book that was to make his name and transform his finances: **The Last Day of War**.

In the introduction to the book Gratton argued that the war between Britain and Germany lasted for exactly one year, from May 10, 1940 until May 10, 1941. Although Britain and France had declared war on Germany at the beginning of September 1939, there was no serious fighting before the following May. Until then there were only skirmishes, some of them huge and destructive but not in themselves representing all-out war. It was the period an isolationist American senator named William E. Borah dubbed the 'phony war.'

On May 10, 1940 three significant events occurred. In the first place, the Germans invaded the Low Countries and France, eventually forcing the British army to evacuate from France. Secondly, the first air bombing of civilians took place, on the German university town of Freiburg-im-Breisgau. Although the bombing turned out to be accidental, it began a series of reprisal raids that led ultimately to the saturation bombing of cities by both sides. Finally, on May 10, 1940 the Prime Minister of Great Britain, Neville Chamberlain, resigned. He was replaced by Winston Churchill.

Exactly one year later, Britain still stood alone against Germany, but the war had moved on into an entirely different and more complex state.

By 1941, Germany was at the height of its military power. German troops occupied most of Europe and with its Vichy French ally dominated a huge area of Africa and the Middle East. Germany also controlled the Balkans, including Bulgaria, Yugoslavia and most of Greece. The first Jews in Poland had been rounded up and were being moved to ghettos in Warsaw and other large cities. Italy had joined the war on the German side. The USA was neutral, but was supplying ships, aircraft and guns to the British. The Soviet Union was in alliance with Germany. Japan, also allied to Germany, was embroiled in a war in China and Manchuria and was severely weakened by oil sanctions imposed on her by the USA.

On the night of May 10, 1941, Britain and Germany launched devastating bombing attacks against each other. The RAF raided Hamburg and Berlin, causing extensive damage to both cities, although particularly to Hamburg. At the same time, the Luftwaffe carried out the most destructive bombing attack of the war, with nearly seven hundred aircraft dropping high-explosive bombs and incendiary canisters on wide areas of London. But out of the sight of most people, hidden also from history, several small events were taking place that night. One of these events had been his own birth, in the very house in Cheshire where he was living once more.

Driven initially by curiosity, later by the sense that he had a good book in the making, Stuart Gratton set out to discover what people had been doing on that day.

5

On May 10, 1941, Pilot Officer Leonard Cheshire, DSO DFC, was on a Norwegian cargo ship, crossing the North Atlantic in convoy from Liverpool to Montreal. He was a serving pilot in RAF Bomber Command, but having reached the end of his first tour of duty he volunteered to act as an air-ferry pilot, flying lend-lease American bombers across the Atlantic to Britain. That night he was playing cards with other volunteers. Cheshire told Stuart Gratton that he remembered that after the game he went up on deck for a breath of fresh air and stood at the ship's rail for several minutes, watching the dark shape of the ship closest to his own, sailing a parallel course a few hundred yards away. Someone was also on the deck of that ship — Cheshire saw the man light a cigarette, causing a sudden flare of light that he was convinced could have been spotted by an enemy plane or ship from a great distance. (Cheshire told Stuart Gratton that because of the armistice he stayed on in the USA until the end of that summer. He helped set up the Commonwealth Flight for the USAAF, in which demobilized RAF aircrew were encouraged to bring their combat experience to aid the USA in its preemptive air strikes against Japanese expansionism. Although tempted to join the USAAF himself, Cheshire instead returned to Britain to take part in Operation Maccabeus, the British sea- and air-evacuation of European Jews to Madagascar. He acted as both a pilot and administrator during the long and dangerous operation. When he returned to civilian life in 1949 he set up charitable homes for critically ill ex-servicemen and others.)

John Hitchens was a telegraph operator for the Post Office, living in the north of England. On May 10 he travelled to London by train to watch a football match. The Football Association Cup had been suspended in 1939 when war was declared. However, by 1941 a certain amount of competitive soccer was being played again. On that day the final of the Football League War Cup was being played at Wembley, between Arsenal and Preston North End. More than sixty thousand fans attended the match, which finished in a

1-1 draw. Most of the crowd came from London, but the ones who travelled down for the match were able to be on their homeward trains by the evening. Hitchens was on one of the last trains to leave Euston Station; he recalled hearing the sirens as the train pulled out. (John Hitchens worked in Eastern Europe between 1942 and 1945, helping to repair and maintain telephone networks in the wake of Operation Barbarossa. He returned to Britain in 1945 and retired from the Post Office in 1967.)

Dr Joseph Goebbels, Reich Minister of Public Enlightenment and Propaganda, spent the day in his office in Berlin. He issued new penalties for illegally listening to BBC broadcasts. He received the latest shipping-loss figures, in which it was claimed the British had lost half a million tons during April. He stepped up his broadcasting effort directed at Iraq. He closed down the German radio service to South Africa. In the evening Dr Goebbels returned to his estate in Lanke. He was visited by people from the film world and they watched a recent British newsreel: they agreed that it was 'bad and in no way comparable with ours.' They then watched two films in colour, one German and one American. A discussion of film-making problems followed, interrupted by an air-raid warning. (Dr Goebbels remained at his position until 1943. He published the first of his *Diaries* in 1944, with subsequent volumes appearing at yearly intervals. He later became a noted documentary film-maker and newspaper columnist. He retired from public life in 1972.)

Flight Lieutenant Guy Gibson, DFC, was based at RAF West Malling, in Kent. On the night in question he and his navigator, Sergeant Richard James, were flying a Bristol Beaufighter on night-fighter patrol over London. A heavy Luftwaffe raid was in progress. He and Sergeant James saw two Heinkel 111 bombers and launched an attack on them, but the Beaufighter's cannon failed to fire. Gibson returned to base, had the weapons checked, then went back on patrol again. There were no other incidents that night. (Gibson also joined Operation Maccabeus after the end of the war, piloting more evacuation flights than any other single volunteer. He was involved in the Toulouse incident, in which the plane he was flying, carrying more than fifty German Jews to Madagascar, was one of several in a formation attacked by French warplanes operated by the National Front. He received civilian awards for his bravery and leadership on this occasion. Gibson afterwards went into electrical engineering, entering politics with the General Election of 1951. He became Tory member for West Bedfordshire and was PPS to a Home Office minister in the R. A. Butler government. Gibson was knighted in 1968. In the early 1970s Sir Guy led the Conservative 'No' campaign against

Britain joining the European Union. He returned to business in 1976 after he lost his parliamentary seat in the General Election.)

Pierre Charrier, a member of the Free French forces based in London, celebrated the feast of Jeanne d'Arc at Wellington Barracks, the first time the festival was commemorated outside France. The ceremonies were completed at Westminster Cathedral, where M. Charrier was still present when the first bombs of the night began to fall. He returned safely to his lodgings in Westbourne Road, although he was badly shaken by the experience. (M. Charrier went back to Paris at the end of 1941, where he became a government official involved in post-war reconstruction. He later became a European Commissioner.)

Philip Harrison, an under-secretary at the British Embassy in Chungking, was working in his office when the building was attacked by Japanese warplanes. Although Harrison was not hurt in the raid, the ambassador, Sir Archibald Clark Kerr and several members of his staff received minor cuts and bruises. The building suffered structural damage but after repairs normal work resumed soon afterwards. (Mr Harrison continued his diplomatic career until 1965, when he retired. He was British Ambassador to the USA during Adlai Stevenson's presidency, 1957-1960. Harrison died in 1966; his daughter was interviewed by Stuart Gratton.)

Kurt Hofmann was a civilian test pilot working for the Messerschmitt company at a small airfield in eastern Germany. On May 10, 1941, under conditions of immense secrecy, Hofmann piloted the maiden flight of a revolutionary new type of aircraft. It was an experimental fighter powered by a jet turbine engine. The prototype Messerschmitt Me-163 flew at 995 kph (621 mph) before landing safely. This aircraft was widely used on the Russian Front from late in 1943 until the end of hostilities, becoming the standard ground-attack fighter-bomber. It was found to be superior not only to early marques of the Russian MiG-15 jet fighter, but also to the North American Sabre that was entering service with the USAAF at the same time. (Kurt Hofmann later rejoined the Luftwaffe, where he flew Me-163s for several months. He was wounded when shot down in 1944. After the Treaty of the Urals brought an end to hostilities he returned to Germany and became technical director of the civil airline Lufthansa.)

Sub-Lieutenant Mike Janson was an officer on the Royal Navy destroyer *HMS Bulldog*. They were in the North Atlantic, returning to Liverpool, carrying in the secure hold an Enigma coding machine, together with the *Offizier* procedures and settings. This invaluable prize had been seized the previous day from U-110 by Lieutenant David Balme, leader of the boarding party from *Bulldog*, after she and the Royal Navy sloop *HMS Broadway* had attacked and disabled the U-boat. Although Mike Janson had not been a member of the boarding party he was officer of the watch when the U-boat had first been sighted. U-110 sank while being towed by the British. The taking of the Enigma was a pivotal moment in the struggle to intercept and decode encrypted orders from the German High Command. (After the war, Mike Janson continued to serve with distinction in the peacetime Royal Navy until his retirement with the rank of Rear Admiral in 1960.)

The RAF was active over Europe on the night of May 10/11, 1941. Five Bristol Blenheims attacked shipping off La Pallice in western France — no ships were hit and no aircraft were lost. (Sergeant Andy Martin was the navigator of one of the Blenheims. To Stuart Gratton he described the flight bitterly in terms of great duration and danger, with no apparent purpose or effect.) The shipyards, power station and central area of the north German port of Hamburg were attacked by a mixed force of one hundred and nineteen bombers. Thirty-one people were killed and nearly a thousand others were injured or bombed out of their homes. Fires were started in several parts of the town, destroying the Kösters department store, a large bank and the Hamburg Stock Exchange. Four British aircraft were lost. (Wolfgang Merck was a fireman in Hamburg at the time of the raid and he described a night of much confusion and activity, but in the morning the authorities discovered there was not as much permanent damage as they had feared while the bombing was going on.) Another twenty-three RAF aircraft went to Berlin, causing damage in widely spread areas. Three aircraft failed to return. (Hanna Wenke, a schoolgirl in 1941, described a hot and uncomfortable night in the shelter beneath her parents' apartment building, with no apparent damage in her suburb of Berlin the next day.) In addition to the main bombing efforts another twenty-five RAF bombers were sent on minor operations, including minelaying in the Kattegat; no losses were reported.

Police Sergeant Terry Collins was on firewatching duty on the night of May 10/11 at the Houses of Parliament, with particular responsibility, along with other members of Westminster Police, for the safety of Victoria Tower. After nightfall the Luftwaffe launched what turned out to be the biggest raid of all on London. Breaking with their normal practice of concentrating on the industrial areas and docks in the East End, the German bombers ranged far and wide across London, with few areas of the capital entirely free from bombing. The most concerted attack took place in the West End and surrounding districts, areas which until this night had been left relatively unscathed by the bombing. More than one thousand four hundred Londoners were killed during the night and another one thousand eight hundred were injured. In excess of sixty thousand homes were destroyed or damaged; many important buildings or famous landmarks were devastated. The debating chamber of the House of Commons was ruined by explosion and fire. The BBC took a direct hit, but managed to continue its activities during and after the raid. Westminster Abbey sustained hits by at least fifteen incendiary devices. Buckingham Palace was hit. The British Museum was bombed. Big Ben was hit by a bomb, halting the chime but not the clock. Shops and offices the length of Oxford Street were burned out. Gas mains, sewers and telephone connections were seriously damaged. Victoria Tower, for which Sergeant Collins was responsible, was at the time shrouded in scaffolding for essential cleaning and repairs. The presence of so many wooden planks attached to the outer structure presented a serious fire risk. Shortly after midnight, a rain of incendiaries fell in the immediate vicinity. Most of those falling on the streets were dealt with swiftly, but one that lodged in the scaffolding close to the top of the tower continued to burn brightly. Sergeant Collins grabbed a heavy sandbag and climbed up the scaffolding ladders and platforms to reach the fire. After a strenuous climb, Sergeant Collins quickly extinguished the fire with the sand and returned to the ground. (He told Stuart Gratton that he thought no more about his actions until the following year, when he was awarded the George Cross. By this time he had moved to the British mandated territory of Madagascar, where he helped oversee civilian security matters during the transition. He remained on Madagascar throughout the upheavals caused by the struggle for independence. When the Republic of Masada was declared in 1962, Chief Superintendent Collins was forced to return home with the other British administrative and diplomatic officials.)

In the early evening of May 10, Rudolf Hess, Hitler's deputy, took off in a twin-engined Me-110D from the Messerschmitt factory's airfield in Augsburg, Bavaria. He carried with him a plan for peace between Britain and Germany, commissioned and authorized by Hitler, which Hess intended to deliver in person to Winston Churchill. He landed his plane in Holland for refuelling. Shortly after taking off again, his plane was intercepted by German fighters, which first attempted to make him land, then later tried to destroy his aircraft with machine-gun fire. Hess managed to elude them and headed out across the North Sea. The smaller fighters gave chase for a while, before dropping back. More Luftwaffe fighters, based in occupied Denmark, also took off in an attempt to intercept his aircraft. They returned to base, claiming that they had shot down his plane over the sea, but in spite of vivid descriptions and corroboration of each other's stories, the pilots were unable to provide conclusive proof. (Hess completed his mission to bring peace.)

Then, latterly, there was Flight Lieutenant Sawyer, RAF Bomber Command. Churchill said Sawyer was a registered conscientious objector who was also an operational bomber pilot. Churchill's memorandum to his departmental staff required them to discover how this came about. No official reply was recorded. Nearly sixty years later, Stuart Gratton, whose own family had a tradition of pacifism, sensed a story. What was it about? In particular, what might Sawyer have been doing on May 10, 1941?

PART TWO
1936—1945

1

I was a serving officer with RAF Bomber Command from the beginning of the Second World War. My entry into the service was by way of the University Air Squadron at Oxford, where I was a rowing blue at Brasenose College. In those early years I had two passions: one was rowing, the other was flying. I had no interest in war, no premonition that I might ever become involved in one. The events of the world went on beyond my restricted area of awareness, as they had done for most of my life. I know I was naïve and therefore badly prepared for the immense war in which we were all eventually caught up.

I should have known better. My father was a registered conscientious objector during the Great War, as the First World War was still called in the 1930s. A reserved and private man, my father would never have tried to force his own convictions on his children. Nevertheless, my brother Joe and I were brought up to believe that war was evil, something to be avoided at all costs. During the Second World War and the years after it, the prewar British policy of appeasing the Nazis became discredited and despicable, but my father would never have that. He maintained that the beginnings of appeasement lay in a humane and pragmatic economic policy, of not forcing Germany to meet her crippling reparations under the Versailles Treaty. Practically every member of the British government of those days had fought in the Great War and felt themselves under a duty to go to any lengths to avoid another. They sensed, perhaps, what Adolf Hitler always claimed: that it was the iniquities of Versailles that led to the second war.

The naïveté was therefore my own fault, because my interest in sport, in rowing, overshadowed everything else. I lived only for the moment and was totally focused on the sport I loved. During the years 1935 and 1936 I concentrated on a single aim: to qualify for the British team that would compete in the Olympic Games. My brother and I trained and practised with an almost obsessive energy.

To anyone who had seen us training, or who saw us competing, it might have seemed a foregone conclusion that we would be selected for the team. We were consistently on form and easily won most of the races we entered, but when you are there at the centre of the obsession you feel you can take nothing for granted. When Joe and I were finally selected, at the beginning of June 1936, it felt that this was quite simply the greatest news we would ever receive. We celebrated with friends in a number of Oxford pubs that night, but afterwards returned with single-minded dedication to our training.

My story of what happened to me during the war therefore begins in July 1936, when Joe and I set off together for the Berlin Olympics.

2

I was nineteen years old and although I had no way of knowing it then, it was not to be my only trip to Berlin. My later visits took place when I was in the RAF, at the controls of a bomber, peering down through darkness, smoke and cloud at the vast city below, releasing incendiaries on to the buildings and streets. That future was unimaginable to me in 1936.

I had been living away from our family home in Tewkesbury for less than a year. I went home most weekends and still collected my mail, clean laundry and a great deal of food for the following week. I had hardly grown up at all, so a journey out of England, especially one to Germany in that eventful year, was an adventure at the highest level.

As we headed for the south coast of England I was at the wheel of our equipment van, in itself another small step for me. I had only recently begun driving, as until then my brother Joe normally drove us around. All the trips I made before this had been short ones, mostly on the familiar roads between Oxford and Tewkesbury. I had gone no further south or east than to London and then in daylight. Now here I was, embarking on our adventure, driving our van slowly in the dark across the Downs towards Dover, with Joe dozing in the passenger seat beside me.

I wonder now if we should have gone on with that trip, but perhaps that is simply the luxury that goes with hindsight. In the small world of rowing, as in most sports, politics was a dirty word. It was easy to close yourself off from international events in the 1930s: there was no television, radio was not the force of journalistic independence it became during and after the war, and for most people the main source of information was whatever newspaper they happened to read. Joe and I rarely read any part of newspapers other than the sports pages. Britons in general closed their minds against Hitler and the Nazis, hoping they would go away. For people like Joe and myself, though, there should have been no such excuses. We were at university, surrounded by articulate and intelligent men and women with views on every subject, frequently aired. We knew well enough what was happening in Germany and that to take part in the Games could be construed as giving aid and comfort to the Hitler regime.

I knew this, but frankly I was not interested. The finest sportsmen and sportswomen from around the world would be in Berlin. It was going to be the only opportunity in my lifetime to compete in my chosen event at the highest level.

Joe did not think entirely alike, I should say. Whenever we discussed what we thought was happening in Germany we vehemently disagreed, but because we were both committed to the sport and had to work as a team we generally steered clear of the subject.

I loved rowing. I loved the strength I had in my body, the speed I could find, the agility with which I could move. I rowed every day that the weather allowed, sometimes alone for endurance development, but usually with Joe, training for speed, for coordination, for the simple familiarity of rowing together. We could never train too much, or enough. I knew I could always improve, always hone my muscles a little more. We competed in a sport in which winning margins were often measured in fractions of a second; there was no possible improvement that was so small we could safely neglect it.

Joe was just as committed. Everything I felt inside myself I could observe taking shape in him. Joe rowed in stroke. As we rowed, his body was only inches away from mine. His back filled my view, shoulders, arms, flowing to and fro, straining back with the main pull, recovering, sweeping forward, slicing the blades down into the water, putting on the pressure for the next stroke. When we rowed Joe's back became my inspiration, the powerful, functional muscles matching every movement I made as if we were somehow synchronized by an invisible power from above. I watched his back in the sunlight, in the rain, on grey days, when our coordination was perfect and when we could get nothing right. I watched it at rest as well as during the bursts of energy. I watched it, yet I rarely saw it properly. It was something on which to rest my gaze, a familiar and undisturbing sight while I concentrated on the mindless task of going faster than ever before. Joe and I became more than a team at such times — it was as if we were one person sharing two bodies.

People said we were the best coxless pairs team in the country. They invested great hopes in us, because rowing was a sport in which Britain excelled. The Olympic coxless pairs gold medallists in Los Angeles in 1932 had been Edwards and Clive, the British team, now retired from the sport.

Edwards and Clive were our heroes, but we were still expected to equal or better them.

So this was the consuming foreground of our lives. Youth is blind to the world around it, but obsessive youth is blinder still. Ignoring everything we trained intensively for the Games through the spring and early summer of 1936. Germany was re-arming, building an illegal air force and Hitler marched in his troops to occupy the Rhineland, but we were training on weights, sprinting and running, bringing our times down, getting the rhythm and the smoothness of the strokes right, learning when and how to burst with speed, when to consolidate our strength, how to take the shortest, straightest line in water that constantly flowed and eddied unpredictably beneath us. Then July came and it was time for us to travel to Germany.

In 1936 there was no combined embarkation of a national team wearing colours, as we see in the modern age. We were expected to make our own way to Berlin, so we carried our equipment in our own van, taking it in turns to drive.

3

I prowled about on the boat deck during the short sea-crossing to France. Joe was inside the lounge cabin and I did not see him again until the ship docked. I was wide awake, exhilarated by everything, but also concerned about the well-being of our two shells, lashed side by side to the roof of the van. We transported them everywhere like that, but never before had we taken them on board a ship. Watching the van being lowered by crane into the hold, the chains swinging, had been an uncomfortable moment of alarm. It reminded me how vulnerable they were and how damage to either of them could put us out of the competition.

I stared restlessly out to sea. I watched the two coasts between which we were slowly crossing. Somewhere in the middle of the Channel, with the lights of both England and France in clear view, it felt as if the sea had narrowed. Both coasts seemed to be almost within reach. I had never before realized how close our country actually was to the mainland of Europe. From this perspective the sea did not seem much wider than a big river. I stood at the rail amidships, thinking such thoughts, little appreciating — how could I have done? — what an important symbol of national security that short stretch of water was soon to assume for everyone in Britain.

Three hours later, with the early dawn breaking ahead of us, we were travelling eastwards away from Calais, along the French coast, heading for the border with Belgium.

Joe was driving. I curled up as comfortably as I could in the passenger seat beside him, closed my eyes and tried to snatch some sleep, but I was too excited. The strange French farmland was drifting magically past our windows, flat fields cultivated in exact, rectangular shapes, tall trees planted alongside the road. Ahead was the prospect of hundreds of miles more of sweet foreignness, Belgium and Holland and Germany.

4

The next day I was driving the van when we reached the border crossing between Holland and Germany.

It was a moment we had been looking forward to with mixed feelings. We were undoubtedly nervous of the Nazis, but at the same time, because our mother had been born in Germany, we had been brought up believing that Germany was a good and beautiful place, with a great civilization and culture. Frankly, we had no idea what to expect.

We had driven through the Dutch town of Eindhoven an hour or two before reaching the German border. The road was straight but perilously narrow, built up on embankments that ran between wide and uninteresting fields. Beyond Venlo we entered an area of woodland. After crossing the River Maas on a long bridge built of girders, we drove into the border zone, hidden where the road ran through a dense thicket of trees.

The officers on the Dutch side dealt with us quickly. After a perfunctory examination of our passports one of the officials raised the barrier and I drove across into the narrow strip of no man's land. We could see the German border post about a hundred yards ahead, where another long pole straddled the road. This one was painted with a triple spiral of red, black and white.

We drew up behind two other vehicles that were already waiting to cross, inching the van forward as each passed through the border ahead. When it was our turn, the officer, a rotund man wearing a uniform of green jacket, black trousers and highly polished black boots, saluted us with his arm raised at a smart angle.

'*Heil Hitler!*'

'*Heil Hitler!*' Joe responded.

Before leaving home we had received a letter sent by the Foreign Office to Games competitors, warning us of the behaviour and courtesies that would be expected of us in Germany. The Hitler salute was the first item on the list. To neglect or refuse to make it could lead swiftly to trouble, including imprisonment and deportation. Like most people in Britain we had seen newsreel film of the Nazis. To us, there was something unmistakably ridiculous and histrionic about it. Back in our rooms in college, Joe and I had Heil-Hitlered each other and our friends, goose-stepping about, laughing and laughing.

The guard lowered his arm stiffly. He leaned down by the passenger window and stared in at us. He was a youngish man, with pale blue eyes and a fair moustache, neatly cropped. He glanced suspiciously into the compartment of our van, where our luggage was stowed, leaned back with his hands on his hips while he regarded our shells strapped to the roof, then held out his plump fingers. Joe gave him our passports.

He looked through both documents slowly, turning the pages with precise motions of his fingers. The sun was beating down on me through the window. I began to feel anxious.

'[These passports are for the same man,]' he said, not looking up. '[J. L. Sawyer twice.]'

'[We have the same initials,]' I replied, beginning what was for us the familiar explanation. Joe was always Joe. I was sometimes called Jack, but usually JL. '[But our names —]'

'[No, I think not.]'

'[We are brothers.]'

'[You are both initialled J. L., I see! Some coincidence. Joseph, Jacob! That is how they name twins in England?]'

Neither Joe nor I said anything. The officer closed the second of our passports, but he did not hand them back.

'[You are going to the Olympic Games in Berlin,]' he said to me, looking across. I was in the driver's seat, but from his point of view the right-hand drive must have put me on the wrong side of the vehicle.

'[Yes, sir,]' I replied.

'[In which event do you propose to compete?]'

'[We are in the coxwainless pairs.]'

'[You have two boats. Only one is necessary.]'

'[One is for practice, sir. And as a reserve, in case of accident.]'

He opened our passports again, closely scrutinizing the photographs.

'[You are twins, you say. Brothers.]'

'[Yes, sir.]'

He turned away from us and walked to his office, a solid-looking wooden hut built beside the barrier. Several large red flags with the swastika emblazoned on a white circle hung from poles standing out at an angle from the wall. There was no wind in this sheltered spot surrounded by trees and the flags barely moved.

'What's he doing?'

'It's going to be all right, Jack. Relax . . . we haven't broken any rules.'

We could see the guard through the wide window at the front. He was before a high desk, turning the pages of a large, ledger-like book. Two other guards were also in there with him, standing back and watching. Behind us and beside us other vehicles were arriving at the border post, but they were being waved through by more guards after only short delays.

Presently our guard returned. He glanced briefly at the trucks grinding slowly past us.

'[English,]' he said. '[You speak German remarkably well. Have you visited the Reich before?]' He handed back our passports, directing his question deliberately at Joe. After the first salute, Joe had not spoken during the exchange. He continued to stare ahead, past the barrier pole, along the road that led into Germany. '[Do you speak German as well as your identical brother?]' the guard said loudly, banging his fingers on the window ledge.

'[Yes, sir,]' Joe said, smiling with sudden charm. '[No, we have not visited Germany before.]'

'[They teach German in your English schools?]'

'[Yes. But we also have a mother who was born in Germany.]'

'[Ah! That explains everything! Your mother is a Saxoner, I think! I knew I was right about your accent! Well, you will know that we are proud of our sportsmen in the Reich. You will find it difficult trying to beat them.]'

'[We are pleased to be here, sir.]'

'[Good. You may enter the Reich.] *Heil Hitler!*'

He stepped back. As we passed over a white line painted across the surface of the road, Joe made a perfunctory return raising of his arm, then wound up the window on his side. He said, with quiet bitterness, 'Heil bloody Hitler.'

'He was just doing his job.'

'He enjoys his work too much,' Joe said.

But soon after that we relapsed into silence, each of us absorbed by the unfamiliar scenery of northern Germany.

The sights we saw have since blended into a few memorable images. A lot of the landscape we passed through was forested, a conspicuous change from the vistas of flat farmland we had seen in Belgium and Holland. Although we went through several industrial towns — Duisburg, Essen, Dortmund, all of them shrouded in a thin, bitter-smelling haze that made our eyes sting — there was not enough variety to provide detailed memories. I was keeping a journal as we went along but of that journey I recorded only a couple of short paragraphs. Most of what I remember was a general sense of *being in Germany*, the place that was always being talked about in those days, and with it the vague sense of dread that the name gave rise to. The feeling was reinforced by the hundreds and thousands of swastika flags that were flying from almost every building or wall, a glare of red and white and black. Many long banners were strung across the autobahns and from building to building across the streets of the towns and villages. They bore inspiring messages, perhaps spontaneously created, but because of the insistent tone more likely to be the product of the party. There were slogans about the Saar, about the Rhineland, about the Versailles Treaty, about *Ausland* Germans — one banner which we saw many times in different places declared: '[WE ARE PLEDGED TO BLIND OBEDIENCE!].' There were few commercial advertisements on display anywhere and certainly there were no messages about the Olympic Games.

We drove and drove, trying to conserve our physical energy for the training and events which lay ahead, but inevitably, by the time we were approaching the environs of Berlin, we were done in. Joe wanted to find the British team headquarters straight away, to let them know we had arrived, but I was tired of driving, tired of being in the van. I simply wanted to find the house of the family friends with whom we had arranged to stay.

We argued listlessly about it for a while. Joe pointed out that we had arrived in the city before noon, that there were many hours of daylight left. I agreed that we should resume training as soon as possible, get our muscles back into competitive trim, but I stubbornly insisted that what I wanted to do was rest. In the end, we came to a sort of compromise. We located the British team headquarters, then went from there to the stretch of water near the Olympic Village at Grunewald, where sculling and rowing teams were to train. We unloaded our two shells and our oars into the boathouse that had been allocated to us. Next we drove to our friends' apartment, in Charlottenburg, a western suburb of Berlin. We did no training that first day we arrived.

5

Five years later, in the early summer of 1941, I was in hospital in rural Warwickshire. My plane, Wellington A-Able, had crashed into the North Sea about thirty miles from the English coast, somewhere off Bridlington. Only one other crew member was still on the aircraft with me when it went down: Sam Levy, the navigator, who had been hit in the head and leg by shrapnel. Sam and I managed somehow to scramble into an inflatable dinghy and we were picked up by a rescue boat many hours later.

I was in a fog of amnesia. I remembered almost nothing of even the bare outline I have described. Moments only of it remained, glimpsed in flashes, like fragments of a terrible dream.

I came slowly back to full consciousness, confused by what was going on in my mind, a conflict of violent images and what I could see around me in the physical world. I was in a bed, suffering intense pain, there were strangers coming and going, inexplicable actions were being performed on my body, bottles and trays were clattering, I experienced a sensation of helpless motion as I was wheeled somewhere on a trolley.

In my mind I saw or heard or remembered the deafening sound of the engines, brilliant flashes of light in the dark sky around us, a loud bang that was repeated whenever I moved my head, a shock of cold as the windscreen in front of my face was shattered by a bullet or a piece of shrapnel, voices on the intercom, the huge and terrifying surge of the sea, the cold, the terror.

I gradually emerged from the confusion, starting to make sense of what I saw around me.

I realized I was in a hospital, I remembered being on the plane, I knew other men had been with me. My legs hurt, my chest hurt, I was incapable of moving my left hand. I was taken from the bed, placed in a chair, returned to the bed. Medical staff came and went. I saw my mother's face, but the next time I opened my eyes she had gone again. I knew I was critically ill.

I tried getting answers about my illness from the staff, but as I slowly improved I realized that they would not give answers unless I asked questions. Before I could do that, I should have to formulate the enquiry in my mind. Before even that, I should have to be clear in my own mind what it was I wanted to know.

I worked backwards to find the memories I needed, learning as I went.

6

While we were in the Charlottenburg area of Berlin we stayed in a large apartment in Goethestrasse. By good chance it was not far from either the Olympic Stadium or the training area at Grunewald. The apartment was owned by close friends of my mother's family: Doktor Friedrich Sattmann, his wife Hanna and their daughter Birgit. They lived on the second floor of a huge, solidly constructed building which on one side looked down on the wide, tree-lined street where trams ran to and fro all day and much of the night, and on the other over an area of open parkland with many trees. Joe and I were given a room to ourselves at the back. We had a balcony where we could sit and enjoy coffee and cakes with the family. It was a home full of music: all three of the family played instruments. Frau Sattmann was an accomplished pianist, her husband played the bassoon. Seventeen-year-old Birgit was a violinist, studying under Herr Professor Alexander Weibl, at the Berliner Konservatorium. Everything, they told us, had been banned — they could not even go to friends' houses to play in their small ensemble, so they played together at home.

Herr Doktor Sattmann and his wife treated us with great generosity throughout our stay, but we were left in no doubt that the doctor's medical practice was no longer prospering. He said nothing about it to us, but every morning that we were staying in his apartment he announced formally that he was leaving to attend to his patients, then he would return only an hour or so later, reporting that only one or maybe two patients had required his services.

Frau Sattmann explained that it was no longer possible for her to continue to work at the publishing house where she had been a translator. Birgit, who was in only her first year of study at the Konservatorium, told us that she had become desperate to leave the country. I was dazzled by Birgit from the moment I set eyes on her: she was dark-haired and pretty and her face became illuminated when she smiled. She stayed shyly away from Joe and me.

Every evening Frau Sattmann would prepare a meal for Joe and myself, but the portions were small and the quality of the food was poor. Nothing was explained or described.

It was during our days in Berlin that I first began to feel the emerging differences between Joe and myself that were to have such a lasting impact on us both. When we were not training together I hardly ever saw him. While I maintained a fitness regime, he went on long solitary walks around Berlin, claiming it was for exercise, but often in the evenings I would hear him discussing what he had seen and the whole area of politics with Doktor Sattmann. I tried to join in, but in truth I was not all that interested, constantly thinking ahead to our race. I began to feel that Joe was not pulling his weight, that our existence as a team was in jeopardy.

Although Joe and I were physically identical, our personalities and general outlook could hardly have been more different. It's difficult to see yourself clearly, but I suppose it would be fair to say that my life from the age of about thirteen was a carefree, fairly selfish one. I enjoyed myself as much as I could, making the most of the advantages with which my well-off and indulgent parents provided me. Sport and flying were my main interests, with girlfriends, beer-drinking and a growing fascination with cars starting to compete for precedence as I grew older.

But Joe was different. He was always more serious than me and he put up an appearance of being more aware, more responsible. He thought about things and wrote them down, sometimes ostentatiously, I believed. He read books on subjects I knew nothing about and whose titles did not even interest me. While I went off and learned to fly, first as a private pupil, then later in the University Air Squadron, he said he was too busy studying and training. His taste in music was classical and serious, he had friends I thought of as secretive and sardonic, and he treated me with contempt and condescension if I tried to talk to him about subjects he was interested in.

Although I was on the receiving end of the rivalry I also understood what he was doing and even why he was doing it. If I was honest with myself I knew I felt much the same. If you grow up with an identical twin you are never allowed to forget it. As twins you suffer endless comments and jokes about the startling resemblance you bear for each other. People say they can't tell you apart, even though they probably could if they took the trouble. They ask you if you think the same things. Parents dress you alike, teachers treat you alike, friends and relatives give you identical gifts or say things that automatically include you both. Superficial differences, if they are spotted, are remarked on out of all proportion to their importance. Buried in this is the assumption that the two of you must also feel alike.

What you want, what you crave, is to be treated as a separate human being. It's almost impossible while you're a child, but as soon you reach your teenage years and adulthood approaches, you start trying to create a distance. You want an independent life, you want to discover information your twin does not have, you want to have secrets from him. It has nothing to do with a failure of love, or a growing dislike of someone once close to you. It is quite simply the need to become an individual.

In Berlin, I began to realize that the Games were all that remained to bind us together. I was often alone, training by myself, or hanging around the Sattmanns' apartment while Joe was out somewhere with the family. In the evenings he and the Herr Doktor would go to the study, while I was left to be entertained by Frau Sattmann and Birgit. I loved their music, the fineness of their playing together, and I relished how close this brought me to Birgit, but I could not stop thinking about what was happening between Joe and myself.

However, we were there to race and at least Joe applied himself conscientiously to that. Every morning we set about our training with energy, making full use of the skills and patience of Jimmy Norton, the British team coach. Once we settled down to the strangeness of the place — the unfamiliar sights of Berlin, the unpredictable currents in the water and, above all, the sounds of so many other teams training in their own languages, the voices echoing across the water from megaphones — we managed to concentrate on what we had come to do.

Gradually, slowly, our times and performance improved. Our first aim was to complete the measured course in a modest eight and a half minutes, knowing that Edwards and Clive had won their medal in a fraction under eight minutes, although that was on a downstream course. Earlier in the summer, similarly downstream on the Thames near Oxford, Joe and I had cleared eight minutes five. We knew that this was not our limit, not the best we could do. Athletic performance is all about gradual improvement, not suddenly achieving an outstanding performance in a fluke that cannot be repeated. For the past three months we had been steadily building our speed, reducing our times.

Mr Norton encouraged us to focus our minds forward to the day of the heats, trying to think ourselves into the first race, leaving the times to set themselves.

The heat was five days away. On the first full day of training our best time was eight minutes thirty, on lake water without perceptible currents.

The next day we covered four full courses: our best time was eight minutes twenty-two.

By the fourth day we could touch eight minutes nineteen every time we tackled the course.

7

Five years later I was in hospital in rural Warwickshire, working backwards to memory. I understand now that my memories arrived in the wrong order. Maddeningly, I remembered the end of the incident first, with no recollection of what had led up to it.

There was a slamming noise, a loud crash made by the shrapnel as it burst through the fuselage a couple of feet behind me, low down, somewhere underneath, bursting through into the Wellington's belly. Just by the navigator's table, close by the wing spar. The rear gunner, Kris Galasckja, crawled forward from his turret and reported over the intercom that Sam Levy looked as if he was dead. There was blood covering his maps, Kris said. I was watching the dials, seeing the airspeed fall away, the altimeter begin a slow, unstoppable circling decline, our precious height being eaten away gradually by gravity's suck.

Down below I glimpsed the irregular black line of the German coast as we limped west, across the North Sea towards England.

A few minutes later Kris came back on the intercom and said he thought Sam was going to be all right. He'd taken a bang on the head but was breathing OK. Kris said he was going to drag him around so he could lie more comfortably on the floor, next to the hatch.

I ordered Kris back into his turret to keep an eye open for fighters. They often patrolled over the sea, waiting for our bombers as we straggled home out of formation. For the next few moments I could feel the crew moving clumsily around in the fuselage behind me, the trim of the plane affected by their changing positions. No one said anything, but I could hear their breathing in the intercom headphones clamped against my ears.

By the time they settled down our height had fallen to below twelve thousand feet and was still dropping slowly. There was no extra power in the engines. The flaps were so stiff I could hardly move the stick. The crew began jettisoning unused ammunition, kit, flares, anything removable, the cold night air blasting in not only through the holes in the fuselage but from the open hatch behind me.

We droned on, following our long downwards trajectory with its inevitable end, delaying it as long as possible. An hour passed, deluding me into thinking we might be going to make it after all. We were down to four thousand feet by then. The port engine began to vibrate and overheat.

Colin Anderson, wireless operator, came on the intercom and said he thought it was time to break radio silence, to send a mayday and how about it?

'We're still a long way out to sea,' I said. 'Still got to be careful. Anyway, what makes you think I'm going to let the kite crash?'

'Sorry, JL.'

We all wanted to get home. We hung on silently.

But a minute or so later the port engine began to falter. I changed my mind and gave Col the order to send the mayday. With three thousand feet to go, the night-dark sea passing in and out of sight through low clouds, I switched on the emergency beacon and ordered the crew to take the rafts and life-jackets and jump. They refused, so I shouted at them that it was an order. I swore at them, yelled at them to get out. It was their only real hope. The intercom was silent after that. Were they still on the plane when we hit the sea, or did they in fact jump when I told them to? I had no time to check again: we were a few seconds away from hitting the sea. The shock, when it came, was an immense physical blow — we might as well have slammed into the ground. Somehow I managed to scramble into the inflatable dinghy, barely conscious, freezing to death. I saw that Sam Levy was there in the dinghy with me. No time had passed.

I must have been in shock. I was confused then, I was confused when I tried to remember it later, I am still confused all these years on.

'Where's the kite?' I said, finding that for some reason I could hardly speak aloud. When Sam gave no reaction I asked him again, this time doing my best to shout.

I saw his shape there, across on the other side of the tiny inflatable. His head seemed to move as if he was speaking.

'What?' I cried.

'She sank,' I heard him say. 'Back there somewhere.'

'How the hell did we get out?'

'The hatch came off in the crash. I was lying close to it and you must have crawled over. Don't you remember?'

I remembered only chaos inside the flooded cockpit of the Wellington. Total darkness, bitter cold, the drenching of icy water that was rising around me. In an instant the cockpit had been transformed into a place I no longer understood. All sense of direction had gone. Was the area behind me up or down? Was I lying or standing? Or still sitting at the controls? Was I face down? My leg hurt like hell. I couldn't breathe because my face was under the water and I was choking. The oxygen mask of my flying helmet had become tangled around my throat. Then the plane lurched and the water drained dramatically away from around my head. A dim light from somewhere came glancing in. I saw two legs vanishing through the hatch. The plane lurched again.

Darkness followed, then a violent struggle. Arms and legs flailing in the water. Somehow I was in the inflatable, on the yielding, water-logged rubber floor of the dinghy, trying to twist myself so that I was face up, my fur-lined flying jacket weighed down by the water it had soaked up, the oxygen mask flapping uselessly against my neck.

'Have you any idea where we are?' I shouted, after what felt like half an hour of painful struggling. I was still staring across in the darkness to where I thought Sam must be lying. There was a long silence, so long that I thought he had passed out or died, or that he had somehow slipped into the sea.

'Haven't the faintest,' he said in the end.

'But you're the navigator. Didn't you get a fix?'

'Shut up, JL.'

The night went on, apparently without end. But dawn came at last in the dinghy, the glint of the sun across a cold grey sea, waves punching up around us. The dinghy moved as if it was stuck to the sides of the waves, rising and falling with the swell, never threatening to tip over but constantly kicking us around. Sam and I sprawled on the slippery rubber floor, our wrists tangled up in the ratlines. We had nothing to say to each other — Sam seemed to be asleep much of the time, his hands and face white with the cold. We both had blood all over our clothes but it was gradually being leached away by the salt water that burst across us every few minutes. It was May, early summer. We were going to die of cold.

Then, after many hours, an Air-Sea Rescue launch found us.

That was all I had to go on, as I lay there in Warwickshire.

I was in a fog of amnesia. What I have described is a worked-out version of many fitful images. Moments only of it, glimpsed in flashes that drifted maddeningly out of reach like fragments of a dream.

I gradually emerged from the confusing half-memories, as what I saw around me started to make sense at last. I was hurting in many places: leg, chest, hand, neck, eyes. One day I was moved painfully from the bed and they sat me in a chair. Medical staff came and went. I knew my mother had been to visit me, I knew we had spoken, but I could remember nothing that either of us had said. When I looked back at the chair where she had been sitting she was gone again.

I worked backwards to memory, learning as I went.

It turned out that time had passed and now it was the end of May. They told me we had been shot down on the 10th. I lay still, recovering. A week later everyone said I was on the mend but they told me I should have to remain in hospital for a while longer. I wanted to see my parents again, but the staff explained how difficult it was for them to travel in wartime. They told me, though, that they were going to move me to a convalescent hospital, closer to home. That would make it easier for my parents.

Another gap of memory follows: perhaps I had a relapse of some kind.

I was inside a Red Cross ambulance, shocked into reality when the vehicle jolted over an uneven patch of road. I braced myself defensively against the knocks and bumps I was receiving, but my waist and legs were held gently in place with restraining straps. I was alone in the compartment with an orderly, a young Red Cross worker I knew was called Ken Wilson. It was difficult to talk in the noisy, unventilated compartment. Ken braced his arms against the overhead shelves as the vehicle swung about. He said we were well on our way in the journey, not to worry. But I was worried. Where were we going? I began to think about my parents. Had they been told I was moving from the old hospital? Would they find me wherever it was I was going to? This was suddenly the most important problem in the world.

Our destination was a large country house, with gardens, steep roofs, gables, tall windows, stone-flagged passageways. The large rooms in the wings at the back of the house had been converted into wards. My parents came to see me on the second day I was there, having managed to find me. I cried when I saw them, I was in so much pain.

During the long summer days we were moved out to a balcony shaded from the sun, where there were lounger seats with big cushions, tables made of wicker and a view of a garden in which cabbages, potatoes, spinach and beetroot were being cultivated in large, neat patches. When my parents came to visit, I would sit there with them, not saying much. I felt the events of the war had removed me from them, grown me up.

I discovered that the convalescent hospital was somewhere in the Vale of Evesham. More days had passed while I was ill and by this time it was the end of June 1941. The news on the BBC reported that the Germans had overrun most of the Ukraine and Byelorussia and were advancing on all fronts into the Soviet Union. The news shook me. War must have broken out between Germany and Russia! When did that happen?

The previous night the RAF had bombed Kiel, Düsseldorf and Bremen.

Damage to all three towns was described as serious. Our attacks had been pressed home with great courage. Five RAF planes were lost, while two more were missing. I was familiar with that kind of news, but I sat quietly after the end of the broadcast, thinking for a long time about the crews they said were missing. I could imagine them in the sea, clinging to rafts and dinghies. Meanwhile Finland, Albania and Hungary had declared war on Russia. Had they invaded too? President Roosevelt was promising aid to the Soviet Union. Did it mean that the USA was also in the war? The BBC said that one of the Nazi leaders, Rudolf Hess, had flown to Scotland with a peace plan to halt the war between Britain and Germany. They explained who he was: Hitler's deputy, one of the most powerful Nazis in Germany.

But for me the name rang a bell: I had met Rudolf Hess while I was in Berlin! Could it be the same man? I knew at the time he was a high-ranking Nazi, but the fact that he was Hitler's deputy had been lost on me.

What had happened to Rudolf Hess's peace plan?

8

Joe and I came second in our first heat, behind France but ahead of Finland and Greece. In the afternoon we took second place in our semi-final heat, which allowed us to scrape through to the main race. The final itself had us ranged against Argentina, Denmark, Holland, France and Germany.

We spent the morning of the big day in training, but at lunchtime Joe suddenly announced that he needed to return to the apartment in Goethe-strasse, meaning that I would be alone, with at least two hours to kill. I was furious with him, because we were so close to the start of the most important race of our careers. We should keep working, stay out on the water for more and more practice. Joe shrugged it off, saying we could over-train ourselves into last place. Then he was gone.

At this time of day, with no events in progress, most people, competitors and crowds, had drifted away to lunch. I stayed by the lake, calming down after my argument with Joe, resting on the grass, watching what was going on around me. I started thinking about Birgit. My last real conversation with her had taken place two days earlier, when I had worked up my courage and asked her if she would like to visit the Olympic regatta arena to watch us race. Like all the athletes, Joe and I had been issued with complimentary tickets for our family and friends. Birgit told me she would love to be present for our race but that it would not be safe for her to be there. Although I was disappointed I had not pressed the point. I wished now that I had. We would be leaving Berlin soon, with no telling when we would be able to return.

A little later I went to stretch my legs. Between the two main grandstands and slightly in front of them was a raised viewing podium, draped in Nazi flags and banners, reserved for dignitaries and officials. So far, whenever we had been competing or training, it had remained unoccupied and our efforts passed unobserved by the important and powerful. This time when I wandered past, though, two armed SS men in their distinctive black uniforms had taken up positions at the bottom of each of the flights of steps that led to the platform. I walked past, staring up at the swastika-draped railings.

'[Move on!]' said one of the guards as I lingered in the area of the podium.

'[I'm a competitor,]' I said mildly, showing him the pass that all athletes were issued with, so that we could gain unrestricted access around the sports complex.

'[Being a competitor is of no importance. It is forbidden to be here.]'

'[Yes, sir!]' I said, having realized during the last few days in Berlin that no one in their right mind questioned the authority of the SS. I added, '*Heil Hitler!*'

He returned the salutation instantly, but continued to stare at me with intense suspicion. I walked away smartly, suddenly a little frightened of the situation.

Down by the river I went to watch the scrutineering of our shell, together with those belonging to the other teams. The German-speaking officials were making no attempt to keep spectators away, so I stood alongside as they methodically selected each of the boats, measured it, weighed it, checked its trim and alignment, then affixed a tiny tag to the helm to certify it was within the set limits.

When I returned to the spectator enclosure I saw a remarkable sight: the crowds were flocking back to the huge grandstands, flooding in from the park area that lay behind. The quiet area where I had been wandering only a short while earlier was now thronged with officials, police, adjudicators, other sportsmen, pressmen and an alarming number of uniformed SS officers, looking out of place in the bright sunlight. A tremendous sense of occasion filled the summer air and I could not help but respond to it.

I was at the Olympic Games and I was about to compete in a final!

Still the crowds poured in, guided towards the narrow entrances to the stands. The officials seemed concerned, over-wrought, chivvying people along as if there was no time to lose. A military band marched impressively into the enclosure, took up position and launched into a medley of cheerful tunes with a bouncing beat. The crowd greatly appreciated this. I sat down on the grass again, watching the band and enjoying the music.

I saw Joe walking along the river bank, looking from side to side. I waved, beckoning him anxiously towards me. We were running out of time. After a moment he saw me and came straight over. He squatted down beside me.

'Look, JL, we have to change our plans,' he said directly, raising his voice over the noise of the music. 'Something's come up. We're going to leave Berlin tonight.'

'You want to go home already?'

'I want to get out of Germany. Whatever it takes.'

'Joe, we're here to compete. Where the devil have you been? Have you forgotten the race? This is the most important afternoon of our lives!'

'Yes, and I feel the same as you. But there are other things we have to worry about.'

'Not now, not just before the race!'

'An hour from now the race will be over as far as we're concerned. There's no point hanging around in Berlin afterwards.'

'But it's in the agreement we signed. We have to stay on for the closing ceremony.'

'It's not safe for us to be here.'

'What could possibly go wrong?' I said, indicating the huge and good-natured crowds, the warm afternoon and the calm river, the oompah band, the squads of officials and adjudicators. I glanced at my watch. 'We should be warming up.'

Joe turned away from me, his attention grabbed by something that was going on. I looked over to where he was staring. Many of the people in the grandstands were getting up out of their seats, stretching up on their toes to see better. The band continued to play, but we were close enough to the musicians to notice that several of them were rolling their eyes while they blew into their trumpets and tubas, trying to see what was happening. I stood up and after another moment so too did Joe.

A group of men in German military uniforms was coming along the pathway that led down to the enclosure between the two main stands. They weren't marching but were walking briskly, staring straight ahead. The way for them had already been cleared, with lines of SS men standing to attention on each side.

Many of the people in the crowd raised their right arms at an angle and a huge racket of shouting, cheering and some screaming was going on. Ripples of excitement were fanning through the crowds in both grandstands. The mood was electric.

'My God!' Joe shouted over the row. 'It's him!'

I stared in amazement. In the centre of the group of men, the instantly recognizable figure of Chancellor Hitler was striding along, acknowledging the excited crowd by holding his right hand slightly aloft, the palm turned upwards. He looked to neither right nor left. He was no taller than any of the other men, dressed in a nondescript pale-green military jacket and a peaked cap, yet somehow his presence had instantly become the focus of interest of everyone.

I was astonished by the effect of the man's appearance on me. Simply by being there, by arriving, by striding into the arena where the regatta was taking place, he commanded our immediate attention. Like everyone else, Joe and I were craning our necks to keep him in sight.

The group of men reached the base of the raised podium. On that hot day in early August 1936, Joe and I recognized none of them apart from Hitler, even though we understood from the way they behaved that they were hugely important men. Without ceremony they climbed the steps to take up their positions on the viewing platform. A few years later, those men on the podium with Hitler would be amongst the most widely known, and feared, men in the world.

The Nazi leaders disappeared briefly from our view as they reached the viewing platform, but Hitler moved forward, flanked by two of the others. He stood by the rail, his back stiff and his head erect, looking from side to side in a calm but imperious manner. He raised his arms with a theatrical motion, folded them in front of him so that his hands clasped his upper arms. He looked around in all directions, silently acknowledging the tumult of acclaim and applause. The noise from the crowd was deafening, yet Hitler seemed detached from it, totally in command of the situation.

After about a minute of this, Hitler swiftly unfolded his arms, raised his right hand briefly in his palm-up salute, then turned and stepped back. As he did so, the crowd noise at last began to fade away.

I looked at my wristwatch.

'Come on, Joe!' I shouted. 'We're going to be late!'

Several minutes had gone by while Hitler and his entourage were entering the arena, attracting the attention of everyone, but we competitors were subject to a strict timetable. We were already nearly ten minutes past the start of our time allocated for warm-up exercises and we knew that the officials would make few allowances for late arrivals.

We dashed up the slope to the warm-up area, thrusting our passes at the German official on duty. Waiting beyond him was one of the British team officials, who was clearly not pleased by our tardiness, nor impressed by our excuse. A brisk, humiliating lecture on national expectations followed. We humbly accepted responsibility, apologized, then finally managed to move away from the man. We settled down quickly to our routine of exercises, trying to close our minds to everything that had just occurred, concentrating on the crucial race that was only a few minutes away.

9

Five years later I was in a convalescent hospital in the Vale of Evesham, working backwards to my memories of the crash and before.

The date they had given me for when we were shot down helped me remember: May 10, 1941. Details began to accumulate around it. On that night we were at thirteen thousand feet, approaching the city of Hamburg on a north-westerly track. I was in a state of terror, my hands and feet pressed rigidly against the controls of the Wellington. I was obsessed by the knowledge that the next two or three minutes could hurt, maim or kill us all. During those moments, with the bombs armed and ready to be dropped, the bomb aimer in position and effectively in command of the aircraft, the rest of the crew tensed against attack, I felt unable to think or speak for myself. All I was capable of doing was to react to the events going on around me, trusting that my instinctive reactions would be the right ones, that my terror would not let me make mistakes. I could keep the plane straight and level, I could respond to the warnings and requests of the crew, but memories of the past and thoughts of the future were impossible. I lived for the moment, expecting death at any instant.

So. Thirteen thousand feet. Clear skies under a bomber's moon. Twenty minutes past midnight, British time. Aircraft A-Able loaded with bombs and flares. City below: Hamburg. We had flown past the city a few minutes earlier at a distance of some twenty miles, trying to mislead the ground defenders into thinking we were passing Hamburg on the way to another target, Hanover or Magdeburg or maybe even Berlin. The RAF had hit Hamburg two nights before and we were warned at our afternoon target briefing that the Germans were bringing in more anti-aircraft guns to defend the city. Return raids were notoriously dangerous for us. We never treated German flak as a minor threat, so we all paid attention to the decoy plan. We used a distinctive curve in the River Elbe near Lüneburg as the assembly point, then turned steeply and headed in on our bombing run.

Ted Burrage, our bomb aimer and front gunner, had crawled into the belly of the Wellington, lying on his stomach, watching the ground through the perspex pane behind the nose. It was a night of clear visibility: great for targeting the ground, but the anti-aircraft gunners could see us just as easily and if night fighters were about we would be visible for miles.

As we approached the centre of Hamburg, distinctive on cloudless nights because of the way the river curved through, the intensity of the flak suddenly increased. Ten or more searchlight beams flicked on, criss-crossing ahead, while tracer bullets snaked up towards us. I tried to ignore the tracer: it always moved with hypnotic slowness while a long way below us, but suddenly speeded up and whooshed past us. I could never get it out of my mind that the tracer was only part of the flak — for every bright firefly of light swarming up towards us there were ten or fifteen others that were invisible. Ahead, bursting in the sky, there was a huge barrage of exploding shells, brilliant white and yellow, flashing on and off like a deadly fireworks display. How could we ever pass through that without being hit a hundred times?

'Bomb aimer to pilot. Are we starting the bombing run?' It was Ted, in the nose.

'Yeah, we're already on it. No need to change track as far as I'm concerned.'

'The sight is settled. Everything calibrated and checked.'

'You can get on with it, Ted.'

'What's our present course?'

'Two eighty-seven. Airspeed one thirty-two.'

'Hold her steady, JL. Right a bit. Thanks, that's fine.'

I could hear the others breathing on the intercom.

'Bomb doors open, skip.'

'Bomb doors open.'

There was a pause, then the plane lurched a little as the air-drag increased.

'New airspeed, sir?'

'One twenty-eight.'

'OK, hold her steady . . . steady . . . hell, we're hitting them hard down there tonight . . . smoke everywhere . . . that's it . . . steady . . . hold her steady . . . bombs gone!'

The plane lifted as the weight of the bomb load fell away. My stomach lurched with it.

'Less get outa here, JL!' The deeply accented voice of Kris Galasckja, the Polish rear gunner, came through raspingly on the intercom.

'You say that every trip.'

'I mean it every trip.'

'OK. Hold on.'

I pushed the nose down to pick up a little speed, then turned the plane through forty-five degrees to port, away from the inferno below. I closed the bomb doors, feeling the plane seem to fly itself as the aerodynamic characteristics improved once more.

'What now, JL? Home?' It was Kris again.

'Not yet. We've got to go round one more time.'

'You joking, skip?'

'Yeah. Relax. But we've got to get out of this place.'

'Anyone see what we hit?' said Sam Levy, who had no outside visibility from the curtained-off cubicle where his navigation table was placed.

Just then there was a loud explosion directly beneath the nose of the aircraft. I was thrown back from the controls and fell sideways to the floor of the cockpit, my left leg twisted painfully in the straps. The plane rolled to the left, tipped over, started to dive. I heard the note of the engine change, as if an invisible pilot had taken my place and was making us accelerate towards the ground. For a moment I was so shaken by the suddenness with which everything collapsed around me that I lay immobile. I was thinking, *It's happened! This is it! We've been shot down!*

My leather flying helmet was still on, although it was wrenched back uncomfortably in some perplexing way across the crown of my head. Somebody was yelling on the intercom — I could hear the sound of the voice through the headphones, but because the helmet had moved I couldn't make out the words. The connection clicked to an even more shocking silence. My left arm was immovable because of the pain — there was some kind of wetness running down my forehead from under the flap of the helmet. I thought, *I've been hit in the head! I'm bleeding to death!* I managed to shift position, got my right arm free and brushed the top of my head with my hand. It was sore but seemed intact. The blood continued to flow. I pulled at my helmet to straighten it, yanking it forward over whatever the wound was. There was a jab of intense pain from the damage up there, but after that I couldn't feel anything.

The plane rocked again, tipping the other way, left wing up, momentarily recovering stability. It was nothing I was doing: the controls were out of my reach and I was in too much pain to move. However, the change in the aircraft's attitude suddenly cancelled the centrifugal force from the spin. Before it started again I levered myself up. I put my weight on my right elbow, rolled to the side, then managed to get my good leg under me. With a further agonizing struggle I was able to clamber back into my seat at the controls. It was easier like that: I could favour the left side of my body, where most of the damage had been done. I could hardly see out of the windscreen ahead: something had burst through it, starring it and opaquing it. A jet of icy air came straight in at me.

I put on full opposite flaps and to my immense relief the plane began to pull out of the turning dive. The stick felt as if it weighed a ton, but by bracing my right leg on the rudder I managed to hold it back as I corrected the spin, fighting the G-force of the recovery from the dive.

I could see something flapping on the upper fuselage in front of the cockpit, but couldn't make out what it was. As the plane first levelled out then swung upwards in its trajectory, recovering some of the lost height, I began a frantic cockpit check. Engines both still running, though the oil pressure in the port engine was below normal. No fires anywhere that the instruments could detect. Controls stiff but working; the plane was yawing to the left, which I could correct with the rudder. Coolant low. Electrics OK.

Crew? At the same time as I was going through the emergency checklist I shouted to the others to report back.

Nothing from Ted Burrage, who was in the damaged nose. Nothing from Lofty Skinner, who had been behind me; nothing from Sam Levy, behind where Lofty had been. Col Anderson said he was OK. Lofty responded on my second try. He said he was helping Kris with Sam, who appeared to have been hit badly.

We flew on, crossing the German coast, over the dark North Sea, looking for home. The plane was losing height as the port engine was not generating full power. I had to keep throttling it back to prevent it overheating. Soon it was inevitable that we were going to have to ditch. Sam Levy and I were still in the plane when it crashed, but we somehow made it out of the aircraft and into a dinghy. I think the others baled out before we hit. Sam and I floated around on the choppy sea for many hours before we were rescued.

I thought repeatedly about this incident as I recovered in the convalescent hospital.

I was still in chronic discomfort, with spells of acute pain, but the doctors said I was healing. At night I dreamed of disturbing events. One nightmare involved me having to crawl head first into a long metal tube, barely wide enough for me to fit. The further I crawled along the tube the hotter it became. I reached a point where the tube curved suddenly downwards, looping back, until I had to crawl upside down. Then the tube began to fill with water, hissing in over the hot metal in front of me. I could not breathe or move my head, could not escape. I woke up. It was the last week in June. The news on the wireless told us that Hitler's army was invading the Soviet Union.

A Royal Navy Lieutenant was brought into the hospital. One of his arms had been amputated at the elbow and both his legs were in plaster. One day they put him on a recliner next to mine, on the verandah overlooking the vegetable garden.

'I was on the cruiser *Gloucester*,' he told me, his voice a mere whisper. He had damaged his throat and lungs when he inhaled hot gases. I told him it could wait until he found it easier to talk, but he was determined to describe what had happened. I encouraged him not to rush his story. We both faced long spells in hospital. Nothing had to be hurried. 'We were stationed off Crete,' he whispered, 'providing cover for the troops who were being evacuated. We came under attack from the air: dive-bombers and fighters. There were U-boats in the vicinity too. I was gunnery officer and we were giving them everything we had. But then something exploded under us and within a couple of minutes the ship heeled over. I think it was a torpedo that got us. The skipper gave the order to abandon ship. I was climbing aboard one of the lifeboats when the magazine went up. I don't remember much after that.'

I told him what I could remember at that point of my own story, incomplete as it was. But at the same time I was thinking: we've lost Crete! That means we must have lost Greece too! I remembered Mr Churchill sending the British army to Greece from Egypt, in an attempt to reinforce the Greeks in their fight against the Italians and the Germans. How long ago was that? What was the cost to our side?

My new friend told me that he'd been hearing rumours from friends who were still serving at sea that one of the German battleships had been sunk. A great triumph, he said. 'She must have been the *Tirpitz* or the *Bismarck*. She broke out into the Atlantic somehow, but the navy chased her and we sank her. We lost the *Hood*, but we got the damned Germans!'

We lost the *Hood* in this triumph? Later we learned that the German ship had been the *Bismarck*.

I was confused and depressed by the news of these events. The world had taken a nasty turn: it was exploding with war. It had not seemed so terrible in the days before I was shot down. The war had gone badly for Britain at first, when Hitler marched across Europe. But under Mr Churchill's leadership we were fighting back and the tide had started to turn. We won the Battle of Britain and there was no longer much of a threat of invasion, we were bombing the German military industries effectively, the Italians had shown themselves to be ineffectual allies of Germany, we were beating the U-boats, even the Blitz had been running down throughout April and May. Now everything was worse again.

Meanwhile I had my own battles to endure. I had a broken leg and a damaged knee, and I had a serious chest wound and a fractured skull. Three ribs were cracked. My left arm and hand were badly burned. I had not died and the medical staff seemed to take my recovery for granted, but all in all I felt that it had been a close-run thing.

My main concern was to get my health back, return to my squadron and rejoin the battle with Germany. Every day I underwent physiotherapy and received medication, and the dressings for my wounds and burns were changed. Every day I sat or lay on the covered verandah, staring at the rows of vegetables, gleaning what news I could from the wireless. Every day more injured servicemen were brought to the hospital or were moved out of it to somewhere else.

'When am I going to be able to return to my squadron?' I asked the senior physiotherapist one day. I was face down on her bench.

She was behind me, leaning down as she worked on my thigh. 'That's not the sort of decision we have to make here, thank goodness.'

'Does that mean you know something I don't?'

'Not at all. Would you really expect them to give us information about our patients that we weren't allowed to pass on?'

'I suppose not,' I said. I asked her no more questions, but I was aching to return to duty.

My idleness gave me too much time to think. One subject that seriously worried me was the fate of the rest of my crew. I found out about Sam Levy: he too was in hospital, but we had been separated. They told me he was going to recover, but that was all I knew about him. The other men were officially posted as missing: that terrible euphemism which inspired hope and dread in equal measure. The only thing I was certain of was that they had not escaped from the plane with me. Either they were killed in the crash, or they had jumped from the plane when I ordered them to do so. What worried me was the silence that followed my order. It could mean, of course, that they had jumped when I gave the order. On the other hand, the intercom might have failed or they had simply decided to disobey me, thinking they'd have a better chance if they stayed on the plane until it hit the water. Whatever the truth, Air Ministry letters had been sent to their families.

War was going on, was getting worse. Thousands more good men like Lofty, Colin, Kris and Ted would have to die before it was over. If I went back, I might have to die too. For a while the war had seemed necessary and inevitable, but now I had heard about it I could not stop thinking about Rudolf Hess and his plan for peace.

The BBC never mentioned Hess any more. After a flurry of excitement, the story of his flight to Scotland had vanished from the newspapers. Surely an offer of peace from the Nazi leadership could not be tossed aside?

I kept remembering Hess, the way I had met him.

10

The race got away at the first attempt, all six teams starting cleanly. The German pair moved effortlessly into the lead within the first few seconds. I had never rowed so hard in my life, driven to maximum effort by Joe's ferocious stroke rhythms. All our thoughts of pacing ourselves, our plan of producing a surging burst of energy in the final quarter of the race, went out of the window. We stretched ourselves to the limit and were rowing flat out from the first stroke to the last. We were rewarded with third place, a bronze medal for Great Britain!

The Germans won with a time of just over eight minutes sixteen; behind them came the Danish team at eight minutes nineteen; Joe and I came in at eight minutes twenty-three. All times were slow: we had been rowing into a headwind.

After we crossed the finish line we collapsed backwards in the boat for several minutes, trying to steady our breathing. The boat drifted with the others at the end of the course, while marshals' motorboats circled around us, fussing about us, trying to make us take the boats across to the bank. My mind was a blank, thinking, if anything, about the medal we had won. Of course, we originally aimed to win the gold. That had been the driving force. However, once we saw the other teams in training in Berlin we realized the enormous task we had set ourselves. For the last few days both Joe and I were haunted by the fear that we would come in last. But third! It was a fantastic result for us, better than anything I had dared hope for.

Eventually, we recovered sufficiently to row back to the bank and we did so with precise and stylish rowing. The first person to greet us as we stepped on to dry land was the coach, Jimmy Norton, who pumped our hands up and down, pummelled us on our backs, treated us like heroes.

About three-quarters of an hour later, after we had warmed down, showered and changed into clean tracksuits, Joe and I were directed to a building behind one of the grandstands and asked to wait. We found ourselves in a small room with the other two medal-winning teams. None of us knew the others, beyond the formal introductions on arrival and seeing each other training during the week. It was difficult to know what to say to one another at this stage. Joe and I tried to congratulate the two Germans who had won the gold, but they only acknowledged our words with dismissive nods.

Eventually, three officials came for us and led us at a quick walking pace across the grassy enclosure to where the Olympic podium stood. It faced the special grandstand used by Chancellor Hitler and the other leaders, but for the moment we were unable to see anyone up there.

Waiting directly in front of the stepped medal winners' platform was a small group of men in black SS uniforms. As we climbed up to the platform and took our places on the steps, one of the SS men moved forward. He was a bulky, impressive figure, his face high-cheekboned and handsome, with deep-set eyes and bushy black eyebrows.

He went first to the German pair and placed their gold medals around their necks as they inclined their heads. There was a huge burst of cheering and applause from the grandstands, so although he was speaking to them we could hear nothing that was being said. Press cameras were bobbing and jutting towards the German rowers. A film camera, mounted on the flat roof of a large van, recorded the whole ceremony.

The SS officer presented the silver medals to the two Danes, then it was our turn.

'[Germany salutes you,]' he said formally, as first Joe, then I, leaned forward to allow him to place the medal around our necks. '[For your country you did well.]'

'[Thank you, sir,]' I said. The applause was merely polite and soon finished.

He straightened and peered closely at both Joe and myself.

'[Identical twins, I think!]' For such a large man he had an unexpectedly soft-pitched, almost effeminate voice.

'[Yes, sir.]'

He was carrying a slip of paper in his left hand. He held it up, consulted it with exaggerated care.

'[I see,]' he said. '[J. L. and J. L. You have the same names even! How remarkable.]' He looked again from one of us to the other, his dark eyebrows arching in a theatrically quizzical expression. His greenish eyes seemed not to be focusing on us, as if his real thoughts were elsewhere or he was unable to think what to say next. It was an uncomfortable moment, standing there on the platform with the cameras around us, while this Nazi official took so much interest in us, peering closely at our faces. Finally, he stepped back. '[You must be playing amusing tricks on your friends all the time!]' he said.

We were about to make our usual response to the over-familiar remark, but at the same time the band struck up loudly with the German national anthem. The SS officer moved quickly back to where a microphone had been placed on a stand. He snapped to attention.

Everyone in sight stood as the flags of our respective nations were raised to the winds on the flagpoles behind us. In the centre, the red, white and black swastika flag fluttered on the tallest of the three poles. It reached the highest point at the exact moment the music ended. The officer stretched his right arm diagonally towards it, straining so hard his fingertips were quivering.

'*Heil Hitler!*' he shouted into the microphone, his voice distorted by the amplifier into a high screech. The salute was instantly taken up in a stupendous roar from the crowd.

He turned to face them, swivelling round in a quick and presumably practised movement that ensured the microphone was still before him. His face was glowing red in the sun. The other SS officers turned too, a synchronized movement, a concerted stamping of their right feet.

'*Sieg heil!*' the officer yelled into the microphone, swinging his arm from a taut, horizontal position across his chest to the familiar slanting Nazi salute. The crowd echoed the call in a deafening shout. Many of them, most of them, had also raised their arms.

'*Sieg heil! Sieg heil!*' he shouted twice more, saluting again, his glittering eyes regarding the huge crowd. He was rocking to and fro on his heels. At the front of the crowd, high on his special plinth, was Adolf Hitler. He stood stiffly as the salutations went on, his arms folded across his chest in the same forced position I noticed earlier. He looked around to all sides, apparently basking in the deafening waves of adulation that were flowing towards him.

Next to us, on the highest step in the centre of the Olympic podium, the two gold-medallist Germans were standing side by side, their right arms raised in salute, their faces lifted towards Hitler's remote figure.

It was simultaneously terrifying and enthralling. In spite of what little I knew about the Nazis, I felt myself responding to the intoxicating thrill of the moment. The sheer size of the crowd, the deafening roar they were making, the almost mechanical precision of the SS men paraded in front of us, the high, distant figure of Adolf Hitler, virtually godlike in his remoteness and power. The urge to raise my own arm, to thrust it emphatically towards the German leader, was for a few moments almost irresistible.

I glanced across at Joe, to see how he was reacting. He was already watching me and I instantly recognized the expression of suppressed anger that Joe adopted whenever he felt cornered, unhappy, uncertain of himself. He spoke some words to me. Although I leaned towards him to hear better I couldn't make out what he said because of the noise.

I nodded instead, acknowledging him.

With a sudden, peremptory swirl, Hitler turned his back on us and moved to return to his seat. The noisy acclaim quickly died away, to be replaced by the band striking up a new marching number. The SS men in front of our stand dispersed. The man who had given us our medals walked back towards Hitler's podium with a measured tread. He went at the same relaxed pace up the steps and after a moment I saw his tall figure leaning over to speak to someone. Shortly afterwards he sat down.

The Olympics officials were clustering around us, making it clear it was time for us to leave. We shook hands with the Danish and German athletes we had raced against, uttered congratulations once more, then stepped down on to the grass. Our moment of Olympic fame had already passed.

11

We walked together towards the British pavilion, where we had left our street clothes and our other possessions. As we approached the temporary wooden building we saw a group of British Embassy officials standing by the entrance.

They were apparently waiting for us, because as soon as we appeared they strode towards us, stretching out their hands in greeting and congratulation.

A man we already knew as Arthur Selwyn-Thaxted, a cultural attaché at the embassy, was the quietest but most insistent in his congratulations. As he shook my hand affably he gripped my elbow with his free hand. 'Well done, Sawyer!' he said. 'Well done indeed, both of you!'

He turned to Joe and said much the same.

'Thank you, sir,' we said.

'It's a great day when Britain wins another medal. You probably heard us cheering for you! It was a hard race, but you did exceedingly well. What a brilliant race you rowed!'

We said what we felt we were expected to say.

'Now, we can't let this remarkable achievement of yours pass,' said Selwyn-Thaxted. 'We'd be pleased if you would join us this evening. Just a little celebration at the embassy. The ambassador would like to meet you and there will be members of the German government present.'

Out of the corner of my eye I detected Joe stiffening.

'What kind of celebration would it be?' he said. 'We were planning —'

'A quiet reception. It's not every day that we have Olympic medal-winners to show off, so we like to make the most of them when we can. Your sculling colleagues will be there, the equestrian team, Harold Whitlock, Ernest Harper, many more. The evening clearly wouldn't be complete without you.'

Joe said nothing.

I said, 'Thank you, sir. We'd enjoy that.'

'Excellent,' Selwyn-Thaxted said, beaming at us as if he meant it. 'Shall we say from about six o'clock onwards? No doubt you know the British Embassy, in Unter den Linden?'

He smiled sincerely again, then turned away towards somebody else, raising a hand in simulated greeting. He went back to the group with whom he had been standing when we arrived. They moved off at once. When I turned to speak to my brother, Joe had already walked away. I saw him striding at great speed past the marshals by the entrance to the enclosure. His head was lowered. I went after him, but within a few seconds he vanished into the crowds that were standing about in the park outside.

I went into the pavilion, changed into my street clothes, collected Joe's gear as well as my own and walked down to the U-Bahn to catch a subway train back to the Sattmanns' flat. By the time I arrived, Joe had already packed his belongings and his bags were stacked in the hallway. He looked impatiently at me then went back into the room we had been using. I followed him in and swung the door to behind me.

Birgit was practising her music in one of the rooms at the front of the apartment. The sweet sound was muted when the door closed.

'What's going on, Joe?'

'I feel I should ask you that. Have you any idea, any idea at all, what's been happening here at the Olympics?'

'I know you don't like the idea that the Games are a Nazi showpiece.'

'So you're not as blinkered as I thought.'

'Joe, we came here to row. We can't get involved in politics. We don't know enough about it.'

'Maybe there are occasions when we should.'

'All right. But any country that hosts the Olympics uses the Games as a way of promoting itself to the world.'

'This isn't just any country,' Joe said. 'Not now, not any more.'

'Look, you knew that before we left home. In effect we both made the decision to be part of it when we were selected.'

'Did you realize who that was, who handed us the medals?'

'I didn't recognize him. I assumed it was someone from the government.'

'It was Hess. Rudolf Hess.'

'Never heard of him.'

'He's one of the most powerful Nazis in Germany.'

'But that doesn't affect us, Joe! It wouldn't have made any difference if Hitler himself had given us the medals. We're of no importance to the Nazis. We're simply here to compete in the Games and when they're over we'll go home. We had to go through with the ceremony. Are you suggesting we should have turned our backs on that?'

'Didn't you even think we might?'

'What good would it have done? President Hoover went to Los Angeles four years ago. You presumably didn't object to that, so how can you object to Hitler turning up at his own Games?'

'How can you not?'

'You didn't say anything at the time.'

'Neither did you.'

We both stood there angrily in that pleasant room overlooking the broad parkland, hot in the late afternoon sun. Birgit's plaintive music could still be heard, a little louder than before: it was a piece she played every evening,

Beethoven's Romance No. 1. I noticed that the draught had moved the door ajar. Because I knew that the family who were our hosts could all speak English, I quietly pushed the door and closed it properly.

We argued on, but there was no shifting Joe from his position. He intended to leave for home more or less straight away. I put up objections: our shells were with the scrutineers, the van was parked close to the Olympic Village, we still had some kit at the pavilion. No matter what, we couldn't leave without saying goodbye to Jimmy Norton, the coach. Joe shrugged the objections away, saying he would deal with them all. He said he was going to retrieve the van, pick everything up and set off for England at once. He planned to drive all night and with any luck would have crossed the border out of Germany by the next morning.

All he would say about my position was that if I wanted to leave with him I'd be welcome. If not, I'd have to find my own way home with one of the other teams.

Meanwhile, I was becoming as stubborn as him. If the British Olympic Committee wanted us to stay on for the closing ceremony, then we should do that. And then there was the reception at the British Embassy, which we would have to attend in less than an hour.

Finally, we reluctantly settled on the inevitable compromise that satisfied neither of us. Joe agreed to delay his departure until after the embassy reception, which I would go to on my own while he collected our property and loaded the van. We would then leave Berlin together. But if I was late meeting him after the party, or missed him somehow, he would set off without me.

While we had been arguing, Birgit's violin had fallen silent.

I settled down in an angry mood to pack my belongings. An atmosphere of resentment hovered in the room around both of us. I put on a clean shirt and jacket and the only necktie I had brought with me. I slipped my medal into my pocket.

I wanted to see the Sattmanns before I left, to say goodbye and thanks. I particularly wanted to see Birgit again, one last time. I went from room to room, but the place was empty. It felt too silent, making me wonder how much of our argument had been audible. To leave without giving thanks to these long-term friends of my mother's was grossly discourteous, it seemed to me. It added to my sense of outrage at Joe, but there was no longer any point in arguing with him.

I went down to the dusty street outside, where the air was still stiflingly hot at this hour. I walked to the S-Bahnhof.

12

At the end of June 1941, nearly five years after Joe and I competed in the Olympics, I was recovering in a convalescent hospital in the Vale of Evesham. Gradually my memory was sharpening up. I was confident that this alone meant that I was on the mend, that I could soon return to my squadron. I was at last walking without crutches, although I did need a stick. Every day I took a turn about the gardens and every day I was able to walk a little further. The solitude gave me the chance to think, to remember what my life had been before the crash. The mental exercise began as a desperate quest to find myself there in the past, but as the days slipped by I took a real interest in discovering what had happened to me.

I remembered, for instance, that on the morning before that last raid I had woken up early. The squadron had not been on ops the night before, having been stood down in mid-afternoon.

In the indescribably heady mood of release that followed a stand-down I drove into Lincoln with Lofty Skinner and Sam Levy to see the early-evening showing of *Santa Fe Trail*, starring Errol Flynn and Olivia de Havilland. Afterwards we went to a fish and chip shop for our dinner, walked around the quiet evening streets of Lincoln for a while, then decided to return to the airfield in time to watch the Whitleys of 166 Squadron — with whom we shared the airfield at Tealby Moor — taking off for their own raid. By ten-thirty the airfield was quiet again and I went to my hut to sleep. I slept so deeply that not even the sound of the Whitleys returning in the early hours woke me.

After breakfast the next morning, May 10, I carried out an air-test on A-Able, flew three low circuits of the airfield, then before lunch Kris Galasckja told me he needed to calibrate his guns in the rear turret, so I flew him in the Wellington across to the gunnery range at RAF Wickenby. We had lunch at Wickenby and were back at Tealby Moor before two in the afternoon.

Then the growing, inexorable pre-raid tension could not be ignored any longer. Everyone was watching for the familiar first signs of raid preparations: staff cars coming and going, trolleys of high-explosive bombs being trundled in from the distant dump, the engineers running up the engines and so on. We saw the various section chiefs heading for a meeting with the station commander: bombing and navigation leaders, met. officers, comms chiefs and so on. By two-thirty we were certain we would be flying that night. For us, though, there was nothing to do until the briefings began in the early evening.

Restlessness coursed through me. In the prewar years I would have gone for a run or taken a boat out on the river to work off any unwanted nervous energy, but in wartime conditions on a RAF station there were few such outlets. The rest of my crew were lounging about in the Mess, playing cards or writing letters, showing their state of tension in different ways from mine, but I knew what they were going through. I left them to it and walked around the aircraft dispersals for a while, killing time.

At last it was time for the pre-raid briefing and I went across to the station hall, almost eager to begin. Once all the crews were settled in place, though, I found it hard to concentrate on what was being said. The target for the night was Hamburg: the station commander displayed the necessary maps of the general area and the city centre. We would be attacking the commercial area and the docks, making an early diversion to Lüneburg in the south to try to put the Hamburg flak batteries off their guard. I forced myself to concentrate: the lives of everyone in the plane could depend on this briefing.

Afterwards, the same sense of quiet agitation continued through the hasty pre-raid meal, through the technical tests and checks on engines, flying controls, guns, bomb-release mechanism, tyres and so on. I was under no illusions about what was causing the nervousness. By this time what we all wanted to do was climb into the plane, take off for the raid and get the whole thing over with as soon as possible.

At just before eight o'clock a WAAF corporal drove us out to the aircraft in the crew bus. It was a warm evening and we were sweating and feeling overdressed in our fur-lined leather flying jackets, heavy boots, padded trousers. The gunners wore more clothes than the rest of us: their turrets were draughty and unheated, so they wrapped themselves up in additional layers beneath their electrically warmed flying suits (which warmed nothing): they wore extra underclothes, pullovers, two or three pairs of gloves and socks.

I hauled myself up through the hatch in the floor of the fuselage and went straight to the cockpit. I squeezed into the seat. Everything was in good working order, the LAC told me informally as I scribbled my name on the sheet of paper on the clipboard to sign off the plane for the ground crew. No problems, nothing to worry about. Take her out and bring her home. Our last raid had been six nights earlier, on the dockyards in Brest, where we had been trying to hit the German warships *Scharnhorst* and *Gneisenau*, so I felt a little out of practice as we went through the rote of pre-flight technical and arming checks. Both engines started at the first attempt. A good sign.

As we were taxiing down from dispersal to the take-off point it seemed to me that the plane felt heavier than usual, but I knew we were carrying a full load of fuel and bombs. I ran the engines up and down, clearing their throats, kicked the rudder left and right, feeling the aircraft responding sluggishly. Tonight was what Bomber Command called a maximum effort. A runway marshal gave me the thumbs-up as we lumbered past him, then turned away with his head bent over and his hand clamped down on his cap. The slipstream from our props bashed against him. Ahead of us was M-Mother with Derek Hanton at the controls — I'd known Derek since the days of the University Air Squadron. Behind us and to the side other Wellingtons were rolling forward from their dispersal positions, turning laboriously on to the side runway, taxiing down, ready to take off. On the other side of the main runway I could see a similar procession of slow-moving aircraft, a gathering of might, ready to go. We passed the caravan where the airfield controller had his station. No lights showed.

As usual a little crowd had gathered at the end of the main runway to wave us off: WAAFs, ground crew, station officers, all turned out to watch us leave. Every night there would be someone there, standing against the perimeter fence where a great thicket of trees pressed close to the edge of the airfield. M-Mother rolled forward, turned on to the main runway, propellers blurring, flattening and shaking the grass in the slipstream. Derek accelerated away slowly. Another Wellington from the side runway opposite moved across to take his place. At last our turn came and I pushed the Wellington forward, swung her around to face down the long concrete strip. The airsock was slack.

I watched the dim outline of the airfield controller's caravan: from this position I could see a steady red light, holding me until the airspace was clear. I waited, waited, the engines turning, the plane rattling and shuddering. My hand on the throttles was blurred by the vibration. I tried to stay calm. The light went to green at last. Our watchers at the side waved cheerfully.

I released the brakes, opened the throttles, adjusted the pitch and we began to move down the runway, slowly at first, so slowly, feeling every bump in the hastily laid concrete, the wings rocking, then a gradual increase in speed, the instruments showing we were going faster than it seemed. At flying speed, with the tail already free of the ground, I pulled back on the stick and the Wellington began its long, shallow climb into the evening sky.

As we ascended slowly through the calm air, circling over the familiar fields to gain a little height before setting off across the sea, I looked down at the quiet meadows and untidy rows of trees, their long shadows striking eastwards. I saw the steeples of churches, clusters of village houses, irrationally curving roads, hazy smoke from chimneys. Lincoln cathedral loomed up a few miles away to the south-east, the tower black against the blue of the evening sky. There were other aircraft in sight: Wellingtons from our own station, below and around us, but also far away, miles off, more tiny black dots lifting away from their own airfields, circling for height around the wide assembly point, seeking the others, aiming to form a broad and self-defensive stream for the long flight across the North Sea.

At last the radio signal came from the ground controller, his final clearance to start the raid. We turned one last time to the east, climbing steadily, away from the brilliant setting sun and towards the gathering dusk. The gunners let off a few trial rounds, their tracers glinting sharply down towards the sea. At five thousand feet the interior of the plane started to feel cold — for a few minutes we were actually more comfortable than we had been on the ground, before the sub-zero freeze of high altitude gripped us. At seven thousand feet I ordered the crew to put on their oxygen masks.

The evening was a deception of calm and beauty, with the steadily darkening sky above us, a plateau of grey clouds below us with a few more white cumulus billowing up, lit by the lowering sun. Germany lay ahead. We flew for an hour, slowly gaining height.

Ted Burrage suddenly came on the intercom. He was on the front guns.

'Enemy aircraft below us, JL! Three o'clock. Approaching fast!'

'How far below?'

'A long way.'

'Can you get a line on them?'

'Not yet.'

'Hold your fire for a moment . . . they might not have seen us!'

Then I saw the aircraft myself. They were at least two or three thousand feet beneath us, crossing our track, south to north. All were clearly visible against the grey plain of clouds below, lit by the last glow of evening light. The leading aircraft was twin-engined. It looked to me like a Messerschmitt Me-110, a guess that was almost instantly confirmed by others in the crew as they also spotted it. Behind it were four single-engined fighters, Me-109s, flying much faster, rapidly overhauling it. I could see Ted swinging his turret round in the nose of the Wellington, bringing his guns to bear, but within seconds it was obvious that none of the Luftwaffe planes was interested in us.

The fighters were diving on the Me-110. I saw tracer or cannon fire flickering across the short space between them. They hit the plane on their first run. One of the Me-110's tanks exploded with a spectacular burst of flame, throwing the aircraft on to its back. Immediately, the Me-109s swung away, turning sharply to each side of the stricken plane. There was a second explosion and this time part of the wing fell away. The plane had lost flying speed and was diving, upside-down, towards the sea. It plummeted into the cloudbase. All I could see of it for another second was an orange diffusion of flame, but then that too disappeared.

The Me-109s continued their sweeping turns, diving down towards the cover of the clouds, heading back to the south, the way they had come. They took no notice of us.

'Bloody hell!' Ted said. Then he said again, 'Bloody *hell!*'

'What was all that about?'

For a moment the intercom was full of voices. Sam Levy and Kris Galasckja had not been able to see what was going on. Lofty, Colin and Ted were describing what we'd seen. I was trying to yell at them to stay on watch. When we were over the North Sea we were never far from enemy aircraft.

As if to underline the point I saw more German aircraft coming towards us. This time they were travelling east to west and were about a mile away from us on the left.

I shouted to the gunners to be ready. 'More bandits! About nine o'clock!'

'Got them, JL!' Ted shouted. 'They're the same ones!'

'Couldn't be. The 109s buggered off as soon as they'd hit the 110.'

'No, I think Ted's right!' It was Lofty, who had come into the cockpit beside me, standing up, peering through the canopy over my shoulder.

I took another look. Once again, the aircraft were silhouetted against the grey cloudbase; once again an Me-110 was flying fast and low against the surface of the clouds, with a small section of single-engined fighters behind him, in hot pursuit.

'What the devil are the Jerries up to?'

'Don't fire,' I ordered the gunners. 'They're not interested in us. Don't change things.'

I saw the 109s turning in for an attack, in two groups of two, one following the other. They peeled off in a sharp turn, flew broadside at the 110, their tracer glittering like jewels, curling around the Me-110. The pilot dived sharply, banked away, reversed the bank, swooped down. The 109s recovered from their attacking pass and swept around for another try. Now the 110 was in a steep dive towards the clouds. Tracer curled towards it.

I could hardly see because our flight was taking us beyond the battle. Lofty moved down the fuselage, went to one of the side windows.

'I still can't see anything, JL!' he reported.

'Kris?' I shouted. 'Are you watching back there?'

'You bet. Rear gunner has the best seat. Germans attacking Germans. Good stuff!'

'Did they shoot him down?'

'Nah . . . they miss. Then they turn away. The 110 was in the cloud and I think it went on.'

Lofty returned to the cockpit and was standing behind me again, crouching forward.

'Do you get it, skip?' he said. 'What were they doing?'

'Haven't the faintest. We were sitting ducks, but they went after one of their own. Or two of their own.'

Sam Levy came on. 'Do you want a position fix, JL?'

'Yeah, where are we?'

'A couple of hundred miles from the German coast and about two hundred and sixty from Denmark.'

'Why Denmark?'

'That was the direction the second lot came from.'

'They could have come from Germany, though.'

'Either way, they would have been at the limit of their range. That's why they didn't hang around out here. The 109s would be watching their fuel.'

'OK, everyone,' I said. 'Keep your eyes open. We've got our own work to do.'

As the darkness finally deepened, the Wellington ploughed on slowly through the gentle air. An hour later we approached the German coast under a full moon, to the west of Cuxhaven. The nervous banter on the intercom died out as we crossed the coastline. Light flak surged up, a long way to the side of us. We watched the glow-worms of tracers, climbing, climbing. A solitary searchlight came on, the familiar bluish dazzle, breaking through the now intermittent clouds. It probed around for about a minute, then went off. We were flying at thirteen thousand feet, the highest altitude we could attain with the fuel- and bomb-load we were carrying.

We were now over Germany and anything could happen. I started jinking the plane, putting it into a long, steady rolling motion, side to side, tilting and swinging defensively, a corkscrew manoeuvre that would in theory prevent night fighters from getting an easy line on us. It had worked so far. The gunners reported tensely every minute or so: there was nothing going on that they could see, no planes around us, no searchlights, the cloud was light, visibility good. A bomber's moon. The dark ground spread out below, marked in places by tightly etched lines of moonlight reflected back from canals, ponds, stretches of river. Lofty Skinner, flight engineer, took the seat beside me, keeping a watch on the engines, the coolant pressures, the hydraulics. He rarely spoke.

We were flying on dead reckoning: a series of timed course changes, calculated before departure and constantly updated by Sam Levy, navigator. He led us to a position north of the German town of Celle (fierce flak briefly came up around us), before we turned through more than a hundred degrees and took a heading on Lüneburg. I went on the intercom, warning everyone that we were a few minutes away from the target. Now we were flying almost due north, with Hamburg less than fifty miles ahead of us. We were looking for a distinctive curve in the River Elbe near Lüneburg.

Ted Burrage, our bomb aimer, had left the front turret and crawled into the belly of the Wellington, lying on his stomach, watching the ground through the perspex pane behind the nose. He yelled up to me when he saw the river. It edged into sight from my blind-spot, directly in front of and below the cockpit: a silvery worm of reflected moonlight, visible for miles. We moved in on Hamburg.

Soon the flak began in earnest and the searchlights came on. Tracer bullets snaked up from below, no longer drifting harmlessly away, miles to the side of us, but targeted on us. Searchlight beams crossed and re-crossed ahead, groping for bombers. As they swept around we caught glimpses of other aircraft in the stream. Every now and again one of the aircraft would be briefly lit from below, but managed to slip away without being coned.

'I have the target in view,' came from Ted, lying in the nose of the aircraft, his hands on the bomb release.

'OK, bomb aimer. Let me know when we're on the right approach.'

Then, at last, bursting in the sky ahead of us — dead ahead, not above our height or below it — a cannonade of exploding shells began, brilliant whites and yellows, like deadly fireworks. How could we ever pass through that barrage without being hit?

We flew on, we opened the bomb doors, we released the bombs.

We turned for home.

Ted Burrage must have died instantly when the shell struck the nose of the aircraft. Shards of shrapnel went through my left leg, above and below the knee. Something else hit my skull. I was thrown backwards from my seat by the explosion and I lost control. The plane immediately went into a dive, turning to the left, while freezing cold air blasted in through the shattered fuselage ahead of the cockpit. Sam Levy was struck by another piece of shrapnel. Lofty Skinner had left his seat in the cockpit during the bombing run, standing by in case there was a problem with the bomb-load hanging up when we tried to release it. His life was probably saved by not being next to me. Colin, wireless operator, and Kris, in the rear turret, were both alive and responded to my call.

I contrived somehow to get the plane back under control. We struggled on for longer than I expected, losing height only slowly. I managed to keep the plane flying for two more hours. We were picking up the radio beacon at Mablethorpe before we ditched, but we were not in verbal contact with our controllers.

Sam and I were rescued from our life raft at the end of the following day: we were soaked through, freezing cold, both in agonizing pain, both probably destined to die had we been forced to spend any more time out there in the open.

Once we were ashore we were taken to separate hospitals and we lost contact with each other.

So, in June 1941, a few weeks after the raid on Hamburg, I was recovering on a verandah overlooking a vegetable garden, contemplating my past.

On the morning after the navy man had told me about the fall of Crete I went for an unaccompanied walk around the hospital grounds. This was not as strenuous as it might sound, because we weren't allowed to go far. Patients were confined to the narrow strips of lawn and the path that surrounded the vegetable patch, a tiny orchard beyond and some further paths that led around the outside of the house. However, I enjoyed the brief solitude, walking slowly through shrubbery that was still sparking with droplets after an early shower, looking back at the impressively gabled house and wondering what it had been used for before the war, what great events it might have seen.

Returning to the convalescent wing, I clambered up the steps to the verandah, squeezed past the other patients and headed for my room.

Three people were waiting for me in one of the downstairs lounges: the matron of the hospital was there with two men, one a civilian, the other an

RAF Group Captain. The matron called me in as I hobbled slowly along the corridor. The moment I saw the officer I stiffened and tried to salute, an action made more clumsy by the fact that my stick was in my right hand, taking my weight.

The officer responded to my salute but seemed amused by my appearance. I was wearing my hospital dressing-gown over a pair of old trousers.

'This is Flight Lieutenant Sawyer,' the matron said.

'Good to meet you, Sawyer,' the Group said. '148 Squadron, I believe. Wellingtons.'

'That's right, sir.'

'Had a bit of a prang over Hamburg, I hear. Well, that can't be helped. You seem to be walking again.'

'It gets better every day, sir.'

'Good. Then we would like you to come with us. No formalities are necessary.'

'Am I going back on ops, sir?'

'Not exactly. Not straight away, at least.'

Half an hour later I was dressed and ready to leave. I found a crisp new RAF officer's uniform hanging in my room, a perfect fit. It bore the insignia of a Group Captain. I supposed that some kind of administrative error had been made: if not, I had been kicked up three levels at once when I had no reason to expect any promotion at all. I was too bemused by the swift change in my circumstances to ask about it, knowing that the RAF would straighten everything out soon enough. When the nurse had seated me comfortably in the back of the Air Ministry staff car, we drove slowly out of the hospital grounds and turned on to the main road outside.

The civilian's name was Gilbert Strathy, he told me, without describing his position in the Air Ministry. Strathy was a middle-aged man with a cherubic face and a shining bald head. He wore a pin-striped suit, immaculately pressed. He was extremely cordial and concerned about my well-being, but gave nothing away about why I had been collected from the hospital. The officer was Group Captain Thomas Dodman, DSO DFC, attached to Bomber Command staff, but again he passed on no more information than that.

I stared away from the two men, out through the window on my side of the car, watching the summery banks and hedgerows slipping past. The roads were deserted, of course, since petrol was more or less unobtainable for most people. The fine weather helped disguise a drabness that had settled over the whole country since the autumn of 1939. At midday the WAAF driver made a halt in Stow-on-the-Wold and we ate lunch in the hotel on the town's main square. The bill was settled by Mr Strathy signing a chit. The hotel proprietor treated us with extraordinary civility. After lunch we continued our journey, slipping through the peaceful countryside, heading south-east in the general direction of London.

13

Looking for the British Embassy, I left the S-Bahn at Friedrichstrasse and walked along the side of the River Spree until I reached Luisenstrasse. The embassy building had been described to me as being on the intersection of this wide street with Unter den Linden. I was apprehensive, feeling that I was being pulled between the unreasonable demands of my brother and the only slightly more reasonable expectations of my country.

As I made for the main entrance of the embassy building I spotted Terry Hebbert, the captain of the athletics team, also walking pensively in the same direction as me. I caught him up and we greeted each other with some relief. He congratulated me on our bronze and told me briefly about his own hopes for the track events that were still to come. He asked where Joe was, but I merely said he was unable to be at the party. While we were talking I took my medal from my pocket and, feeling a little self-conscious, slipped it around my neck. We found the correct entrance and followed elegantly lettered signs towards the Imperial Ballroom. We were duly announced from the door.

The reception was being held in a long hall with a highly polished floor and glittering crystal chandeliers. A four-piece orchestra was playing on a dais at the far end and uniformed waiters moved deftly with trays of drinks and snacks held aloft as they wove between the large number of guests already there. The noise and heat were tremendous. Everyone seemed to know everyone else, chattering in both English and German and laughing with increasing vivacity and noise. Several high-ranking German officials were present, wearing their distinctive black or dark grey uniforms even in this unventilated and crowded room. I saw a couple of fellow athletes I recognized from Oxford, deep in conversation. Under pressure from Joe to stay at the party as short a time as possible, I resisted the temptation to go over and say hello. As we slowly worked our way across the congested floor of the ballroom, somebody in a small party wheeled round and touched Terry Hebbert's arm and he promptly joined them. I wandered on, alone. I soon emptied my first glass of champagne, and exchanged it for a full one.

The orchestra finished a piece and silence was called from the rostrum. A tall British gentleman made a short welcoming speech, alternating between English and near-perfect German. He mentioned the Olympic athletes who were competing so successfully, singling out the British, of course, but also generously praising the athletes of the host country. Germany was already so far ahead in the medals table that no other country was likely to catch up. He also paid tribute to the German government, for ensuring that the Games were being played in such a spirit of fairness and sportsmanship. He concluded with the earnest hope that the Games would be the beginning of a new and lasting spirit that would imbue the German nation with a sense of brotherhood towards the other countries of Europe.

Halfway through the speech I realized that of course the speaker was the British ambassador. Behind him on the little stage I also spotted Arthur Selwyn-Thaxted. When the ambassador had finished speaking and the band struck up again, he stepped down from the dais and walked quickly through the throng towards me.

'I'm so glad you could be here, Mr Sawyer!' he said loudly. 'Which of the JLs are you?'

'I'm Jack, sir. Jacob Lucas.'

'And is your brother here too this evening?'

'I'm afraid not. Something came up at the last minute.'

'That's a tremendous shame. Well, at least you have been able to make it. There's someone here who is anxious to meet you. Could you spare a moment to say hello to him?'

'Of course.'

I put down my half-empty glass of champagne and followed him as he squeezed politely through the crowd. A number of long tables covered in white cloths were arranged along one side of the hall. Clustered behind, separating themselves from everyone else, were several German officials. Prominent among them was the man who had made the presentation of medals to Joe and myself. He noticed us as we walked towards him and at once came forward.

Selwyn-Thaxted said, '[Herr Deputy Führer Hess, I have pleasure in presenting Mr J. L. Sawyer, one of our Olympic medallists.]'

'[Good evening, Mr Sawyer!]' Hess said at once and made a jocular gesture towards the medal hanging on my chest. '[Of course I remember you. Please, you will join us for a drink.]'

The table where he had been standing was laden with a large number of tall steins and lidded tankards. Several huge glass jugs of a foaming black liquid were standing there, while two waiters stood ready to serve. Hess clicked his fingers peremptorily and one of the waiters filled a tankard.

'[You will enjoy this,]' said Hess.

I took the heavy pot, raised the lid and sipped the frothy liquid. It was sweet and cold and had a strong but not unattractive flavour. I noticed that Hess himself was not drinking the same stuff but was holding a small tumbler containing fruit juice.

'[Thank you, sir. It is a pleasant beverage.]'

'[You have tasted Bismarck already?]'

'[Bismarck?]' I said.

'[It is a great favourite, I am told, at your Oxford. Maybe you know it by its English name, which is Black Velvet?]'

'[No, I've never tasted anything like it. Because I have been training for the Games I drink only beer, and that in modest quantities.]'

'[This Bismarck is popular in the Reich with many people. Most of them like to drink it when you Britishers are here, as today. You have a good black beer, as you know, which you bring from Ireland. It is called Guinness? Then we mix the Guinness with champagne from France. So we are all friends in Europe, as your ambassador advises us!]'

Selwyn-Thaxted was still standing beside me, smiling attentively, while the banal conversation proceeded.

'I have other guests I must attend to,' he said, speaking softly and quickly in English. 'I shall be on hand if you need any advice.'

'Advice?'

'You never know. Do excuse me.' He nodded with deep courtesy to Rudolf Hess. '[We are greatly honoured by your presence here this evening, Herr Deputy Führer. You must make yourself feel welcome. Do let me or one of my staff know if there is anything you require.]'

'[Thank you, my gentleman.]' Hess turned directly to me, in a gesture of dismissal to Selwyn-Thaxted. Hess had already removed his jacket and was wearing a khaki shirt tucked into grey trousers. An Iron Cross on a ribbon hung at his throat. He moved his burly body closer to me. '[Why have you not brought your brother with you this evening?]' he said in his rather disconcerting tenor voice.

'[He was unable to be here.]' I saw from Hess's reaction that it was not a satisfactory answer, so I added, '[He is training alone this evening. Only one of us felt able to take advantage of the invitation.]'

'[That is a great pity. I was looking forward to seeing you together again. Your bodies are so healthy and muscular. And you are so alike! It is a marvellous deception and a great novelty.]'

'[We never try to deceive anyone, sir. Joseph and I feel that —]'

'[Yes, but surely you realize how useful it must be, if you wish not to be somewhere! To be there in your twin brother's guise so that others you do not know think that you are somewhere else or that you are not what you appear?]'

I barely followed that. I thought to take a sip of the drink in order to cover my confusion, but when I raised the tankard to my lips the sweet, malty smell deterred me.

'[We are either seen together,]' I said, thinking how pointless all this was. '[Then people know we are twins. Or we are seen apart when no one need know.]'

'[That is so true, Mr Sawyer. Do you do everything together, even those things that —?]'

'[We lead separate lives, sir.]'

'[Unless we speak of your rowing! You could not do that alone!]'

'[No, sir.]'

'[Where and how did you learn to speak German?]' He was moving closer to me. '[It is excellent and almost without fault.]'

'[My mother is from Saxony, sir. She emigrated to England before the last war. That is where I was born, but I grew up speaking both English and German to her.]'

'[So you are half German! That is good. Half your medal is ours, I think!]'

He laughed uproariously and repeated his observation to some of his associates, standing close behind him. They laughed as well. I looked around to see if Mr Selwyn-Thaxted was anywhere near, but I could not spot him. I needed what he had called his advice. The small talk went on.

'[Herr Speer is an oarsman also. You should meet him perhaps.]'

'[Herr Speer?]'

'[Speer is our leader's architect. Look around you when you are in Berlin. Herr Speer is designing most of our great buildings and arenas. But he is fanatical about talking of boats.]'

'[I should like to meet him, of course,]' I said, but as vaguely as I could. '[What about Herr Hitler? Is he interested in sports?]'

'[He is our leader!]' Hess was suddenly alert and upright, and for a moment I thought he was going to raise his arm and salute. His deep-set eyes stared away across the room, apparently not focusing on anything in particular. Then he said, '[After the reception we are going on to a private dinner. Will you and your handsome brother accompany us?]'

'[My brother cannot be present at all this evening,]' I said.

'[Then you will come alone. We have good drinks and you will eat wild boar for the first time and we will explain many interesting things about Germany to you.]'

I was becoming increasingly anxious to escape from this man. I knew Joe was waiting for me in one of the streets outside the building. The longer I delayed the more furious he would be with me.

'[I'm sorry, Herr Deputy Führer,]' I said. '[It is not possible. I am really sorry.]'

'[We will make the arrangements for you. In the Third Reich all things are possible!]' His voice had taken on a bantering quality, which gave it a threatening undertone. '[What else is there for you to do in Berlin, while you are here? You will come with us when we leave in a few minutes. You will enjoy the rest of the evening. There will be no women, no one to interrupt what we wish to do. You understand, of course! We all have a good enjoyment and you can show me how you stroke. I your little boat shall be!]'

He laughed again, his eyes squeezing momentarily closed beneath his jutting eyebrows. I felt a wave of confusion, embarrassment, uncertainty, fear. His associates were watching for my reaction.

Hess tipped up his glass and finished the fruit juice. As he placed the glass on the table beside me, leaning forward so that his shoulder pressed against me, Selwyn-Thaxted materialized beside me with marvellous deftness.

'Ah, Sawyer,' he said. 'I see you need another drink.' My tankard of champagne-Guinness was still almost full, but Selwyn-Thaxted took it from me and put it down on the table. He flipped the lid closed. '[The ambassador has specifically asked if it would be possible to meet you, Sawyer,]' he added loudly in German, for Hess's benefit. '[Nothing formal. Do come with me straight away.]'

Hess was looming beside us.

'[We have decided already to leave, my gentleman,]' he said to Selwyn-Thaxted, then looked directly at me with his dark, worrying eyes. '[Come, we will depart, I think!]'

'[The ambassador presents his compliments, Herr Deputy Führer,]' said Selwyn-Thaxted. '[With your permission he asks if he might have a private audience with you also, but in a few minutes' time?]'

'[That is not possible.]'

'[Then His Excellency will not insist.] Come, Sawyer.'

With his hand firmly gripping my upper arm, Selwyn-Thaxted led me at a relaxed pace across the ballroom, then through a pair of double doors to a small room adjacent to the hall. He closed the doors behind him, cutting off most of the noises of the reception.

'May I assume you will be staying on in Berlin until the closing ceremony?' he said.

'I don't think that's going to be possible.' I told him about my brother's unexplained but urgent need to set off for home, to which Selwyn-Thaxted listened intently. He thought for a moment, staring at the ornately woven Persian carpet.

'Yes, I think that's probably wise,' he said. 'I don't know what your brother has in mind, but as far as you are concerned it's probably sensible not to see Herr Hess again.'

'May I ask why you encouraged me to meet him?'

'He asked for you by name. We also knew that you are a fluent German speaker, which suggested there might be an extra dimension that would possibly be useful.'

'It was small talk,' I said.

'Nothing at all of any interest?' Selwyn-Thaxted asked mildly.

'In what respect?'

'Well, did he happen to mention anything about Chancellor Hitler's plans, for instance?'

'No, that didn't come up. He is intrigued that my brother and I look so much alike. And he said that Herr Speer was interested in rowing.'

Selwyn-Thaxted smiled fleetingly. 'I don't think we knew that.'

'Is it important?'

'Probably not . . . but you never know.' Without being obvious about it, he was already steering me towards the door. 'I'm grateful to you, Mr Sawyer. I hope you didn't mind speaking to him.'

'No, sir.'

In the outer hall Selwyn-Thaxted asked one of the under-secretaries to conduct me out of the building by way of the main entrance.

By this time it was twilight but the air remained warm. I saw a line of open-top Daimlers waiting in Unter den Linden, ready to collect Hess and his colleagues, but of the Nazis themselves there was no sign. I walked quickly along Unter den Linden in the direction of Brandenburger Tor, beyond which I had agreed to meet Joe. I saw the van from a distance: the two shells were lashed once more to the roof. As I walked closer I saw Joe himself, pacing impatiently. He greeted me without more than a gruff acknowledgement and went quickly to the driver's side.

In no time at all we were driving at speed through the darkening streets of Berlin, going north. I said nothing. Night fell as we left the outskirts of the city and headed out into the German countryside, using the new autobahn that led towards Hamburg. It was not the same road as the one on which we had arrived. I mentioned this to Joe. He made no reply.

14

The Air Ministry car made several more stops during our long drive south from the hospital: for fuel, for Gilbert Strathy to make a telephone call, and finally for a snack and a cup of tea in a pleasant market town somewhere on the way. Without road signs it was difficult to recognize towns if you did not already know them. Neither of the other men commented on the route.

After our final stop I fell into a doze, rocking uncomfortably in the back of the car, my head lolling forward. I was in that peculiar state of non-sleep that it is possible to achieve while travelling, in which you remain partly aware of your circumstances yet able somehow to rest. I heard the other two men discussing me, presumably thinking I might not hear them.

I heard Mr Strathy say, 'I've managed to arrange a place for Group Captain Sawyer to stay tonight. It's a great asset that he doesn't need nursing.'

'Is he staying where we're going?'

'No, that wasn't possible. He has to be in London after this. There's a room in the Officers' Mess at Northolt. He could make that his base for as long as he needs.'

'Northolt's still a long way.'

'I know, but it's the best I could do. I have to return to London, so I can give him a lift as far as Northolt. After that, Downing Street will have to take over.'

I dozed on, interested but not interested, feeling exhausted after the long drive, with my left leg starting to hurt like mad, my neck stiff. The unfamiliar uniform, which at first had felt like a good fit, now proved to be cut too tightly under my arms and at my crotch. The fabric felt prickly where it pressed against uncovered skin: my legs, my neck, my wrists. I waited until the other two fell silent again, then popped an eye open surreptitiously, looking through the passenger window on my side. It was dark and the car was moving slowly, the shielded headlight beams throwing only a restricted glow forward. I thought sympathetically of the young driver in her glassed-off compartment at the front: she had been driving all day along narrow, difficult roads without town or direction signs, without many traffic signs, now without daylight. She too must be exhausted.

Mr Strathy reached over and gently touched the back of my hand, to rouse me.

'Are you awake, Sawyer?'

'Yes, I am,' I said, instantly alert. I realized that I had been dozing more deeply than I had thought. I felt myself plunged back into reality. The car, the other occupants, bulked large around me. The engine noise sounded much louder. I was aware of a draught flowing from the door and playing around my leg.

'We will be arriving shortly,' Strathy said. 'I thought you would like time to compose yourself.'

'Where are we?'

'We are about to drive through Wendover, which is not far from Chequers. I'm able to inform you now, Group Captain Sawyer, that the P.M. has asked to see you. Naturally, we could not tell you before.'

'The Prime Minister?' I said. 'Mr Churchill has asked to see me? I can't believe he even knows I exist.'

'Mr Churchill knows, I do assure you.'

The real Group Captain spoke. 'It's a short-term staff secondment, Sawyer. You'll be told the details when we arrive, but from time to time the Prime Minister's office makes personal appointments from within senior echelons of the forces. Many young men like you are chosen from the armed services for this kind of experience. It'll stand you in good stead later on.'

'What will I be expected to do?' I was still slightly dazed by the news.

'The P.M. or one of his people will explain that to you. Tomorrow you'll receive a more detailed briefing from the staff at Admiralty House. Tonight, you are simply to meet the P.M. for a few moments. After that we'll drive you to your quarters, which will be at RAF Northolt. You'll be based at Northolt for the time being.'

'Sir, I thought I was going back on ops.'

'You will be soon. This is a temporary posting. The promotion is also an acting one, although if you acquit yourself well in the next few weeks I dare say you won't be returned all the way to your former rank.'

The driver suddenly braked the car and swung it to the left, as if until then she had not seen the turning she was looking for. As I lurched sideways in my seat I glimpsed tall, brick-built gateposts in the quick glare of the headlights, then wrought-iron gates. Uniformed police officers stood beside each gatepost, saluting as we passed through. Beyond the gate itself there was a more familiar military-style checkpoint, with a guardhouse next to it. Here the car halted and an army sergeant leaned down and examined everyone's papers with careful movements of his torch. It was almost impossible for me to see what was going on. Strathy and Group Captain Dodman waited patiently. I carried no papers: my service identification had been lost or destroyed when the Wellington crashed into the sea. However, there appeared to be no problem as to my identity.

We drove on down the unlit driveway, passing between mature trees, with white-painted stones set at intervals on the sides of the track, each one gleaming briefly as we passed.

I remember those few seconds vividly. No one in the car spoke from the moment we left the barrier until we were inside the famous house called Chequers, giving me an opportunity to collect myself and prepare for what was to come.

As I write these words it is many years since the Second World War ended. I live in a time when it is fashionable in some quarters to be cynical about patriotism, bravery, political leadership, national purpose. I feel it myself sometimes, as in a properly sceptical democracy who should not? In 1941 things were different, for which I make no apology.

Winston Churchill then was an incomparable figure, almost unique in British history. For those of us who were alive at that time, we happy few, Churchill was the man who mustered the nation's spirit when everyone expected defeat. We held out alone against Hitler's Germany, then the most powerful military nation in the world. The result, a few years later, was the eventual military victory of the Allies, although in 1940 and 1941 there were few who would have seen victory as inevitable, or even likely. When the war ended in 1945, everyone was so relieved to be able to put the war behind them that they turned their backs on the years they had recently lived through. The war was over. What had mattered most then suddenly mattered not at all. Churchill fell spectacularly from power and languished in Opposition while much that he predicted came to pass. He returned as Prime Minister in 1951, for one more short term of office when he was physically enfeebled by old age. It is also true that for many years before he came to power in 1940 Churchill was a controversial figure on the margins, unpopular in some quarters, distrusted by most of his political contemporaries. But he rose to the moment. Churchill, in those long and dangerous months before the USA, the Soviet Union and Japan were involved in the war, quickly became a legend to most ordinary British people. He seemed to sum up a certain kind of British spirit, a symbol of British willingness to fight, perhaps never before identified until that need arose.

I was of that world, that generation. I was serving in the RAF when war broke out, with the rank of Flying Officer. Our early attempts to launch daylight bombing raids were met with fierce resistance. We suffered terrible losses and the raids were soon discontinued. The Blenheims we flew were too slow and badly defended for daytime use and did not have the range for deep-penetration night flying, so for most of the first winter and spring of the war we restricted ourselves to anti-ship 'sweeps' across the North Sea, rarely engaging, or even seeing, the enemy.

With the invasion of France, the war entered a deadly earnest phase and Britain's safety was at risk. As the dangers loomed, Neville Chamberlain's reputation as the man who had appeased Hitler made him an unsuitable war leader. He stood down, Churchill took over and a new spirit swept through the nation. Never was the peril greater, never were the British people so willing to face it. If you were there, if you lived through those times, you were in awe of Churchill. There is no other word for it, and it was awe that described my feelings as we drove slowly up to the main entrance of the Prime Minister's country residence.

I was stiff from being cooped up in the car all day and it took me a long time to ease myself out on to the gravel surface, supporting myself with my stick. The two men I was travelling with watched with some sympathy, but I was determined to manage on my own. Sharp daggers of pain stabbed into my legs and back.

Gradually the pain eased. Group Captain Dodman was by my side as we went through the door, his hand lightly supporting the elbow of my right arm. We were met by a man wearing black trousers and a white shirt, neatly pressed, not in the least casual. He greeted all three of us by name, then asked if we would please wait a while.

We were shown to a side room: a long, dim, panelled chamber, with dark landscape paintings, trophies and bookcases lining the walls on each side. A table ran down the centre of the room, well polished, with a great number of chairs arranged neatly around it. The windows were draped with thick tapestry curtains, the dark fabric of blackout material visible behind them, covering the glass panes. The three of us stood in a nervous group just inside the door, waiting for what I at least assumed would be a summons in the next few minutes.

We were still there two hours later, having long since taken seats at one end of the table. During the time we were waiting callers to the house came and went, some merely delivering or collecting various things, others arriving on apparently urgent missions and being conducted straight away to other parts of the building. About an hour after we arrived we were brought a tray of tea and biscuits. We conversed little, all drained by the long day in the car and expecting to be called at any moment.

At about twelve-fifteen the summons finally came.

Stiffly again, I climbed to my feet. Leaving the other two in the waiting room I hobbled after the man who had come for me, feeling I should hurry so as not to keep the Prime Minister waiting, but put under no pressure to do so.

We crossed the hall where we had entered, then went along a short, darkened corridor. I was led into a room where there were four desks bearing large typewriters, with women working on two of them. The room was sparsely and cheerlessly furnished: bare floorboards, no curtains apart from the inevitable blackout screens, harsh overhead lights, a multitude of filing cabinets, telephones, in-trays, trailing wires, paper everywhere. Again, I was asked to wait. The secretarial work went on around me, with the two typists paying no attention to me at all. The clock over the door said that it was twenty minutes past twelve.

'The Prime Minister will see you now,' said the man who had brought me from the waiting room, holding open the door. As I limped through he said, 'Mr Churchill, this is Group Captain J. L. Sawyer.'

After the bright unshaded lights of the office I had left, the large room I entered felt at first as if it was in darkness. Only the centrally placed desk was illuminated, by two table lamps placed at each end. In the light reflecting up from the papers I saw the famous visage of Winston Churchill leaning forward across his work. Cigar smoke shrouded the air. As I walked painfully towards the desk he did not look up but continued to read through a sheaf of papers, a thick fountain pen in one hand. He held a cigar in the other. An almost empty cut-glass tumbler was on the desk, glinting in the light — a decanter of whisky and a jug of water stood beside it. Mr Churchill was wearing half-moon reading spectacles. He read rapidly, pausing only to inscribe his initials at the bottom of each page, then turning the sheet with the hand that held the pen. On the last page he wrote a few words, signed his name and turned the sheet over.

He tossed the papers into an over-full wire basket under one of the lamps, then took another wad from his dispatch box.

'Sawyer,' he said, looking up at me over his spectacles. I was only a short distance away from him, but even so I wondered if he could see me properly, so deep was the shade in the room. 'J. L. Sawyer. You're the one named Jack, is that it?'

'Yes, sir.'

'Not the other one.'

'Do you mean my brother, Mr Churchill?'

'Yes. What's happened to him? My people had the two of you muddled up for a while.'

'My brother is dead, sir. He was killed last year during the first few weeks of the Blitz.'

Churchill looked startled. 'I hadn't heard that dreadful news. Words are always inadequate, but let me say how appalled I am to hear it. I can only offer you my sincerest condolences.' The Prime Minister was staring straight at me, saying nothing. For a moment he seemed genuinely lost for words. He put down his pen. Then he said, 'This war . . . this bloody war.'

'Joe's death happened several months ago, sir,' I said.

'Even so.' He shook his head slightly and pressed his hands flat on the desk. 'Let me at least tell you why I have asked to see you. I'm in need of an *aide-de-camp* from the RAF, and your name was put forward. You won't have much to do for a while, but I might have a more interesting job coming up for you later. For now, when we go anywhere I would require you to walk behind me, stay visible and keep your trap shut. I see you're on a stick. You can walk, can't you?'

'Yes, sir.'

'The staff here will give you the passes you need. Be at Admiralty House first thing tomorrow morning, if you will.'

'Yes, sir,' I said again. Mr Churchill had returned to browsing through his papers, the hand and the pen moving steadily down the margin. After a few seconds of indecision I realized that the interview had ended, so I turned round painfully and went as quickly as I could towards the door.

'Group Captain Sawyer!'

I paused and looked back. The Prime Minister had put down the papers and was now sitting more erect behind his desk. He added whisky and water to his glass, more of the former than of the latter.

'They tell me you and your brother went to the Berlin Olympics and won a medal.'

'A bronze, sir. We were in the coxless pairs.'

'Well done. They also tell me you were introduced to Rudolf Hess afterwards.'

'Yes, I was.'

'Was that you alone, or was your brother there too?'

'Just me, sir.'

'Did your brother ever meet him?'

'Only briefly. Hess handed us our medals at the ceremony.'

'But I gather you spent some time with him after that. Did you form any kind of impression of the man?'

'It was a few years ago, Mr Churchill. I met Herr Hess at a reception at the British Embassy. I didn't spend long with him, but I would say that I didn't like him.'

'I didn't ask if you liked him. I'm told you speak fluent German and held a long conversation with the man. What did you make of him?'

I thought before answering, because since that evening so long ago I had not dwelt on my memories of what happened. Larger and more interesting events had followed.

Mr Churchill took a sip from his glass of whisky, watching me steadily.

'From the way he was acting I would have thought him drunk, but he was not drinking alcohol. I came to the conclusion he was used to getting his way by bullying people. He was with a crowd of other Nazis and he seemed to be showing off in front of them. It would be difficult for me to say what I really learned about him.'

'All right. Would you recognize him again if you saw him now?'

'Yes, sir. I'll never forget him.'

'Good. That could be invaluable to me. As you possibly know, Herr Hess has acquired a certain notoriety in recent weeks.'

I had no idea what Mr Churchill meant by that last remark. The news of Hess's sensational arrival in Scotland had apparently been overtaken by events. I was stunned by the realization that the Germans were seeking peace, but after the first blaze of publicity there was no follow-up in the papers and Hess was never mentioned on the wireless. I had discussed it with some of the other patients at the convalescent hospital, but none of them knew any more about it than I did.

Mr Churchill put down the drink, took up his pen and returned to the papers. I waited for a few seconds but once again it was clear that he had finished with me. I opened the door behind me and returned to the outer office. One of the secretaries was waiting and she handed me a folder containing several pieces of paper and card. She explained what they were, where I should sign them and when I would be expected to show them.

A few minutes later, reunited with Group Captain Dodman and Mr Strathy, I went back to the car waiting on the gravel drive outside the house. The WAAF driver was asleep, hunched forward uncomfortably over the steering wheel.

15

Joe was tense and silent as he drove away from Berlin. He checked the rear-view mirror constantly and reacted nervously if any other vehicle overtook us. Of course I asked him what the matter was. As before, he would say nothing.

We left the huge sprawl of the city behind us and were driving along the autobahn through the dark countryside when I heard a muffled knocking from the back of the van. It sounded like a mechanical problem to me, but Joe shrugged it off.

'Hold on, will you?' he said to me harshly.

A few minutes later we approached a turn-off, signposted to a place called Kremmen, and after further checking in the mirror Joe slowed the van. There was no traffic around. We left the autobahn and joined a narrow road, leading across hilly country and through tall trees. Joe drove for another two or three minutes before he spotted a narrow lane that led off to the side. He pulled into it, switched off the engine and doused all lights.

I said into the sudden silence, 'Joe, what's going on?'

'I sometimes think you must be blind, when so much occurs around you that you don't see. Come and give me a hand.'

Outside the van we were in almost total darkness. Whatever light there might have been from what remained of the dusk was blotted out by the canopy of trees. There were no sounds of traffic, no lights from houses, no sign of anything happening anywhere. A warm, piney smell embraced us. Over our heads we could hear the branches brushing lightly against each other as the breeze soughed through the forest. Our feet crunched on dried needles. Joe opened the rear double doors of the van. He reached in, felt around for a moment, then located what he was looking for. It was our torch, which he switched on and passed to me.

'Hold it steady,' he said.

He clambered up into the van compartment, bending double, and pushed our bags of kit away from the side where they were piled up. There seemed to be several more cases and boxes than I remembered bringing with us when we left home.

'Over here!' he said, waving his hand with an annoyed gesture. 'Don't point the light at me.'

A mattress had been placed on the floor of the van, concealed until now by the bags and cases Joe had stacked alongside it. The mattress itself was covered by a wooden board of some kind, leaning at a forty-five-degree angle against the wall of the van to make a cramped, triangular space beneath. Joe was kneeling on the edge of the mattress, pulling the board away. As soon as he did so I realized that there was someone lying underneath it. The figure exclaimed loudly in German and made an irate movement, pushing at the board from below and sitting upright as soon as there was enough space to do so.

It was a young woman, but because of the angle of the torch beam I did not recognize her at first. Joe took her hands and helped her out, and as soon as I was able to see her properly I realized it was Birgit, the daughter of the family we had been staying with in Berlin.

Joe tried to embrace her but she pushed him away angrily.

'[Why have you taken so long?]' she cried. '[I've been trapped for hours! I couldn't move, couldn't breathe, I'm dying of thirst!]'

'[I stopped as soon as I thought it would be safe,]' Joe said. '[I was held up in Berlin, waiting for him.]'

He jabbed his thumb in my direction. At least some of Joe's earlier impatience was explained, but many other questions remained glaringly unanswered. For a few minutes there was a noisy scene between the three of us, there under the darkness of the trees, with Birgit angry and Joe defensive, while I was thoroughly confused and unable to get replies to the string of questions I felt had to be asked.

Birgit's unexpected appearance caused an explosion of feelings in me that I could never explain to Joe. I had never discussed her with him, so I assumed, partly because it suited me to assume, that he had no interest in her. However, thoughts of her had haunted my every moment since we had arrived in Berlin. She was the most beautiful young woman I had ever seen or met. Her lively, amusing personality had smitten me, provoking wild fantasies which I reluctantly suppressed. When she picked up the violin and became absorbed in her music I simply doted on her. I managed a few short conversations with her, but most of our contact had been during the family meals. I had not been able to take my eyes off her. She ravished me with her looks, her laugh, her sensitive intelligence. When I was away from that apartment in Goethe-strasse I could hardly dare think of her, so turbulent were my feelings about her, yet I could barely think of anything or anyone else.

Things eventually quietened down. My eyes began to adjust to the gloom so that it was no longer so profoundly dark around us. I could see that Joe and Birgit were standing side by side, leaning back against the van.

I said, 'Would you mind telling me what's been going on, Joe?'

'[Speak in German so Birgit can follow what we're saying.]'

'She speaks English well enough,' I said, sulkily.

'[We're still in her country. Let's make it as easy for her as possible.]'

'[All right, Joe. What's happening?]'

'[Birgit is going to travel back to England with us. She has to leave Germany as soon as possible.]'

'[Why?]'

Joe said to Birgit, '[It is exactly as I was telling you. People like JL haven't the faintest idea what Hitler has been doing to the Jews in this country.]'

'[You needn't patronize me,]' I said, stung by his words, but more so by the way he tried to belittle me in front of Birgit. '[I can read the newspapers.]'

'[Yes, but you don't act on what you read.]'

'[How can you say that?]' I retorted. '[If you felt as strongly as that, you wouldn't have come to Germany for the Games.]'

'[I couldn't tell you before,]' Joe said quietly. '[I was going to try to convince you we should stay away. After all the training we've done I wasn't sure how I could tell you, or what I could say to persuade you, but that's how I was feeling. Then Mum told me about Birgit, how desperate the situation had become in Berlin for Jews, and that she was desperate to help. You know she and Hanna Sattmann were brought up together. The truth is that the main reason I came to Germany was not to race, but to try to bring Birgit out with us.]'

'[JL, he's right about the situation,]' said Birgit, her head turning from one of us to the other. '[You can't know what it's been like for us. But neither can you, Joe. No more than any of the visitors who have come from abroad for the Games. The Nazis have been pulling down their banners, cleaning slogans off the walls, allowing Jewish shops and restaurants to open up again, to make foreigners think that what they've been told about the persecution of Jews is untrue. As soon as the Games are over, they'll start up on us again.]'

She gulped, then fell silent. In the darkness I could see she was pressing her hands over her eyes. Joe leaned towards her, apparently trying to console her, but she pushed him aside. In the gloom I saw her move away from the van, stepping into the darker area beneath the nearest trees. I could hear her crying.

My heart impelled me to run across to her, hold her, comfort her, but in the last few minutes I had started to realize how little I really knew about her or her life. For that matter, too, how little I understood about what the Nazis had been doing to the Jews in Germany.

Here again, the time I am describing seems an age ago. Post-war hindsight threatens the accuracy of my memories, in particular the reliability of my remembered sensibilities. This was 1936. The concentration camps and the extermination camps, Himmler's *Einsatzgruppen*, the vile medical experiments on prisoners, the forced labour and starvation, the gas chambers, all these lay years ahead. To say that Joe and I could not have known about the growing persecution would be facile, but even had we been blessed or cursed with foresight, who could have believed how it would in reality grow?

Yet the clues were in place. They were nakedly exposed in the speeches of Adolf Hitler, there for anyone to understand them, if they took the trouble. Rudolf Hess was no better, but he was not so well known at that time outside Germany. Although it was Hitler who announced the Nuremberg Laws, the series of measures that removed all civil, legal and humanitarian rights from the Jews, and which Birgit was in effect beginning to tell us about, it was Hess who had enacted them and it was Hess's signature on the orders.

Again, Joe and I were two naïve young men from a relatively sheltered background, whose principal interest was sport. Perhaps I was more naïve than Joe, but it was true of us both. We were not untypical. Even those who should have known better, the politicians and diplomats of the Western democracies, clearly did not realize the enormity of what was happening in Germany. Perhaps they suspected more than they admitted, but they have claimed since that they did not. There was some mitigation: nothing like it had ever happened before, or not on such a scale, so it was easier to try to believe something else, to hope for the best. But those few minutes, in the hush of the silent forest, turned out to be the beginning of an education for me.

I sat down on the carpet of pine needles, away from the other two, thinking that my presence was only adding to the confusion. I certainly realized that the turbulence of my feelings and wishes meant that I was likely to say or do something I would quickly regret. I watched the indistinct dark shapes of the other two, visible against the white-painted background of the van. Birgit was sobbing quietly; Joe was talking to her. Either I could not hear what they were saying, or I closed my mind to it. Gradually she calmed.

A little later I went to the rear compartment of the van and found the Primus picnic-stove that Joe and I had brought with us from England. I set it up with some difficulty and managed to light the burner and heat up water from our canteen. I made coffee for all three of us, dark and strong, the way we knew the Germans liked it. Birgit sat on the van's floor, between the open doors, cradling her cup and sipping the hot drink. Joe and I stood before her.

Joe told me what he and Birgit were planning. We spoke in English.

'Birgit has no money with her, no passport, no documents of any kind,' he said. 'Just about everything has been taken away from the Jews in Germany. She is forbidden to travel and if she is discovered with us we will be in the most serious trouble. But we think we can get out of Germany OK. Her parents found out that there's a Swedish ship sailing for England tomorrow, leaving from Hamburg. If we drive tonight and tomorrow we can catch it.'

'What if we miss it?'

'That's when things might become more difficult. Doktor Sattmann thought that if we miss the ship we should attempt to drive across the border to Denmark and try our luck there, but it might be impossible.'

'Joe, what in God's name are we getting involved in here?'

'We have to take Birgit to England. She's not safe in Berlin any more.'

'What about her parents?'

'They're in the same position as Birgit, of course. They've decided they must escape from Germany too. They've been warned by friends in Berlin that if they travelled as a family they would probably be stopped at the border, so Birgit has to leave with us. As soon as they know she's safe in England, they're going to try to travel separately to Switzerland, where her father has a little money. With luck they'll be able to get to France from there, then make it across to England. They might even leave next week. No one's sure what's going to happen to the Jews after the weekend, when the Games finish.'

'Wouldn't Birgit be safer staying with her parents?'

'No. They've heard stories about other German Jewish families caught trying to escape.'

We were already committed to a desperate plan, with no safeguards except the most elementary ones. Joe and I agreed that Birgit could travel in the front of the van for as long as it was dark and we were not trying to cross any borders. As soon as we got near Hamburg, though, she would have to return to her hiding place and stay in it until we were on the ship and clear of German territorial waters.

Time was passing. We knew that we should cover as much distance as possible in the darkness of the short summer's night. I offered to take the first turn in the cramped rear compartment of the van, settling myself on the mattress to make myself as comfortable as I could, with the board Joe had used as a cover stacked out of my way on the other side. It was hardly cosy, but after while I was able to doze a little.

After midnight Joe found another place in a side road to make a brief halt, and he and I changed places. I was stiff from being confined in the noisy, shaking rear of the van and was glad of the break. Birgit, sitting to my left, hunched down in the passenger seat with her knees drawn up against her chest. I said nothing as I turned the vehicle around and headed back towards the autobahn. The engine felt rougher, noisier than before. Every shift of the gears made the van jerk and shudder.

Once on the wide, modern road I was able to drive at a steady cruising speed, with few of those disruptive changes of gear. I hoped that Joe, silent in the compartment behind my seat, was finding it possible to sleep. I wanted to talk to Birgit, to make the most of our temporary companionship, but I already knew that for all the noise and vibration in the vehicle it was possible for someone in the back to hear what the two in the front were saying.

Whenever another vehicle went past in the other direction, I used the momentary glare of its headlights to steal a glance across at Birgit.

She remained awake, staring forward into the night. She gave no hint of what she was thinking. Eventually she did shift position, twisting her body and switching her legs so that they were on the other side. This put her head and shoulders closer to mine. When the next vehicle roared past on the other side of the autobahn, I glanced towards her and found that she was looking at me. Still neither of us said anything. Quite apart from Joe's silent presence, asleep or awake, a few inches away, Birgit had the power to strike me dumb, to make me feel clumsy, to inspire me to think and say the most foolish and impetuous things. I sensed that it was a crucial night in my life, one that I should not ruin with hasty words, so I kept my silence. My senses reached out towards her. I was aware of every tiny movement she made, every small sound. I imagined I could feel the warmth of her face radiating across the short space between us so that my own cheek felt the glow of her. I craved to hear a first word from her that I could respond to, even a grunt or some other kind of semi-voluntary noise, a reaction to something which I could in turn react to. She remained silent. I drove on, completely obsessed with her, driven mad by her silent presence, but beginning to enjoy what we were doing. In the monotony of the almost deserted highway I could pretend to myself that Birgit and I were alone in the van, that Joe was no longer with us, that she and I were eloping together, driving through the warm European night to some romantic destiny.

I began yearning for every next vehicle to appear from the distance ahead of us and pass with a flood of its headlights. Whenever it happened I turned to Birgit and found her looking towards me. Her eyes were serious and calm, seeking mine with some unstated private message.

The few hours of darkness passed slowly before light began to glimmer against the clouds low on the eastern horizon. Birgit became aware of the coming dawn at the same moment as me, as if realizing that the intimacy of the night would pass with daylight. She leaned even closer to me and placed her hand on mine, where I was holding the steering wheel.

She said, in English, 'JL, I am most happy to be here with you and Joe.'

I grinned back at her, unwilling to speak in case it brought a response from Joe, hidden behind me. I could see her now, without needing the lights of a passing vehicle to show her to me. She was smiling; a conspiratorial flicker of her eyes towards Joe's position seemed to confirm my own feelings about not wanting Joe to be a part of it.

She did not remove her hand from mine. I drove on and on, as smoothly as I could, north-west towards Hamburg, savouring every second of the long moment of intimacy with the girl I thought of as the prettiest in the world. Gradually, morning came.

16

I was woken at 6.30 a.m. in my room in the Officers' Mess at RAF Northolt. I had slept for less than three hours. I forced myself out of bed, reeling with the need to sleep, fighting back the compulsion to stay lying down for a few minutes more. I showered, shaved and dressed, stumbling, dropping things, yawning. I was stiff with fatigue and my leg was aching. Breakfast was the standard RAF fare for non-operational officers: as much toast as I could eat, spread with the yellow gunge the mess called butter but which tasted of fish and was widely rumoured to be refined from the sumps of trawlers.

The car was already waiting for me outside the mess. It was a large black Riley with the crest of the House of Commons imprinted on the doors. A WAAF driver — not the same one as before — was standing beside the passenger's door. As I approached she stood to attention, saluted smartly and held the door open for me. It had started to rain: a warm but depressing drizzle, slicking down over the roads and trees from a sky the colour of lead.

The WAAF drove swiftly towards central London, expertly negotiating through what little traffic there was.

It was my first visit to London since the early months of 1940, when I had spent a weekend leave with some of the other officers from 105 Squadron. We were in the West End for two nights, carousing our way through the pubs and nightclubs, taking a break from what we thought at the time to be the unspeakable horrors of war. Like most people we had no conception of what was to follow within a few weeks. After the invasion of France and the Low Countries, the Germans were able to move their bomber squadrons to within a short flying distance of the British coast. Every major city in Britain was suddenly within range. For most people the war changed from an anxious time of distant skirmishes to a battle in which they found themselves in the front line. The nightly Blitz had begun in the first week of September 1940 and continued more or less without a break for eight months. London suffered the most, but almost every provincial city was attacked at one time or another. By November, casualties among civilians and rescue workers were numbered in the thousands. One of those killed was my brother Joe, who died when the Red Cross ambulance he was driving in London took a direct hit from a bomb. Months later, I had still not become reconciled to the shock of his loss.

Today was my first visit to London since the Blitz began. I stared out of the car as we drove to the centre, appalled by the sheer scale of destruction. Everyone in Britain knew the capital had taken a beating during the winter. Even though what the newspapers printed was controlled by government overseers, so as not to give information or encouragement to the enemy, there was enough for most people to gain a pretty vivid idea of what was going on. The weekly newsreels at the cinemas were filled with images of flames, smoke, gutted and collapsing buildings, snaking hosepipes in the roads and torrents of water jetted against the fires.

But to see some of the damage for myself was horrifying. As we drove along Western Avenue I saw street after street where houses had been blown to pieces, where rubble-mountains of brick and plaster and jagged beams of charred wood had been created by the bulldozers. In Acton I saw a whole street that had been destroyed: it was just a rough, undulating sea of broken bricks and other rubble. Windows everywhere were broken, even where there was no other visible damage. There was a pervasive, squalid smell: something of drains, smoke, chalk, oil, soot, town gas. Along the main road itself there were many places where the surface had been cratered by an explosion or was being dug up to repair water mains, electricity supplies, telephone connections, gas pipes, sewers. These constant obstacles slowed our progress. In a few places, where the damage was worst and bombed buildings hung perilously awaiting demolition, there were police warning signs, tapes, boards hastily erected to prevent pedestrians from wandering into areas where the paths or the road surface had been undermined. The rain still fell lightly, streaking the car windows with muddy rivulets and creating areas of shallow flooding across the roads and pavements.

We were held up by a large truck blocking the road. Accompanied by a team of workmen, it was reversing slowly into one of the bomb sites. I stared out at the dismal scene, the shattered bricks and pipes lying in the muddy puddles, the filth of charred wood, the glimpses of broken and crushed household items, the pathetic remains of wallpaper visible where inner walls still happened to stand. I tried to imagine what the street must have looked like before the war, when it was full of homes, harmlessly lived in by ordinary people, going about their lives, worrying about money or jobs or their children, but never imagining the worst, that one night their house and all the houses around it would be blown apart by German bombs or incinerated by phosphorus incendiaries.

I also tried to imagine what those former inhabitants must have thought about the men who had bombed their houses, the Luftwaffe fliers, coming in by night. The fury they must have felt, the frustration of not being able to hit back.

I recoiled from the thought. The popular press depicted the Luftwaffe crews as fanatical Nazis, Huns, Jerries, shorthand codes for an enemy impossible to understand, but sense told me that most of the German fliers were probably little different from me and the young men I flew with. Our own bombing missions to Bremen, Hamburg, Berlin, Kiel, Cologne were no different in kind from the raids that had brought the German bombers here to Acton and Shepherd's Bush. Today, in Hamburg, there would inevitably be piles of rubble, fractured water-mains, homeless children, where A-Able's high-explosive bombs had fallen.

There was surely a difference, though? What everyone hated about the German raids was that they were indiscriminate, the bombs falling on every part of the cities that were attacked. Women and children were as likely to be killed or injured as soldiers — more likely, indeed, since cities are full of civilians. By contrast, it was repeatedly argued that the British bombing of German cities was a matter of careful targeting, of meticulously chosen aiming points on military installations distant from civilian centres.

War cannot be fought except with lies. I knew the dispiriting reality of the RAF's bombing campaign. I had experienced at first hand the impossibility of aiming accurately at targets shrouded in cloud or smoke, I remembered so well the crews' inability in the dark to find the chosen town, let alone the specific target: the power station, the military camp, the arms factory. I had tried to fly through anti-aircraft fire without losing my nerve, listening on the intercom to the terrified reactions of the other men, knowing that sometimes bombs were released early in panic, that sometimes the bomb-load was jettisoned in frustration after a target could not be found, believing it preferable to drop bombs on anything German — even a German field — than to return home with a full load of unused weapons.

We left the suburbs, passing the White City stadium, then turned south towards Holland Park, heading for the part of central London close to the river. The nature of the damage changed noticeably. Where in the suburbs there had apparently been few attempts to clear the wreckage, in the central parts of the city, where several raids had been concentrated, much had been done to keep the streets clear. Where the bombing was worst I saw gaps in the rows of buildings, and the streets, if they were cratered, had been effectively repaired and smoothed. Everywhere I looked I saw piles of sandbags guarding the entrances to buildings or shelters and windows criss-crossed with sticky tape to try to prevent glass splinters flying. Directions to the nearest air-raid shelters were everywhere, painted on walls or printed on paper placards pasted to shop windows.

In some respects London life was continuing as it had before the war: there were many red double-decker buses driving along, as well as more than a few taxi-cabs. Apart from the general absence of other cars, there were whole stretches where for a few moments you could believe that nothing much had been changed by the war. It was an illusion, of course, because as soon as you convinced yourself that you were seeing a part of London the bombers had somehow missed, the car would turn a corner and there would be another burnt-out ruin, another gap, another hastily erected wooden façade concealing some scene of devastation beyond. The sheer magnitude of the damage was a shock to me: it extended for mile after mile, with every part of London apparently affected.

I guiltily remembered a night when we had been despatched to bomb Münster, a town that had been difficult to find. When we finally located the place, it turned out to be covered in cloud. Because A-Able was starting to run low on fuel, we dropped the bombs blind, through ten-tenths cloud cover, down on Münster below, then headed for home. Where did those bombs fall, what did they destroy, what human lives had they permanently disrupted?

We crossed Hyde Park Corner then went along Constitution Hill, past Buckingham Palace, which was almost unrecognizable behind the mountains of sandbags placed against every visible door and window. Green Park, to the left, was a curious sight: much of the open space had been ploughed under and replanted with vegetables, but at frequent intervals I saw emplacements of anti-aircraft guns, or winching stations for the multitude of silvery barrage-balloons that floated five hundred feet above the trees.

We turned into The Mall, where more anti-aircraft guns pointed upwards through the summer-leafed trees on each side. The car was moving alone, unhindered by other traffic. I realized that I had crossed over into a part of London that was closed to normal traffic, that my new status as one of Churchill's ADCs was already letting me move in places, and around people, that I would not have dreamed about even two days earlier.

Admiralty House is part of the great archway that separates The Mall from Trafalgar Square and the warren of offices it contains had provided Mr Churchill with a London headquarters that was more practical for the conduct of a war than the cramped quarters of 10 Downing Street, a short distance away. The WAAF driver took the car to the rear entrance of the building, in the wide area called Horse Guards Parade, in peacetime a place of pageantry and commemoration of great national events, now in wartime a huge open-air depot for military vehicles, supplies and temporary buildings. The inevitable brace of anti-aircraft guns stood among the trees adjacent to St James's Park.

I walked from the car towards the only entrance I could see, wondering what I was supposed to do and to whom I was supposed to be reporting. My orders said only to attend the building by the stated time. However, as soon as I limped to within sight of the door, a Regimental Sergeant-Major marched out to greet me, snapped to attention, saluted me and, after briefly checking my identity, conducted me to a room close to the main entrance. Here, already waiting, was a small group of men, presumably civil servants, dressed in suits and carrying bowler hats, two senior policemen, and two other serving officers: a submarine captain from the Royal Navy and a colonel from the Brigade of Guards. Everyone was extremely cordial and welcoming and I was offered a cup of tea while we waited.

At about eight-thirty we heard a great deal of noise in the corridor outside and a number of men and women hurried past. A few moments later, entirely without ceremony, the stocky figure of Winston Churchill appeared at the door of the room.

'Good morning, gentlemen,' he said, glancing around as if checking that we were all present. 'Let us be done with this task as quickly as possible, as I have to be elsewhere this afternoon and out of London tonight.'

He turned smoothly and walked out of the door. We followed, making way for each other. It was only a few hours since my interview with Mr Churchill at Chequers. Before he appeared I had been thinking that he might acknowledge me personally, perhaps make small-talk about the late night that he must know we had both had. In fact he barely glanced at me. I noticed that for someone of his age, who in the early hours of this morning was still awake and working and who, like me, could have snatched only two or three hours' sleep to be in central London by this early hour, he looked remarkably fresh. I had seen him only in the glow of his desk lamps — in the bright light of morning his face, the familiar rounded outlines, so reminiscent of a baby's features, looked vigorous and untroubled.

Outside, he was standing beside the first of three cars that were waiting for us. He was wearing his familiar black hat and coat and already held a fat Double Corona cigar in his hand, as yet unlit. Like all of us, he carried a gas-mask in a pouch slung over one shoulder. As the civil servants and the other military men started to dispose themselves in the three cars, Mr Churchill signalled to me.

'Group Captain, this is your first tour with me, is it not? You should travel in the front car today. Get the feel of things.'

He climbed into the rear compartment and I followed. One of the civil servants clambered in beside me and the three of us squeezed into the back seat. I held my walking-stick between my knees in front of me, exactly in the same way, I suddenly noticed, as Mr Churchill was holding his own cane.

Without further ado the convoy of cars set off, first wheeling around Horse Guards Parade, then passing through Admiralty Arch into Trafalgar Square. A crowd of pigeons scattered noisily as our cars rushed along. We headed east.

It was for me an extraordinary experience to be sitting so close to, indeed crushed up against, this most famous and powerful statesman, to feel the warmth of his side and leg pressing casually against mine, to feel his weight lean against me as the car went round corners. He said nothing, his hands resting on the handle of his cane, the unlit cigar jutting up from his fingers. He stared out of the passenger window, apparently deep in thought, his lower lip set in that familiar expression of stubbornness.

I had heard that Churchill was normally a talkative man and the silence in the car was becoming one of those that you feel must be broken. What had Mr Churchill known about me and Joe before we met, that had made his staff confuse us?

Joe and Birgit had moved to the north of England soon after they married at the end of 1936, renting a house on the Cheshire side of the Pennine hills, near Macclesfield, but I had seen hardly anything of either of them since I left university. The last occasion was when we met at our parents' house during one of my leaves. That was the week of the first Christmas of the war, an occasion of bitter arguments between us which ended up with my leaving the house in a rage, infuriated by Joe's intractable attitude and beliefs, and feeling, wrongly as it turned out much later, that my father was taking Joe's side against me.

I had not seen or spoken to Joe after that: in our different ways we became caught up in the war, I more obviously in the RAF. At the beginning of 1940, Joe successfully applied to be registered as a conscientious objector, afterwards starting to work for the Red Cross. I was bitterly regretful that he and I had not been able to patch up our differences before he died, but that was not to be. Much of what he had gone through in his last months was unknown to me.

Our motorcade was passing through areas of much heavier bomb damage, where many burnt-out buildings stood looming over the road with their smoke-darkened walls and blank windows. The sky could be glimpsed through their roofless shells. Not all such damaged buildings remained: many had been demolished and the rubble cleared away, allowing new vistas across to other parts of the city. I saw St Paul's Cathedral, still more or less intact, having famously survived the worst nights of the Blitz, but it was surrounded by acres of levelled ground, ruined buildings and bulldozed heaps of rubble.

At last I spoke.

'Mr Churchill, last night you mentioned my brother Joseph. May I ask what you knew about him before he died?'

For a moment Churchill did not seem to react. Then he turned to look at me.

'I'm sorry, Group Captain. I know nothing more of your late brother than what I told you last night.'

'You implied he was known to you in some way. You said your staff had been confusing the two of us.'

Mr Churchill looked back out of his window, not burdening himself to answer.

The man who was in the seat beside me, presumably a member of Churchill's staff, suddenly spoke.

'Group Captain Sawyer, we are passing the Bank of England. It remains undamaged, as you can see. And the Mansion House. I think you'll find as we move further down towards the docks that the destruction gets worse.'

I nodded politely. The Prime Minister's answer had piqued rather than satisfied my curiosity. He had in fact told me nothing at all about Joe during our short meeting.

'Is this your first visit to London since the Blitz?' said the man beside me, persisting.

'Yes . . . yes, it is.'

'The damage must seem terrible to you. Did I hear you say you had a brother who was killed in action?'

'No, it wasn't like that,' I said, distractedly. 'Not in action. He was a civilian.'

'I'm sorry to hear that. My own brother's in the Royal Navy, you know. Commands a destroyer, out on the Atlantic convoys. Nasty job sometimes.'

'Yes, so I hear.'

'Did you ever fly any naval liaison missions, Group Captain? My brother speaks highly of the RAF.'

'I'm not attached to Coastal Command,' I said. 'I've never worked with the navy.'

'I must arrange an introduction for you to the C.-in-C. Western Approaches. Good man. I'm sure he'd be fascinated to meet you. Look,' he said, pointing across me and the Prime Minister into the distance, over another field of rubble. 'Tower Bridge is still standing. The Luftwaffe uses it as an aiming point, you know. They line up on the docks by using the river and they know where they are when they see the bridge. They could knock it out if they wanted to, but it's probably more useful to them left as it is.'

So it went on, the flood of chatter from the man beside me, removing any possibility of my pressing Mr Churchill on what he might have known about Joe.

After we passed through the City the visible damage became even more extensive than before, at one point the road narrowing to a single lane that wound between two immense heaps of rubble. Policemen were on duty here, waving our convoy through. They saluted the P.M. as our car went by. Afterwards we crossed the Mile End Road — my companion the civil servant smoothly identified it for me — then joined a narrower road leading down to the river. Here the car slowed to a gentle halt. The other two cars pulled up behind us.

Two uniformed policemen emerged from one of the intact buildings at the side and together with our driver set about lifting back the convertible roof and folding it into its special place at the rear. The drizzle, still misting down as it had done since first light, began to settle on us.

The Prime Minister watched the operation of removing the roof calmly. When the driver was back in his seat at the front of the car, he stood up, bracing his weight on the long metal handle that was at the front of the compartment.

'Gentlemen, it's usually left to you to decide whether you should stand with me or remain seated,' he said. 'Because of the weather today, from which there's no escape, you might prefer to take it on the chin with me up here. It's actually rather more comfortable to be standing for short distances. You'll discover, Group Captain, that a firm grip on the handle in front of you will keep you steady.'

The civil servant and I both stood up, finding, as Mr Churchill said, that with all three of us on our feet it was possible to stand in some comfort. Churchill felt around in his pockets, but the civil servant was already ahead of him. He produced a box of matches and struck one of them. He held the flame steady so that the P.M. could light his cigar.

Churchill took two or three deep pulls, turned the end around in his mouth to moisten it, then declared himself ready. The car moved forward at about ten miles an hour.

Behind us the other ADCs were also standing up in their cars. Steadily our little motorcade headed down into the wasteland of blasted homes, warehouses and dock installations.

We came around one particular corner and I saw that the Women's Voluntary Service had erected a large tent, from which hot food and drinks were being handed out. A large crowd was clustering around it, but a sizeable number of the people on the edge of the crowd were looking expectantly towards us. The moment our car came in sight, an immense cheer went up and everyone began waving and yelling enthusiastically. People inside the tent rushed out to join the crowd. Everyone was waving. Some people were clutching Union flags. The noise was tremendous.

Mr Churchill immediately raised his hat, waved it in a jovial fashion and held up his big cigar for everyone to see. The cheers redoubled.

'Are we downhearted?' he cried.

'*NO!!*' came the immediate response.

'Give it to 'em, Winnie!'

'We can take it!'

'Dish it out, Mr Churchill!'

'Give the Jerries all we've got!'

The car drove steadily on. A smaller crowd beyond the tent heard the noise and as soon as we hove in view another great commotion arose. Mr Churchill waved his hat, beamed at the crowd, puffed expressively on his cigar.

'We can take it!' he said loudly.

'We can bloody well take it!' they responded.

'Give 'em as good as we got!'

'Give old Adolf what he deserves!'

'God Save the King!'

'Hoorah!'

'Are we downhearted?' cried the Prime Minister, waving his hat and puffing on his cigar.

This continued for about a mile, with unbroken crowds along the side of the roads, well marshalled by alert police officers, all of whom, I noticed, were eager to take a look of their own at the famous visitor. We reached an area of total destruction where even the bulldozers had not yet started work. It was shocking to realize that the undulating, broken mass of concrete slabs, splinter-ended beams, broken brickwork, millions of shards of glass, large pools of water, rampant weeds already poking up through the rubble, had all of it once been people's homes and places of work. There were no crowds here, probably because there were no homes left, no reason for anyone to be about. We remained on our feet, silent as we passed along the navigable track that was cleared on the edge of the Luftwaffe's night-time work.

Eventually the car entered a less damaged area and drew to a halt outside a tall Victorian edifice. Apart from a few boarded-up windows and the ubiquitous sandbags, it appeared to be comparatively untouched by the bombs. From a sign near the main gate I saw that the building was Whitechapel Hospital. A squad of uniformed police was waiting in the yard to greet us, saluting as Mr Churchill stepped down. We walked at a smart pace into the building, my injured leg giving me difficulty for the first time that day, but I managed to keep pace. A huge roar was going up: people had crowded into the yard to welcome the Prime Minister, and seemingly hundreds more were leaning from all available doorways and windows, waving and shouting and cheering.

Mr Churchill raised his hat, beamed about in all directions, puffed cheerfully on his cigar.

'Are we downhearted?' he shouted to the crowd.

'*NO!!*' they yelled back, waving their flags enthusiastically.

We toured the wards, spoke to doctors, nurses and porters, chatted to patients. Mr Churchill spent extra time in the children's ward, meeting not only the children but their parents too. At every point his message was the same, endlessly repeated, with only minor variations: 'We're going to see it through to the end, we'll never give up, we've got Hitler on the run now, we can take anything he throws at us, he's in for a few surprises.'

After the hospital we drove to a large school in Leytonstone which had taken a direct hit from a German parachute bomb. After that we drove down the badly bombed High Road in Leyton, where people were crowding on both sides of the street. Wherever there were crowds, Mr Churchill repeated his performance with the hat, the smile and the cigar.

We were back at Admiralty House by lunchtime. With a curt nod to us and a word of thanks Mr Churchill hastened away into the interior of the huge building. By this time I was exhausted after the morning of crowds and noise and the long walks among them. Mr Churchill remained spry and energetic to the end. I was given a light lunch with the other ADCs, then our respective cars arrived to take us home. I went to my room at RAF Northolt and fell asleep at once.

Nothing happened the next day, but the day after I was summoned again to Admiralty House. This time the tour Mr Churchill took was to the south of the river, visiting the areas of Southwark and Waterloo that had been devastated in a raid at the end of April. The next day we returned to the East End and dockland. Two days later the entourage travelled north for tours of the worst-hit parts of Birmingham, Coventry, Manchester and Liverpool. Back in London after a week, we immediately set off touring Battersea and Wandsworth.

I served as a Churchill ADC for just under three hectic weeks, by the end of which time I was convinced of two things about the Prime Minister.

The first was that he was a truly great man, inspiring belief in the impossible: that Hitler could and would be beaten. In that summer of 1941, the Germans were massively engaged in the first phase of the invasion of the Soviet Union, so for a while the pressure was off the British Isles. But the danger of air raids never really went away and the submarine war in the Atlantic was entering its most dangerous phase for Britain. The fighting in North Africa, which had been thought to be almost over when the Italian army collapsed, suddenly took a new and more worrying direction as Rommel assumed command of the Afrika Korps and moved swiftly on Egypt and the Suez Canal. Most of Europe was occupied by the Germans. The Soviet Union was in retreat. The Jews were being moved into ghettos; the extermination camps were built and ready. The Americans were still not involved. Whichever way you looked at it, the British were not in reality winning the war, nor did the prospects look at all good. Churchill, however, would have none of that. Britain has never had a greater leader at a worse time.

But I was also convinced of an altogether different matter.

I quickly realized what the other ADCs must also have known, but which none of us ever admitted or discussed. The cheerful, charismatic man who toured the bombed-out streets and homes of London's East End, who smilingly received the cheers and shouts from the crowds, who gamely puffed his cigars and uttered the familiar words of patriotic encouragement and defiance, was not Winston Churchill at all.

I do not know who he was. Physically he was almost identical to Churchill, but he was not the great man himself. He was a double, an actor, a paid impostor.

17

I returned to my college in Oxford at the end of September 1936, fêted as a hero and briefly the subject of great interest and curiosity. The fame was only brief, though, because a bronze medal is not the same as a gold, and sporting achievement is ephemeral when you cannot follow it up. That is what happened to me, because Joe showed no interest in returning to Oxford. My career as one half of a coxwainless pair immediately ended.

For a while I tried to find another rowing partner, meanwhile concentrating on solo rowing, but it was not the same without Joe. Gradually, my practice sessions grew shorter, less frequent, until the cold spell in January 1937 when I no longer rowed at all.

Instead, I turned to flying, the other obsession of mine that rowing had for a long time overshadowed. I had joined the University Air Squadron as soon as I arrived in Oxford for my first year, and even through the long months of my most intensive training before the Olympics I managed to keep up my flying training hours with the squadron. After the Games I spent more and more time flying, neglecting my academic course. Everyone at Brasenose College knew that I was at Oxford because of my skill at sport, not because of academic brilliance, but I had become a rowing blue who no longer rowed. Flying was no replacement, so I turned reluctantly to the books. I came down from Oxford in July 1938 with a third-class honours degree in German History and Literature.

Through the adjutant of the University Air Squadron I applied for a permanent commission in the Royal Air Force, intending to become a fighter pilot. I had already logged many solo flying hours and I was qualified to fly single-engined aircraft. It seemed to me that I possessed all the natural aggression and quick reactions needed in a fighter pilot and that the RAF would welcome me with open arms.

Nothing, of course, is ever as easy as that. After my first medical examination I was told I was physically unsuited for fighters: I was simply too tall and big-boned and would not fit into the cockpit of any of the aircraft in service. Instead I was selected to fly bombers.

After my time at Cranwell, the officer college for the RAF, I ended up as a trainee Flying Officer with 105 Squadron, equipped with the Blenheim light bomber. By the time war broke out, at the beginning of September 1939, I was in command of my own aircraft and I was ready for operations.

When the Germans launched the Blitz, Britain at first tried to respond with bombing attacks on German targets. I was part of that effort: I had been posted to 148 Squadron, equipped with Wellingtons, and I began flying operationally from the end of 1940. At first our targets were the French ports occupied by the Nazis — Brest, Boulogne, Calais, Bordeaux — but with increasing frequency we were sent to attack targets in Germany itself: Gelsenkirchen, Emden, Wilhelmshaven, Cologne, Berlin, Hamburg. Over Hamburg it ended for me, on May 10, 1941.

I saw nothing of my brother Joe during the early months of hostilities and was completely out of touch with him at the time he was killed. After our falling-out at Christmas 1939 we went our separate ways, cursing each other, misunderstanding each other. We were no more deeply alienated from each other at the time of his death than before, but our separation added an extra ingredient of despair to my loss.

Our row had simmered for years, ever since our escape from Germany with Birgit. In practical terms, that adventure turned out to be greater in anticipation than in reality. When we arrived in Hamburg, we went to the docks area and located the ship we had been told about, the Swedish motor vessel *Storskarv*. We reported to the shipping office, still with no concrete plans about how we hoped to smuggle Birgit aboard, and discovered that Herr Doktor Sattmann had managed to make arrangements by telephone ahead of our arrival. Our passages were booked, the papers were in order. We crossed the North Sea in some luxury, our equipment van buried deep in the hold of the ship.

The real upheaval did not begin until we were safely back in Britain, and then it took me some time to realize what was going on.

The ship docked after midnight. Our parents were waiting in the bleak dockside buildings in Hull to greet us. It became a family event: Mum and Dad had been on a trip to Germany four years earlier when they had stayed in Berlin with the Sattmanns. While we were waiting for our van to be lifted out of the ship's hold we sat in the dreary hall of the waiting area and Birgit passed Mum a long letter written by her parents. My mother glanced through it and began to cry. Then she put it aside, most of it unread, and cheered up suddenly. Everyone was speaking German, hugging each other.

Joe told them of the way Birgit had hidden, the daring escape from Berlin. I felt removed from the reunion, increasingly conscious that most of these arrangements had been made without anyone telling me. It made me see myself in the same way that they perhaps saw me: Joe was obviously to be trusted with the task of helping Birgit escape, while I was kept in the dark.

I contented myself by watching Birgit, wondering how I could claim her now we were all safe in Britain.

We drove home to Tewkesbury. Joe and Birgit travelled in the back of our parents' car, while I drove the equipment van alone. I was filled with excitement: hopes and plans circled around insistently in my mind, all focused on Birgit, my fantasies of love and romance, of easing her away from Joe and taking her for myself.

All this was to be quickly dashed. Long before three months were up Birgit was married, but not to me. She and Joe married quietly in Tewkesbury Register Office and went to live temporarily at my parents' house. By then I was already back in Oxford, in turmoil, fretting about my life, about Birgit, about Joe, about having been forced to give up rowing, about wanting to fly, about the mounting pressure on me to take my studies seriously. It was too painful to think about Birgit, so I tried to close my mind against her.

With the outbreak of war, everyone's life changed. Like many people, I found a renewed purpose to my own life in fighting a war I had not started, did not want and barely understood. War simplifies problems, sweeping up a multitude of small ones and replacing them with great concerns. To many people the shift in personal priorities was almost welcome. I was among them. A process of immense social and political change was about to flow through the country, and there was no stopping or questioning it. Of that process I was a tiny part, as were we all. No one understood at the time what was going on, even though we experienced it every day. All we knew was that Hitler had to be fought and the war seen through to the end. Only afterwards would we be able to look back and begin to comprehend what had happened, what had changed.

18

In a way that had rapidly become familiar to me, my first warning that I was required for duty came in a telephone call from the Air Ministry. I was in the

Officers' Mess at RAF Northolt, relaxing with some of the other officers. Even though I was in a somewhat anomalous position compared with theirs, because they were on operational duty while I obviously was not, I was starting to get to know the other men. The war brought circumspection to us all, so apart from the most general enquiries when I first arrived no one asked me what I was actually doing. To them, I was the group captain on staff duties, who came and went in official cars. Now it was about to happen again.

The mess steward approached me discreetly and told me I was wanted on the telephone. I went to a small office at the back of the building, where a certain white telephone was located.

After I identified myself with the usual codeword, I was told that a car would be collecting me at six o'clock that evening. I was to pack for at least two overnight stays, perhaps longer. It was unusual for them to call for me at this time of day, but apart from that there did not seem to be anything special about the mission. I assumed that another provincial tour was about to take place. I went to my room, bathed and shaved and put on my uniform. The Air Ministry car arrived at exactly five minutes to six.

As soon as we left the base and turned away from London I guessed that we were going to Chequers again, but we drove on into the evening shades for much longer than I had expected. It was dark when we arrived at our destination, but once again there was a ritual with an armed guard post set in the grounds of what was apparently a large country house.

Once I was inside the house I was informed that dinner was about to be served. A manservant showed me to a tiny guest-room where I deposited my overnight bag, then he led me downstairs to the dining room, a long hall, panelled and tapestried, high-ceilinged with a gallery running around three sides. Two long tables were set, side by side, with many people already sitting down and sipping a watery brown soup. Winston Churchill was one of the diners, seated about halfway along the table next to the huge, blacked-out windows, talking rapidly to the heavily bearded man sitting at his left.

I was ushered to a place on the second table, with my back to the Prime Minister, but I could clearly hear his voice over the general hubbub. Because of the echoes in the high-ceilinged room I could not make out his actual words, but the sound of his familiar voice was unmistakable.

Later, when the party moved to a large lounge next to the dining hall, where after-dinner drinks were served, we were sitting or standing about in a much more informal way and I was able to take a good look at the Prime Minister.

By this time I had spent many hours in the company of his double. The resemblance between the two men was uncanny. The famous baby face, the wispy hair, the pugnacious jaw and down-turned lower lip, the way of walking and using his hands, all these made the two men almost indistinguishable. When we were out in public, more obvious props would misdirect the eye: the distinctive high-crowned hat, the cane, the bow tie, the cigar. Now that I could see the real Winston Churchill, though, the differences were easy to spot. The Prime Minister was a slightly smaller man, his head closer to his shoulders, his waistline more stocky. He turned his head with a particular mannerism the actor had not mastered and his expression changed in many lively ways when he spoke.

I fell into conversation with a tall and rather handsome middle-aged woman, who said she was from the Cabinet Office, ultimately working for the Prime Minister but only indirectly responsible to him. She had never in fact met him before this weekend and said what a thrill it was for her. She told me that the house was called Ditchley Park, in Oxfordshire. It was a privately owned house sometimes lent to Mr Churchill for his working weekends. One of her duties was making practical arrangements for visits like this one. She in turn asked about my role in the RAF, so I gave her a general account of flying with a Bomber Command squadron. I realized that even here, in this inner sanctum, I was on my guard.

As we were speaking a number of ATS girls were moving around the room, shifting the armchairs and settees into lines, while two young women army officers were setting up a film projector and screen. Although nearly a month had passed since I had left hospital and I was able to walk without a cane, I quickly grew tired if I stood still for too long. I therefore sank gratefully into one of the armchairs in readiness to watch whatever we were going to be shown. The Cabinet Office woman chose a seat in the same row as mine, but not next to me. I saw her starting a conversation with another woman. I stared at the pale screen, waiting for the film to begin. I was expecting some kind of newsreel or information film, which would inevitably be followed by a talk or lecture.

I could hardly have been more wrong. When everyone sat down — Mr Churchill took pride of place in a settee all to himself in the front row, with a large ashtray, whisky decanter, water and glass close by his hand — one of the ATS girls started the projector and the film began. It turned out to be a comedy called *The Lady Eve*, starring Barbara Stanwyck and Henry Fonda. I settled back to enjoy it, noting that the Prime Minister, who was only a few feet away from me, smiled and laughed all the way through. Clouds of cigar smoke billowed up into the projector beam. When the film ended, Mr Churchill led the applause.

As the lights came up, many of the guests began to disperse. I moved uncertainly, wondering why I had been invited. Was it for a specific meeting with the Prime Minister, or was I here for the same reason as everyone else, apparently part of a weekend house-party? I hesitated, allowing some of the others to leave first.

Churchill walked up to me. He was wearing spectacles with round lenses, which glinted with the reflections of the overhead lights.

'Group Captain Sawyer!' he said. 'We're planning to post you back to your squadron next week. I believe that's still what you wish to do?'

'Yes, sir.'

'Well, it's up to you, my boy. I hear it's becoming more dangerous over Germany. I've just been given a note of our bombing losses for last month, which are most concerning to me. We could find you a permanent job on the Air Ministry staff if you'd like one. You've done your bit for the effort, so you need have no fears on that score.'

'I think I'd rather be flying, Mr Churchill.'

'Well, I must say I'm with you there, Group Captain. I respect your decision, but if you should change your mind, let my office know. We'll arrange something.' We had started speaking in the centre of the room, but now he led me across to one side, away from the others. 'Before you return to your squadron, there's one more job I'd like you to carry out for me. I don't want to make it sound more dramatic than it is, but I've come to the conclusion that the less you know about it in advance, the better you will be able to come to a sensible conclusion about what you find.'

'All right, sir.'

'Speak English as much as you can while you're there, but your German will be invaluable. A car will pick you up from here after breakfast. All I ask you to do is make up your own mind about what happens, then provide me with a full written report as soon as you can. Spare no details. Say what you think, no matter what. I am eager to soak up intelligence from you, however trivial it might seem to you. Are you clear on that? Time is of the essence, so I should like to read your report by the end of the week, if possible.'

'Yes, sir,' I said, but in the second or two it took me to draw breath and utter those two syllables, Mr Churchill had turned away from me and was crossing the room towards an inner door on the far side.

The next morning, when I was still feeling stiff and half asleep, and weighted down by a stodgy breakfast of yellow powder concocted into something that only faintly resembled scrambled eggs, I was in the back of another Air Ministry car being driven along the leafy Oxfordshire roads. I opened the window and breathed in the air thankfully. It was a misty morning, one that would later turn into a hot day, but the early coolness was a foretaste of autumn, now not many weeks away. I was thinking about what Mr Churchill had said about returning to ops, wondering what the winter would bring, where I might be sent, whether I would live to see the end of it. Winter nights were the open season for bombers and their antagonists: extended flights across German territory were possible in the long hours of darkness, with night fighters to contend with most of the way. The thought of the risk was like sniffing a dangerous intoxicant. Death remained an ever-present prospect but one that usually felt acceptably distant. I wanted to live, wanted no more injuries, but I was also desperate to return to the work I had chosen: the planes, the rest of the crew, the tracer bullets, the horrifying sight of an enemy city in inferno a few thousand feet beneath me. While the war went on, everything else was secondary.

We drove for about an hour after leaving Ditchley Park. I was not paying close attention to the route, absorbed in the thoughts of my other concerns. Other than the codename of my destination — 'Camp Z,' which was typed on my new identity card, valid for the next ninety-six hours — I had no idea where I was being taken. I calculated from the position of the sun that we must be heading generally back in the direction of London, if by a southerly route.

We were passing through wooded countryside, with tall conifers shading the road, when I noticed that the driver was peering from side to side as she drove, as if trying to find a landmark she had been told to watch out for. The car slowed. We passed down a short village street, one with cottages and shops, a car-repair workshop, a pub, a church. The name of the proprietors was painted on the overhead sign of the general store, *A. Norbury & Sons*, while underneath the words *Mytchett Post Office and Stores* were written in smaller letters. If Mytchett was the name of the village, it meant nothing to me, but in a moment we arrived at an unfenced driveway where the words *Mytchett Place* were dimly visible in faded paint on a brick gatepost.

Beyond was the now familiar guard post, although in this case there were high metal gates, surmounted by coils of barbed wire. Sturdy fences, with dense tangles of more barbed wire, ran off in both directions into the surrounding trees and shrubbery.

I handed my papers to the sergeant, together with the sealed envelope I had been given by a member of Mr Churchill's staff before I left Ditchley Park that morning. The sergeant took the envelope unopened to the guard post and I saw him speaking on a telephone.

The driver and I sat in the car, the engine idling smoothly.

After about five more minutes I saw a young Guards officer walking briskly down the driveway towards us. He glanced in the direction of my car, saluted quickly but courteously, then joined his sergeant inside the guard post. He emerged a moment or two later, holding a sheet of paper and the envelope it had been in.

He came to the car, saluted again, then leaned down towards me.

'Group Captain Sawyer?'

'Yes,' I said.

'Good morning. We have been expecting you. Captain Alistair Parkes, Brigade of Guards.'

'I'm pleased to meet you, Captain Parkes.'

I reached through the open window of the car and we shook hands. I opened the door and climbed out.

'Let's walk across to the house,' said Captain Parkes. 'Your driver can wait for you there. Gives us a chance for a brief chat before we take you in.' He slipped my letter of accreditation into his pocket and set off along an earthen path that ran through the trees, roughly parallel with the main drive. Once we had walked far enough for the guard post to be out of hearing, he said, '[Do you speak German, my gentleman?]'

'[Yes, I do,]' I said.

'[We speak English to the prisoner, partly as a matter of principle but also because we have reason to believe he understands more English than he admits to. It won't hurt him to learn a bit more, since he's likely to be with us for some time. But he sometimes insists on speaking German only, so it's useful to have some.]'

'[I'm fluent in German,]' I said and explained about my mother.

Captain Parkes seemed to assume that I knew as much as he did about the German-speaking prisoner, because he added no more information. He said, '[In my own case, I was sent to school in Berlin because my father was military attaché at the embassy. Another language comes more easily when you're a child. I never thought it might be an advantage one day. How about you?]'

We chatted for a while in German about growing up bilingually, then slipped back naturally into English. On the way through the woods we passed a defensive position consisting of slit trenches, a small concrete pillbox and a lot of camouflage netting. There was also a sophisticated system of telephone communications, with wires strung high between the trees.

We emerged at last into sight of the house, which was an unprepossessing building. My life recently seemed to have become a progress from one large country residence to another. Many of the great English estates had been requisitioned and made over to war use for the duration; this one, Mytchett Place, was a Victorian manor house built of pale brick with a red-tile roof. One wing looked as if it was in need of renovation, although the main part of the house was in good repair. The grounds had not been tended properly for some time and long grass and weeds grew in profusion. Untidy creeper spread over most of the walls that I could see, covering some of the lower windows of the neglected wing. A number of temporary buildings had been erected in the grounds and around them visible efforts had been made at tidying up and instituting the customary sense of military order. I saw several soldiers on guard duty.

'We have two or three unique problems here,' said Captain Parkes. 'It is technically a prisoner-of-war camp, so naturally we have to be sure we can keep the prisoner locked up inside. At the same time, in this particular case we think there's a reasonable chance someone might get it into their head to try to push their way in and snatch him, so we have to be ready for that too. There are other special features, as well.'

'Such as?'

'You'll be monitored the whole time you're here. All the parts of the house you'll be visiting are wired up with hidden mikes. Conversations are recorded. We're trying to get whatever information we can out of him, so long as there's still a chance he might have something we can use. Also, there are several MoD intelligence officers in the building. You'll meet them before you go in to see the prisoner. They will brief you with anything you need to know.'

I was intrigued by what the captain was telling me, but even then it did not occur to me to guess who the solitary prisoner might be. I think I was assuming it must be a captured senior German officer who needed to be interrogated in his own language. It did not occur to me to wonder why this agreeable young army officer was not qualified to do the job himself. Once again, I remembered what my brother Joe often said in the past, that I did not fully connect with what was going on around me.

I was led up to the first floor of the house, where I was introduced to the three Ministry of Defence intelligence officers on duty that morning. At last

I was led through a solidly constructed metal door and along a short hallway to the rooms where the prisoner was being kept. As I entered the first of the two rooms, he was lying on his back in the centre of the floor, full-length on the bare boards. He was dressed in the uniform of a Luftwaffe Hauptmann. His eyes were closed and his hands were folded across his chest.

It came as a considerable shock to discover that the man being held in the building was Deputy Führer Rudolf Hess.

19

In the first nine months of the war, until the beginning of May 1940, I notched up only eleven sorties against the enemy. After the German invasion of France and the Low Countries I was posted to 148 Squadron, which until recently had been operating the obsolete Fairey Battle in France, with horrific losses of both men and machines. Now back in the UK, based at Tealby Moor, the squadron itself was being re-manned and re-equipped, this time with the Wellington night bomber. Although the summer of 1940 was a period of maximum danger for Britain, the squadron had been pulled back from the front line while the process of reconstruction went on. Everyone was anxious to do what we could, to give back to the Germans what we were taking from them, but for several weeks the squadron to which I was attached did not even have aircraft to fly.

At the beginning of August, when I was going through a dull refresher course on night-time navigation, I received a letter from Birgit.

The last time I had seen her was during the disastrous family reunion the previous Christmas, during which she hardly spoke to me or even looked in my direction. After that I had not expected to hear from her again, although I had in fact received an earlier letter from her, back in May. It was a short, semi-formal note telling me that Joe had been beaten up by some off-duty squaddies. They apparently took exception to his not being in uniform. That at least was how my mother described it when I phoned her to find out more. She told me that Joe was not badly hurt and that after a short spell in hospital he would be back to normal.

But now Birgit had written to me again. When her letter was brought round during the daily distribution at the airfield, she was so far from my thoughts that I did not recognize her handwriting on the envelope.

The letter was short and written in her plain, almost formal English. I could sense her straining to write carefully and correctly to me. Without explaining why she had decided to write at that particular moment, she told me the circumstances of her present life. She said she had not heard from her parents for more than three years and feared they were dead. She was trying to find out what might have happened to them, but the war made communications with Europe almost impossible. A problem that seemed to her connected was that she was in danger of being interned by the British authorities, as she was known to have been born in Germany. She had already been visited twice by the police but on both occasions Joe had persuaded them to let her stay at home. Now there was a new danger: she said that Joe had been sent to London to work for the Red Cross and he was therefore away for weeks on end. Travel was so difficult with all the fears of invasion, the defensive preparations going on, that he had been home for only one weekend since he left. Being alone terrified her, but because of everything else that had happened she felt especially vulnerable.

That was all her letter said: she made no requests, no suggestions, asked for no help.

It threw me into an emotional quandary. I was living with the idea of her marriage to Joe by ignoring it. The latest row between Joe and me made that easier, of course. Because Birgit did not intervene at the time, and because she was after all his wife, I assumed she was allied with him on whatever it was, whatever new thing we rowed about that evening. She was still Birgit, though. Now she was in her early twenties, Birgit, as I witnessed from a distance during the Christmas reunion, had matured both physically and emotionally. The slightest thought of her would tip me into a long reverie about what might have been had events worked out differently.

Now I had a whole letter from her.

I wrote back to her the same day. I composed what I intended to be a thoughtful letter, one that was helpful and sympathetic without trying to interfere in any way. At the end I said, as blandly as possible, that if she thought it would help I could probably obtain a short leave and make a hurried trip across to see her.

Two days later I received a one-sentence reply from her: 'Come as soon as you can.'

I immediately put in an application to the station commander's office for a forty-eight-hour pass, but at the same time I felt I should take a final precaution against the impulses of the heart. I too wrote a one-sentence letter to her.

'If I come to visit you,' I said, 'am I likely to see my brother Joe?'
She did not reply. As soon as my leave was confirmed I went anyway.

20

My meetings with Rudolf Hess at Mytchett Place extended over three days. As soon as I realized who the prisoner was, I assumed that I had been sent because he remembered me from our meeting in Berlin, or he had asked to see me for some other reason. Nothing could have been further from the truth. He showed no sign of recognition at all, was suspicious of me and for the first day the only responses I had from him were hostile or uninterested.

Hess's circumstances had changed a great deal in five years. In 1936 he was one of the most important and feared people in Germany, but by the time he was incarcerated in Mytchett Place he had become a prisoner of war allowed only the minimum of comforts or privileges. The easy bullying manner had gone. The small talk did not exist. When he spoke at all, it was to complain about his treatment or to make demands to which I was simply unable to respond. For most of that first day he was sullen and silent, unwilling even to acknowledge my presence in the room.

Matters changed and improved on the second day. Although his suspicions remained, I think it finally sank in that I really had been sent by Churchill himself. For that day, and the next, I made much more progress than at first. It wasn't an ideal meeting, because of the circumstances, but by the time I finished I felt I had gained some important information for the Prime Minister.

I left Mytchett Place on the fourth morning, immediately after an early breakfast. I did not see Hess again before I left. The car drove swiftly to London, taking me to Admiralty House. My mind was swirling with a heady mixture of excitement, intrigue, anticipation and the more prosaic memories of many hours of awkward boredom. Whatever the circumstances, Hess was the worst of social company.

As soon as my arrival at Admiralty House was known I was taken to a two-roomed suite of offices which had been set aside for me on the top floor of the building. That my investigation was something of a priority was borne in on me because, as well as being allocated the rooms, I also had assigned to me a secretary and a translator. I was promised that the archivists in the library would treat any requests from me as a priority. Still feeling as if I had been thrown suddenly into a world of intrigues I barely understood, I settled down to assemble my thoughts and try to write them down in a coherent form.

I worked solidly for the next few days, travelling into central London every morning from my base at Northolt. In that time, two reminders came through to me from the Prime Minister's office, asking when my report might be ready. Time was of the essence and I was not to be allowed to forget it.

I had never been involved in this sort of work before, so organizing the material sensibly was a serious problem. My first version of the report was a lengthy and ill-arranged affair. I presented it as a verbatim account of each of my several meetings with Hess, including unedited transcriptions of the recordings of our conversations (translated into English when we had spoken in German) and supported by much other detail and elaboration that I was able to obtain from the library archives. I tried to produce a comprehensive account, a definitive record, comparing my own observations of Hess with what facts I could find about him in the Foreign Office archives. They had been observing him for years and the files were stuffed with information.

Miss Victoria MacTyre, the War Office secretary who was assigned to me, took the report away and had it typed out in full. She distributed it among four typists downstairs in the pool. If I say that it took them a day and a half of intensive typing this will give some impression of how many pages the report comprised.

Miss MacTyre brought the finished report to my office. While the secretarial work was going on, she managed to read the whole thing. She complimented me generously on it and told me that in the two years since the outbreak of war she had never read such an interesting piece of work. However, she said, there was a particular problem.

'Group Captain, I must warn you that Mr Churchill will not read it,' she said.

'I think he will. He commissioned it personally and has been pressing me to deliver it to him as quickly as possible.'

'I do understand that, sir. The fact remains that he will take one look at it and send it back to me.'

'Why should he do that?'

'It's far too long,' she said. 'It presents a brilliant analysis of the subject and I've never read any report that is so well cross-referenced and supported by evidence, but the plain fact is that Mr Churchill does not have the time to read anything so lengthy and detailed.'

'There are an incredible number of ramifications,' I said. 'Until I went to the place, to Camp Z, I had no idea how complex the situation is. It wouldn't do justice to the problem if I left half of it out.'

'What the Prime Minister requires,' Miss MacTyre said, with what I belatedly realized was immense patience, 'what he needs is a succinct and reliable summary of the salient points. You should add detail where it is necessary, but wherever possible the supporting material should be contained in a separate report. That is the version the officials will analyse and retain as the basis for whatever actions the Prime Minister decides to take.'

Still feeling the pressure of Mr Churchill's expectations on me, I stared gloomily at the thick pile of typewritten sheets on my desk, wondering how I should ever be able to organize such rambling and discursive material. Everything in it needed to be there, because everything I had learned about Rudolf Hess had a bearing on what I had discovered. I began sifting through the pages, trying to see what I could distil from them.

After leaving me for an hour to work on the problem alone, Miss MacTyre returned and briskly offered me the solution. She brought with her a copy of a report commissioned by the Admiralty into what had gone wrong during the Narvik campaign at the beginning of 1940. It was four pages long.

'This took more than three months to prepare,' she said, laying it on my desk. 'The original depositions amounted to over five hundred sheets of paper. What Mr Churchill read is the first four pages, from which he gained an accurate summary of the main points. The rest of the report was distributed to the various departments who needed to act on the lessons learnt from what went wrong.'

I glanced through the four-page report. It looked so easy, so plain and straightforward. It consisted of a number of fairly short sections, each one of which was preceded by a question.

It was such a practical and obvious solution that I was amazed I hadn't thought of it myself.

Miss MacTyre said, 'As you know, sir, I've read your report and I think I have drawn from it a number of different leading questions. I've taken the liberty of suggesting some for you.'

She passed me the sheet with a list of questions neatly typed. The first was: *Before you arrived at Camp 'Z,' did you know the identity of the prisoner you were going to meet?*

The second question was: *Did you recognize the prisoner when you met him?*

The third read: *Why did you recognize him?*

The fourth: *What were your first impressions of the prisoner?*

'Thank you,' I said simply.

'You can leave some of them out if you wish,' she said. 'Or you could add some of your own.'

'But not too many of them, I suppose,' I said.

'No, sir.'

I settled down to work.

21

Birgit and Joe were living in a rented house in a tiny village on the western side of the Pennine hills, overlooking the Cheshire Plain, with a longer view to the north-west across a large part of the city of Manchester. This much I knew from my mother's description. Otherwise, I had only the address on Birgit's letter to guide me.

I borrowed a motorbike from Robbie Finch, another pilot with 148 Squadron, scrounged some petrol, then rode the bike at high speed on the almost traffic-free roads across the breadth of England. The main part of the journey took me less than two hours, but I spent another hour driving around in the general area of the village before I found the house.

Birgit opened the door to me, ushering me in coolly and politely. When the door was closed I held out my arms towards her. We pecked a kiss on each other's cheek.

My first words to her were, 'Is Joe here?'

'No. I don't know where he is.'

She pulled herself away but smiled encouragingly at me. She showed me around the house, which she kept in a state of scrupulous cleanliness. It had many rooms, some of a good size and with stunning views across the countryside below. She had made one of the upstairs rooms into her studio, where there were music-stands, a glass-fronted cabinet to hold her sheet music, a large gramophone, a wireless, a long couch. Her violin lay in its case on top of a low cupboard.

In spite of its generous proportions the house was in dilapidated condition, with several holes in the roof, windows that would not open or close properly and floorboards that were uneven and in places rotting away. There was running water and a crude inside toilet, but the water-heater, run from bottled gas, had stopped working several weeks earlier. The house had no proper heating. There was no cooker, just a small hob with two gas rings, which used the same bottled gas as the water-heater. As we went around from room to room I noted all this, thinking how cold and uncomfortable the place must be in winter. Even on the sunny day in August when I arrived, the inside of the house felt draughty and damp.

With the tour of the house soon out of the way, we sat together in her stone-flagged kitchen drinking tea. She had no coffee, said how much she missed it, how much she would like to offer me some.

We had much to talk about. We spoke mostly in English and although her manner to me was warm she was clearly holding her feelings back. She treated me like her closest friend, but a friend she kept at a distance. To me, she had never looked more attractive, more so because I could see the signs of recent stress in her appearance. She looked thin and her face fell easily into a troubled look, but to me she was as beautiful as I ever remembered her. Now that I was there with her, though, it was the beauty of reality, not of some lonely, wishful dream. During my noisy motorbike ride across the country I had been harbouring a vision of a passionate, loving reunion with her, but once I was really there all that changed. She made me happy, but it was the happiness of being with her, not of yearning for her.

She told me about her troubles and worries: Joe's frequent and long absences, the loss of contact with her parents, her fears that they were dead or in one of the Nazis' concentration camps. More pressing still was her situation here, in England. Our youthful adventure, in which we had smuggled her out of Germany, seemed long ago in the past, but it was a small indicator of the worse trouble that was to come.

When the war broke out, her German birth meant that she faced internment with many other German nationals. Only the fact that she was married to a Briton and had taken out British citizenship saved her from the first round of internments. A second round had followed, two months later, at the time of Dunkirk when the country was rife with rumours of a fifth column. She again managed to avoid that, partly through the intervention of the Red Cross in Manchester, for whom Joe was working. She and Joe had assured the police that she was pregnant, though in fact she was not. Now once again, with the air battles in the south-east of England going on every day and huge numbers of invasion barges being assembled by the Germans in the Channel ports, the British authorities were again casting their net. She had come increasingly to see Joe as her last defence: so long as he was there with her, she had a form of security. But Joe's work had taken him to London, from which he was rarely able to return. She was existing from one day to the next, waiting for the police to arrive.

'I am British!' she said to me desperately, as she wept. 'I became British because of what I had been. When I was growing up . . . [I thought I was German, because that's how we thought of ourselves, a German family. An ordinary German family. I was a German first who was born a Jew, but still a German]. Then I found out I was *only* a Jew, not a German at all. So I came to England to escape being German, to escape being Jewish. But here I am not British, not even Jewish, but German again! [I fled from Germany because of what the Nazis were doing. Now I am to be persecuted again because they think I am a German spy, a Nazi! I am just a woman with an English husband. Can't they leave me alone?] Who will look after me, now that Joe is away all the time?'

I had answers to none of this, but I comforted her as well as I could.

She gave me lunch: a simple snack of bread and cheese, with some lettuce she said she had grown in the garden.

Afterwards she said, 'JL, I want to ask you a favour. A big, *big* favour.'

'What would it be?'

Then she retreated, wouldn't tell me what it was. I didn't need to be asked, because for Birgit no favour would be too big. A few minutes later, she started again, building it up before she would tell me what it was, explaining that she was so reluctant to ask because she did not want me to think that it was the only reason she was pleased to see me. I assured her that I would not think that. Finally, she came out with it.

'I want you to walk around the village with me, so that everyone can see me with you. I want them to see you too. They will think they see Joe. Will you do it?'

'You want me to pretend to be Joe?'

'A little walk,' she implored me. 'Down the lane, past the houses, so people can see I'm not alone. Will you do it for me?'

No favour was too big for Birgit.

But in my RAF uniform I was wrongly dressed for the role of Joe, which meant I would have to change into his clothes. Birgit had already chosen and laid out some of them, which underlined the fact that she had planned the whole thing.

Once we were in the lane she slipped her hand through my arm, squeezing her fingers lightly around my elbow. She leaned affectionately against me. We walked slowly along in the sunshine, looking around at the scenery. The light pressure of her hand on my arm was like a glowing imprint of her. To be seen with this lovely woman, to feel her affectionate touch, her closeness, to see her smile, was like a fantasy come true, even in an imposture. I slowed our pace, wanting to prolong the harmless physical contact with her. If to have her as close as this meant I had to be Joe, then Joe I would be for as long as it took.

Back at the house, we pushed my borrowed motorcycle out of sight and discussed how, in future, I should come and go when I visited. We agreed that unless it was night-time I should change into civilian clothes before I arrived, then be seen in them when I was with her or around the house and garden. The quiet assumptions implicit in these arrangements sent a thrill of anticipation through me.

In the evening Birgit played to me: a Mozart serenade, more Beethoven, the emotionally stirring cadenza from Mendelssohn's violin concerto.

I stayed overnight, sleeping uncomfortably in an armchair in the living-room. During the day that followed I tackled some of the most urgently needed repairs around the house. I replaced a broken window pane in Birgit's studio. I sealed up many of the places where draughts came in through the loose-fitting window frames. I rehung the front door so that it closed properly. I managed to clear the blockage in the water heater so that Birgit did not have to heat water on the gas ring. The bathroom, where the walls were being invaded by cracks and a spreading damp mould, was another urgent job to be done, but there was no time for it then.

While I worked, Birgit assisting and cleaning up around me, we talked about Joe, endlessly about Joe. He was an obsession we shared, if for different reasons.

The words poured out of us both: we described what we knew about him to each other, talked about fond memories of good times with him, expressed our thoughts about what he was trying to do with his life and how it felt when he hurt or abandoned the people who loved him most. I told her of the pain I suffered caused by the separation he and I were going through, but also about the ambivalence of the separation, the contradictory needs for closeness and individuality. Birgit said that from the time the war began, when he became a conscientious objector, he had seemed to her remote, awkward, stubborn. She desperately needed and wanted him, but he had become so difficult to live with.

I left her as the evening drew on, hastening back to Tealby Moor at the eleventh hour. I dashed in through the main barrier at the guardhouse with only a few minutes of my leave remaining. After another night of restless sleep I turned my mind to the concerns of the squadron, where the Wellingtons were at last starting to arrive.

Crews were assigned to planes and testing began immediately. All bomber squadrons were under pressure to become operational as quickly as possible. As a result, 148 Squadron was moved back to front-line status when only a handful of the aircraft were ready. My crew was not assigned to one of the first planes, so for a little while longer I was still relatively idle. With another weekend coming I was able to arrange a second forty-eight-hour leave, borrowed Robbie's motorbike again and rode at high speed to see Birgit. She welcomed me with tears of relief, putting her arms around me and holding me close. She was looking even thinner than before. Exhaustion lined her deep-set eyes and her long dark hair hung shapelessly around her shoulders. My mind's eye overlaid what I saw with what I knew she was really like. I still thought she was beautiful. I could never forget what had once briefly flared up between us.

That Friday evening we sat together in her dimly lit kitchen and talked again about Joe. It was August, but the weather had suddenly turned cool. The hilly countryside was silent around us, but for the blustering pressure of wind against the windows. The blackout shades moved with the draughts. Birgit was looking tired, desolated, worn down.

The next morning I rode the bike across to Buxton to visit the estate agents who collected the rent money. They told me that the landlord had moved to Canada for the duration of the war and there was no hope that he would accept responsibility for the physical deterioration of the house. While I was in Buxton I did some food shopping, then found a hardware shop and bought nails, paint, lengths of timber, electrical flex, a couple more tools. I rode back to the house, the side panniers at the back of the motorcycle packed to overflowing, the timber carried precariously under one arm. There was a limit to the number of repairs to the house I could tackle on my own, but I did what I could. I changed the broken lock on the front door and replaced light bulbs and dangerous wiring. I borrowed a ladder from a neighbour and clambered unsteadily over the roof, knocking loosened tiles back into place, repairing the flashing against the chimney stack, clearing leaves out of the gutters, stopping up holes everywhere, fixing, patching, sealing.

I began to relish the cool airy heights of the Pennines, the gusting winds with their constant threat of rain, the clouded view of the great Cheshire Plain below, the fields and towns and drystone walls, the dark sprawl of industrial Manchester lying to the north. It made me think of the post-raid briefing I had listened to half-enviously a few nights earlier, when the other crews returned from the squadron's first full raid. They had attacked Emmerich, a German town on the border with Holland, and returned with vivid descriptions of flying over the buildings, watching the bombs exploding beneath them. The madness of the war I still had not properly fought was infecting me: from this elevation I imagined how the land down there on the plain would appear from the air, what it would be like to fly over it at night and drop bombs and incendiaries on the people who lived there.

Then, after dark, the race back to the airfield.

That week I was assigned to a new Wellington, A-Able, and began training hurriedly with the rest of the crew. We had waited so long that we were eager to throw ourselves into the campaign. We were not made to wait long. As I was an 'experienced' pilot, with eleven full sorties on my record, our first raid was against a target in Germany: an industrial area in the Ruhr valley. The next night, while we were still exhausted from the previous raid, we were sent to attack an airfield in Holland that had been taken over by the Luftwaffe. The following night we were sent out again.

Meanwhile, in the south of England, the Battle of Britain was growing in ferocity. British airfields and military bases were being attacked every day, while larger and more dangerous dogfights took place high above the Weald of Kent and the Downs. At last we were fully engaged with the enemy!

Leave became difficult to obtain while we were so intensively in action, so two or three weeks went by when not only did I not see Birgit, but I was hardly able even to think about her. She wrote to me every week: short, factual letters, with no hint of special affection, but informing me in a quiet away of her everyday concerns. One letter sent a small, guilty thrill through me: she told me that Joe had turned up unexpectedly at the weekend and stayed for three days before returning to London. That particular weekend was one when I had been angling for a two-day pass, but it was cancelled at the last moment. What might have happened if Joe had walked into the house when I was there, dressed up in his clothes, alone with his wife?

After the first rush of sorties, the powers-that-be must have realized that if we maintained that level of activity for long we would be too exhausted to function properly. Crews were therefore put on a duty rota: not a rigid timetable as such, but the staff officers worked it out so that each crew flew on average just over once a week, or about three times a fortnight. This more calculated use of resources continued for the rest of the war, disrupted whenever Bomber Command demanded 'maximum effort' for certain targets. From my own point of view, it meant that most weeks, with careful planning and a bit of luck, I could arrange a thirty-six-hour pass, or even a whole weekend away.

Birgit and I soon settled into a kind of cautious familiarity, even though I had to be away from her so often, for so long. I would try to take her little extras that I knew were difficult for her to find or afford: tins of meat, powdered egg, chocolate, coffee, sometimes a few pieces of fresh fruit, all scrounged from the base. There was little she could give me in return, but my satisfaction lay in seeing her starting to look better. She put on a little weight, her face lost its haggard look, she seemed less careworn, less despairing. She remained unhappy without Joe, and she was still scared of being rounded up by the authorities, but I was beginning to sense a hopeful future for her. She looked increasingly beautiful to me. I was obsessed with her.

One weekend in September, while I slept as usual on the ancient armchair in her parlour, Birgit woke me up. I opened my eyes, saw her in the dim light spilling into the room from the hallway. She was kneeling beside me, her face close to mine. Her cold fingers were resting on my arm and her long hair brushed against my cheek.

'I can't sleep, JL,' she said, her voice wavering as she shivered. 'It's so lonely upstairs.'

I swung myself from the chair and stood up. I took her in my arms and instantly we were kissing and caressing each other passionately. Her mouth bruised against mine. She forced herself against me so vigorously that I almost fell backwards. I was still half asleep. I had not planned or expected what we started. Dreaming of it and hoping for it were not the same. It simply started to happen and afterwards I did not try to justify it to myself. We became ardent lovers, delirious with a desire for each other that we could scarcely satisfy. For the remainder of that short weekend we left her bed only for brief spells: food, bathroom visits, then back to our nest and our frantic love-making.

The single most difficult thing I have done in my life was to part from Birgit at the end of that leave. I delayed until the last possible moment, then rode at headlong speed along silent roads to the base. The following night our squadron flew to the port of Antwerp, where the Germans had amassed many invasion barges.

September and October went by slowly, the war becoming more bitter and destructive in every direction. After two or three weeks of effective bombing attacks against British airfields, the Germans inexplicably changed tactics. Had they continued to hit our airfields, they might well have overcome us, but they shifted their attention to bombing the cities, in particular to bombing London, and inadvertently they spared the RAF. The military benefits were not realized for several months, because in the short term the change in tactics meant that ordinary members of the public were now in the front line. Night after night the Luftwaffe bombers droned in above London and indiscriminately released hundreds of bombs on residential areas. Soon they were making for other cities, bringing a feeling of imminent danger to everyone in the country. Nowhere was safe from the raids.

Joe was still in London, working for the Red Cross. We heard little about what he was doing, except indirectly. Red Cross workers gained occasional mention in the newspapers or on the wireless. It was clear they were in the thick of events. Concern about Joe's well-being was a constant in my life, but as the Blitz worsened, the damage to the cities increased, the deaths mounted, Birgit became obsessed with his safety.

Even so, our passionate affair continued. I went to see her when I could and after the first few times I no longer worried if Joe might be at home when I arrived, or that he might arrive when I was there. All pretence that I was visiting Birgit for her company or to tackle repairs around the house was abandoned. We were lost in our fervent, passionate need for each other.

Then, suddenly, it changed. One day, at the beginning of November 1940, I received a message from the adjutant's office that there had been a long-distance telephone call for me, from Mrs Sawyer. She had left a number for me where I could contact her. Full of alarm, I raised the operator and booked the call, person-to-person. Within half an hour Birgit and I were speaking and she told me the news straight away: Joe was dead. He had been killed in London when a German bomb hit the Red Cross ambulance he was driving.

22

Joe's body was cremated after a secular ceremony in Gloucester. The service of remembrance consisted of a reading of a poem by Wilfred Owen and an extract from Erich Maria Remarque's novel *All Quiet on the Western Front*. Joe's short life was described in moving terms by a man from the Quaker Society of Friends. Joe was not a Quaker, but apparently his work had brought him into contact with Meetings in Manchester and London. The speaker described Joe as friend to the Friends. Mrs Alicia Woodhurst, who was Joe's boss at the British Red Cross Society in Manchester, gave an emotional account of the quietly heroic rescue work he had been carrying out in the Blitz in London.

Birgit, standing next to my father, leaning on his arm, sobbed all the way through. I, standing next to my mother, my arm around her shoulders, was stiff with grief and the sudden realization of loss, inexplicable and final. Afterwards, when we returned to my parents' house, Birgit would not look at me or speak to me. I was thankful she would not. Waves of guilt consumed me. I was devastated, shocked, deeply depressed by Joe's death, but as well I felt sick at heart when I thought about my affair with Birgit, behind his back, in his bed, dressing up as him to delude his neighbours, taking his place in his own house. Of course!, of course!, Birgit and I could not have known or guessed what was going to happen — perhaps we would not have been deterred by the foreknowledge if we had — but even so. We did what we did, but now that we had done it we were left to agonize in a mire of guilty feelings.

The squadron had given me eight days' compassionate leave and my parents pleaded with me to stay with them for the whole of that time. I was there at their house on the night after the funeral, but the next day I could stand it no more. I hopped on Robbie Finch's motorbike — which had become mine ever since a raid on Cuxhaven, two weeks before, during which Robbie and his crew baled out over Germany and were now prisoners of war — and headed back to Tealby Moor as quickly as I could.

What happened next made sense only in the callous context of wartime. Joe's death was the worst and most emotional experience of my life and for a time I thought I might never recover from the complex feelings of guilt, lost love and misery. But wars are filled with deaths, both remote and close at hand. Every night that the Luftwaffe bombers came to a British city, thousands of people were injured or killed. Ships were being sunk at sea with frightful loss of life, sickening news that came in daily. And every time the aircraft of our squadron, or of any of the front-line squadrons, took off for Germany, inevitably there was a loss to contend with in the morning. Some mornings there were several losses. Four of our Wellingtons were destroyed in a single night in a raid on Bremerhaven in December of that year, a disaster within the squadron, demoralizing and depressing us all, but the young men who died were simply more to be added to the war's tally. We never became blasé about death or immune to its shock, but as the war went on we grew to accept that deaths were the price we were paying. This was the context, this was the world in which Joe had died.

For me, the war was the only distraction I had from my private troubles. Now that the heady affair with Birgit had been taken from me, I gave myself up entirely to fighting the war. In doing so I realized the danger in which I had inadvertently been placing my crew. Those men were my closest friends and allies, yet for half the time I had been flying with them my mind had been on Birgit. I changed. I dedicated myself to war.

We went through the winter of 1940/41, one raid following another: Bremen, Wilhelmshaven, Sterkrade, Düsseldorf. We learned what there was to learn about night bombing, but in that period of the war our techniques were crude and our successes uncertain. The only certainties were that we went out to Germany and that some of us never came back.

On May 10, 1941, after bombing the port and city of Hamburg, my aircraft A-Able became the latest plane from our squadron not to make it home and my crew the most recent to be posted missing or wounded.

23

Following the question-and-answer format suggested by Miss MacTyre, I wrote a shorter version of what I had learned about Rudolf Hess during my visit to Mytchett Place. The typewritten copy prepared in her office then went straight to the P.M., with copies of that and the full version sent to the Foreign Office, the Home Office, the Admiralty and the War Ministry. All those copies, short or long, vanished into the government labyrinth.

Of all the actions in which I was involved during the war, preparing my report on Hess seemed the most important, certainly at the time and still, in some ways, even now. There for a few days, by what seemed like happenchance, I was acting as a kind of intermediary between two of the most powerful men in Europe, investigating one of them for the other, with whatever conclusions I drew being likely to affect the way the war would be conducted. That is how it felt at the time.

Yet in the end my work made no difference, or none that I could discern. The war continued and what I had discovered about Hess appeared to have no impact on it. Perhaps that was what Churchill wanted. With post-war hindsight I realize that the presence of Hess in Britain must have been a serious embarrassment to the British government: as soon as Stalin found out that Hess had landed in Scotland, he leapt to the conclusion that Britain and Germany were conducting secret negotiations. In papers released by Churchill soon after the end of the war it was revealed that at this time Britain was putting a great deal of effort into reassuring Stalin that the Anglo-Russian alliance was intact. The German invasion of the Soviet Union was in full flow at the same time as I was at Mytchett Place, with the Red Army retreating on every front.

Those published papers never included anything that even remotely resembled my findings. I have always been curious about why this might be, since what I discovered about Hess should have thrown everyone's assumptions about him into turmoil. At first I assumed it was simply the way governments worked, but once I made serious efforts to find out what happened after I met Hess I realized that there must have been a decision to cover up the details.

Because I am telling my own story, not an official one, I don't feel bound by the political imperatives of half a century ago. Although I can't locate the original report I wrote, I do vividly remember the meetings, and because I have kept my own handwritten notes from which the report proper was typed I can reproduce a fair copy of it here. My days with Hess were long and often tedious, with many interruptions, distractions and obscurities. He often confused me and frequently annoyed me, but for a lot of the time he simply bored me. My report boiled everything down to the salient facts, thanks to Miss MacTyre's advice. Some details might have become blurred by the passage of time, but the main conclusion is identical to the one I reported to Churchill in 1941. This report is still an accurate summary of what I discovered.

Report:	To Prime Minister
Author:	Group Captain (Acting) J. L. Sawyer
Date:	August 26, 1941
Subject:	Prisoner 'Jonathan,' currently held at Camp 'Z,' Berkshire.

Q Before you arrived at Camp 'Z,' did you know the identity of the prisoner you were going to meet?
No. When I arrived, officials of the Ministry of Defence told me that Camp 'Z' contained a single prisoner of war, whose codename was 'Jonathan.' That is all I knew in advance.

Q Did you recognize the prisoner when you met him?
I immediately recognized the prisoner as being Walther Richard Rudolf Hess, Deputy Führer of the Third Reich.

Q Why did you recognize him?
I recognized him because I had previously met Rudolf Hess on two occasions in 1936, when I was in Berlin as a member of the British Olympics team. Hess is a man of distinctive physical appearance. He is tall and fairly broad. He has a high forehead beneath dark, wavy hair. He has prominent cheekbones. He has deep-set eyes, coloured greenish-grey, with large black eyebrows. That is an exact description of the prisoner.

Q What were your first impressions of the prisoner?
Although I instantly knew who he was, I was surprised by Hess's appearance. He did not look well. He has been in captivity in Britain for several weeks and he complains of mistreatment and insufficient food. If his complaints had any substance they might explain the deterioration in his appearance, but as far as I could tell they are unsubstantiated, as I describe below. From his present appearance he appears to have lost a great deal of weight, more than you would imagine possible after only a few weeks in captivity. His cheekbones have become more prominent and his jaw looks bony. He stands with his shoulders stooped. His front teeth protrude slightly. He is not as tall as I remember him and his voice is deeper in pitch.

Q Did the prisoner recognize you?
I spent a total of three days with Hess. At no point did he say that he remembered meeting me before, even when I deliberately raised the Berlin Olympics as a subject and we discussed them for several minutes.

Q In which languages did you and the prisoner converse?
German and English, although predominantly German.

My own first language is English; my second language is
German, which I speak fluently.

Our spontaneous conversions were in German.
Whenever Hess was reading from his notes or lecturing me
on Hitler's plans for supremacy, he spoke in German.
When I asked questions in English he appeared unable to
understand them. However, he spoke English on several
different occasions. I gained the impression that he had
memorized in advance much of what I heard him say in
English.

Hess is an 'Auslander,' born to German parents in
Alexandria, Egypt. He spent much of his childhood and
young adult life in Bavaria and he speaks German with a
'southern' accent. However, I detected several words and
phrases more commonly used by Swiss or some Austrian
German-speakers. In Germany, his unusual accent would
make him stand out. I can find no reference to it in the
Foreign Office profile of Hess that I have since consulted.

*Q Did the prisoner describe the circumstances in which he was
captured by the British?*
Hess said that he had flown to Britain with a proposal for
peace between Britain and Germany. He called it a
'separate' peace, one which would exclude all other parties,
notably the USA and the USSR. While he was looking for
somewhere to land, his plane ran low on fuel and he was
forced to escape by parachute. He was arrested before he
could contact the people he was intending to meet. He
repeatedly referred to a 'peace party' in Britain, which at
first I took to mean an opposition party in Parliament. Of
course, no such party exists. He said he was carrying a letter
addressed to the Duke of Hamilton, which has since been
mislaid or stolen. He expected that after he had read the
letter, Hamilton would introduce him to the Prime
Minister. Peace negotiations would begin immediately. He
frequently expresses in most bitter terms his frustration at
not being able to present his proposals for peace.

I explained to the prisoner (as I was authorized to do)

that I was a personal emissary of the Prime Minister, Mr Winston Churchill. I showed him the letter of accreditation supplied by the P.M.'s office. He read it closely.

For a few minutes afterwards he treated me with noticeable deference and courtesy. Then, without explanation, he suddenly refused to speak to me. It lasted for the rest of the first day. When our conversation resumed, the following morning, he was more guarded in his responses and seemed suspicious of me. (Transcripts in German and English of all conversations are included in the full version of this report.)

Q Did the prisoner 'Jonathan' bring any messages with him to Britain?
The prisoner carries a sheaf of handwritten papers, which he consults from time to time. On two occasions I was allowed to see short extracts, but the pages were handwritten illegibly. When reading from these papers, or speaking extempore while referring to them, Hess invariably spoke in German. The subject was a long-winded history and justification of Nazi ideals, which I found tedious and sometimes offensive.

When the prisoner spoke in English, he was less wearisome but often more ambiguous.

Q When the prisoner 'Jonathan' flew to Britain, was he acting on his own or was he on a mission authorized by Adolf Hitler?
Hess was never clear on this subject. He sometimes said that the Führer had ordered him to negotiate a separate peace. (He used the German verb *befehlen*, 'command.') At other times he referred to it as 'my' proposal or 'our' proposal.

To try to clarify the matter I asked the prisoner if the proposal was being made by him personally or if it came with Hitler's backing and therefore could be treated as an official approach from the German state. The prisoner replied in German that in wartime the two were the same. He then said that he was acting on his own initiative on behalf of the German government and that a separate peace with Britain was the personal wish of Chancellor Hitler. It had his full backing and authority.

I felt this did not clarify the situation in any way.

On another occasion, the prisoner said that Hitler had made a number of public pronouncements about his wish for peace with Britain. He drew my attention to several of Hitler's speeches, in particular the one to the Reichstag on July 19, 1940. In the speech Hitler pleaded for common sense to prevail in both countries.

Q What are the details of the peace proposal from Germany?
After much discussion with the prisoner it appears that the offer of peace is based on the following five principles:

> The United Kingdom is to concede unconditionally that the war against Germany is or will be lost.

> After the UK has made that concession, Germany will guarantee the independence of Britain and her right to maintain her present colonies.

> The UK undertakes not to interfere in the internal or external affairs of any European country. In particular, Germany is to be allowed a free hand in Eastern Europe.

> The UK and Germany are to enter into an alliance for a minimum of twenty-five years.

> So long as war continues between Germany and other states, the UK will maintain an attitude of benevolent neutrality towards Germany.

Q What was your response to these proposals?
None. I said merely that I would pass on the proposals to the Prime Minister's office.

Q Did you form any views as to the prisoner's sanity or otherwise?

I have no medical or legal training so I can only offer a general or informal impression.

In the first place, there is no question but that the prisoner acts in a peculiar way. His behaviour is often puerile, especially at mealtimes. Like a child, he plays with his food, refuses in a bad-tempered way to eat, deliberately spills food and drinks. It could mean anything: that he has a puerile personality, or that his hold on sanity is slipping, or that he is acting in a way that he hopes we will think means that he is losing his sanity.

He is a persistent complainer. He says that people open and close car doors outside the house at night. He says that motorcycles are revved up outside his window to keep him awake. He even complained that for several nights running he was woken by gunfire. I might add that I slept in the same house as Hess for three nights and, although there were many comings and goings, I considered noise levels normal. The house is close to a large army base where there is a range. I came to the conclusion that his complaints were made as a part of the larger picture concerning his dislike of being held prisoner.

He is convinced that his food is being poisoned. During the meals I shared with him he elaborately examined and sniffed the food before eating it. At one meal he demanded that I exchange plates with him before we started eating. (I refused.) He claims that the people holding him prisoner are starving him, but while I was there he was given substantial portions — somewhat bigger, I might point out, than most serving RAF officers are currently being offered — which he ate with speed and relish. He told me several times that he was a vegetarian, yet he ate meat of some kind at every meal, without complaining about it. (According to the Foreign Office file, Rudolf Hess has been a vegetarian for many years.)

From time to time he breaks off a conversation to indulge in yoga-like exercises (such as lying on the floor or folding his legs) but the clumsiness of his movements makes it appear that he has not been practising it for long. (According to Foreign Office intelligence, Rudolf Hess began practising yoga while he was still at school.)

The prisoner claims to be losing his memory and makes unspecified accusations that his captors are drugging or influencing him in some way. When questioned on potentially sensitive matters, the prisoner frequently claims that he cannot remember, while at other times his memory is exact and detailed.

Q What are your general observations about the conditions in which the prisoner is being kept?
The regime at Camp 'Z' is efficient, thorough, clean and restrictive. The prisoner is treated humanely and has access to writing materials and German-language books. He is allowed a copy of *The Times* each day. He is addressed with firmness but courtesy.

Given that we are in a war and the general populace is having to put up with severe rationing of ordinary supplies, the food the prisoner is offered is plentiful, well prepared and reasonably varied.

The prisoner is allowed several periods of exercise every day. Camp 'Z' has large grounds. There is a tennis court in good condition which is used by several of the staff while off duty. The prisoner shows no interest in exercise other than short, undemanding strolls on one small lawn. (According to the Foreign Office file, Rudolf Hess is a keen tennis player and an advocate of healthy exercise. The prisoner has apparently stated to one of his captors that he dislikes tennis and will not play.)

As far as I can see, the prisoner's larger complaints about mistreatment are unfounded.

Q What conclusions do you draw from what you have seen and what the prisoner has said to you?
(1) THE PEACE PROPOSAL:
I believe it to be genuine in the sense that Rudolf Hess

sincerely wants to offer peace to the UK.

Without Hitler's endorsement, such an offer would be worthless. Although the prisoner sometimes asserted unequivocally that Hitler had 'commanded' it, I was left feeling unsure whether Hitler even knew about it.

Rudolf Hess left Germany on May 10 — Germany invaded the Soviet Union six weeks later, on June 22. Hess said nothing in my presence about the invasion that he could not have found out since from reading the newspaper. He revealed no special insights into Hitler's strategy, military intentions, etc. His peace proposal makes no mention of the war against Russia, other than a vague reference to 'other states.'

My conclusion is that the prisoner knew nothing of the invasion before he left. This alone underlines the probability that he was not privy to Hitler's plans in the weeks leading up to his flight. It in turn suggests that his plan does not have Hitler's backing.

(2) THE PRISONER:
All through my meetings with the prisoner I felt there was something 'wrong' about him. I made a conscious effort to think back to my earlier meetings with Hess in 1936 and to compare the man I remembered with the man I was interviewing. In doing this I kept in mind the prisoner's greatly altered circumstances.

Throughout our meetings, the prisoner 'Jonathan' struck me as impulsive, naïve and afflicted with a persecution complex. In 1936, Rudolf Hess showed none of this. At that time he struck me as clever, calculating, intimidating, sinister and something of a bully.

Rudolf Hess is a leading Nazi who enacted several anti-Jewish laws before the war began, the notorious 'Nuremberg Laws.' He made several well-reported speeches with distinct anti-Jewish sentiments. However, other than using his documents to quote Hitler's record and express Nazi policy, the prisoner revealed no anti-Semitic attitudes.

While it is known that Rudolf Hess was brought up by prosperous middle-class parents within a Germanic expatriate community, the prisoner 'Jonathan' displays vulgar table habits, frequently remarked on by the staff at Camp 'Z.' For example, he invariably drinks soup by tipping the edge of the bowl against his mouth, he belches loudly between courses, he leans over his food with his elbows resting on the table, he chews with his mouth open and so on. Rudolf Hess is well known to be a vegetarian, but 'Jonathan' routinely eats meat without complaint.

'Jonathan' bears an uncanny physical resemblance to Rudolf Hess, claims to be Rudolf Hess and by his act of bringing a proposal for a separate peace he is arguably acting *as* Rudolf Hess, but I am left in real doubt as to his identity.

I have no idea why a substitute should have been sent on the mission, nor how such an imposture might have been arranged and carried through, nor why the prisoner, now the game is up, does not reveal his true identity. Even so, I can state categorically that the prisoner in Camp 'Z' is a physical double, an impostor. The prisoner 'Jonathan' is not the Deputy Führer, Rudolf Hess.

[REPORT ENDS]

I returned to Northolt. After two days I received my posting back to 148 Squadron at Tealby Moor. A week later I was summoned to the Station Commander's office and given a sealed envelope which had been delivered by a motorcycle despatch rider. Noticing the insignia on the back flap, I took it to my room and opened it in private. It contained a short, typewritten note:

Dear Squadron Leader J. L. Sawyer,
The Prime Minister is grateful for your diligent attention to the task you undertook on his behalf. He wishes you to know that your report has been studied in detail and is currently being acted upon. You are of course aware of the highly confidential nature of your findings and conclusions, which confidence must not be breached within the foreseeable future for any reason whatsoever.

Yours sincerely,
(signed) Arthur Curtis
Principal Private Secretary to the Prime Minister

Underneath was another note, this one written with a broad-nibbed fountain pen. It said:

Hess will no doubt receive what he deserves, as will in the
end Herr Hitler. Yr. report is a great credit to you. I wish to
apologize once again for my insensitive remarks concerning
yr. late bro., which were based on a misunderstanding
within my department. I held him in the highest regard.
WSC

(I never again saw the man who stood in for Rudolf Hess. He remained a prisoner in Britain until the end of the war, with no information about him being released to the public. He frequently feigned amnesia and madness, but always maintained he was Hess. He was taken to Nuremberg in October 1945, where he was indicted under all four Counts as a war criminal. He was found guilty on Counts One and Two — Conspiracy to Wage Aggressive War and Waging Aggressive War — but not guilty on Counts Three and Four — War Crimes and Crimes Against Humanity. He was sentenced to life imprisonment. Because of Soviet suspicions about Hess, he was not allowed remission against his sentence. He therefore served forty-two years in prison — forty-six years when the time spent in Britain is included. For the last years of his life he was the sole prisoner in Spandau Prison, West Berlin. He never appealed against his sentence on the grounds of wrongful conviction or mistaken identity. He refused to see Frau Ilse Hess or her son Wolf for many years, finally relenting in 1969 when he mistakenly believed he was near death. At the time he was seventy-five years old. Frau Hess had not seen her husband for more than twenty-eight years. Medical examination of the prisoner in 1973 could find no trace of the scarring that would have been caused by rifle bullet injuries known to have been sustained by Rudolf Hess during the First World War. This is the only forensic evidence made public that supports my own belief about the imposture, because scars caused by bullet wounds never disappear. The prisoner died in mysterious circumstances while he was still being held in Spandau, in August 1987. A suicide note found by the body appeared to have been written many years earlier. Post-mortem examination of the body did not establish conclusive cause of death, other than asphyxiation. In some quarters his death is regarded as murder. Again, no sign of heavy scarring from war injuries was found on the body. Soon after the death of the prisoner, Spandau Prison was demolished to prevent it becoming a shrine for neo-Nazis. The body was laid to rest by the family in a secret location. Some time later, it was moved to the family plot in Wunsiedel. The prisoner's real identity, if known, was never revealed by the authorities.)

24

After my spell working for Churchill I was posted back to 148 Squadron in September 1941 and in theory resumed operational flights in December. In reality, because of my long absence, I was sent on a flying refresher course to an airfield on the Welsh coast near Aberystwyth. When I returned to Tealby Moor I was assigned a new flight crew, but almost at once the news came through that 148 Squadron was converting to four-engined heavy bombers.

Once again, the squadron was taken out of the front line and many of the personnel started to disperse to other postings. While I was working with Churchill I heard a report that 148 Squadron had been selected for conversion to the new Lancaster bomber. For that reason I opted to stay on. I was posted to an RAF base in Scotland used by an HCU (Heavy Conversion Unit), where I was introduced to the new plane, first by training on its immediate two-engined predecessor, the Manchester, then by practising on the Halifax, another four-engined plane of slightly older design. I was therefore one of the first RAF pilots to fly the Lancaster operationally, the plane that over the next few years was to become the backbone of the RAF's bombing campaign against Germany.

In 1942 the Lancaster represented a radical breakthrough in bomber design. It could fly faster, higher and further than any existing type. It was strong, well defended and carried a much larger and more varied payload of bombs. It was equipped with Rolls-Royce Merlin engines B the same unit that powered the famous Spitfire fighter — and it flew like a dream, laden or empty.

After two weeks of familiarization training at the HCU, working with my new crew, we were sent back to Tealby Moor. In due course the squadron started taking deliveries of Lancasters from the factory and by mid-May we were ready to become operational again. My first Lancaster raid was on the German town of Mannheim, but after that 'blooding' we were once again taken out of operations. Two weeks later, during which rumours were constantly circulating that the Air Ministry was preparing a 'spectacular,' I took part in the first so-called thousand-bomber raid on the city of Cologne on May 30, 1942.

These two missions, to Mannheim and Cologne, were in some respects routine affairs: we experienced no technical difficulties with the aircraft, we came under no sustained attack, we dropped our bomb load as close as we could to the target area and we returned home safely. Apart from an extra feeling of nervousness, as it was more than a year since I had flown on a raid, the main practical difference was the fact of flying the Lancaster. However, both the raids had a signal effect on me, if for different reasons.

The day after we went to Mannheim we received photographic evidence of our bombing results. As I was a senior operational pilot in the squadron I went to the debriefing session where the photographs were produced. The pictures revealed that the raid had been an almost total failure: most of the bombs we dropped fell in open countryside or forest, some of them many miles from the town. Only a handful of bombs fell where intended and these had started fires in a small industrial area. There was a scattering of bomb or incendiary damage over the rest of the town, all of it minor. At the same time, we already knew that of the two hundred RAF aircraft sent to Mannheim that night, eleven had been shot down. No parachutes were seen.

Each plane carried a crew of five or seven men, depending on the type of aircraft: around seventy young men were dead. By any standards it was a disaster, with unknowable but all too imaginable impact on the families, friends and colleagues of the dead men. Seventy men dead for what?

While the raid on Mannheim was a 'failure' in strategic terms, the attack that followed was a 'success.' It was carried out as a show of Bomber Command's strength, to demonstrate to the enemy that we possessed the ability to put a thousand bombers into the skies above a German city and bomb it into oblivion.

A thousand planes were in fact sent, although less than half were from front-line operational squadrons. Most of the aircraft were found elsewhere: mostly from OTUs (Operational Training Units) or HCUs. Some of these planes were piloted by instructors, but many others were flown by trainee pilots. The Germans were not to know this, however, and the effect of the raid was devastating, both as propaganda and in terms of damage to the target.

148 Squadron was despatched to Cologne late in the evening, so when we arrived over the city much of the bombing had already been completed. We were at twenty thousand feet, close to the Lancaster's operating ceiling. We took advantage of this to stay above the general level of activity. As we turned in to start our bombing run the city lay ahead of us, already blazing and smoking, fires spreading out in all directions. Planes below us were silhouetted against the terrible conflagration. Pinpoints of brilliant light, our incendiaries, lay like ten thousand glinting beads on the streets, roofs and gardens below. Flares tumbled down, spitting magnesium light like immense escaped fireworks, illuminating the horrors on the ground. Whole districts were ablaze, as individual fires reached out and joined up with others, the flames dazzling yellows, whites and reds, mottled by the bulging, rising smoke. Explosions continued in every part of the city, shattering the buildings, blasting them open so that the incendiaries might take a better hold.

Anti-aircraft shells exploded around us, shaking us and unnerving us, but we came through unscathed. It seemed to me that the flak was much lighter than I had known it on earlier raids. We were flying higher, we arrived later. Our bomb aimer called up to report that we had released our load. I heard the voices of the rest of the crew speaking in relief. I flew on according to plan, heading south across the city, not daring to swing round and across the path of the planes in the bomber stream.

As soon as we were clear of the main inferno I turned the Lancaster through a hundred and eighty degrees and we went back. Now we were flying north, heading for the first navigation marker on our route home, the town of Mönchengladbach, near the Dutch border. We passed Cologne on our right, staying well away from the centre of the city, not wanting to attract the flak. More British planes were arriving to drop their bombs. Even from this distance we could see their bellies shining orange with the light from the fires on the ground. The explosions and flares continued. The fires were much bigger already, spilling across the city like floods of flaming liquid.

I noticed that most of the searchlights were out and the anti-aircraft fire from the ground had almost ceased — the last RAF planes were flying in unchallenged to drop their bombs. I looked again at the inferno: who could be down there still, manning the guns, loading and aiming them, firing them off at the sky? Fire and smoke were everywhere. Turmoil had consumed Cologne. The RAF planners called it 'overwhelming' a city: it happened when the level of bombing reached saturation point, one bomb following another, wiping out everything, obliterating the searchlights, silencing the guns.

I remembered the guns I had seen in London, poking up through the trees of Green Park and Hyde Park, and alongside Horse Guards Parade, their ineffectiveness against even a small force of a hundred planes apparent. We were a raiding force ten times that size. How can any city defend itself against air bombing? After only a few nights of the Blitz, London became a chaotic tangle of broken gas- and water-mains, disrupted electricity supplies, cratered streets, burned-out buildings, fallen rubble, homeless families. Our single raid on Cologne was by several factors larger than anything London had suffered during even the worst of the Blitz. We used ten times as many bombers, which were bigger, stronger and carried three or four times as many bombs. Cologne was a compact city, while London sprawled. Cologne had a population less than one-tenth the size of London's.

The only point of trying to destroy a city would be to attack the morale of the ordinary people, to make them wish to give up the war.

I could never forget the hundreds, the thousands of ordinary English people I met when I was with Mr Churchill's double, touring the most damaged parts of our cities. I saw again and again how manifestly unbeaten they were, how resistant they had become to loss and destruction, how keen they were to pay back the Germans in their own coin. They did not want to give up. Their morale was intact. They wanted to hit back, to bomb German cities in the way they had bombed ours, but with a force ten or a hundred times greater.

So there I was on their behalf. Cologne lay overwhelmed beneath me.

I could not put out of my mind the look in the eyes of Rudolf Hess, the captive Deputy Führer, when he told me he had flown to Britain to stop the war, to forge a peace between our two countries. He finally accepted that Churchill himself had sent me to hear what he had to say — until then Churchill had not listened to him, and now I was there to listen on his behalf. But after I left, Hess remained in prison, silenced for the rest of the war.

We flew on, high above Germany. The land was dark beneath us. Occasionally, a squirt of tracer fire would rise up towards us from some isolated gun position, but mostly we flew unchallenged. Half an hour after we left Cologne and were flying across Holland towards the coast, the rear-gunner came on the intercom and reported that he could still see the glow of the burning city, far away behind us.

We headed out across the North Sea, thinking of home. Soon we were there.

Later we learned that more than forty British bombers had been shot down during the raid on Cologne before the German guns fell silent. Each plane had carried five, six or seven young men. The arithmetic of loss was all too easy to work out, but impossible to understand.

Two nights later, June 1, we went back to Germany. Once again Bomber Command put up a force of one thousand bombers, the target this time the industrial city of Essen in the heart of the Ruhr valley. Later in the same month we returned to Essen, then twice more. We called it 'turning over the rubble,' thinking that after the first raid there could be nothing left standing, but whenever we went back the German guns blazed out with terrific ferocity. The morale of the German people remained intact, their wish to take revenge on us more sharply defined with every raid. So we overwhelmed them, then flew home in the dark. What were we achieving?

I was approaching the end of my tour of duty, the one that had started at the outbreak of war. There was one more mission I had to fly. This was to Emden, a port on the north coast of Germany that was easy to locate because of its unique position: it faced south across an inlet bay. Even so, with such a compact target, so readily identifiable, the raid turned out to be another 'failure' for Bomber Command. Most of the bombs were later discovered to have fallen in the open countryside between the target and Osnabrück, some eighty miles away. Nine British aircraft were shot down for the sake of it. At the end of the raid I landed the Lancaster safely at Tealby Moor, and the next day I went on leave. By the time I returned to the squadron a week later my crew, whose own tours still had several missions outstanding, had dispersed.

I was re-posted within a few days, this time to 19 OTU, based near Liskeard in Cornwall. Like all pilots who completed a tour, I was to act as an instructor of new pilots for the next few months. A second tour of active duty would follow. I travelled down to Cornwall full of misgivings. For the next few weeks I went through the motions of being an instructor, but I was not good at it. Some people are born to be teachers, others are not. The only consolation during those weeks was that I was not the worst instructor at the unit.

Deeper worries were nagging away inside me, though. My recent experiences had made me think about the way we were fighting our air war, what we were trying to achieve with it, whether or not it was the right thing to be doing.

I began to question my own motives and abilities. I suspected that such a mental process was part of the reason why crews were taken out of the front line: after thirty operations most aircrew were in a state of burn-out. A spell at an OTU gave you an opportunity to recover, rebuild your morale, think things out, then, in theory at least, return to operational flying not only refreshed but with a wealth of experience. Experience was a key to survival. The wastage of new crews was terrible. Even by mid-1942 it was known that the average number of sorties a crew-member would survive was only eight. After three raids you were considered to be a veteran. Few men completed thirty flights.

As I worked with the new pilots I could not get these facts out of my mind. I knew that most of the young recruits I was working with would soon be dead.

So there was that burden. But in addition my own fears were growing. So long as I kept flying, I did not think about it. The fear was there all the time, but once a mission was under way, once the plane was on track and working well and the target was in sight, then I could take the dangers in my stride. Away from the action, though, there was too much time to think.

Why were we constantly attacking civilian areas of cities while tactical raids were comparatively infrequent? Why did we seem never to attack the U-boat construction yards or their service pens? Why were aircraft- and tank-factories, oil refineries and pipelines, shipbuilding yards, power stations, army bases, fighter stations never targeted, except when they happened to be in some more general target zone? Surely these were the very engines of Hitler's war machine?

Why were we trying, night after night, to damage civilian morale when every ordinary person in Britain knew from their own experience that the effect on civilians was to make them more, not less, determined? What was the point of it all?

25

After my spell of duty at the OTU I reported to my new squadron, this one being 52 Squadron, based at RAF Barkston Ash, in Yorkshire. Not long after arrival I was assigned to a Lancaster and a crew, and I returned to operations.

We were at the end of summer in 1942 and Bomber Command was stepping up its campaign against Germany. There was a new commander-in-chief: the legendary, notorious and widely feared Air Marshal Arthur Harris, 'Bomber' Harris to the press, but 'Butch' (short for 'Butcher') to the crews who flew under his command.

Harris reorganized Bomber Command and introduced many changes. For all the increased danger to which Harris exposed us, morale began to improve. A sense of purpose surrounded what we were doing. Not only was the size of the bomber fleet increasing rapidly, the planes were being fitted with ever more complex electronic navigation, defence and target-locating devices. Certain top squadrons were designated as 'pathfinders,' reaching the aiming zones ahead of the bomber stream, finding the targets, then laying down markers for the other planes to bomb. All pretence that we were trying to hit industrial or military targets was finally abandoned: the RAF followed a clear policy of area bombing, in which the houses, schools, hospitals and jobs of the German civilian population were what we were out to destroy.

I settled down to my second tour of duty with a sense of grim determination, closing my mind as far as possible to my doubts.

Gradually my number of completed missions began to notch up. I went to Flensburg, Frankfurt, Kassel, Bremen, Frankfurt again. At least two hundred bombers visited every target, and sometimes twice that number were sent, or even more. Our accuracy was improving, the percentage of aircraft we lost on each raid began to decline. The cities we visited were hit with increasing ferocity. They fought back when we arrived, they glowed like hot coals when we left.

It did not bear thinking about, so we thought only of ourselves, of our own survival. There was no end in sight to the war, so we were not due to finish yet.

In the middle of September 1942, after a raid on Osnabrück, I was given a weekend leave. I rode around the country lanes for a few hours on the motorbike before returning to the airfield. There was nowhere else I wanted to be. Two nights later, 52 Squadron was one of a dozen squadrons that visited Berlin. The big city, we called the place. Its size made it seem indestructible, but every time we went there we did our best to destroy it. That night we left the big city behind us, glowing in the dark, the smoke pouring into the moonlit sky.

I flew back to Germany another night and dropped bombs and incendiaries on the people who lived in Kiel. Later we went to Ludwigshafen, to Essen, to Cologne, to Düsseldorf, doing to them what we had come to do, overwhelming them from the air, then abandoning them to burn behind us as we flew home through the long nights. Next was Wuppertal. With three hundred other RAF planes, we dropped bombs and incendiaries on the people who lived there. We overwhelmed the defences, then left the place burning in the night as we set off for home.

Two days after the Wuppertal raid we received a visit from one of the senior officers in 5 Group and were briefed on Bomber Command's strategy for the next few months. Our raids were to intensify: more aircraft would be despatched on every mission, more and better bombs would be dropped, accuracy would be improved by electronic aids, a number of innovative defensive measures were to be introduced. New and recently revised maps of Germany were handed out and we were shown aerial photographs of industrial and residential complexes. We would become an irresistible force that would bomb the German people into surrender.

That night we set off in the company of some two hundred and fifty other RAF bombers to Stuttgart, a place notorious among the crews for being difficult to find and bomb accurately. When we arrived, the area was shrouded in thick cloud and ground mist, but we saw the fires that had been started by the first waves of aircraft, so we bombed those. Hundreds of explosions flared beneath us, brightening the clouds with shots of brilliant light. The areas of flame began to spread, their glow suffused. We dropped our bombs, continued to the end of the targeting track and turned for home.

As I banked the plane, a huge blast from somewhere shattered our starboard wing. The Lancaster immediately went into a dive, turning and spinning, flames soaring back from the main fuel tank in the broken wing. I hunched down in terror, crashing my hand involuntarily against the joystick in front of me. My head bashed against the canopy at my side. I shouted an order down the intercom to bail out, but there was no response from anyone.

I struggled out of my seat, crawling towards the hatch in the fuselage floor behind the cockpit, climbing up against the pressure of the diving spin. The noise inside the aircraft was tremendous. I became obsessed with time, thinking that there could be only a few more seconds to go before we hit the ground. Where the navigator's table had been was a gaping hole in the side of the fuselage, with white flames roaring against the metal struts. The rest of the fuselage, the dark, narrow tunnel that was always so cramped, was filled with smoke glowing orange from the light of fires further along.

I could see none of the other crewmen. I kicked the floor hatch open, thrust my legs through and after a struggle I was able to push myself out. The plane fell past me as a hot torch of blazing fuel. I was plunging through the night, the wind in my face and battering against my ears. I found the ripcord, snatched at it and a moment later felt a violent jerk against my spine as the chute opened above me.

My instinctive need to escape quickly from the crashing plane was borne out, because now that I was in the air I could see that I had not much further to fall before reaching the ground. I had already passed through the layer of cloud. I could see the burning city beneath me, still suffering many explosions and bursts of fire. I instinctively shrank away from it, not wanting to land in the worst of the inferno. After a few seconds it became clear that the wind was carrying me away from the biggest fires. I drifted down into a plume of smoke, suddenly blinded and choking for breath. Something hot and yellow was swelling and moving beneath me. I was terrified of falling into a blaze. Then I drifted out of the climbing smoke, breathed clean air and looked around to get my bearings again, but almost at once I hit the ground, rolling across a paved surface of some kind, my leg an agony of pain. The parachute dragged me along until I was able to release it. I lay still, unable to move, paralysed by pain. I could smell the smoke, and the fires were a huge orange radiance behind the buildings away to my right, silhouetting them. For a while there were explosions in the near distance, but I could not tell if they were bombs going off or anti-aircraft guns firing.

As the raid ended those noises faded quickly away. In their place I heard sirens, engines, signal whistles blowing, people shouting, others weeping.

I lay wounded, somewhere in the heart of the glowing city, as the remaining bombers flew for home.

I was soon discovered, arrested and taken into captivity at gunpoint. My leg was giving me hell and my blood had made a mess of my uniform, but the damage to me was mainly superficial. I had cuts to my hands, face and chest, bruises on my arms and back. As I landed awkwardly in the parachute I inflamed the old injuries to my left leg and at the same time twisted the other ankle.

After a few days in a German military hospital I was transferred by way of a slow, two-day train journey to a prisoner-of-war camp, Stalag-Luft VIII, situated in the heart of a pine forest somewhere in central Germany. (I eventually found out that it was about twelve miles to the west of the town of Wittenberge.) It was in that camp that I was destined to spend the remainder of the war, from the beginning of November 1942 until the camp was liberated by the US Army in April 1945.

Looking back to that now fairly distant period of my youth, I realize that my captivity lasted just over two and a quarter years, not after all such a huge chunk of my life. That's not how it felt at the time, of course. I was young, physically fit — once my injuries healed — and desperate to escape somehow from the drab wooden huts and barbed wire of the camp, make my way back to Britain and resume the fight.

Many of the men with whom I was in captivity had been in the camp for a long time before I arrived. Some of them had already attempted to escape and a few of them had made repeated attempts. One or two of them got away for good, or so we believed. In some sections of the camp the talk was constantly of escape. I sympathized, but I was never a candidate for being included in one of the attempts. At first it was because of my difficulty with walking, but later, when most of the damage healed, I realized I had adjusted to captivity and no longer wanted to run the risk of being a fugitive in Germany. I decided to stay put, sitting out the war.

Hunger was the worst enemy in the camp, with boredom running it a close second. On the whole we were not treated badly by the Luftwaffe guards and although there were long periods when food rations were sparse, we survived. I lost a great deal of weight, which I regained within a few weeks of returning to England in 1945. My ability to speak German was undoubtedly a valuable asset to many in the camp: I was often called upon to act as an interpreter or translator, I tutored the men who were preparing for their escapes and during the last twelve months of captivity I ran regular language lessons. It was all a way of passing the time.

Soon after I arrived in 1942 I wrote the permitted single-page letter home through the Red Cross. I wrote to my parents, telling them the news that they would most want to hear, that I was alive, safe and well. At the end I asked them to pass on my best wishes to Birgit and to tell her that I'd like her to write to me.

More than two years had passed since Joe's death. For much of that time I had barely thought about Birgit: she was a sore spot in my life I shrank away from. All the signs were that she felt much the same about me. Our guilt feelings obviously ran deep. While I was still in England, from time to time I asked my parents how she was but they always looked embarrassed, said that she had closed herself off and wanted no further contact. I never knew how to press for more information, so I never did. But already, in the first week of imprisonment, I found that one of the problems of idleness was constantly thinking back over your life, reminding yourself where you had gone wrong.

Frightened by the experience of being shot down a second time, hurting because of my new injuries, lonely in the prison camp, I soon began thinking back to my love affair with Birgit and wondering what the real reasons were that ended it. It seemed to me that nothing had actually gone wrong between the two of us, that what drove us apart was the awful accident of Joe's death and our resulting guilt. In the special circumstances of isolation in a prison camp, when I became the focus of my own interests, it seemed to me that perhaps it was time to try to patch up the friendship with Birgit. Of course there was no chance of seeing her or speaking to her until after the end of the war, but I thought it might be possible for us to write letters to each other. Somewhere there was a residue of hope.

Within a few weeks I received a reply from my mother, saying, amongst much else, that she had passed on my 'request' to Birgit. However, months went by without any kind of response from Birgit.

Her silence created a difficult time for me. At first I irrationally expected, hoped, assumed, that she would reply within a few days. Some of the men who had been in the prison camp longest warned me that letters could sometimes take weeks or months to travel to and fro through the international agencies and neutral countries. I struggled to control the torment and settled down to wait, hoping intensely that in this case the system might work more quickly and that Birgit's reply would soon arrive.

It was nearly a year before I heard from her, by which time I had assumed that no letter would ever come. When I realized who the letter was from, and what it might contain, I ripped the envelope open immediately and read the contents with my heart pounding. Written in the careful English handwriting that for a short time had been so familiar to me, it said:

> *My dear JL,*
>
> I am so pleased to hear you are safe that I cannot find the words. Your parents told me as soon as they heard from you. I think of you with love and excitement and deep gratitude for the kindness you gave me. I shall never forget you. I hope you will come home to England soon and that you will find a nice wife of your own and that the rest of your life will be what you want it to be. I am safe now and also happy with a new husband and a new life. I hope you understand.
>
> *Yours sincerely,*
> *Birgit*

It had been foolish of me to harbour even vestigial hopes, but when I read her letter I discovered that those hopes had been powerful. Against all the odds I had been counting on Birgit.

Hers was the kind of letter, I gradually realized, that was received by many of the men in the camp. The arrival of the Red Cross mail and parcels was always an event which was highly anticipated, but it was invariably followed by a mood of restless quietness everywhere. This was what it was like to be a prisoner: the lives of the people you loved at home went on without you and it was hard to accept that. A brushing-off of hope is terrible to suffer. For weeks after I received Birgit's letter I was depressed and disconsolate. I kept away from the other men as much as I could.

The worst of my disappointment eventually passed. I accepted at last that it was over. I wanted her to be safe and happy and could live without her so long as I did not have to see her. When I thought of her as part of my life, I went through terrible rigours of rejection, misery, jealousy and loneliness. But she was out of my life for good.

Some of the men in Hut 119 had built a radio from spare parts stolen from the Germans. With this it was possible to pick up the news from the BBC. From the middle of 1943 we were able to follow the progress of the war: the carnage and suffering on the Russian front, the difficult campaign across the islands of the Pacific being fought by the USA, the invasion of Italy and the collapse of Mussolini's regime. After the D-Day landings in June 1944 our craving to go home was intensified by the knowledge that the war was at last being won by the Allies. Again, hopes of a swift conclusion to our predicament loomed over most of the captives. We could do nothing but wait impatiently for rescue. The days and months dragged by.

26

One night towards the end of the war, in January 1945, the air-raid siren sounded and the floodlights surrounding the compound were abruptly extinguished. It had happened dozens of times before, so this was nothing unusual. According to the rules of the Kommandant, prisoners were to stay inside their huts and not to move into the compound for any reason until after the all-clear had sounded and the lights were switched on again.

We knew though that the German armies were retreating on all fronts, that the Luftwaffe as a fighting force was almost defunct, that the Russians were advancing at formidable speed across the northern plains of Europe. The British and Americans were poised to cross the Rhine. When that happened, the only question would be which of the Allied armies would reach us first. We were certain the war could not last much longer. The Kommandant and his rules were still a powerful presence, but we no longer feared for our lives. Small freedoms crept inexorably around us, presaging the larger liberty that lay ahead.

I had been out for a stroll around the compound late that afternoon, the weather fine and still. After dark the sky cleared and a full moon was high overhead. The air was bitterly cold but there was hardly any wind. It was possible to stay outside without feeling the worst effects of the cold. I was restless inside the hut, so that night, when the lights went out, I pulled on a thick pullover and a coat. I moved in the darkness from my shared room within the hut, down the short corridor to the main door. In defiance of the Kommandant I stepped out quietly into the Appell compound, where the roll-call was taken every morning. The dark, tall trees pressed in on all sides, beyond the camp barbed wire. The wooden watch-towers were outlined against the sky. I breathed the air deeply, feeling it sucking down sharply over my teeth and throat, a bracing coldness. I stood on the hard, bare gravel by myself, listening to the sounds of the night. I could hear some of the guards talking restlessly; somewhere the guard dogs were barking; there were quiet sounds from many of the huts. Few of us could relax when we knew an air raid was expected.

I stood alone in the gravelly compound for about five minutes. After that, some of the other men emerged one by one from the huts and walked out into the compound to stand with me. I knew everyone in our part of the camp by sight, but in the unlit square the men were just dark shapes. We acknowledged each other in English, muttering tentatively, not wanting to draw the attention of the guards. Most of the British prisoners were RAF officers and most of those were Bomber Command aircrew. In the same camp, but in their own huts largely by choice, were Polish, French, Czech and Dutch officers who had flown with the RAF. The Australians, Canadians, Rhodesians and New Zealanders tended to mix with the British. We were a cross-section of what the Allied air force had become. There were also many American crewmen, who were kept in a separate compound of their own, but a few of them had managed to transfer themselves across to our part of the camp, and they mixed in with us. The Yanks were popular with everyone but they were generally more fretful about being held prisoner than any of the Europeans. I think some of them still saw the war as a European sideshow, something they had been called in to help with, not a war that was truly their own. They were a long way from home. Their food parcels were bigger than ours and contained foods and treats that seemed to us exotic, but the Yanks who were with us were generous, so we readily forgave them that sort of thing.

That night we all stood together silently in the dark, watching the sky.

A few minutes after midnight we heard the first sound of engines, far away and high above us. In silence we scanned the sky, hoping for a glimpse of the planes. The sound grew louder, a deep-throated roar, a throbbing noise that was more felt than heard. The aircraft came steadily closer.

Then someone said, 'There they are!' and we turned to look away behind us to the west. Against the stars, against the moon-bright sky, the distant bombers began to appear. At first they came singly, then in increasing numbers, high and tiny, flying relentlessly on. The stream thickened and widened. We tried to keep a count of them: fifty, a hundred, two hundred, no, more over there, at least five hundred, maybe six or seven! We craned our necks, looking and looking, expertly identifying them from the engine sounds as Halifaxes and Lancasters, bombed up and ready. The bomber stream went on, a seemingly unstoppable flow, unchallenged, dreadful, unhesitating. The droning of the engines seemed to blanket everything else. In the moonlight we could distinguish the Luftwaffe camp guards emerging from their command positions, standing as we were standing, staring up at the sky.

The bomber stream passed over us for twenty minutes, rocking us with the deep, pulsating sound of their engines, a terrifying armada in the moon light, until finally the tail-end bombers flew on and out of our sight. Silence slowly returned.

I stood in the dark, feeling as if I was straining to catch the last particles of the engine noise, the last tiny pressure of the droning sound the planes had made.

One by one the other men returned to the warmth of the huts, but I stayed put. Soon I was alone, standing in the open space at the end of the ranks of huts, my head tilted back, searching the sky. I was shaking with cold.

How many more cities did Germany have, that the Allies might visit to destroy? What was left? Who could still be alive in those flattened ruins, those acres of turned-over wreckage and rubble, cold and broken, overwhelmed?

Once again, thinking of the war's futility, I remembered the prisoner everyone thought was Rudolf Hess. I had not at that time forgotten the man I met at Churchill's behest, half out of his mind, a captive in a foreign country, clinging to the past, offering a kind of future that no one wanted, that no one was prepared to discuss with him. I had not solved the mystery he presented — perhaps no one ever would.

I was to glimpse him again in the months ahead, though only in the newsreels. Towards the end of 1945, by which time I was back in England, the Nuremberg war crimes trials began and the man who looked like Hess appeared in the dock with the other surviving Nazi leaders. He sat in the front row between Goering and Ribbentrop, wearing an inane, friendly expression — there is film of Goering openly mocking Hess, who sat through most of the trial without the translation headphones, quietly reading books. Whereas most of the Nazis received the death penalty, Hess was given a life sentence, his crimes mitigated by his attempt in 1941 to forge a peace. He vanished from public gaze after the end of the trial, going behind the walls of Spandau. Once there, he was not seen again. He was never again in his lifetime called by his own name: from the moment the sentence was handed down he was addressed invariably as Prisoner 7. When his death was reported in 1987 I was shocked to discover he had remained alive until then, but shocked as well that I had all but forgotten him until the news broke.

By January 1945, it was irrelevant whether or not he was an impostor, or even whether he had tried to bring a genuine peace proposal to Churchill. Peace was not made in 1941 and the war went on, becoming immensely more dangerous and complex than it was when Hess flew to Britain. In that long winter of 1945 the war was at last heading towards its bitter end, and for people like me all that really mattered was how soon I would be able to return home.

Dreams of escape, which had once charged the thoughts of the prisoners of war, became dreams of repatriation. After the Americans finally arrived to free us from the camp we were soon being transported by trucks to the north of Germany, where the British army held the ground. From there we were flown back in small groups, crammed uncomfortably into the fuselages of the same bombers in which many of us had flown.

Home turned out to be a state of mind rather than a reality in which I could live. Everything I knew had gone or was going. As soon as I reached my parents' house I learned the truth about Dad that my mother's intermittent letters had deliberately skirted: he was in the advanced stages of prostate cancer and he died at the end of July, shortly before the atomic bombs were used against Japan. My mother's own death from angina followed soon afterwards. Joe of course was dead; Birgit had remarried.

I tried to obtain a job in civil aviation, thinking that I should put my flying skills to use, but there were many ex-RAF pilots around with the same idea, and flying jobs were few. A small number of dead-end jobs followed but

I was only twenty-eight. I still felt youthful, still able to look forward to a future. I took a decision that many men of my age and background were taking at the time and in March 1946 I bought an assisted-passage ticket to Australia. I had to wait four weeks before the ship left.

With one more week to go before I sailed, I borrowed a friend's car and drove across to the Cheshire side of the Pennines. I entered the village, drove down the lane and passed the house where Birgit and Joe had lived, where she had still been living on the day she wrote me her final letter. I halted the car a short way down the lane, turned it around so that I could look back at the house and switched off the engine. It was a fine day, with thin clouds and intermittent periods of sunshine. From the quick glances I took as I drove past, and from this more distant but steady look, the house had not changed much. The roof still needed retiling and the flashing I had amateurishly fixed in place against the chimney stack was the same.

The sight of the house evoked in me a strange mixture of feelings: it had become the love nest where Birgit and I spent those still memorable weekends, but it was also Joe's house, a place I should have been forbidden to enter. I sat there in the car for an hour, wondering all that time whether I should stay or leave. If Birgit was there, then one thing; if she was not, then another. Both seemed likely to hurt. To be honest, I really had no idea why I was there at all. I had finally decided to drive away when I saw a movement by the front of the house.

Birgit appeared at the front door, reaching back inside to hold the door open, looking downwards. She was smiling. Her hair was short and she had put on weight. I stared at her, my feelings suddenly awoken by the sight of her. She was facing towards my car but apparently had not noticed me. A small child ran past her and out into the garden and promptly sat down, out of my sight. Without even glancing towards me, Birgit went back inside the house, leaving the door ajar. She had been in sight for only a few seconds.

I left the car and walked down the lane. As I approached the house I saw that a chicken-wire fence had been put up to create a play area. Someone had dug a shallow pit in one corner of the sloping lawn and filled it with white sand. The child, a small girl dressed in brown dungarees, was sprawling in the middle of the sandpit, making tiny shaped piles with her hands. Her hair fell forward across her face, as Birgit's had often done when she concentrated on her violin. As I reached the fence and stared down at the little girl, she glanced up once, looked straight at me, then immediately lost interest and continued with her game.

I was thunderstruck by the child's appearance. She had the look of my family: I could see my father's face in hers, his eyes, his mouth. Her colouring, her hair were the same as mine. The same as Joe's. She had the Sawyer look, whatever that was, but it was instantly recognizable to me on some instinctive level. I tried to guess the girl's age — I was inexperienced with children but thought she might be about five. That would mean she was born in 1941, which itself would mean that she must have been conceived in the latter part of 1940.

I was still standing there, mentally reeling, my gaze locked on the playing child, when the door of the house burst open.

'*Angela!*'

Birgit was there, in a desperate mood. She dashed across the lawn, snatched the little girl up, shielding her head and face with her hand, and moved quickly back into the house. She did not look at me once.

As the door slammed behind her, I heard the child starting to wail in protest at the rough way in which she was being handled. The door did not catch properly but swung back open. I could see a short distance into the narrow hall that lay beyond. I heard Birgit's voice again, shouting: '*Harry! Harry! There's someone out there!*'

So I had a name for the child. I held the knowledge to me like a coveted prize. Angela, her name was Angela. My daughter — I felt a thrill of intoxicating excitement — my daughter was called Angela!

A moment later the door opened fully again. A man stepped through with a rough movement of his shoulders. I had never seen him before in my life: he looked to me as if he was about forty or fifty, with a weather-beaten, unshaven face. In the house behind him I could still hear the child crying. The man stood there on the threshold of his house, staring steadily at me, his silence and the resentful set of his head radiating a stubborn aggression.

I backed away, returned to the car and drove away down the hill.

The following week my ship sailed from Southampton and I set off on my fresh start in Australia. During the six-week voyage, itself an adventure like nothing I had known before, I made a conscious decision that if I was going to make a go of my life in Australia I must leave the old emotional baggage behind. Of course, such a decision is easier to plan than to carry through, but I sensed that many of the people who were on the boat with me, emigrating for similar reasons to mine, were undergoing something of the same feeling themselves. We talked about our hopes and plans, about the challenge of starting again in a new and young country. We were silent about our past lives.

As we sailed across the calm swell of the Indian Ocean, I felt all that starting to slip away.

I arrived in Australia. In that beautiful and exhilarating country I lived my new life, working hard and long. First I was a part-time pilot for a crop-dusting concern. There was a great deal of work available because Australia had vast fields. Soon I graduated from part-time hired pilot to full-time salaried pilot; later I became a manager in the company; within fifteen years I owned the whole firm. After that I moved into other aviation businesses, usually involving the chance for me to keep flying, something that burned up energy, if not always my own.

I returned to Britain in 1982, when I reached sixty-five. By then I had earned and saved plenty of money and I bought the flat where I have lived until recently. I settled down to retirement, not really thinking what it would mean until I had time to sit still long enough. Sitting still long enough turned out to be what I was least good at.

I went through a period of physical restlessness, endlessly travelling, constantly trying to meet people and make new friends, opening up possible non-vocational interests and projects. I made tentative contact with some of my colleagues from the RAF and prison camp days, even visiting one or two of them. I realize that this can be predictable behaviour in some recently retired people, those whose lives have been full of activity. In my case it achieved little — and anyway it was brought to a sudden end by a minor heart attack. Whether one thing led to the other is not for me to say, but the result was that since then I have been taking things much easier.

In the time of reflection that necessarily came while I recuperated, I started thinking back over my life. Reflection was something that seemed timely, now that I was in my seventies, living with a heart that had given me an unwelcome reminder of my own mortality. It was time to think matters through.

Writing this down, looking back on my life, it seems plain to me that I am one of that generation whose lives were permanently marked, perhaps blighted, by involvement in the Second World War. To be young and to live through a war is an experience like no other. It was enough experience for a lifetime, but if you survived, as I survived, there was more life to come but it was not the same thing at all.

For me the war, and therefore my early life, ended in January 1945, as I stood there in that freezing prison compound, somewhere in Germany, waiting alone.

It was the last time in the war that I saw a bomber stream flying overhead, as Bomber Command went about its deadly business. I did not know which city the planes were visiting that particular night, but I do know that it was not to be the last of their visits. Great and terrible bombing raids still lay ahead, of which I was to know nothing until long after the war ended: the devastating raids on Dresden, Pforzheim, Dessau, many other towns and cities, now almost without defences as German resistance collapsed, lay in the weeks ahead.

I sensed some of this as I shivered in that bitter night — I wanted to see the planes for the last time. The other prisoners had returned to their huts, the guards had moved away. There was no reason why the aircraft would fly back by the same route they used on the way in. Usually, in fact, to avoid the risk of night fighters the planes would scatter and take different routes. But at this stage of the war, every crew probably chose the shortest, most direct route. The long silence continued.

Then, as I was about to give up, I heard at last what I was waiting for: the sound of distant engines. I scanned the sky and before long I was able to pick out the first of the bombers returning. More followed, then more. Soon the same hundreds were flying overhead. They were no longer in a stream but were flying at different heights, most straggling alone, sometimes in pairs or small groups. It took more than an hour for them to go by. They were heading towards the west, back to their bases, home to England. Somewhere behind them, a German city whose name I did not know was lying overwhelmed in the night, glowing and smoking.

PART THREE
1999

1

Five months after he met Angela Chipperton at his signing in Buxton, Stuart Gratton finished work on his latest non-fiction book, **Empty Cities of the East**. It was another oral history, this one dealing with the experiences of the men and women who had been sent to Ukraine between 1942 and 1948 to build and populate the new German cities, as part of the Nazi *Lebensraum* policy. He sent the manuscript and a floppy disk to his literary agent, caught up with the usual backlog of messages and mail, then took a short holiday. He went first to visit his son Edmund (twenty-seven, working for a telecom provider in Worcester, married, pregnant wife called Hayley, child expected in October) then after a few nights drove across to Yorkshire to see his other son Calvin (twenty-two, completing his doctorate at Hull University, single, living with a young woman called Eileen). Ten days later he was back home. The agent acknowledged his new book but said she hadn't yet had a chance to read it all. The editor at his publishers was meanwhile said to be reading the book: on an impulse Gratton had e-mailed it to him before he went away.

So far he was following his normal post-book pattern. What he usually did next was to start work immediately on a new project, a kind of psychological bulwark against the possibility of some kind of problem with the one just delivered.

As he drove back across the Pennines from Hull, he was trying to decide which book to start. He had two projects in mind, but both were problematical, if for different reasons.

One would involve a major investment of time and research: he planned to write a social history of the USA since 1960/61, when Richard M. Nixon was elected to the US presidency after Adlai Stevenson's term of office. The Nixon administration, voted in on a bring-our-boys-home ticket, in fact more than doubled the size of the American military commitment to Siberia during its term of office. Nixon's over-ambitious, ill-judged and corruptly financed foreign policy measures were widely regarded as a principal cause of the economic stagnation which still afflicted the USA to the present day. Gratton's idea was to travel to the US and carry out detailed interviews with the surviving main players, illustrating their testimony with an up-to-date profile of the present state of the country. He knew that the book could be sold without any problems: he had already received serious offers from three publishers, and the Gulbenkian Foundation had committed itself to providing a lucrative financing package for the many months of research it would entail. All Gratton had to do was instruct his agent to set up the deal from the best offer on the table and he could start whenever he liked.

However, the sheer size of the book daunted him. Although much of it was mapped out in his mind and he had received outline agreement from most of his proposed interviewees, it was a vast project that would probably require two or three years of his undivided attention. Above all, it would mean him having to spend several months living in and travelling around the USA. His new book, **Empty Cities**, had involved a total of three visits to the US, tracking down and interviewing survivors from both sides of the Ukrainian uprising of 1953. There were tens of thousands of East European expats who moved to the USA throughout the '50s and '60s. Now he found it discouraging to contemplate going back again. There was much to like, admire and enjoy in the USA, but from the point of view of a traveller or researcher from Europe, time spent there involved endless hassles and wearying reminders of the Third War mentality that still held American political life in its thrall. He simply did not look forward to several months of having to cope with suspicious bureaucracy, crooked currency deals, technology that didn't work and the need to register with the police or FBI whenever he arrived in a new town or county. He remembered the first time he had visited the US, in 1980. Struggling with the pervasive isolationist mentality, the xenophobia, the blatantly censored media, the cities managed by criminals, the fuel shortages and the inflated prices had felt like perverse fun at the time, almost like a trip back to the Depression of the '30s. Two decades on since his first visit, with nothing better and everything the same or worse, the novelty had gone out of it.

The other possible book for him to work on would be the one he was idly planning about Sawyer, but because of the time spent on **Empty Cities** he had done virtually nothing about it. By chance, his route back from Hull led him through Bakewell, the small town where Angela Chipperton lived, and he was reminded of her and the notebooks she had lent him. Compared with the American history, the book about Sawyer held all the appeal of smallness of scale, a puzzle to elucidate then ideally solve, a minimum of travel and perhaps a few weeks of soothing archive or internet research.

The main problem with the Sawyer project, apart from the general lack of response to his advertisements, was that Angela Chipperton had failed to reply to his efforts to contact her since their brief meeting. He had already sent the photocopied pages to the transcription agency, anticipating her response. The agency returned the clean copy to him a short time later, but she had not yet sent him the original notebooks, nor had she given him formal permission to use the copyright material. He had still not found the time to look at the long text. All he knew about Mrs Chipperton was her postal address. No phone number was listed and she appeared not to use e-mail.

Meanwhile, no reply had ever come from Sam Levy in Masada: Levy had always been a long shot, because for one thing there was no guarantee that the old man was even still alive. Levy's link with Sawyer could anyway be a red herring. However, over the years Gratton had learned that there was rarely such a thing as coincidence. Everything was ultimately connected. He had a hunch that Levy's offhand remark about the Sawyer he knew in the RAF meant that they were quite likely the one and the same, but with or without a response from Levy there was still no guarantee he would be able to 'find' the real Sawyer.

He realized that the Sawyer book could rapidly become a waste of time, involving a lot of fruitless research for a book that he might never be able to write, let alone publish. The puzzle could turn out to be not a puzzle at all, but a misunderstanding by Churchill, even a mistake or a misprint. It wouldn't be the first time that an idea for a book led nowhere. Nor would it be the first time historians had been misled by Churchill, that arch manipulator of twentieth century history.

2

Then the decision was made for him. A few minutes after he arrived home and was still unloading his car, his neighbour brought round the various large postal packages she had taken in for him while he was away. Among them was a small, firmly packed parcel with Masada stamps and postmark.

Gratton attended to his necessary chores. As soon as he could, he settled down in his office and opened Sam Levy's package. He then went back and read, at last, the Sawyer notebooks.

The next morning, after a night of shallow sleep, he was out of bed early. He telephoned his agent, leaving a message on her voice-mail to put the American social history project on hold. He went to his car and set off across

the Pennines, speedily retracing his route of the day before, back through
Buxton towards the town of Bakewell.

3

Bakewell was a place with which he was unfamiliar, somewhere he passed
through in his car from time to time, with no reason to stop. While Wendy
was still alive they occasionally used Bakewell as a base for walks, parking
their car in the town then exploring the countryside around, but since her
death Gratton had given up that sort of thing, endlessly promising himself he
would return to taking regular exercise as soon as his current workload eased.

He was looking for Williamson Avenue, an address that sounded
straightforward enough. Bakewell was a small town, so when he arrived he
began cruising the streets, looking for the road. He stopped at a newsagent's
to buy a street plan, but they had sold out. He asked the man behind the
counter if he knew where Williamson Avenue was. He was directed out of
the town, towards Monyash. He turned back when he reached the countryside without seeing the road.

He located it in the end, surprisingly close to the centre of the town: it
was a residential road off another residential road, with fairly modern houses
down one side and a parade of recently built shop units on the other. The
address Angela Chipperton had given him was number 17, which was a laun-
dromat. The maisonette above was empty. According to the man who ran the
pharmacy next door, it was used for storage by a firm of magazine distribu-
tors. Clearly no one lived there.

Gratton drove to the information centre at the town hall and carried out
a systematic search. First he discovered that houses in Williamson Avenue
had been demolished about ten years earlier to make way for the shops, but
they had stood, derelict and uninhabited, for several years before that. There
were no Chippertons in Bakewell, no Sawyers and no Grattons. Nor were
there any Chipperfields, Sayers or Grattans, or at least not any with names or
initials even close to those of the woman he was trying to locate. He cast his
net wider, scouring through the directories for towns or villages in the area
with names similar to Bakewell: he found a Blackwell, a Baslow, a Barlow and
of course a Buxton. He drew a blank in all of them: there was no one with a
name even remotely similar, certainly not in any Williamson Road or Street
or Lane or Avenue.

In the car he again studied Angela Chipperton's covering letter. There was no possibility of mistake: her address was printed on the notepaper in an unambiguous typeface.

He drove home, feeling irritated rather than intrigued. The attraction of the Sawyer story was the puzzle it presented: Mrs Chipperton merely added another layer of enigma that seemed designed only to waste his time.

That evening, putting aside his irritation, he re-read the Sawyer notebooks, then looked again at the material Sam Levy had at last sent to him.

4

Mr Stuart Gratton, Cliffe End, Rainow, Cheshire, UK
August 3, 1999

Dear Mr Gratton,

I hope you will quickly understand why I've taken such a long time to answer your letter of enquiry about Flight Lieutenant Sawyer. I apologize for that, also for not even responding with an acknowledging postcard. I can explain the delay by asking you to look through the enclosed, which I've been working on ever since I received your letter. You will understand where most of the time has gone, perhaps. However, I can read between the lines of your letter so I'll assure you I'm still in pretty good health, in spite of being eighty-one next year. The wounds I received during the war, after being latent for many years, have come back to haunt me. Walking is difficult, as is getting in and out of bed, sitting down or standing up, etc., but once I'm in place somewhere I don't feel inconvenienced. My wife Ursula died last year, so I have had to leave the house you mentioned. I'm now living in some style with my niece and her family. I have a room to myself, my library is intact, I have online access, my brain still feels sharp enough and overall I have a pleasant life. I hope to be good for a few more years yet!

Turning to the subject of your letter.

I'd already come across that remark about Sawyer by Churchill. In fact, the memorandum is part of the dossier I was compiling at the time you wrote to me, so we are clearly thinking alike. (I've included it in its approximate chronological place.) Yes, the Sawyer he mentions is almost certainly the Sawyer I flew with for a time. I can only say 'almost certainly,' though, because you are correct in thinking that there's a mystery about the man.

It was Sawyer's strange behaviour during the war that personally involved me. At first it was a mild irritation, then it became a potential threat to the safety of the whole crew, then, after the war, it became the small mystery it still is. I don't pretend to have solved it, but I do think that what I've found may help lead you to an answer. However, not everything is as clear as even that might seem to make it. Churchill had it both wrong and right, as he often did.

The first-person account attached to this letter is my own short description of how I met JL (Flight Lieutenant Jack L. Sawyer), what happened while we flew together in the RAF and how it ended in tragedy. The rest of the pages make up the dossier I've compiled: the various photocopies, internet downloads, tear-sheets, newspaper cuttings and so on, that I've been collecting for some time. Some of them were fairly hard to locate, but if you have access to the internet and as much spare time as me, it's amazing what you can turn up with a little perseverance. I imagine you're an old hand at this kind of thing, but for me it has been an interesting journey through the past. Perhaps I should warn you that my dossier raises more questions than it answers.

And I should also warn you that you'll probably not enjoy everything you learn from the papers, but I know that as an historian you can take that sort of rub.

You use the phrase 'intense interest' in your letter to me. I can understand that. I too shall be intensely interested if you can fill me in on the rest of this unfinished story.

Finally, let me emphasize that irrespective of whether or not you want to interview me again, you'll always be welcome to visit me here in my tropical paradise. Don't be put off by recent news of the fighting and terrorism on this large island. We are well aware here how our country sometimes appears from abroad. The government has got the measure of the insurgents and the problem is well in hand. The native Malagasy are largely confined to their area of the island and next year they'll be given a measure of self-government. That should almost certainly satisfy their demands. In the meantime, life in the big cities is modern, convenient and extremely pleasant. I look forward to your coming here again and seeing for yourself. 'Masada' is no longer a state of mind for our people.

Sam Levy

PART FOUR
1940 — 1941

Statement of Samuel D. Levy to Stuart Gratton, July 1999.

Subject: Flight Lieutenant J. L. Sawyer, 148 Squadron, RAF.

1

My first impression of Jack ('JL') Sawyer was entirely favourable. I'd been posted to 148 Squadron and along with the other people in the same position I was going through the RAF's rather eccentric and informal method of crew selection. Everyone was sent to the drill-hangar and left to sort themselves out into crews. I noticed JL soon after we walked in, partly because he was an officer — at that early stage in the war most of the men who were picked for operational flying were 'other ranks' like me, so JL was already unusual — but also because he was a career officer, not from the Reserve. I immediately assumed I'd be far too humble to be in his crew. He'd been chatting with a tall young Warrant Officer wearing the insignia of a flight engineer but then he came up to me, a friendly expression on his face.

'You're a navigator, aren't you?' he said.

He spoke with a good voice, in those days the sort of thing people like me called a BBC accent, but he gave it an amused lilt, conveying the impression he was slightly mocking himself. He was a big chap: he had broad shoulders, long back, strong arms, an athletic way of walking. I found out later that he had competed in the Olympics, but I didn't know that at the time. All I knew that day was that he gave off a self-confident aura, suggesting a kind of inner strength. I instinctively liked him, felt I might be safe in his aircraft.

'Yes,' I said. 'Sergeant Sam Levy, sir.'

'We don't use ranks when we fly together,' JL said. 'How did you get on with the training?'

'All right, I think. I was only lost once.'

'What did you do about it?'

'We found an airfield and landed, then phoned back to the base. They gave us the right course to find our way home. It was the first time I'd guided a plane on my own and it hasn't happened since.'

'At least you're honest about it! Where do you come from?'

'I'm a Londoner,' I said. 'Tottenham.'

'I was born in Gloucestershire. I'm JL Sawyer. Would you like to take a chance in my crew?'

'Yes, I would!' I said. 'They said at nav school that everyone gets lost once. It's not going to be a habit.'

He laughed at that, slapped an arm around my shoulders and took me to meet the flight engineer, Warrant Officer John Skinner, or 'Lofty,' as we learned to call him. In the same casual way we soon found the rest of the chaps needed to form a crew: I'd been chatting earlier with an Aussie bomb aimer called Ted Burrage, so he joined up with us — he already knew a Polish gunner called Kris Galasckja and a young bloke from Canada called Colin Anderson, a wireless operator. With the crew selection complete the six of us trooped off to the canteen to have a cup of tea and to start sizing each other up.

JL struck me as a typical RAF 'type:' he was handsome, wore his cap at a rakish angle, he was obsessed with flying, used RAF slang with an easy familiarity, moved his hands around to simulate aircraft movements, he was battle-experienced, knowledgeable about targets and bombing methods and full of good advice for us inexperienced recruits. He even told us he'd been to Germany before the war and had seen Hitler in person. Before I went to bed that night I was congratulating myself on having found a first-rate captain.

Four weeks later, after we completed intensive navigation, gunnery and bombing trials, we were feeling as if we were a proper crew. JL's experience was invaluable. He'd been on daylight ops, for one thing, which earned our respect: we knew how dangerous those trips had been. Then he'd been on several shipping sweeps, again a background that gave him a great deal of experience of flying over the sea, which was handy for us. By RAF wartime standards he was an old hand at the bombing game, already partway through his first tour with eleven completed raids under his belt. He was a natural leader and gained our respect from the outset.

After the trials we were assigned our own Wellington: A-Able. We flew on our first proper mission as a crew in the last week of August 1940, a raid on somewhere in the Ruhr. I don't mind admitting I was terrified by the experience. Even at the time I'd no idea if we hit the target or not. The next night we were sent to attack an airfield in the Low Countries. More raids followed, and that became the way we lived our lives in the next few weeks and months: a constant round of training, preparedness, stand-bys, raids. It was a hard, cold, frightening and exhausting time, but I think I can speak for all of JL's crew during those weeks when I say that none of us would have changed a thing.

2

For several weeks during the winter and spring of 1941, though, I was convinced JL was cracking up under the strain. Strange behaviour went with the job we were doing. They used to say that you had to be crazy to volunteer for active duty, but that was only partly serious, almost an embarrassed excuse. A lot of us were recruits but we were willing recruits, knowing we had to do our bit in the war. We were attracted by the feeling of defiance to Hitler that was such a feature of life in those days. As for volunteering for ops: if truth be known, most of us secretly thought we had the best of it. None of us would swap our lot for what the ground crews had to do, for instance. They weren't in much danger but they worked long, hard hours, slaving outside in all weathers, a daily round of chores with not much chance of excitement. We wanted a bit of action, a bit of glamour, and although the reality of being aircrew was not in the least glamorous, we were the only ones who knew that. Being aircrew was a surefire way of impressing girls, for one thing.

The real problem was the stark contrast between the inactivity of most of the days and the dangers of some of the nights. Many of the men developed a reputation for odd behaviour, verging in some cases on eccentricity or weirdness. After a while you took no notice of the air-gunner who went everywhere in his balaclava helmet, the man who whistled quietly through his teeth through the briefing sessions, the flight engineer who adamantly refused to take off his flying jacket, even when he went to bed. Everyone carried personal good-luck tokens — hours could be spent in frantic searching when one of those little mascots went missing. Some people became withdrawn or aggressive between ops, yet transformed themselves into wild extroverts before we actually took off. On the nights when we were not on operations, most of us would go down to the mess and get smashed: drunken revels were not only tolerated by our senior officers, in the end we came to think they were expected of us.

So odd behaviour was normal, nothing you would comment on. Unless, that is, it showed itself in a member of your own crew. Then you began to worry if your own safety in the air might be at risk.

This was what started to worry me about JL. I noticed that he often went off the airfield without telling us he was going, sometimes, as far as I could tell, without arranging official leave. He was secretive about these activities and other matters. Things came to a head when Kris Galasckja, our rear gunner, commented that he'd accidentally overheard JL on the telephone one morning and thought he'd heard him speaking German.

Lofty Skinner was the second most senior member of the crew, so I had a word with him first. It turned out that he too had been observing JL's behaviour. We therefore cornered JL one evening in the bar and asked him straight out what was going on. He was surprised at first, then he looked relieved and admitted he was glad we had asked him. He said that there was something he had been trying to keep quiet, for all sorts of reasons. He asked us to keep it under our hats too.

He told us that he was married and that he had been since before the war. He knew that it didn't create a special situation, but he said he and his wife had been trying for some time to start a family. Now she was pregnant, with the baby expected at the end of May.

'The first two or three months were relatively trouble-free, but she's been having a lot of problems recently. Her blood pressure's up and there are other symptoms. Because of the war, because of the difficulties of my being away from home, I'm going crazy with worry about her.'

'Shouldn't she be in hospital?' I said.

'Yes, of course. But we live close to Manchester and because of the bombing the hospitals are stretched to the limit. Pregnant women are being kept at home as much as possible.'

He explained how isolated their house was, in a village on the Cheshire side of the Pennines, no telephone, not much in the way of modern comforts. JL said that he was using a motorcycle borrowed from one of the other pilots. Whenever he saw the chance, he said, he hopped on the motorbike and rode home as quickly as possible. He always made sure he was back at the base in time and, like us, he treated the safety of the crew as a priority.

'Skip, that's not good enough,' Lofty said. 'Some of the other officers are married and several of them have brought their wives to live close to the airfield. Why can't you do that? There are all the maternity facilities at Barnham Hospital she would ever need. And why haven't you said anything about it before?'

'I didn't want to concern you.'

'It is our concern, JL. If your mind is on something else while we're on a raid, if you're tired out from riding a motorbike half across England to be back in time, you won't be up to the mark.'

'Have you ever felt I have endangered you?'

'No,' Lofty said and I had to agree with him.

'Then can't we leave it at that?'

'I'm still not happy about it. Why do you have to be so secretive? Does the Wingco know what's going on?'

'No,' JL said. 'No, he doesn't.'

'Then why not?'

'I haven't got around to mentioning it.'

Lofty spoke again. 'JL, do you speak German?'

'Yes, what's wrong with that?'

'Sam, tell him.'

'The other day, Kris overheard you on the phone. He said you were speaking German.'

'I was probably making one of my regular calls to Adolf Hitler, tipping him off about the next raid.' JL grinned at us, then took a deep swig of his beer. 'All right, I'll tell you the rest. My wife was born in Germany. I sometimes speak to her in her own language.'

'Your wife is German?' I said, amazed by the revelation.

'No, she's British, but she was born in Germany. She moved to Britain in 1936 and she was naturalized as soon as we were married. There's a lot I could tell you about her, but since the war began I've felt that the less said about her background the better. We're in a bit of a jam over it. You've heard the rumours about a fifth column. Because of the rumours the government is interning German nationals, or anyone with even a remote connection with the place. Well, my wife is on that list, I'm sorry to say. Only the fact that she's pregnant and is married to a serving RAF officer is keeping her safe from internment. Or, at least, that's what I suspect is the case.'

We sat in silence for a while. I for one was wishing we'd kept our fears to ourselves, but at least everything was out in the open now. Whenever I tipped up my glass to drink from it I used the movement to look at JL. Something about him appeared to have changed: he seemed smaller, more human and vulnerable. He'd exposed something of himself to Lofty and me and in the process he had lost some of the flair that had impressed me so much. I decided I wanted to hear no more about his private life. I was thinking ahead to the next time when we would need to pin our faith on his judgement and flying skills, be able to accept his orders without doubt or question. It would be risky to take this clumsy interrogation of him too far if it threatened to undermine the authority he enjoyed or the willing compliance we normally showed.

3

We went through that part of the war OK. There were a few nasty surprises: one night, over Gelsenkirchen, a flak shell took away part of our tailplane. Kris Galasckja in the rear turret swore for half an hour — after all, the part of the tail that was hit was only a few feet from his head — but other than causing the plane to swoop with a stomach-heaving lurch whenever we made a turn, no real harm was done. On another night, returning from an otherwise incident-free trip to Kiel, our Wellington was attacked by a German intruder fighter as we tried to land at the airfield. JL managed to keep control, aborted the landing and by the time we had circled round before making our second attempt the intruder had been frightened away by our ground fire.

Gradually the nights were getting shorter and the weather, at least on the ground, was becoming warmer. Shorter nights were good news for us. They meant that we were sent to targets that required less time flying over Germany itself: we went instead to the North Sea ports, military bases in the occupied countries or the industrial towns in north-west Germany.

JL's odd behaviour continued, but now it took a slightly different form.

One afternoon, for example, I hitched a lift into Barnham, the nearest town to the airfield. I'd finally grown fed up with suffering cold feet during our long flights. The standard-issue socks were too thin. Even if you put on several pairs under your flying boots you still weren't warm enough. I was looking around the shops, hoping to find some woollen socks. They'd been in short supply throughout the winter — shortages of just about everything was something we had to put up with. I saw JL walking along the road on the other side, coming towards me. We were too far apart to speak to each other, but it was certainly him and because he was looking around our eyes briefly met. I raised my hand in greeting. He made no response and walked on.

This encounter struck me as odd for a couple of reasons. We were due to be on an op that night, which was incidentally why I'd picked that afternoon to try to buy some warm socks. JL was on the base with the rest of the crew. I'd eaten lunch with him in the canteen and in fact I'd been talking to him by the main gate before I hopped on the truck for a lift into town. He hadn't travelled with me, so I was surprised to see him again so soon. Finally, and this was what made an impression: he was out of uniform, wearing civvy clothes.

I carried on, found a shop, used my clothing coupons to buy a couple of pairs of the socks I wanted and was back at the airfield in time for a cup of tea with the others. I saw JL soon after I arrived, but the incident hardly seemed worth remarking on and was soon forgotten. That night we went to Brest docks, trying to hit the German battlecruiser *Gneisenau*.

The following day, during the afternoon, I ran into Lofty Skinner, who asked me if I'd seen JL anywhere about. I said not. Lofty told me there was a message for him from Group, but he was nowhere in the Officers' Mess, nor in his room, the ground crew hadn't seen him and according to the guard-room he'd not left the base. The next day we saw JL again, talking to one of the other pilots outside the NAAFI.

One evening around the middle of April, Lofty and I came up on the rota for one of the regular perimeter patrols. Perimeter checks had to be carried out twice a day and were one of the more unpopular routine duties, especially in winter. All the crews had to take their turn. It involved a long walk around the airfield, taking the best part of two hours, checking not only that the fence was still intact and that there were no obvious signs of anyone trying to get in, but also testing the navigation and landing lights. In fact these lights were used only rarely or selectively, because of the risk from enemy intruders, but they had to be switched on for night landings and in emergencies, when they were of course invaluable.

We were at the furthest, western end of the airfield, about as far away from the admin and ops buildings as it was possible to get. Here the runway ran out into the countryside, with a main road some distance away on one side, separated from us by a field and some hedgerows, and with several dense patches of woodland on the other. Lofty suddenly touched my arm.

'Look, Sam,' he said, pointing ahead. 'That's the skipper, isn't it?'

We could see a male figure dimly distinguishable ahead, standing among the trees that grew up thickly against the fence. He was too far away for us to make out his features clearly, but his size and the way he stood were familiar and we both immediately recognized him as JL. He was not in his uniform but was wearing a large, dark brown overcoat. At the moment we first saw him he appeared not to have noticed us, but as we drew nearer he glanced quickly in our direction then stepped back into the trees. By the time we reached the part of the perimeter closest to him, there was no sign of him.

Now, what might seem peculiar is that neither Lofty nor I said anything about what we had seen. At the time I found it difficult, particularly Lofty's lack of a reaction: did he know something I didn't?, had I been mistaken in identifying the man?, was Lofty waiting for me to say something about it?, and so on. Three-quarters of an hour later we were back at squadron headquarters.

Soon after we had turned in our guard rifles, we were walking back to the mess and almost the first person we saw was JL. He was wearing his RAF uniform again. He said nothing about the incident in the wood.

Afterwards, I said to Lofty, 'That was JL standing in the trees, wasn't it?'

He obviously knew at once what I meant.

'Yes. Have you any idea what he was up to?'

'Haven't the foggiest.'

'I was talking to Ted this morning. He said he'd seen JL hanging around outside the guard post at the main gate.'

'No reason why he shouldn't,' I said.

'That's right. But also, there's no reason why he should.'

'Bloody hell,' I said. 'He's still a good pilot, though.'

'Yes.'

4

In the last week of April I was given a weekend pass, so I went to stay with my parents in their house in north London. One of my sisters, Sara, had joined the Auxiliary Nursing Service and was being posted to a hospital in Liverpool. She was also passing through that weekend, before heading up north. We were concerned for her because at that time the Blitz was at its height and the seaports were being attacked regularly. Churchill was still in full control and everywhere you went you heard and saw the effect he was having. Germany could never beat Britain so long as that extraordinary mood of bravery and resilience survived. Sara and I felt stirred by it, but also humbled. You could only do a bit yourself. Dad took us down to a part of Green Lanes that had been flattened in a recent night raid. We walked around for a while, looking in horror at the damage to the area we knew so well, where we grew up. On the Saturday night the whole family went out to a pub, followed by a dance.

My dad was a sports fan and over lunch on Sunday, shortly before I was due to set off on the slow journey back to the airfield, he mentioned that he'd seen our squadron mentioned in one of the newspapers. A former sporting hero had become a bomber pilot with the RAF and was based at Tealby Moor. He asked me if I knew who they meant. Of course, without more clues than that it could have been anyone. Dad said he'd kept the newspaper and he started hunting around for it, determined to show me and to find out the name of the man. He was still searching when I had to leave.

The following evening, when I was back at the base, Dad phoned me from a callbox. His voice was faint and we were limited to three minutes, but his excitement was almost tangible.

'That chap I told you about,' he shouted down the line. 'His name is Sawyer, J. L. Sawyer. Do you know him?'

'JL's our pilot, Dad,' I said. 'I told you that ages ago, when I first got here. He'll be in that crew photograph I sent you.'

'Name wouldn't have meant anything to me then. But listen, I've been looking him up in a book in the library and he took a bronze for Great Britain.'

'A bronze medal?' I said stupidly. 'Like in the Olympics?'

'That's right. He was out in Berlin in 1936. The Jerries came first, but it was a hard race and we came in a good third. Has he ever talked about it?'

'No, never. Not to me, at any rate.'

'Why don't you ask him? That was something, going over to Germany like that and winning a few medals.'

'What event was he in, Dad? Was he a runner, or what?'

'He was a rower. Coxless pairs. It all comes back to me. I heard it on the wireless at the time. It was him and his brother, identical twins called Sawyer. They did well for England, they did.'

'Does it say what his brother's name is?' I said.

'They didn't put first names in the book. All the competitors are there under their initials. That's the funny thing about those two: they had the same initials. "J. L." That's what they were both called.'

'Does it say one of them was called Jack?'

'No . . . just "J. L." for them both,' my father said, but our conversation ended peremptorily when the money ran out.

5

Then came the evening of May 10 1941, the night our plane was shot down.

It began as one of those long evenings of early summer when light seems to hang around for ever, even after sunset. During the long winter we had grown used to the idea that we would take off in the dark and never see day-light again until we woke up the next day, after the raid. But now we were in May and double summer time had been introduced the weekend before. We took off while the sun was still just above the horizon and as we circled for height and set out eastwards across the North Sea we were flying in a serene evening light. The air was soft, free of turbulence. Whenever I went to the navigator's dome to take a positional fix I could see the long twilight linger-ing around us.

We were about a hour into the flight, still climbing slowly towards our operating altitude, when Ted Burrage in the forward gun turret suddenly yelled into the intercom.

'Fighters! German fighters down there!'

'Where are they, Ted?' JL's voice came immediately. He sounded calm. 'I can't see them yet.'

'About twelve o'clock, sir. Dead ahead, quite a long way off.'

'I still can't see them.'

'Sorry, there's only one. Me-110, I think. Way below us, heading west, straight for us.'

'Is he acting as if he's seen us?'

'I don't think so!'

I was standing at the side nav window at the time and had a clear view around and below us. No other aircraft were in sight. As soon as Ted called his warning I moved forward, clambering up into the cockpit behind JL's seat so that I could look through the main canopy. Moments later I too could see the plane: a small black shape, some way below us, fully visible against a silvery plateau of clouds.

It was unusual to meet any German fighters so far out to sea, even more so to see one at low altitude. Luftwaffe pilots normally gained the advantage of height before diving to attack.

'Permission to open fire on him, skip?' Ted said. 'He's almost in range.'

'No, keep an eye on him, Ted. No point letting him know we're here if he hasn't spotted us yet.'

I suddenly made out a movement beyond the Me-110.

'There are more of them down there!' I said. 'Look! Behind him!'

Four single-engined fighters were rapidly catching up with the larger air-craft, swooping down on it from the east. Even as I watched they went into a steep turning dive and accelerated towards the twin-engined plane. I could see the firefly flicker of their wing-mounted cannons, the lines of tracer curving towards the Me-110. The pilot of the twin-engined plane responded at last, making a climbing turn, briefly presenting a plan shape of his aircraft against the grey clouds, but then twisting around, diving away from his attackers. I saw a spurt of flame from one of his engines.

Our own track was taking us on past the fight. We were almost on top of the German aircraft. I dodged back to one of the side windows, but could see nothing.

'Boom! Boom!' It was Kris's distinctive voice, loud in my earphones.

'What's up?' said JL.

'They got him! I see it all. Four Me-109s and a 110. They got him! Boom!'

'Is he down?'

'Bloody big bang! Big flames, big smoke! Down in the sea, skip!'

'What about the 109s?'

'Can't see. They scattered.'

'Kris, are you certain you saw the 110 crash?'

'Rear gunner has best seat. Germans attacking Germans. Good stuff!'

'OK, everyone, keep your eyes open for more bandits.'

I clambered awkwardly up through the fuselage, past Col's radio kit, and returned to the cockpit, intending to talk to JL about what had happened. He was fully alert, scanning the sky in all directions. He registered my presence and unclipped the mike so we could speak direct.

'Did you see the 110 go down, Sam?' he shouted over the roar of the engines.

'No. We've only Kris to go on.'

'Good enough for me,' JL said, and I nodded vehemently. We both clipped our mikes on again.

'More Messerschmitts!' It was Ted again, from the front turret. 'About three o'clock. Below us again.'

I craned forward, trying to see down and to the right-hand side. JL kept the Wellington on a steady track, still climbing slowly.

'I can see!' I shouted. 'Same thing as before . . . another Me-110, this one heading due north. He'll cross under us in a moment.'

'Has he seen us?'

'Doesn't look like it.'

He was a long way off to our right, flying low against the clouds, crossing our track.

'Hold your fire, gunners!' JL said crisply. 'They're not looking for us.'

'What's going on down there, JL?'

'Haven't the faintest.'

'There are the 109s again!' This was Lofty, from somewhere down the fuselage. 'They must have circled round.'

'No, the last lot buggered off,' I said. I could see the smaller fighters now, flying fast and low from the south, catching up with the 110. Apart from the different direction from which they appeared, it was an almost exact replay of what we had seen a few moments before. I saw the fighters go into a diving turn, accelerating towards the larger aircraft. Cannon fire glinted on their wings. Tracer curled across the short gap between them.

But once again our track was taking us over the dogfight.

'We're losing sight of them, Kris! Can you see what's going on?'

'Rear gunner has best seat. Yeah! They go for him!'

I moved back from the cockpit and found Lofty pressing his face against the thick perspex of the port-side nav window. I crammed up against him, trying to see.

'They miss!' It was Kris again, from the rear turret. 'He's OK!'

'They'll go round again, won't they?'

'I lost them. Wait!'

JL came on. 'Don't forget, if any of those crates see us we're in trouble. No one relax!'

'Yes skip.'

'Sam, can you get a fix for us? I need to know where we are, how far from the coast.'

'OK, JL. Give me a few minutes.'

From the rear, Kris said, 'I can't see them no more. The 110 was OK. I saw him fly on.'

'Which direction was he going in?'

'Due north.'

'What about the Me-109s?'

'Like you say, they bugger off.'

We remained fully alert, knowing for certain that there were German fighters in the vicinity, knowledge no bomber crew liked to have. A strange sense of purpose settled on us. With remarkable efficiency the gunners reported at regular intervals on what they could see in the skies around us and I completed the fix I had been taking.

When I had worked out our position, I reported the information over the intercom to JL.

'How far does that put us from the German coast?' he said.

'A couple of hundred miles,' I replied. 'About two hundred and sixty from the Danish coast, though.'

'Why do you say that?'

'Because that was the direction the first lot were coming from. That would place their airfield somewhere on the Danish mainland.'

'They might have come from Germany.'

'It looked to me as if the second lot did. Either way, the Me-109s would have been close to the limit of their range.'

'Presumably that's why they buzzed off as soon as they could.'

'Right. So what were they up to, trying to shoot down their own?'

'Beats me.'

We were closing on the German coast and we said nothing more about the strange incident. Other business was more pressing. By this time it was completely dark outside the aircraft and I needed to take another positional fix to be certain of where we would be crossing the coast. I worked it out and reported it to JL: our landfall would be a few miles to the west of Cuxhaven.

Not long after, Ted Burrage reported flak coming up from below and the familiar sick feeling of fear rose in me. While we were under attack from anti-aircraft fire, or while we were on a bombing run, I had to sit tight inside my little cubicle, unable to see what was happening outside. All I had to go on was the movement of the aircraft, the change in the pitch of the engines, the explosions of the flak and the often incoherent shouts from the rest of the crew coming through the intercom. On those flights in which we penetrated deep into German or occupied territory the racket could continue for several hours.

That night, though, our target was Hamburg, a port about fifty miles inland from the coast on the long estuary of the River Elbe, so we wouldn't have to be over enemy territory for long. I plotted the route from the coast to our turning point and reported the bearing to JL. After that I worked out the course that would take us directly over the Hamburg docks, the intended drop-zone for bombing. After the plane had manoeuvred round to the new course I heard the voices of the rest of the crew changing when they reported in. As we neared the target everyone spoke more quickly. Their breath rasped noisily in my headset and sentences were left unfinished. They all seemed to be on the point of shouting.

While we were still on the way to the bombing zone I began to work out the best course for home: the shortest route back to the German coastline, a dog-leg to take us around the known positions of certain German flak ships moored offshore, then, once we were safely out to sea, swinging round to take us by a direct westerly route towards the beacon on the Lincolnshire coast and after that to our airfield. All the time the aircraft was shifting attitude and position and bucking violently whenever a flak shell burst close to us, but from the sound of Ted Burrage's voice, and from JL's responses, I gained the impression that things were going as smoothly as could be expected. Those last moments before the drop were the worst for most of the crew, but it was a time of great concentration for the bomb aimer and pilot.

I forced myself to be calm, staring down at my maps and charts and trying to calculate angles and distances, but in reality what I was waiting for was the blessed moment when we felt the bombs being released from the bomb-bay.

'Let's go home!' someone shouted as soon as the aircraft gave its familiar judder of relief. The plane was rising, free of the weight of the bomb load.

'Keep your eyes peeled!' JL said brusquely. 'There's a long way to go yet.'

'Can't we lift above this lot?'

'Bomb aimer, get back to your turret.'

'Yes, skip.'

'Christ! That one was close!'

'Everyone all right?'

'Yes, skip.'

'Both engines normal.'

'Anyone behind us?'

'Another couple of Wellingtons.'

'OK, hold on. We can't turn yet. Searchlights ahead. Some poor devil has been coned.'

'Can't we go round them?'

'They're on all sides.'

Releasing the bombs had that effect. For a few minutes everyone was talking at once, the held-back fears and excitement rushing out of us. I waited for the others to quieten a little, then I read out our new course to JL. He repeated it back to me.

'Turning now,' JL said. I felt the plane moving to port, the engines' note changing as they took up the temporary strain of the turn. It was all right, it was going to be all right. It felt all right after you dropped the bombs: illogically, because the plane was lighter and you were heading for home, you believed the gunners on the ground couldn't see you. If there were any fighters up they wouldn't be looking for you any more. The worst was over.

6

Except that on that night the worst was yet to come.

Something struck us explosively at the front of the plane. I felt the shock of the impact, was thrown against the wall of the aircraft by the blast and scorched by the sudden glare of white flame as it ballooned briefly down the fuselage. I fell to the floor as the plane tipped over.

'That's it! Bail out, everyone!'

I heard JL's desperate words through the intercom, but they were followed by a dead silence on the earphones. The intercom lead had jerked out of its socket as I fell. I think I blacked out for a few seconds. Then I was back, in an agony of pain. Blood was running down over my eyes, gluing my eyelids. Something must have hit me in the leg, high up, close to the hip. When I put my hand down to see what damage there was, I could feel more blood all over my trousers and tunic. Freezing cold air was jetting in through a large hole in the floor, below and slightly to the side of my desk. All the lights were out. The engines were screaming and the angle of the plane's dive was rolling me towards the front. My injured leg banged against something jagged that was sticking out from the floor and I yelled with pain.

Suddenly terrified that I alone had survived the explosion, that I was trapped inside the plane as it plunged towards the ground, I dragged myself from under the remains of my navigation table and pulled myself along the uneven floor of the fuselage. Because of the plane's steep angle it was easier than it would otherwise have been, but I had to get past the large hole that had appeared in the floor. The broken spars of the plane's geodetic hull jutted up sharply.

I had managed to squeeze past the hole when I heard the note of the engines change. They throttled back, under control, and I felt the downward pressure of G-force on me as the plane levelled out of its dive. I'd rolled forward so that I had fetched up against the back of the pilot's seat. I hauled myself up and saw JL sitting there, silhouetted by the dim light from the instruments. He was at a crooked angle, but reaching forward with both hands to hold the control stick. The front of the aircraft had suffered great damage: most of the fuselage ahead of the cockpit had been blown apart. Freezing air battered in against us.

Seeing the difficulty he was having with the controls, I reached over and tried to help him by taking some of the weight of the column, but he brushed my hand aside. My intercom lead had followed me down the fuselage so I plugged it into the socket on the instrument panel.

I shouted, 'Are you hurt, JL?'

'No!' His voice was high with tension. I glanced up at him, but his face was unreadable behind the oxygen mask and flying goggles. 'Well, nothing serious. It got me in the gut,' he said. 'But I think it's OK. More like a big punch than a wound. What about you? You're covered in blood.'

'Head wound. Something wrong with my leg.'

'What about the others?'

'I haven't seen anyone else.'

'I told everyone to bail out.'

'I heard that. What about Ted Burrage? Or Lofty?'

'I don't know. Remind me of that course to get us home!'

'Do you think we can make it?'

'I'm going to have a damned good try!'

The plane was apparently responding to the controls, although there was extensive damage to the fuselage. Both engines were running OK, but JL said that the port engine was starting to overheat.

The shock of the explosion wiped all thoughts from my mind and I couldn't remember the course I'd worked out. I crawled back to the remains of the nav cubicle, holding the emergency torch. By some miracle my pad was on the floor beside the hole, the pages fluttering stiffly in the gale. I grabbed it and hauled myself back to the cockpit. I read out the two courses and JL confirmed them. For a moment it felt as if we were flying normally.

By the time the plane was back on a more or less even keel we had long since crossed the German coast and were heading out over the North Sea. Our course no longer had to be exact, because once we were close to British air space there were direction-finding aids we could use. Getting lost was the least of our worries. Of greater concern was the condition of the port engine, which had obviously taken a hit somewhere. JL throttled it back to ease some of the strain, then a few minutes later he pulled it back a little more.

'How long before we lose too much height?' I shouted.

'An hour maybe.'

'Are we going to make it?'

'What's the distance to the coast?'

'More than a hundred miles.' It was only a guess. Without my charts and instruments I couldn't be sure of anything.

'I think at least one of us will be OK,' JL said, but he knew as little as I did.

Those were the last clear words I heard him utter. Suddenly, the dark sea filled our forward view, pale ripples reflecting the moonlight. We were already much lower than I had realized. Our dive had taken us to about a couple of hundred feet above the sea. JL leaned the weight of his body to the side, shoving the control column to the left — the plane briefly steadied, but we were so close to the surface of the water that we could see the surging shape of the waves.

JL shouted something, but I was unable to understand him.

The engines throttled back, the nose dipped. I could see the waves through the gaps in the fuselage ahead of us where the nose of the aircraft had been blasted away. I stared ahead, filled with a terrible despair. I could smell the salty sea on the freezing air that was rushing in at us. It reminded me, with shocking clarity, of childhood holidays at the seaside. Windy days, huddling out of the rain in a hut on the edge of the beach at Southend, the wide flat sands damp from the ebbing tide. That cold salt wind. I was certain I was about to die. This turned out to be how it was when you died: you died with your childhood before you. I was immobilized with fear, the sight of the sea, the huge black surface rising up towards us at a crazy angle and at a terrifying speed, believing that the end was upon me and that all my life this finality had been selected by that one moment in childhood.

There the flight ended. I cannot remember the moment of the crash or how I was thrown out of the wreck. I next remember I was in the water, floating face down, surrounded by the appalling, unlimited coldness of the sea. I was rising and falling with a sick sensation. Water was in my face, ears, nose, mouth, eyes. When I tried to draw breath I felt an awful fullness in my lungs, a sensation that I couldn't open them any more to draw in air. Somewhere, from deep and low inside me, a last bubble of air choked out of my throat and burst briefly around my eyes. I snapped into awareness, thinking that I had lost even that, that last gasp of air. I raised my head backwards out of the water, to a black nightmare of heaving, swelling waves, then down again beneath the surface. But I had been in the air so I struggled and floundered again in the dark, pushing my face out of the water, my mouth out of the water, trying to suck in air, trying to empty my lungs of the sea.

Every attempt to breathe was a struggle against death. I coughed, spurted water, sucked at the air, but too late! I was under the waves and taking in more water. I choked it out somehow, breathed again, sank again. I thrashed my arms, trying to lift myself out of the water long enough to live.

I was surrounded by floating debris from the plane. As I flailed my arms about, struggling for life, they sometimes banged against these small pieces of wreckage. I snatched at whatever they were, trying to interrupt the endless deadly sequence of sinking and resurfacing. Most of the flotsam was too small to hold my weight and anyway slipped from my grasp.

I was tiring rapidly, wanted to end the struggle, to give up and let death take me. I choked once more, tasting vomit-flavoured salt water as it jetted out through my nose and mouth. I thought that was it, that I was breathing only water. I let go, slipped backwards, relaxing at last, feeling the weight of my flying gear drag me under. It was a relief to give way to death, to glimpse the darkness that was waiting for me beyond life. The rage to live had gone.

But a wave washed over my face and as it did so I felt air bubbles bursting from my mouth. Somehow I had taken in air.

Once again I struggled to the surface and gasped for breath.

There beside me, dark and silent, was the round shape of the emergency dinghy, self-inflated on impact. I swung an arm up, clasped one of the rat-lines, got my elbow through it, then after another long effort, fighting the pain that was erupting from my leg, I managed to hook my other arm through the rope.

I clung there, my head at last safely above the surface of the water, breathing in with a horrible gulping desperation, but breathing. Gradually my panting steadied. Breathing became almost normal and whenever the choppy sea raised itself high enough to splash a wave across my face, I was able to hold my breath for a second or two, shake off the water, then breathe again. I was not going to drown after all.

The next enemies, clamouring to take me, were the cold and the pain.

It became vital that I should somehow manage to pull myself out of the water, flip myself over the inflated wall and fall into the rubber well of the dinghy, where I might lie in comparative dryness until rescue came.

Somehow, in that freezing May night, against the huge swell of the sea, against the pain and weakness in my body, I must have done that, because my next memory is of the breaking dawn, a rubbery smell, a soft and shifting floor beneath me, a curve of bright yellow rubber against a dark blue sky, a sense that the sea was distant, that I was tossing somewhere alone, perhaps in some after-life limbo.

Yet when I hauled myself to the inflated yellow tube that was the wall of the dinghy and raised myself up with both elbows so that I could see over the edge, there was the great endless sea around me, everywhere, heaving and grey. The sun glinted low and yellow from between dark clouds on the horizon.

I felt the touch of wind.

I lay there, probably in great danger of dying but no longer in any condition to know or care, when at last my dinghy was spotted by an aircraft. I heard the engine but I was too weak to wave or set off the flares. The pilot tipped the plane's wings, swooped down over me, turned at a distance, flew low across me again. Then the aircraft headed away. By that time it no longer mattered to me whether it was British, German or any other nationality, but it turned out that it must have been British. Two hours after the plane flew away an RAF Air-Sea Rescue launch came out and saved my life.

I was alone on that sea, the only survivor from our plane. If there was a miracle that night it was one that saved me. Of the others, Ted, Col, Lofty, Kris, JL, they were killed when the aircraft was shot down, or if they survived that then they must have drowned after the plane hit the sea.

That was the end of JL, the last I knew of him. 'I think at least one of us will be OK,' he had said to me in the last moments before he died.

PART FIVE
1940 — 1941

1

Extract from Chapter 3 of The Practical Conscience — The Red Cross in
The German War *by Alan J. Wetherall, published by George Allen & Unwin,
London, 1958:*

. . . it was in this way that I first encountered J. L. Sawyer, a remarkable figure of the war years. At the time I was still working as a staff Red Cross official, attached to several offices in the north-west of England. Although I was
not personally involved with his exploits, my early encounter with him was
memorable and in view of events is worth describing in detail. In anecdotal
fashion it may provide insights into his later work.

J. L. Sawyer was at that time an obscure figure, unknown not only to the
general public but also to the authorities. He lived in Rainow, a small village
on the western edge of the Pennines close to the town of Macclesfield. He
was married but at that time childless. His wife was a naturalized Briton who
had emigrated from Germany during the 1930s.

Sawyer appeared before the Macclesfield Local Tribunal on Thursday
morning, March 28, 1940. It was here that I saw him for the first time. My
role at that time was to observe the proceedings on behalf of the Red Cross.
Pacifism pure and simple is not a part of Red Cross policy, even though in
times of war the Society is often associated with it.

In 1939 the British government had reintroduced conscription, the first
call-up going to men in their early twenties, the aim being to raise the
strength of the armed services to about three hundred thousand men.

Experience with conscientious objectors during the 1914-18 war forced
the government of 1939 to prepare the ground carefully. Under the circumstances the authorities established an enlightened and indeed tolerant
approach to the problem. It should not be forgotten that in the months leading up to the outbreak of war in September 1939, Nazi Germany was seen as
a major threat to peace and stability throughout Europe. If war broke out,
devastating air raids on British cities were expected. All through 1940 there
were realistic fears of an invasion from across the English Channel. The fact
that by March 1940 none of these had taken place was seen by most people
(correctly, as events turned out) as only the calm before the storm. In this
climate it took political sophistication and firmly liberal instincts to

implement an official policy that gave a humane hearing to would-be objectors.

Needless to say, in the same atmosphere of war preparations it took an act of special courage for those with anti-war sentiments to present themselves for the hearings.

In 1940 a central register of conscientious objectors (COs) was created and maintained by the authorities. A man could register as a CO on one or more of the following loosely defined grounds: The first was that he objected to being registered for military service; the second that he objected to undergoing military training; the third that he objected to performing combatant duties. There was no onus on him to prove his pacifist credentials. For example, the objector did not have to belong to a recognized religion or church, nor did he have to show a past commitment to pacifism, nor did he have to come from any particular political affiliation. The rules were left deliberately vague, allowing each applicant to present his own case in the way he thought best. At the same time, it encouraged the tribunals to judge each man and his case on merit.

J. L. Sawyer appeared at the first hearing I monitored on behalf of the Red Cross in Macclesfield, although it was not the first Local Tribunal that I had monitored.

Sawyer was a young man of striking appearance: he was tall, muscular and powerful-looking, with a comfortable stance and what appeared to be a calm, self-confident manner. His name meant nothing to me when I was given a list of attenders, although when I later found out that he was an Olympic medallist it came as no surprise.

The courtroom being used for the hearings was a small but imposing room, panelled in oak, with a high bench and a deep well, the clerk's desk being placed at a level somewhere between the two. There were no windows, only skylights. The lighting was dim, in accordance with wartime practices. For anyone walking into the room for the first time, even as an observer, the overall impression was intimidating.

Sawyer's application was heard halfway through the morning session. The tribunal had already turned down half a dozen applicants and give only conditional registration to two others. The members of the tribunal, a businessman, a local councillor and a vicar, struck me as constitutionally intolerant towards pacifists and suspicious of the motives for being one, determined to give each of the applicants as difficult a time as possible. I was taking extensive notes because I considered the Society would interest itself in the appeals, should any be lodged.

Before Sawyer was called, the clerk handed up to each member of the tribunal a typewritten copy of his statement. They scanned it briefly, before saying that they were ready.

Sawyer entered, glanced around the courtroom with evident nervousness, then took up the position he was directed to, standing in the cramped space of the back row of seats in the well of the court.

Asked to identify himself, Sawyer said, 'Joseph Leonard Sawyer, aged twenty-three, of Cliffe End, Rainow, Cheshire.'

'The members of the tribunal have read your statement, Mr Sawyer,' the clerk said. 'You do not have to take an oath unless you wish to. Do you wish to?'

'No, thank you.'

'Is there anything you want to add to what you have written in your statement?'

'Yes, sir. There is.'

'Is it going to be relevant, Mr Sawyer?' said the chairman of the tribunal, a man I knew to be Patrick Matheson, the owner of a large insurance brokerage in Manchester.

'I believe so, sir,' Sawyer replied, facing the bench squarely.

'All right, but keep it brief. We've a lot to get through this morning.'

Sawyer glanced at the public gallery where I was sitting to take my notes, together with three other members of the general public, then at the press bench, where a reporter from the local newspaper was paying close attention to everything that happened.

'As this is for the public record, sir,' Sawyer said, 'I will need to go over some of the material you have read in my statement, so that the rest of what I have to say will make sense to other people.'

'Very well, but be quick.'

'Thank you, sir.' Sawyer shifted position, trying to ease his muscular legs within the narrow confines of where he had been made to stand. 'I have been a pacifist since 1936, when I travelled to Germany on behalf of my country and competed in the Olympic Games. Before then, I was too young to take much notice of world affairs, having been at school, then at university —'

'Which university was that, Mr Sawyer?' Mrs Agnes Kilcannon asked.

'Brasenose College, Oxford, ma'am.'

'Thank you. Carry on.'

'While I was staying in Berlin I came into contact with Chancellor Hitler and other members of the Nazi ruling party. I also saw at first hand the effects of their ruthless control over the country. My father was a conscientious objector during the last war, and what I saw made me remember what he always said, that the Treaty of Versailles was merely stoking the fires of future troubles. I saw much that alarmed me. Germany was controlled by the police and army, also by groups of armed militia who did not seem answerable to the authorities. Newspapers had been closed. Certain minority groups, like the Jews, were unable to work and were being constantly harassed by officials. Many shops owned by Jews had been burned. My friends in Berlin, with whom I was staying, were formerly a well-placed family, the man a doctor, his wife a translator, but because of the Nazis they were virtually unable to work. There were extensive laws which affected their most basic rights and freedoms. As well as that, I was shown convincing evidence that the Nazis were secretly expanding their army and had created a modern air force, in breach of the Treaty.'

'If I may say so, Mr Sawyer, it is for reasons like these that most young men have taken up arms to fight Hitler.'

'I know, sir, but I'm trying to show you that I'm aware of the danger Germany presents.' Sawyer paused to look down at his own copy of his statement, which he was holding. I could see the page trembling. He cleared his throat and went on, referring to the statement but speaking from the heart. 'I am personally convinced that war is wrong, no matter how good the cause. I am also convinced that although a war can be fought for what is believed to be an honourable reason, such as with the intention of forming a peaceful society, the war itself, by causing so much death and destruction, defeats its own object. Human suffering, pain, misery, separation and bereavement are inevitable when wars are fought. Violence, when opposed by other violence, creates a set of circumstances in which more violence will inevitably follow. Revenge, retribution and reprisal become predominant in people's minds. They seek to hurt others because they themselves have been hurt. I know that views like mine are unpopular in wartime, sir, but they are sincerely held and openly expressed. I am applying for complete exemption under the Act and request you to register me unconditionally as a conscientious objector.'

After a short silence the chairman said, 'Thank you, Mr Sawyer.'

The three tribunal members briefly consulted in whispers. The only woman on the bench, Mrs Kilcannon — later to be Lady Kilcannon but at that time the deputy chairwoman of Macclesfield Town Council — spoke up.

'Do you have any evidence to show us that you have not trumped up your beliefs in the last few weeks, merely to avoid military service?'

Strictly speaking, Sawyer was not obliged to answer such a question, but he faced her steadfastly.

'I do wish to avoid military service, but I have been working actively for peace since 1936. As soon as I returned from Germany I set up home with my wife and took a job as an adviser working with homeless refugee families in Manchester. I joined the Peace Pledge Union and committed myself to housing and prison reform. I began to work more closely with Canon Sheppard of the PPU and was appointed a national organizer. I was on the paid staff until the outbreak of war. I am still an unpaid member of the PPU National Council.'

'Do you have another job?'

'I have been working as a trainee printer, but I am actively seeking a more useful occupation that would be in tune with my beliefs.'

'Do you have any religious faith?'

'No, sir.' Sawyer looked directly at the Reverend Michael Hutchinson, the third member of the tribunal, who had fired the question at him. Again, such a question was not normally admissible, and I noticed the clerk of the tribunal turn to glance warningly up at the bench. Sawyer did not flinch, though. 'I am an agnostic pacifist, my objection to the war being based on moral or ethical grounds, not religious ones.'

'I see. So how would you distinguish between moral and religious grounds?'

'I do not believe in God, sir.'

'You are an atheist?'

'No, I'm an agnostic. I'm full of doubts.'

'Yet you have written in the preamble to your statement that you are a Quaker.'

'No, sir. With respect, I say there that I am attracted to the moral framework of Quakerism and share many of its ideals. I have worked on several projects with the Society of Friends. However, theirs is a system of belief and mine is a system of doubt. In your terms I remain Godless.'

Revd Hutchinson noted something on his pad of paper and indicated to the chairman with a tilt of his pencil that he had no more questions.

'All right, Mr Sawyer,' said Patrick Matheson. 'I should like to ask you a few questions about practical matters, so we can find out the extent of your objections. As you know, we are here to decide the level of registration for which we think you are suitable. This can be subject to various conditions, or it can be unconditional. At the same time, we might decide that you should not be registered at all. Do you understand that?'

'Yes, sir.'

'Let me ask you first, is there any kind of war to which you do not object?'

'No, sir. I object to all wars.'

'Can you say why?'

'Because a country at war is pursuing its aims by means of violence. That must be wrong, no matter what.'

'Even if its aims are to resist the violent aggression of a dictator like Hitler?'

'Yes, sir.'

'Then do you propose that this country should stand idly by and let Hitler do whatever he wants?'

'I don't know what the answer is to that. I can only speak for myself.'

'All right, then let me ask you this. Is there any part of the present war effort in which you might be willing to take part? Serving in the RAMC, for instance?'

'No, sir.'

'So you would not help a wounded man?'

'Not if I were made to serve in the Royal Army Medical Corps.'

'Why is that?'

'Because the Corps is part of the army. The people who serve in it are subject to military discipline and are bound to obey orders. The main purpose of the army is to fight the war, which I cannot accept.'

'But what would you do if you came across an injured man in the ordinary course of your life?'

'I would naturally do whatever I could to help him.'

'Do you oppose the activities of the Nazis?'

'Yes, I do. Utterly.'

'Then why will you not fight to defeat them?'

'Because I believe that the system of Nazism can only be dismantled by the German people themselves.'

'And if the Nazis were to invade Britain, bringing their activities with them, would you still see it as a matter for the German people alone?'

For the first time since the interrogation began, Sawyer was lost for words. I saw him swallow hard and his hands were fretting with the piece of paper he still held. Then he said, 'I don't know, sir.'

'Surely you must have thought about the possibility?'

'Many times, sir. The fear of it haunts me every day. But the truth is that I don't know what the answer is to your question. I told you I am full of doubts.'

Mrs Kilcannon suddenly said, 'If there was an air raid going on, would you use a public shelter to protect yourself?'

'Yes, I would.'

'Then would you be prepared to take on ARP duties?'

'What's the connection, ma'am?'

'If we were to register you as a conscientious objector, on condition that you worked for Air Raid Precautions, helping other people to take shelter during air raids, would you accept that?'

Again, Sawyer appeared unable to answer. He continued to stare rigidly at his three interrogators, but I could see no clue in his expression as to what he might be thinking.

'I'm not a coward, ma'am,' he said finally. 'I do not mind exposing myself to danger. I understand that if air raids begin, the ARP are likely to be in great peril. That would not bother me unduly. But if I felt that the ARP work was helping towards the war effort I should not be able to undertake it.'

'So your answer is no.'

'The answer is again that I don't know.'

'There are a lot of things you don't know. Could it be that you are wrong in your opposition to the war effort?'

'I am here because I have a conscience, ma'am, not because I have thought things out according to a plan.'

Mrs Kilcannon appeared to approve of his answer, because I saw her make what seemed to be a tick mark on the paper in front of her.

Patrick Matheson returned to the questioning.

'Sawyer, suppose we gave you what you want, an unconditional registration, what would you do with it?'

'Do I have to commit myself, sir? I've been trying to find a job —'

'Just a general answer.'

'I'd like to do humanitarian work.'

'Do you have special expertise in that?'

'No, sir.'

'Or any qualifications?'

'No, sir. I left Oxford before I completed my degree.' Mr Matheson continued to stare bleakly at him, so Sawyer went on, 'I thought I might look for work in a hospital or a school, or maybe on a farm. I have never been with-out a job before. I'm unemployed because the printing company where I was working took on war work, so I felt I should leave.'

For a moment I saw Mr Matheson looking across the well of the court-room at me.

He said, 'Have you ever thought of working for the Red Cross, Sawyer?'

'Well, not so far —'

Of course, it was not long after the tribunal hearing that J. L. Sawyer became a Red Cross official, after a dangerous spell as a paid employee of the Society. On the day I am describing there was nothing I could do to inter-vene on his behalf, as my presence in court was merely that of an observer, but soon afterwards I did mention this remarkable young man to our branch in Manchester, whence the first approach to him was made.

That hearing in Macclesfield ended satisfactorily as far as Sawyer was concerned. Against my own expectations, the tribunal awarded Sawyer unconditional registration, news he greeted with an impassive nod.

I continued to observe Local Tribunals throughout the remainder of 1940, but for the British Red Cross that year was a busy and stressful one . . .

2

From the holograph diary of J. L. Sawyer (Collection Britannique, Le Musée de Paix, Genève; www.museepaix.ch/croix-rouge/sawyer)

April 10, 1940

Yesterday, Hitler sent his armies into Denmark and Norway. I'm convinced the warmonger Churchill was ultimately behind it. Less than a week has passed since the Prime Minister put him in charge of the British war effort, as Churchill immediately claimed for himself. He made no secret of the fact that he intended to mine the Norwegian fjords. Neutral shipping, according to Churchill, was using the fjords for the delivery to Germany of iron ore. Neutral shipping, according to common sense, was also using the fjords for the delivery to Germany of medical supplies, food, clothes, essential fuel. Germany is as dependent on such things as any other country. No wonder the Germans have gone in to take control of the sea lanes. Churchill would do the same if the situation was reversed.

I have been trying to put the vegetable patch into shape. The one thing that seems clear is that Britain will run out of food as soon as the war worsens and the U-boat blockade begins to be effective. I worked outside all afternoon with B until it started to rain, but the soil up here on the hillside is shallow and full of stones. I can't see how anything will grow, unless it's grass or moss. Mrs Gratton and her peculiar middle-aged son Harry live in a house along the lane from us and they seem to grow vegetables pretty well. If I see Harry I'll ask him what I'm doing wrong.

Last night I had another of my dreams about my brother, Jack. I dreamt that he came to visit B and me at the house, that while he was there I walked away on my own and when I returned he had gone again. I often wish that Jack and I could settle our differences, as I miss his companionship. I know the arguments would only start up again, though. I don't judge him — why should he judge me?

Tomorrow: more job interviews. One is for a porter's job at a hospital in Buxton, which I think I can get. It has not been so easy finding jobs. Britain has gone over to a total war economy. All businesses, large or small, are making guns, shells, planes, engines, uniforms, boots, or any of a million smaller components or parts. There seems to be no part of British life that is not touched by war.

April 13, 1940

I belatedly discovered that the hospital in Buxton has set aside two wards for injured servicemen, so I had to turn down the porter job. B was furious with me when she found out. I found it so difficult to explain, even to myself. I sympathize with her sometimes.

April 19, 1940

Against my better judgment I wrote a letter today to the Foreign Office, asking them if they can help trace B's parents. She believes that they must have arrived safely in Switzerland as planned, but they have been unable to let her know because of the war. I suspect the reality is much darker than that and I worry how B will react if she hears the worst. I have seen stories in the newspapers of Jewish refugees on their way to Switzerland, only to be intercepted by the SS or to be refused entry by the Swiss border guards. Of course I have never let B see these stories.

Her parents made their first attempt to escape at the beginning
of 1937, but something went wrong and they returned to Berlin.
Because they had many good friends in Berlin they were able to
stick it out until things took a turn for the worse last year. They
made a second attempt to flee to Switzerland, but nothing has been
heard of them since.

I am concerned that writing to the British government will
draw attention to B's origins. There is such an intense anti-German
mood in the country that it amounts to hysteria. Already young
men of German birth who live in Britain — including many who
escaped here because of the Nazis — have been rounded up and
interned somewhere: out of temptation's way, as someone nastily
put it. Now the politicians, and some elements of the press, are
talking about what to do with the rest of the German nationals:
older men, but also the women and children.

April 29, 1940

When I came in this evening, wet through from the drizzling rain,
after the long bicycle ride up the hill from Macclesfield, B showed
me something that had been pushed through the letterbox while
she was out at the village shop. It was a large brown envelope with
my name written on the front in childish capitals. Inside was a
white feather.

B had opened the envelope. She said she burst into tears when
she realized what was in there.

My father warned me that something like this was likely to
happen, but what really troubles me is that it must have come from
someone in the village, someone we know, perhaps even a neighbour. Few people outside the immediate vicinity of the village know
anything about me. I have been trying not to dwell on the mystery
of the identity of the sender, but I can't help it. It is the first event
of the war which has made me angry, made me want to do something about it.

I went out into what we hope one day will be our vegetable
garden. I kicked at some stones, felt violence rising in me like a
mad drug. I was ashamed of myself afterwards.

When it was dark I walked down the lane to the telephone box
outside the shop and tried to speak to Jack at the phone number

Dad had told me was the RAF station's. The man who answered would not say where Jack was. I could imagine what that might mean.

Afterwards, walking back along the dark lane, the drizzle settling on my hair and shoulders, I did wonder if it might have been Jack himself who had sent the feather.

Now, while I am writing in my notebook, I feel my hatred of war rising all over again. This time the anger is against the effect war has on men's thoughts. The effect it has on my thoughts.

May 3, 1940

I have a new job and that has been my main concern for the last few days. For all that time the news from the war has been almost too horrible to bear. Every night on the wireless it seems there is more bad news. There have been losses on both sides, huge losses. Ships have been sunk, aircraft have been lost, men have been killed and wounded, civilians have been uprooted from their homes. The British troops are giving up in Norway at last. It is not their fault. The blame lies with that menace Churchill, the man who was responsible for the disaster in the Dardanelles in the last war. History will go on repeating itself so long as warmongers lead us.

I can't help feeling we are being told only part of the story.

My new job is with the British Red Cross, in a building in the centre of Manchester. My first task there is to compile an inventory of the surgical materials, dressings and medicines they hold in stock. This is part of a national effort by the Society, so that should bombing of the cities begin, or if there is an invasion, the Red Cross will at least know what stocks they hold.

B says that she has had one answer to the postcard she placed in the Post Office window in Macclesfield: a child of eight needs violin lessons once a week. I am relieved that B will at last be doing something she loves and is good at, and that takes her out of the house for a few hours.

So far, we can be thankful that few civilians have been affected by bombing. There are rumours that bombs have been dropped on the Orkney Islands, but it is impossible to find out about casualties. Because of the Royal Navy base up there, secrecy obscures everything.

Another envelope with a white feather has been shoved through our door, this time while we were asleep last night. I managed to conceal it from B and later put the feather in the chicken run, where I hope she will not notice it.

May 4, 1940

This being a Saturday I had to go to work in the morning but I was home again after lunch. B and I attempted more work on the vegetable plot. This time we made progress because during the week B arranged for a local farmer to deliver some dung. We scooped it on to the patch and dug it in.

Late in the afternoon a number of twin-engined aircraft flew low over the hills, their engines making a loud, throbbing noise. We assumed they were British by the slow and unaggressive way in which they were being flown, but neither of us could identify them for sure. B is terrified by the thought of German aircraft coming anywhere near her. I still cannot even begin to imagine what she suffered while she was in Berlin. I know that she is in constant dread of finding out what happened to her parents. I can give her no hope beyond the blandest kind of reassurance.

I am becoming obsessed with the belief that the war must be ended as soon as possible. Europe, which has been driven mad by Hitler's ambitions, must come to its senses. I feel a steady fury about the ineffectual way I am living my life. Still I count the rolls of bandages and lint dressings. My mind says that Europe needs soothing ointments to heal its wounds, but increasingly my heart seeks a terrible revenge against the men who are conducting the war.

Pacifists, Canon Dick Sheppard once said to me, are more interested in war, and better informed about it, than the most bloodthirsty of warriors. The reason is because we think of it endlessly and because the warmongers think of it not at all.

The Red Cross has enough plasters and bandages to wrap around the entire population of Manchester, should the need arise. I know, because I feel as if I have personally counted most of them.

May 6, 1940

Everyone in the Red Cross office seemed tense today, presumably sensing that the war is about to take a turn for the worse. There is talk of a detachment of Red Cross volunteers being sent to France. I cannot decide if I should like to be one of them. I do not want to leave B alone, but the restlessness and raging that goes on inside me is not being quelled by the clerkly preparations we are making in Manchester. My immediate supervisor, Mrs Alicia Woodhurst, seems pleased with me and said today that she will find me more interesting work in future. I shrugged, pretending not to care.

Austerely, I tell myself that to work with the plasters and bottles of antiseptic is pacifist enough. If I am bored by the task, then that is the price to pay for my beliefs.

But in truth I am desperate to be doing something more active. Today, briefly, I found myself envying Jack. He at least has a clear role in the war. I stand to one side.

May 7, 1940

I was moved to Mrs Woodhurst's office today, now that the inventory is complete. She set me to catching up with her filing. I worked slowly through it, reading as much of it as I dared, trying to find my way around in what I realize is a vast international organization.

Later, Mrs Woodhurst asked me if I would stay late at the office. She had to go out while I was to stand by in case anyone telephoned us. The evening wore on, making me hungry, tired and increasingly anxious to go home. The telephone did not ring once. Mrs Woodhurst finally returned after eight o'clock and I set off to London Road Station, stopping on the way to buy some fish and chips, which I ate from the paper as I walked along. It was almost dark by the time I reached Macclesfield, the blackout complete across the streets. Only a residual glow remained in the western sky. As I left the station I noticed a group of older men standing around outside the pub next to the pedestrian tunnel beneath the railway tracks — I have to push my bike through the tunnel to reach the main road. They saw me with my bicycle and from the way they moved their heads and shoulders, shunning me, they apparently knew who I was. I had to weave my bicycle between them to get past.

May 8, 1940

Today a consignment of tents, long awaited, in a road/rail/sea
shipment that originated months ago in Switzerland, arrived at
Manchester docks. I had to spend most of the day arranging for
them to be cleared through Customs and prepared for collection
later by Red Cross trucks. The sheer number involved gave me an
insight into the scale of damage that the Red Cross is expecting.

May 9, 1940

Two more of the officials from our Red Cross branch have moved
away, apparently to France. We are now short-staffed. Mrs
Woodhurst asked me this afternoon if I thought I could drive an
ambulance, which I immediately said I could. That would not
conflict with my views and might well give me a sense of the action
I am starting to crave.

I was not late leaving the office. It was still daylight as I pushed
my bike out of the station and headed for the dark tunnel that led
to the road. As I did so, a couple of men in working clothes walked
directly at me, their shoulders set and lowered. They barged into
me, one on each side, knocking me over. The bicycle clattered to
the floor. I landed heavily on one shoulder. As soon as I could
recover my breath I shouted after them, asking them why they had
done that. They were already at the far end of the tunnel but they
turned and looked back. For a moment I thought they were going
to return and attack me again. 'Yellow bastard!' one of them
shouted at me, and the other yelled, 'Coward!' Their voices echoed
down the curved brick roof of the tunnel.

At least it was only that. My bicycle was undamaged so once I
was sure the men weren't lying in wait for me further along I rode
home. I have said nothing about it to B.

3

Downloads from The New European Press Library (www.new-libeuro.com/UK):

From *The Times*, London, May 14, 1940:

> Yesterday the Prime Minister, Mr Winston Churchill, addressed the House of Commons on the grave crisis that faces the country, following the German invasion of the Low Countries at the weekend.
>
> To a packed Chamber, he said, 'On Friday evening last I received His Majesty's Commission to form a new Administration. In this crisis I hope I may be pardoned if I do not address the House at any length to-day. I would say to the House, as I said to those who have joined this Government: "I have nothing to offer but blood, toil, tears and sweat." '
>
> This was Mr Churchill's first appearance in the House since he took office on Friday. His new war cabinet has been chosen and remaining government appointments, where necessary, will be announced in the next few days. Mr Churchill has declared he will draw his ministers from all parties, forming a government of national unity.
>
> Referring to the overwhelming successes of the German forces, Mr Churchill warned, 'We have before us an ordeal of the most grievous kind. You ask, what is our policy? I will say: It is to wage war, by sea, land and air, with all our might and with all the strength that God can give us; to wage war against a monstrous tyranny, never surpassed in the dark, lamentable catalogue of human crime. That is our policy. You ask, what is our aim? I can answer in one word: It is victory, victory at all costs, victory in spite of all terror, victory, however long and hard the road may be; for without victory, there is no survival.'
>
> Information released earlier by the War Ministry revealed that the German army is making progress on most fronts. The Belgian and Dutch armies are falling back and the Maginot Line is being circumvented. British and French troops are putting up stiff

resistance but such is the speed with which events are occurring that it is so far not possible to predict where the resistance will hold.

Mr Churchill concluded his short announcement on a note of rallying defiance.

'I take up my task with buoyancy and hope,' he declared. 'I feel sure that our cause will not be suffered to fail among men. At this time I feel entitled to claim the aid of all, and I say, "Come then, let us go forward with our united strength." '

From *Stockport & Macclesfield Advertiser*, Stockport, May 17, 1940:

A Rainow man was attacked by unknown assailants last Friday in Moor Road, Macclesfield. He is said by doctors at Stockport Infirmary to be 'comfortable' and has recovered consciousness.

The victim, Mr J. L. Sawyer, of Cliffe End in Rainow, was returning from his work in the centre of Manchester when he was attacked by a gang of at least four men.

A police spokesman said that the attack took place after nightfall. Because of the blackout it has been difficult to trace witnesses.

Detective-Sergeant Stephenson of Macclesfield police has appealed for anyone who was in Moor Road between 9 and 10 p.m. last Friday evening, and who might have seen what happened, to come forward.

Mr Sawyer suffered multiple cuts and bruises, including a blow on the head. He is expected to make a full recovery.

A spokeswoman for the Manchester branch of British Red Cross, where Mr Sawyer is employed as a clerk, said at the weekend, 'We cannot imagine who could have carried out the attack. Mr Sawyer is a valued member of our staff. We believe it must have been a random attack on an innocent man.'

There have been several night-time attacks on pedestrians in various parts of Britain since the blackout was imposed last year, but it was the first to take place in this part of Cheshire.

Mr Sawyer is married. His wife Brigit has been at his bedside since the attack.

4

From holograph letters of J. L. Sawyer and family (Collection Britannique, Le Musée de Paix, Genève; www.museepaix.ch/croix-rouge/sawyer/bhs)

The letters of Birgit Heidi Sawyer (née Sattmann).

i

May 12, 1940 to Flt Lt J. L. Sawyer, c/o 1 Group, RAF Bomber Command
Dear JL,

I have been unable to reach you by telephone, which is always so difficult for me to use in the phone box. Have you received the messages I sent you? If not I must tell you that Joe has had an accident. He was attacked by a gang on his way home from work and is in hospital. He has many injuries, but they are mostly on the surface. His pride has been hurt most. If you can arrange some leave to see me he is in Stockport Infirmary. (He does not know I am writing to you, of course.)

With love, your close friend, who would like to see you,
Birgit

ii

May 14, 1940 to Mrs Elise Sawyer, Mill House, Tewkesbury, Gloucestershire
Dear Mrs Sawyer,

Joseph has improved since you and Mr Sawyer visited him at the weekend and he is expected to come home in a few days' time. He already is looking much better.

Please, I want to set aside the many arguments we have had in the past, and please, to ask you a great personal favour. Even if you will not do this for me think of it for Joseph.

There are people in the village whispering about me because of where I came from before I was married to your son. I can't say the words but they think I am working for the other side. They only hear my accent! I am alone here and the house is isolated and after what happened to Joseph I am terrified for every minute of each day. Please *please* may I come to stay with you for a few days, until Joseph is well again? You do not have to come here to fetch me. I can travel by train on my own. It would only be until Joseph is out of hospital. I am begging you.

> *I am, your loving daughter-in-law,*
> *Yours faithfully,*
> *Birgit Sawyer*

iii

June 3, 1940 to Mrs Elise Sawyer, Mill House, Tewkesbury, Gloucestershire
Dear Mrs Sawyer,

I am pleased you and your husband were able to visit Joseph and me at the weekend and that you could satisfy yourself about the care I am giving your son. Of course it would be impossible to live up to your high standards, but I do my best. Always we are short of food and even medicines. The difficulty is caused by the rationing but also because it is so hard for us to reach the shops in Macclesfield. This will change once Joseph is able to ride his bicycle again. You are probably correct to point out my mistakes in the kitchen and you may be sure that in future I shall make greater efforts to provide Joseph with the kind of food and clothes that you think he should be having. You need not inform me of this again.

I have been talking to Joseph and we are agreed that in future it will be best if he visits you on his own, at your house in Gloucestershire.

> *Yours sincerely,*
> *Birgit Sawyer (Mrs)*

5

From the holograph diary of J. L. Sawyer (Collection Britannique, Le Musée de Paix)

June 4, 1940
This evening I found that I was moved to tears after listening to the Prime Minister on the wireless. B was there with me, listening

too. She tried to comfort me but I don't think she understood. I certainly couldn't have explained to her, mainly because I don't understand myself. I'm still amazed by my reaction. That odious man Churchill moved and inspired me. For a moment he even began to persuade me that it was right to fight.

But I am in an impressionable state of mind, depending on B for everything, still in pain. Churchill's warmongering rhetoric has had a disproportionate effect on me. In spite of it, I feel I am almost better. I hobble around on my stick, I am even able to stand unsupported as I use the toilet. B says I should rest as much as I can. I use the time to prepare my recovery: each day I plan to make progress, aiming to be back to normal by the end of next week. Is it possible? Mrs Woodhurst is coming to visit me next Thursday afternoon, which I hope will mean that I can get back to work quickly.

Winston Churchill apparently took over from Neville Chamberlain on the same day as I was beaten up. It was confusing to wake up in hospital and find so many changes. The war has lurched further into unstoppable chaos. Churchill's speech tonight made a clear distinction between the German people and the Nazis who are their dictators. He seems to be almost alone in maintaining that. Ordinary people can only commit themselves wholeheartedly to fighting a war when they demonize the enemy. Dad said this is what happened in the last war: the German people became Fritz, the Hun, the Boche. Now it is starting again: they have become Jerries, Nazis, Huns.

It was difficult enough to argue for peace before the latest events. In the present climate, with Churchill whipping up war fever, bracing the country for the worst, it is impossible. I simply do not know what to do any more.

His speech ended with simple words of calm determination: we will defend our island against invasion whatever the cost, fighting in the streets and fields and hills, never surrendering. His words mysteriously and powerfully evoked an England I know and love, a country it is right to defend and one that is worth dying for. Churchill made me proud of my heritage and nervous of losing it. He aroused my eagerness to hold my home safe. Without being able to resist, I started to cry.

June 21, 1940

Today I went to the Society office in Manchester, in preparation for my return to work in four days' time, on Monday. I was not nearly as nervous as B at the prospect, but she went with me to Macclesfield Station and insisted on being there to meet me when I returned. We agreed the time of the train I would catch home, while she would do what shopping she could in the town.

All signs and place-names have been removed or obliterated, windows have been taped up as a precaution against blast, sandbags are heaped against many doorways. Everywhere there are posters and notices, warning, advising, directing. In the centre of Manchester, public air-raid shelters have been opened at the end of almost every street. Most people carry gas masks or steel helmets. Many are carrying both. You see people in uniform everywhere. This is what it is like to live in a country at war. Now it is in earnest.

Tonight is by chance the shortest of the year. It is nearly 11 p.m. and it is not even fully dark outside yet. The sky is mostly black but there is a band of silvery blue touching the horizon in the west. A deep-grey, beautiful light washes across the plain below my window. No lights show, but in the charcoal shading of the long twilight most main features are visible. If the German bombers were to come now, they would find all the targets they want. The thought makes me nervous and I realize that this must be what everyone else is going through at the moment.

France surrendered to the Nazis today.

June 30, 1940

I have been back at work for a week, while the threat of invasion continues to worsen. Everyone talks about it, where and when it will happen, what Churchill will do about it, how strong our army might be after the disaster at Dunkirk. The newspapers and wireless report that German forces are gathering in France, that invasion barges are being prepared, that the Luftwaffe is massing its aircraft in the thousands. Every day we hear that shipping in the English Channel has been attacked by dive bombers. The harbour in Dover has been bombed several times.

All this talk of war. Few people seem to know that talk of peace is also in the air!

It is being kept out of the newspapers, but through my work at the Red Cross I know for certain that Hitler has made two peace offers to Churchill this week. One was sent by way of the Italian government. The other was passed through the Papal Nuncio to Red Cross HQ in Switzerland. Churchill immediately rejected both offers.

I was despairing and furious when I first heard about it, but I have been having a think.

Churchill loves war. He makes no secret of it, even boasts about it. When he was a young man, 'eager for trouble,' he pulled strings and even cheated his way into the front line of the wars in India and Africa. His reaction to the disgrace of the Dardanelles in 1915 was to join the British army and fight on the Western Front for several months. It is clear that he sees the present war as a culmination of his passion for fighting.

At the moment, though, Churchill is cornered. No warmonger will entertain an offer of peace while his back is to the wall. He would interpret it as capitulation or surrender, not peace, no matter that common sense would tell him that worse punishment is to come. Churchill undoubtedly believes that he needs a military victory of some kind, before he will talk to Hitler.

No sign of that, so how am I going to feel when England is invaded, as surely she must be? For all my beliefs I remain an Englishman. I can't bear to think about a foreign army, any foreign army, marching across our land. Thought of the Nazis worsens that imagining by many degrees. B is more scared than I am — better than most people, she knows what the Nazis are capable of doing.

July 25, 1940

Several airfields in the south-east of England have been bombed by the Luftwaffe, with many casualties and a great deal of damage.

The Red Cross is in a state of official readiness. Tomorrow I will be joining three other chaps from our depot and driving one of two ambulances and a mobile field surgery to our South London branch. It will probably take us two days to drive to London, bearing in mind how hard it is supposed to be to get around the country at the moment. It's difficult to obtain reliable information, but we hear that many roads have been blocked with crude barricades.

It means I shall be going into the front line of the war, an idea I find inescapably romantic and terrifying, although there is in reality little danger of my being caught up in the fighting. All four of us will be returning to Manchester by train immediately we have handed over the equipment.

Of course, it also means that I have to leave B alone here until after the weekend. She is feeling much stronger than she was and says that I must do what I believe is right. There is food in the house for her until next week. Since the weather has been so warm she has been spending more time in the garden. Teaching the child has given her a new interest in playing and she has been learning new pieces. She says she will be so busy she will hardly notice I've gone.

July 29, 1940

I returned from London late last night, after long but uneventful journeys. B was asleep in bed when I arrived, but she woke up. She was obviously pleased and relieved to see me home safely again. We have spent a quiet, contented day together in the garden, as I was given today off work after the trip. In the evening B played me a new piece she has learned, by Edward Elgar.

British fighter aircraft are constantly active in the skies around here. I wish that reassurance was not what they bring, because that translates, I must admit, to their ability to shoot and kill.

I get so confused by the strength of feelings the war induces in me. I write down in my diary what I feel, but in truth I no longer know exactly what I feel. Was it the bump on the head? Or am I simply responding to the changing circumstances, which I would never have predicted?

July 30, 1940

We have to deliver more ambulances to the south, so tomorrow I am once again driving to London. My immediate concern was with B and how she would cope during my absence, but she has assured me she will be all right on her own for as long as I have to be away.

I have spent today packing the vehicles with emergency supplies. We will be setting off to London first thing tomorrow morning.

August 6, 1940

I am still in London after a week. I cannot begin to describe the confusion that the Society is having to deal with, a terrible warning of the chaos that will follow should hostilities really get going. Every day the fighting seems to worsen, although for the moment much of it is skirmishes between warplanes. The bombing is confined to attacks on military bases. Naturally, the damage spreads far and wide, so civilians become casualties too. This is where we come in. For the last four days I have been driving my ambulance to and fro across the south-eastern counties, acting as a relief to the regular ambulance services. Mainly I am simply expected to be the driver, but inevitably I have to help out with many of the injured. I am learning fast about the work.

I have left a telephone message for B at the post office in Rainow, so she knows where I am and that I am safe.

I am staying at the YMCA in the centre of London. I wondered at first if I might meet other COs doing similar work to mine in the capital, but as far as I can tell I'm the only one. Almost without exception the men here are in the forces, in transit from one part of the country to another. Most of them are only staying overnight while changing trains or arranging to be picked up, so it is difficult to strike up friendships with any of them. The few civilians appear to be merchant seamen, en route to one of the ports to find a berth. It leaves me feeling isolated and wishing I could be at home with B.

At the end of last week, Hitler made a speech to the Reichstag, in which he made public an offer of peace to Britain. German aircraft even dropped leaflets over London reporting what he said:

'At this hour I feel before my conscience that it is my duty to appeal once more to reason and common sense in England and elsewhere — I make this appeal in the belief that I stand here, not as the vanquished, begging for favours, but as the victor speaking in the name of reason. I can see no grounds for continuing this war. I regret the sacrifice, and I also want to protect my people.'

Whether or not we should believe him was swept aside yesterday, when the Churchill government formally rejected the offer. The war goes on, presumably to Mr Churchill's deep satisfaction.

August 12, 1940

I am *still* here in London, torn between my urgent wish to go home for a few days and the growing realization of the emergency the country is in.

I am on duty for most of the daylight hours, dealing with an ever-increasing number of casualties. More and more of them are our airmen, shot down and wounded in the violent aerial dogfights taking place overhead. The authorities constantly warn us that the 'blitzkrieg' tactics used in Poland, Holland and France must soon break upon us. That is a terrifying prospect.

Today I managed to speak to Mrs Woodhurst on the telephone. She is arranging for someone to come down from Manchester to relieve me for a few days. All the excitement of being in the thick of the war has faded: I want only to see B again.

August 15, 1940

Home at last, in the uncanny peace and quiet of the Pennine hills. The war suddenly seems remote from me. I slept for twelve hours last night and have woken refreshed. B certainly seemed pleased to see me yesterday evening and we have had a happy reunion. She woke me this morning at about ten when she put her head around the bedroom door to tell me she was about to catch the bus into Macclesfield.

I dozed for a while longer, then pottered contentedly about the kitchen, eating toast, drinking tea and looking through the letters that arrived while I was away. After that I took a bath. Because it is a fine, warm day I stood for a while in our garden, enjoying the sunshine, looking down at the plain of Cheshire, relishing the silence.

Later on in the morning I made an unusual find. I'm still puzzling over what it means.

Some of the furniture in this house was here when we moved in. Among the better pieces is an immense old oak wardrobe in our bedroom. (We can't imagine how anyone got it into the house and up the stairs, except in pieces.) We keep most of our clothes inside it. This morning I was searching around on the deep shelf that runs from side to side across the top, hoping to find an old jacket of mine, when my hand rubbed against something made of fabric, but stiff and round. It had been placed right at the back of the shelf, apparently put there deliberately so it would be hard to find. I had to stretch right in to get hold of it. It was an RAF officer's peaked cap, complete with badge.

I looked at it with interest, turning it around in my hands. I had never been so close to any part of a military uniform before. The cap was almost new, in excellent condition, with only a couple of small darkened streaks on the inner sweatband to show that it had been worn a few times. I tried it on, experiencing a *frisson* of something (embarrassment? excitement?) as I did so. It was a perfect fit. I looked at myself in the mirror, startled by the way it seemed to change the shape of my face.

I didn't want B to find me with the cap, so I put it back where I found it. I have said nothing to her about it, but I can't help wondering if she knows it's there.

August 18, 1940
The war has taken a new turn: the German bombers are ranging more extensively across the country, seeking other targets. So far they appear not to be aiming deliberately at civilians, but there have been many reports that some of the German planes jettison their bomb loads as soon as they are attacked by British fighters. As a result, a number of bombs have gone off in the countryside. We have always thought that the remoteness of our house would give us a measure of safety from the bombs, but we are forced to recognize that nowhere is safe. The German raiders appear almost everywhere: we have heard of air raids in Scotland, in Wales, in the London area, in the extreme south-west. Of course, the towns along the south coast are attacked almost every day. Then there is the fear of a parachute attack. For obvious reasons, parachutists will land in open countryside in remote areas. The country is already rife with rumours about parachutists being seen. So far there has been no substance to any of these stories, but with an enemy like Hitler anything is possible.

Shortages in the shops continue and are getting worse.

Tomorrow I have to return to London.

September 2, 1940

Many more days have slipped by, unrecorded here. I am stuck in London, with no hope of a return home for as far as I can see ahead. I had no idea of the sheer chaos war could bring.

Every day I travel to the Red Cross depot in Wandsworth, where I am assigned to an ambulance. With at least one trained medical orderly, sometimes with two, I then drive all day, ferrying victims of the fighting to whichever is the closest hospital.

Like many other married couples, B and I have been forced into war separation. When you find a few minutes to chat to the people you're billeted or working with, the consequences of being away from home are the most pressing subject. Most people now see their home life as something that is possible only for short periods of time, a weekend snatched from the everyday chaos, an overnight stay while passing through. Almost everyone you meet has been mobilized away from their own districts. Women are on farms or working in factories, while many of the men are in the forces or in one of the support organizations: manning the anti-aircraft batteries, patrolling for Air Raid Precautions, on nightly fire-watching duties, drilling with the Home Guard, on stand-by with the Emergency Rescue teams or working with the fire service. Everyone is on the move, with no permanence or stability. We are obsessed by the threat of invasion, by the air raids, by the battles going on overhead. Every day, they say, the country is growing stronger, is becoming better prepared. Every day that Hitler does not send his invasion forces is another day gained, a bonus, a growing of strength.

I feel no fear. Nobody feels fear. I remain a pacifist but pacifism is not based on fear. Nor is it based on the opposite. Churchill remains in power, leading the country with suicidal defiance, almost taunting Hitler to try his best to destroy us. He was born to fight war. Every so often we hear on the wireless the words that Churchill chooses to say to us. You cannot ignore what he says because of the poetic grace and power with which he speaks his unpretentious and inspiring words. Everyone you speak to is moved by his speeches. I do not know what I think any more. Except the basics, which never change.

Rumours abound: distant cities have been raided, with horrific results, tonight a thousand bombers will be coming to London, Dover has been bombed flat, German troops have been seen in the Essex seaside towns. For a while you believe the stories. Then the BBC news gives another version of events and you believe that instead. I'm fortunate in that the Red Cross is well informed. It is fairly easy for me to establish the truth, or something close to it. So far, things do not seem to have been too bad for civilians.

Shipping and airfields are bombed every day. At night the German bombers fly across all parts of the country, but they are more of a nuisance than anything: the sirens go off in the evening, so that people's lives are interrupted. Little damage is done. A few bombs are dropped here and there. In places they drop propaganda leaflets, which instantly become objects of derision. You grow tired of hearing jokes about people using them as toilet paper.

So, each morning comes. I take out the ambulance and its medical crew, liaise with our army escort — needed in case we are sent to a crash-landed German plane in which crew members may have survived — then head for the towns and suburbs on the edge of London: to Croydon, Gravesend, Bromley, Sevenoaks. This is where most of the battle casualties are found. We pick up airmen who have been shot down, staff who were working at the factories and other installations under attack, those civilians unfortunate enough to have been injured by a crashing plane or a stray bomb or fallen shell.

Most of the bombing continues to be against 'military' targets — airfields, oil-storage depots, factories — but in an increasing number of incidents it looks as if the Germans deliberately cast their bomb loads wide. Houses, schools and even hospitals in the general area of the main targets are being damaged or destroyed with increasing frequency. And as is obvious to all of us, more and more towns are being treated as targets.

At first the bombing attacks were confined to the ports: Dover and Folkestone have suffered terribly, but they are the nearest British towns to the Luftwaffe bases in France and have an obvious strategic value. Then the areas of attack spread rapidly along the coast: Southampton and Portsmouth were bombed. After that the Germans turned on the towns alongside the Thames estuary, the threshold of the capital. What next?

September 8, 1940

It is a Sunday afternoon. I woke up an hour or so ago after one of the hardest and longest days of my life.

I spent the daytime in the usual round of duties, this time in Chatham on the south side of the Thames estuary. Because of its naval yard the town has become a regular target for the Luftwaffe. As evening came I drove back to London, returned my ambulance to the yard in Wandsworth and caught the Underground back here to my lodgings at the YMCA. I had been home no more than a couple of minutes when the air-raid sirens started again. I was summoned back to Wandsworth immediately. Within half an hour a major attack was taking place on the docks and warehouses in the East End. I was there all night, finally reaching my bed at 5 a.m.

September 19, 1940

I can no longer stand it here in London and need a rest. I have applied to return to Manchester.

German bombing tactics have changed drastically. Every night the Luftwaffe bombs London. Occasionally, they send second or third waves to other industrial cities, briefly sparing the capital. The first sirens are heard soon after sunset and the bombing continues, with varying degrees of violence, until well into the small hours. The planes first drop incendiary devices in their hundreds and thousands. They land everywhere — on roofs, in streets, gardens, parks — and almost immediately discharge a burst of white-hot fire that ignites anything it touches. Firewatchers are on duty along every street and on every tall building that has an accessible roof. Many of the devices are doused with sand before they can do much damage, but there are limits to how many can be tackled. It's dangerous and difficult work. Not long passes before many dozens of fires are taking hold. Soon afterwards the second phase of bombing begins as the Luftwaffe planes drop high-explosive bombs and parachute mines, shattering the streets and buildings and blasting the already burning debris in every direction.

Many people are killed outright, hiding under the staircases of their houses or huddling in their garden shelters, or if they are caught out in the open. The public shelters are safer, and the deep platforms of the Underground system are safer still. Every night more and more people are said to be moving down to the platforms to sit out the raids. Hundreds of people are injured in every raid. Among those casualties are members of the fire service, the police, the rescue workers, the air-raid wardens, the firewatchers and the ambulance drivers.

I have myself been close to death or serious injury many times. When the night raids began I intended to use my notebook as a first-hand record of what the experience is really like. I felt at the outset that there should be some evidence, some authentic first-hand account, of what happened to London when the bombers came. Someone, eventually, will be called to account for what is being done to this great city. The bombing of cities is clearly criminal. I am a witness; I am here in the thick of it.

But I am always too exhausted after my night-long shift of duty even to feel like lifting the pencil. It is etched in my memory but I have written none of it down. And memory is unreliable: after the first few bombs exploding in the street where you are, after the first few burning warehouses, the incidents run together.

I am already sick of the heat, the explosions, the shock of sudden flares of flame as the incendiaries crash to the ground, the smells of burning, the cries of injured children, the sight of bodies buried in the rubble, the hideous wounds, the dead babies, the grieving parents. I am deafened, half blinded, frightened, angry, scorched. My hair, skin, clothes stink of smoke and blood. I truly walk in hell.

6

From letters of J. L. Sawyer and family (Collection Britannique, Le Musée de Paix)

i

The letters of J. L. Sawyer.
September 2, 1940 to Mrs Birgit Sawyer, Cliffe End, Rainow
My dearest Birgit,

It has become easier to arrange a weekend pass. I am so sorry I have had to stay away for the last two or three weeks. If I were to visit you again this weekend, arriving on Friday evening and leaving on Sunday morning, is there any likelihood I would see my brother Joe?

  Yours ever,
  JL

ii

The letters of Birgit Heidi Sawyer (née Sattmann).
  September 4, 1940 to Flt Lt J. L. Sawyer, C/o 1 Group, RAF Bomber
  Command
  My dearest JL,
    No. Come quickly.
    As always,
    Birgit

  September 9, 1940 to J. L. Sawyer, Poste Restante YMCA, London
  WC1
  Dear Joe,
    I miss you so much and wonder when you will be coming home again. Are you able to give me any definite dates? I am able to tell you that you need not worry about me. I am all right in the house and can get by without you a little longer. You must not feel I am constantly asking you to come home. You know I will like nothing more than to have you home again with me, but I understand if your work in London must keep you away from me.
    Always with love, my darling,
    B

7

Papers of Institut Schweizer für Neuere Geschichte, Zürich

The letters of A. Woodhurst, British Red Cross, Manchester
  November 4, 1940 to Mrs J. L. Sawyer, Cliffe End, Rainow
  Dear Mrs Sawyer,
    Although your husband Joseph has been with the Red Cross for only a comparatively short time, he has rapidly become one of

our most valued and dedicated workers. In particular, the medical and rescue aid work he has been carrying out in London has drawn praise from all quarters.

The Superintendent of Whitechapel Police has written to me personally to state that amongst many other acts of great courage, Joseph was personally responsible for saving the lives of six children who were seriously injured by a German bomb that exploded close to the entrance of one of the shelters in Stepney Green. Although suffering cuts to his face and hands, he pulled all six of the children to safety and drove them to hospital. Afterwards, he continued to drive his ambulance through the streets for the remainder of the night, constantly in danger. On another occasion, the Superintendent tells me, Joseph helped evacuate an area under immediate threat from an unexploded parachute mine. The bomb exploded moments after everyone had moved to safety and no doubt would have caused many deaths and horrific injuries.

Joseph's name has been put forward three times to the authorities, drawing attention to his bravery. He has been an inspiration to everyone working with him in those dangerous circumstances.

You will therefore recognize the depth of our concern which we must share with you (although certainly not to the same extent), after he was posted as missing during the devastating air raid on Bermondsey two nights ago. We know that this distressing news has already been sent to you by telegram. I hope this personal letter will be a small comfort to you.

Although Joseph's ambulance took a direct hit from a bomb, there are no signs that anyone was inside. All of us here are drawing great hope from this knowledge. Joseph was certainly seen in the area immediately before the second wave of the attack and one of his medical crew said he believed Joseph might have gone to one of the public shelters. A full search of the area has been concluded, including a close inspection of all the shelters and damaged properties in the area. There were no unidentifiable bodies found and the lists of the other casualties have been checked thoroughly.

In the confusion that follows a large raid at night a lot of people are temporarily listed as missing, but most of them turn up again soon afterwards. We are treating him as missing, but let me

assure you that it is only a technicality. The police remain confident
he will be found. In Joseph's case, most of our concern is caused by
the amount of time that has elapsed.

We shall of course contact you immediately we have any firm
news.

Yours most sincerely,
A. V. Woodhurst (Mrs)
British Red Cross Society — Manchester Branch

8

From letters of J. L. Sawyer and family (Collection Britannique, Le Musée de Paix)

i

November 5, 1940 to Mr J. L. Sawyer, Cliffe End, Rainow
Dear Mr Sawyer,

We refer to your letter of April 19, concerning the possible
whereabouts of a family named Sattmann, formerly of
Goethestrasse, Charlottenburg, Berlin, now thought to be refugees
within the Federal Republic of Switzerland.

We regret to inform you that no trace has been found of the
family, either by the Swiss authorities or by the Embassies of
Sweden and the Irish Republic, acting on our behalf elsewhere.

Yours sincerely,
K. M. Thomason — Foreign Office
Assistant Under-Secretary

ii

The letters of Birgit Heidi Sawyer (née Sattmann).

November 8, 1940 to Flt Lt J. L. Sawyer, C/o 1 Group, RAF Bomber
Command
Dearest JL,

Joe is alive! He was found yesterday in a hostel for homeless
men, suffering from concussion. Apart from that he is not
physically harmed. The Society is bringing him home today or
tomorrow.

My darling, it will be all right for us again. Soon, I promise. For now I must care for Joe.

My fondest love, which I renew in my heart day by day,
Birgit

iii

November 8, 1940 to Mrs Elise Sawyer, Mill House, Tewkesbury, Gloucestershire
Dear Mrs Sawyer,

I am pleased to tell you that my husband Joseph, your son, has been found unharmed and is on his way home. I will ask him to contact you as soon as possible.

Yours sincerely,
Birgit Sawyer (Mrs)

9

Papers of Institut Schweizer für Neuere Geschichte, Zurich

The letters of A. Woodhurst, British Red Cross, Manchester
November 11, 1940 to Miss Phyllida Simpson, 14 Stoney Avenue, Bury, Lancs.
My dear Phyllida,

I'm so glad you came to my office earlier today, to tell me yourself what happened in the ambulance on Saturday night while you were driving back to Manchester. The incident must have been upsetting to both you and Ken Wilson. You are certainly not to blame in any way for having fallen asleep while supposed to be caring for Joe Sawyer. I know how exhausted you must have been. I have nothing but admiration for the dedication you and hundreds of other young Red Cross workers have been showing during the Blitz on our cities.

Be sure that you may come here to speak to me at any time. In the short time he has been working for us, we have all become very attached to Joe.

Yours sincerely,
Alicia Woodhurst
British Red Cross Society — Manchester Branch

10

Extract from Chapter 9 of The Greatest Sacrifice — British Peacemakers in 1941 *by Barbara Benjamin, published by Weidenfeld & Nicolson, London, 1996:*

. . . which is where the Duke of London emerges unexpectedly from his past to stride the world's stage for a few crucial months. No one man — politician or general or diplomat — did more to affect the course and outcome of the German War than the Duke. 'If I encounter a man with a mind of his own I see it as my prompt duty to change it for him,' he once said, describing a condition that he might well have applied to himself. Although a man of apparently unshakeable convictions, the Duke of London was for years considered politically untrustworthy because of his habit of changing sides.

In this we can see the first clue to what many people interpreted at the time as an inexplicable volte-face, one which turned out to be the most important and historically significant of the last hundred years.

If there had been no war with Hitler's Germany, the Duke might have remained in the political wilderness for ever, perhaps thought of as a complex, innovative but inconsistent politician who was never able to fulfil his potential. The fact that war came when it did was his making. He rose magnificently to the challenge. Had the war continued and had London led the conduct of the war to the military victory he always promised, one may only guess at the terrible consequences. Because London reversed his policy, though, a real and lasting peace became unexpectedly possible.

In such a way arises the great historical dilemma over which the Duke presided. When is it right to fight? When is it right to lay down your arms? When the chance arose in 1941 to alter the course of history, it required a man of greatness to know whether that chance should be seized or spurned.

The Duke of London, who was half-British, half-American, was born Winston Leonard Spencer-Churchill on November 30, 1874, the elder son of Lord Randolph Churchill. His mother was Jennie Jerome, daughter of a businessman from New York City. He built substantial fame and popular support while still young by filing colourful and sensational accounts of British wars in his role as a correspondent for the *Daily Telegraph*. The books later published which were based on these accounts became best-sellers. During his experiences — in Cuba, the North-West Frontier of India and in the Sudan — he displayed the first signs of impatience, impetuosity and inconsistency: as a serving officer, in his case with the 31st Punjab Infantry, he should not have been allowed to write for the press. It was only his personal charm and family contacts with the great and the good that enabled him to break the rules so much to his own advantage.

He first ran for parliament in 1899, unsuccessfully contesting the seat for Oldham. The following year he gained the seat for the Conservatives in a by-election. By 1904 Churchill had fallen out with the Conservative establishment and crossed the floor of the House to become a Liberal. It was the first of many such shifts of political loyalty, a habit that endured for most of his career. A gifted speaker and orator, Churchill made a number of anti-Conservative speeches at this time which members of the Conservative establishment liked to quote back at him many years later when his judgment was so often in question.

Winston Churchill held several of the main offices of state over the next three decades. His first Cabinet appointment, as Home Secretary, was in Herbert Asquith's Liberal government of 1910. Controversially, as Home Secretary he took a leading personal role in a police siege of two gunmen in East London, putting himself in the line of fire and bringing in armed troops to deal with the problem. It was the first indication that he would allow his reckless nature to colour his political judgment. The second was far more serious and affected the lives of thousands of men. As First Lord of the Admiralty in 1915 he bore personal responsibility for the disaster that occurred in the Dardanelles. Churchill always maintained that the bungled campaign on the Gallipoli peninsula was the collective responsibility of Lloyd George's cabinet, but history has identified it as an incautious adventure in the familiar Churchillian mould. It seriously damaged his political career and for a time he rejoined the army and served on the Western Front in France. By the end of the Great War, though, Churchill returned to government and was Secretary of State for War. In this position he became an advocate of British intervention to quell the Russian Revolution. In 1941, Josef Stalin was quick to remind Churchill of this by-then inconvenient fact. The breakdown in relations between the United Kingdom and the USSR in the summer of 1941, and the catastrophic consequences when Britain remained neutral during the German invasion of the Soviet Union, are traced by many historians to this solecism by Churchill.

After the Great War he lost two more elections, returning to Parliament only in 1924 as a Constitutionalist member for Epping. The same year he changed political allegiance yet again, returning to the Conservative party and becoming Chancellor of the Exchequer under Stanley Baldwin. As Chancellor he argued repeatedly for reducing Britain's defence spending, a political stance which his later anti-appeasement arguments totally contradicted. In 1926 he bitterly attacked the leaders of the General Strike, from his office as editor of the officially published *British Gazette*. As he had used soldiers as strikebreakers in 1910, against striking miners and dockworkers, his contribution was seen as unduly threatening.

A ten-year period followed, 1929 to 1939, when Churchill was again out of high office, though he remained a backbench Member of Parliament. He changed his attitude to military spending and became a strenuous advocate of rearmament, being in effect the only voice raised in public to warn of Adolf Hitler's ambitions. Cynics in the political establishment said then, and continued to say after 1941, that Churchill helped to stir up the war for his own political ends. Indeed, in 1939, on the outbreak of war in September, the Prime Minister, Neville Chamberlain, appointed Churchill for the second time to the Admiralty, a triumphant return to power, recognized as such within the ranks of the Royal Navy. In the first months of the German War, the navy bore the brunt of military operations, which with hindsight is not coincidental.

In spite of the fact that events in Germany from 1936 onwards seemed entirely to have vindicated his militaristic stand, Churchill was by this time regarded by his political contemporaries as unreliable by nature and a warmonger by instinct. Churchill was unpopular with most of the other MPs, few of whom were able to say they trusted him. He appeared to remain popular in the country, but by modern standards the sampling of popular opinion was only approximate at best.

Winston Churchill became Prime Minister on May 10, 1940, the day the Wehrmacht marched into the Low Countries. Chamberlain felt obliged to resign because he knew a national government had become necessary and he could no longer count on the support of Parliament. Because experience of high office was essential, only two men were deemed to be qualified to replace him: Churchill or the then Foreign Secretary, Lord Halifax. Churchill's disadvantage was his most recent military fiasco: the British had been ignominiously thrown out of Norway by German forces after an adventure in which Churchill's actions arguably breached Norwegian neutrality. As First Lord of the Admiralty, Churchill enthusiastically engineered the action and so was ultimately responsible for its failure. Halifax's disadvantage was that he was a peer and therefore sat in the House of Lords. He was also well known for his appeasement policies, a serious drawback in May 1940. In a private meeting at 10 Downing Street between the three men, Churchill opted to say nothing. Breaking the long silence, Halifax eventually yielded. Churchill immediately accepted that the duty fell on him. By the evening he had been asked by the King to form a new government. Churchill's own reaction, recorded in his post-war account of the war years, was that he felt as if he were walking with destiny, that all his past life had been but a preparation for that hour and trial. So his twelve-month premiership began, as did the process by which he would take Britain out of the war.

By the late summer of 1940 it would seem that Churchill was in an unassailable position, both within the government and in the country as a whole: in a series of brilliant speeches he stiffened the sinews of the British nation with plainly spoken messages of unshakeable defiance against the German enemy. Neither defeat nor surrender was an option: he was determined to prevail against Hitler's machinations. Meanwhile his political standing had improved immeasurably. Before the end of 1940 most of the men who served in Chamberlain's prewar cabinet, still identified as appeasers, were gone from the government and Churchill commanded almost universal respect and loyalty.

By the following May, the fortunes of war had started to swing in Britain's favour. The Italian army was defeated in Africa. The Battle of Britain had been won. The threat of invasion across the English Channel had receded. The Blitz against British cities was slowly reducing in intensity, with both sides realizing that the bombing of the cities had been a blessing in disguise for the Royal Air Force, which in the meantime built up the strength of both its Fighter and Bomber Commands. The British had cracked the German codes. From decoding those ciphers, and from other intelligence sources, Churchill knew that Germany was planning to launch a huge attack on the Soviet Union. The USA seemed likely to come into the war on the side of the British, later if not sooner.

On the face of it, the war situation looked like a formula for eventual military success, a different prospect indeed from the days of the previous summer, when Adolf Hitler had disingenuously offered peace. To accept Hitler's terms then, in the state of weakness that existed, would have been to capitulate.

In this more advantageous spring of 1941, thoughts of formulating any kind of peace with Nazi Germany must have been a long way from Churchill's mind as he contemplated the reports from his Chiefs of Staff. His principal concern at the time, as recorded in his *London Wartime Diaries* (1950), was to persuade the Americans to convert their brand of Britain-favouring neutrality into a full-blooded military alliance that would rid the world first of fascism, then of communism.

The USA, meanwhile, was tormented by the situation in China and Japan. It was by no means certain that President Franklin Roosevelt would be able to swing the USA to Churchill's assistance. Had the Japanese expanded eastwards, with some kind of provocation against the USA, then Churchill's plans might well have borne fruit. Japan was in alliance with Nazi Germany, so the USA would have had to come into the German war on Britain's side.

Instead, after Churchill's final and most sensational reversal of policy in May 1941, the USA felt itself released from all obligations to the British. Within four weeks of the British armistice, and two weeks before the beginning of Operation Barbarossa, they launched their series of pre-emptive attacks on expansionist Japan and the Japanese-occupied areas of mainland China. When Japan had been defeated, and the Bolshevist threat posed by the Maoist revolution had been crushed, the USA's opportunistic alliance with Chiang Kai-shek's Kuomintang enabled them to move swiftly on Manchuria and, eventually, across the vast eastern reaches of the Soviet Union.

Churchill always claimed after the event that the destruction of communism was for him a higher priority than the defeat of Nazism, the latter being but a step on the way to the former. There is, however, no real historical evidence that this was the case. All contemporary records reveal Churchill's obsession both with his own central position within British history and with the relatively straightforward war with Germany.

The infinitely more complex and dangerous war against communism was in effect fought by the Germans invading Russia from the west and the Americans from the east. With the dismantling of the Soviet Union after the cease-fire at the Urals, the two former superpowers then settled into the Third War stalemate. They both collapsed into economic and social stagnation as the incalculable costs of their wars were counted. From this ruin, only Germany so far has recovered — and then only with the aid of the denazification programme from the European Union. For the USA, the half-century of stalemate has been a disaster, still with no solution in sight. At the beginning of the twentieth century the USA was shaping into the newest and perhaps best democracy in the Western world. Instead, because of bad military decisions, corrupt civilian governments and a level of political inwardness that puts prewar isolationism into the shade, it has become a shaky but authoritarian republic, run in effect by capitalist adventurers and armed militias, and undermined by social dissent, organized crime and a heavily armed populace.

By the time the Third War stalemated in the early 1950s, Britain was by contrast in a supreme military alignment with the democracies of Western Europe. With her uncontested access to the oilfields of the Middle East, Britain remains to this day a dominant political and economic power in world affairs. Those who support the Churchill version of history ascribe Britain's supremacy to the warmonger's ambitions in the middle of the twentieth century, but they do not, of course, explain his volte-face.

For an understanding of that, we have to re-examine the events leading up to the sudden armistice. It was at the beginning of May 1941 that the only recorded meeting took place between Churchill and the young British Red Cross official, J. L. Sawyer.

Little is known of Joseph Leonard Sawyer before he met Churchill. He competed in the 1936 Olympic Games in Berlin, when it is believed he met the German Chancellor. Later, he was a registered conscientious objector and pacifist who worked as a volunteer ambulance driver throughout the Battle of Britain and the London Blitz. He received injuries several times during air raids, in one case suffering concussion. His conduct is known to have been exemplary: he consistently showed bravery and resourcefulness, saving the lives of many people caught up in the inferno of the Blitz, with little regard for his own safety but never risking the lives of his colleagues. Although his name was unknown to the public, his gallant behaviour under fire had already been noticed by several civil authorities.

The crucial meeting between him and Churchill came as the result of an initiative from Dr Carl Burckhardt, president of the Swiss Red Cross. Because the Society was a non-combatant recognized by both sides, the Red Cross was in a unique position to attempt to negotiate an armistice. Such proposals had been put forward at regular intervals after the outbreak of hostilities. As the fighting spread across Europe and Africa during 1940 and the early months of 1941, the war becoming more intense and violent, neither side was in any mood for a cease-fire and the Red Cross proposals were turned down at the same regular intervals.

At the beginning of May 1941, however, Churchill suddenly and unprecedentedly acceded in principle to the latest formal proposal and Sawyer was one of those who were summoned to a top-secret meeting. No public record exists of what was said or agreed during this meeting. Confidential Cabinet minutes about the armistice do not fall under the thirty-year rule and are therefore under indefinite embargo, but in recent years pressure has been increasing for them to be made public. Until then we can only conjecture as to the meeting itself.

If not much is known about Sawyer before he met Churchill, even less is known about him afterwards. That he participated in the armistice is certain, for his signature appears in the treaty document. There are also the photographs taken at the time of the signing, in which Sawyer may be glimpsed standing on the periphery of the group. After that, there is no further trace of him.

His unprecedented influence on Churchill, and to a lesser extent on the German Chancellor, is unquestioned, but also unexplained. One naturally wishes to know more, but we can be content that as a result of it the peace deal was forged. The enigma deepens because of his subsequent disappearance, the intrigue heightened by the fact that there were only two recorded sightings of him while on Red Cross business, both of which were made while he was abroad . . .

11

Holograph notebooks of J. L. Sawyer — University of Manchester, Department of Vernacular History (www.man.ac.uk/archive/vern_his/sawyer)

i

I remember exactly the moment when I came to my senses after the accident. Memory reappears like a scene in the middle of a film, an abrupt jump from blankness. I was inside a Red Cross ambulance, shocked into reality when the vehicle jolted over an uneven patch of road. I braced myself defensively against the knocks and bumps I was receiving, but my waist and legs were held gently in place with restraining straps. I was alone in the compartment with an orderly, a young Red Cross worker I knew was called Ken Wilson. It was difficult to talk in the noisy, unventilated compartment. Ken braced his arms against the overhead shelves as the vehicle swung about. He said we were well on our way in the journey, not to worry. But I was worried. Where were we going?

As awareness dawned on me, something must have changed in my manner, because Ken raised his voice over the racket of the ambulance's engine and tyres. 'Joe, how are you feeling? Are you OK?'

'Yes,' I said, realizing that I was indeed feeling all right, whereas until a few seconds before I had not been feeling anything. The world was suddenly in focus. 'Yes, it's starting to make sense again.'

'You had a nasty shock, old man. Do you remember anything about that?'

'A bang on the head, was it?' I reached up and gently felt the top of my skull, but I could feel no sensitive areas where a wound might have been.

'You took quite a knock,' Ken said. 'We're not sure exactly what happened to you. We think you were a bit too close to a bomb going off. Blast can knock someone out without causing any obvious physical damage. The doctor said we needed to get you to a hospital.'

'The doctor said . . .? I'm not ill, am I? When did this happen?'

'A week or so ago. You were down in Bermondsey. In fact, a lot of us were there that night. A big raid, one of the worst so far. At the end, when we reported back to the Wandsworth yard, we did a head count and you hadn't returned. You were posted as missing, but the police didn't find you until three days ago. You don't seem to have suffered any physical damage, but the doctor who examined you said they had already come across several similar cases. Blast can cause internal damage without visible wounds. You need a proper check-up, but the hospitals in London are stretched to the limit. We thought it would be safe to take you home, so you can see your own doctor, go to your local hospital. Things aren't too bad yet in Manchester.'

After the shock of renewed self-awareness faded, I began to orientate myself. It seemed to me that my memory, as I prodded experimentally at it, was not too badly affected: I could remember the weeks in London, the endless anxious hours driving the ambulance, the scores of injured people we picked up. I vividly remembered the hundreds of fires in the narrow London streets, the ruined, gaping-windowed buildings on each side, the piles of wreckage, the flooded craters and snaking fire-hoses. I remembered Ken Wilson, too. Ken and I had always rubbed along well together. As the ambulance continued on its way, he told me more about what the people at the Red Cross thought might have happened to me, where I could have been until I managed to find my way to the men's hostel.

Although my memory was already starting to piece itself together, behind the calm appearance I was trying to project to Ken I was terrified. Concussion creates a sense of unfilled blankness behind you, one you know in reality must have been made up of experiences which at the time were perfectly normal, but which have since become unreachable by memory. Discovering what is there in your memory, and what might not be, is a painful process.

I want to emphasize the reawakening in the ambulance (why did it occur there?, why at that exact moment?) because it is a point of certainty. My conscious life began again, there and then. What was to follow is the crucial period of my life and I want to record it in my notebook, but much of what I can say is less certain than I would like. I can only describe what happened to me in the way it seemed to happen. I am sure about that moment of awakening. It is certain and it is a sort of beginning.

Some time after midnight we took a short break from the journey in Birmingham, where there was another main Red Cross depot. I tried taking some steps without using the sticks Ken gave me. It came quite naturally, but I felt nervous without their support and was quickly short of breath. We carried on to the canteen and sat at a table with the young woman who had been driving our ambulance, Phyllida Simpson. We huddled together in the cold canteen, getting to know one another.

When we returned to the ambulance, Ken took over the driving, while Phyllida loosely secured my legs and waist with the straps in case I wanted to sleep. Soon we had passed through the heavily bombed centre and inner suburbs of the city, and were striking northwards into the countryside. Phyllida lay back on the stretcher shelf on her side and began to doze.

I too was exhausted, but the exhilaration of having an identity was coursing through me. I settled down to pass the rest of the night on the uncomfortable ledge, wrapped in a couple of blankets, bracing myself with my elbows and staring up at the van's ceiling. It was cream-painted, made of metal, held in place by a line of tiny painted-over rivets. There were few comforts in the vehicle. How many damaged lives had expired on a hard shelf like this, with a similar dreary view? I knew of some of those people myself. I could not forget the feeling of despair and regret that arose whenever we arrived at a hospital casualty bay, only to find that the injured person must have died as we were driving frantically through the blacked-out streets.

ii

We arrived in Manchester as dawn was breaking. Someone unlocked the door of our building and we went inside. Ken and Phyllida went to the kitchen and one of them put on a kettle to make tea while I walked around the deserted floors, familiarizing myself with the place once again. I knew it had been some time since I worked in the building, but my faulty memory was imprecise about details. I was anxious to go home to see Birgit again. The first train out to Macclesfield did not leave until after 8 a.m. but as we drove into the centre of Manchester Phyllida told me she thought there might be someone who could give me a lift home before then.

In the end, after hanging around in the centre of Manchester, I caught the train. I left Macclesfield Station, walked through the tunnel, crossed the Silk Road and began the climb up the hill towards Rainow. It was a long walk, with many reminders of the times I had laboured home the same way, pedalling my old bicycle.

I took a shortcut across the fields on the slopes below our house. It was a lovely autumnal morning, with mist shrouding the hills, but the thin sunlight was already on my face and the view across the plain was coming into focus as the day moved on. I could see our house ahead of me, outlined against the pale blue sky. I thought of Birgit in there somewhere, not suspecting that I was almost home. Because we had no telephone in the house I had not been able to send a message ahead. I briefly imagined her sitting alone at our kitchen table, perhaps drinking milk or tea, reading the morning newspaper.

I had been away so long — I no longer knew how many weeks it had been since I left. Birgit was living by herself for all that time, alone in a house and in a country where she never really felt she belonged. I had hardly been able to contact her: no telephone conversations except short ones by arrangement in public call-boxes, our letters delayed by the disruption the bombing caused. She was so young, so beautiful. I had left her alone, neglecting her for the sake of trying to do something about the war.

I broke my stride. For the first time ever, I was stricken by doubts about my wife. Could she have turned to someone else for comfort in my absence? While I was in London I had met so many other people whose lives had been disrupted by the war, whose minds were full of anxious thoughts about sexual betrayals and jealousies. Separation, loneliness, mistrust, infidelities, these were the real consequences of war for most people. The marriages of two of the men in the small group I worked with in London had already collapsed under the strain of war.

I realized I was panicking, a reaction usually alien to me, and I decided at that last moment to send out a warning. In those few seconds I had convinced myself that if I marched unannounced into my house I might interrupt something that I would rather not see. I was less than fifty yards away from the house.

I cupped a hand around my mouth.

'Birgit!' I shouted. 'Can you hear me? I'm home!'

My voice sounded to me like an explosion in the quiet morning. It seemed that my words echoed across the slopes, back from the tranquil hills, loud enough to make people miles away turn their faces and crane their necks. I glanced around at the misty, sunlit view. I called again and continued to climb up the uneven grassy slope.

'I'm home, Birgit!' I yelled again.

Then there was movement. I saw one of the curtains in the main living-room twitch quickly to one side. Had it been Birgit?

The front door opened, the one that led out to the muddy lane running past the house. I stumbled forward, tripping, pressing my hands briefly on the dew-cold grass for balance, then levering myself up again. I saw someone step out of the house.

It was not Birgit. It was, in a terrible fulfilment of my worst fantasy, a young man. He was in uniform, in RAF uniform: smart blue trousers and tunic, pale-blue shirt and dark tie, a peaked cap. He looked across the muddy ground towards me, the shock in his face reflecting the shock that I myself felt.

It was my brother Jack, there at my house.

I half crawled, half climbed up the slippery grass towards him. He was standing stiffly with his hand stretched out towards me. I kept stumbling and sliding, pushing myself desperately towards him, but somehow I was unable to make any more progress. Birgit came through the door behind Jack and stood peering past his shoulder as, like a fool, I blundered and slithered on the muddy slope.

iii

I opened my eyes and the cream-painted metal ceiling of the ambulance was there above me. The noise and vibration of the engine rattled through me. My back was stiff from straining for balance against the lurching of the van.

Phyllida was standing in the aisle with her legs braced, leaning down over me. She was holding my wrist in one hand; the other pressed coolly on my forehead. I tried to sit up, deeply confused by the suddenness of the transition. She pushed me down again, gently but not allowing me to resist. I realized how physically weak I was feeling.

'You were shouting,' she said. 'I couldn't catch what you said.'

'I don't know,' I said. In my mind's eye I could still see the steep slope, the bright morning sunshine, the figures of my brother and my wife, high and unreachable above me. 'I wasn't asleep! Was I shouting?'

'Joe, try to relax. We'll get you to Manchester as soon as we can. Let me give you something to drink.'

She held out to me one of the lidded cups we gave the patients when the ambulance was moving at speed. What had been going on in my house? Jack and Birgit together? I took the cup from Phyllida and sucked at the metal mouthpiece. Cold water ran pleasantly into my mouth. I took two or three gulps and passed the cup back to her.

'Better?' she said.

'Better than what? I can't imagine what's happened to me! I thought we had arrived. We went to the building in Irlam Street, where we work! You were there and so was Ken Wilson. Just now! Isn't that right?'

'Joe, make yourself comfortable.'

She rapped her heel sharply three times against the metal bulkhead dividing the back of the van from the driving cab. In a moment I felt the vehicle slowing down. Eventually it came to a halt and the engine fell silent. I heard the driver's door open and close. Ken Wilson walked round and let himself in through the main doors at the rear. There was nothing but darkness outside.

'What's the problem? Is everything OK with you, Joe?'

'Yes —'

'He suddenly started shouting,' Phyllida said. 'You must have heard.'

'I think I was dreaming,' I said, as I realized how unexpectedly seriously they were treating my outburst. 'A nightmare, something like that.'

The words sounded unconvincing as I spoke them. It had not felt like a dream at all, but flowed seamlessly from the same reality in which I now inexplicably found myself for a second time. Dreams are odd but concise, but that had been different. I remembered lying for long, empty hours on this hard shelf while we drove through the night, halfway between sleep and awareness, bored and restless, anxious to be home. It had been so unexceptional that it had not occurred to me to question it. When we reached Manchester — as I thought — I was numb with exhaustion, but relieved to be there. I took a second wind, walking slowly to the main station to catch the first train out to

Macclesfield. It had been dull, everyday, with a background of lucid thoughts, not concise, not at all odd, not dreamlike in any way that I usually experienced dreams. Had I dreamt the cold train with the dirty windows? Had I imagined walking up the long hill of Buxton Road, in that revitalizing autumnal morning?

It was as if I had slipped suddenly back in time, out of one reality into another. But which reality, now, was the one I should believe in?

Ken and Phyllida were watching me, concerned. They made me feel as if I were a patient in a hospital bed, called upon to describe mysterious symptoms. I tried to make myself sound as ordinary and conversational as possible.

'How far have we travelled?' I said. 'I mean, since we stopped in Birmingham?'

'Not far,' said Ken. 'We went through Walsall about fifteen minutes ago. That's only a few miles north of Birmingham.'

'I think I had a bad dream,' I said. 'I'm sorry if I've alarmed you both.'

'I'll stay awake with him, Ken,' Phyllida said. 'Let's get back to base as soon as we can.'

I wanted to protest that they were treating me like a patient, but in fact I had no idea what had been happening to me in the last few days. In this sense, like so many real patients, I was to a large extent at their mercy. Phyllida lived in Bury, north of the city, and Ken, who was due to be posted back to London, was planning to lodge with her and her parents for the next two days. After a look at the map, they decided they could make a detour and drop me off at my house. I was relieved to hear it. I ached to be home. I didn't want to have to experience the long wait in Manchester all over again, or the slow train journey home afterwards. I had only just done that.

We were soon under way again. Phyllida tried to keep me talking as we drove along. We were both worn out. I was thinking that so long as I maintained awareness, watched what was happening, kept answering Phyllida's questions, then the continuity of my real life could not be broken. Inevitably, though, Phyllida's conversation lapsed. She lost her train of thought several times and I knew she was struggling to stay awake. I told her I was feeling OK, that if she wanted to take a nap I'd be fine lying there on my own. She shook her head and said that she and Ken had been advised to keep me under observation all the way home, but her voice was slurred. After a few more minutes she did stretch out on the hard shelf, pulling one of the blankets over her. Soon she was asleep, lying there with her mouth open, one arm dangling over the side of the shelf. I became introspective, thinking about that lucid illusion and wondering what it might mean.

iv

We rumbled into Macclesfield as dawn was breaking. I moved around on the shelf of the ambulance as soon as I noticed daylight starting to show through the high slit windows, sitting up so that I could peer through the small window that looked out to the front, over the driver's head. Not surprisingly, perhaps because of the hour, there was virtually no other traffic out there. The one or two vehicles we did see were military ones. It was a grey, cold morning, with a sharp wind sending raindrops against the ambulance's windscreen in short, diagonal lines, jerkily moving until swept away by the wipers. A few hours earlier, when I had dreamed or imagined so clearly this same morning, it was sunlit and mist-shrouded, promising autumnal brightness. Not now. The appearance of the countryside was more or less unaffected by the war, but in the towns many houses had their windows boarded up, their gates and doors padlocked. We saw no evidence of bomb damage in Macclesfield, but dreary signs of the war were everywhere: shelters, concrete road barriers, the general drabness created by the lack of advertising signs and shop-window displays. We were approaching the second winter of the war and there was little relief from the grimness. Ken halted the ambulance in Hibel Road, opposite the courthouse, its memories still fresh for me of the tribunal I had been forced to attend earlier in the year. I walked around to the front of the vehicle and sat in the cab with Ken for the last part of the way.

As we drove noisily up the long hill I was looking ahead for the first glimpse of the house, wondering again, this time with a low feeling of dread, what I would find when I arrived. At such an early hour Birgit would almost certainly still be asleep. I let my thoughts drift no further than that.

At Ken's insistence we drove along the narrow lane to the front of the house. I clambered down from the ambulance and collected the small bag of belongings I had brought with me. The noise of the idling engine seemed to me loud enough to wake everyone in the village. Phyllida moved forward to take my place in the driver's cab. I waved and mouthed my thanks to them both, and turned to the house. I opened the door with my key.

Into the familiar sense of home. Everything looked tidy, clean, attended to. I heard footsteps on the boards above me and Birgit appeared at the top of the stairs. She was a light sleeper and the sound of the ambulance had woken her. She was pulling on the long dressing-gown I had given her the previous Christmas, wrapping it around her nightdress. Her hair was awry, her cheeks were flushed. My first impression was how happy she looked, how well. Still beautiful! I realized how much I had been missing her, how much my absence turned in on itself, creating a vacancy in my life. She was smiling, hurrying down the stairs, greeting me with arms upraised.

I took her in my arms, smelling her familiar scents, the touch of her face against mine. She still felt warm from the bed. Without saying anything we kissed and held each other, touching, tasting, clinging on. She was soft and large in my arms.

Then she laughed and pressed my hand against her belly.

'Can you feel the baby yet?' she said. 'This is my surprise for you, my darling!'

'What?' I said stupidly.

'I have just found out! Only since two days ago. I am already nearly two months pregnant!'

That was her surprise for me, that cold November morning.

v

It was a cool, rainy autumn that year, the wind battering constantly against the west-facing side of the old house, insinuating bitterly cold draughts into every room. The view of the Cheshire Plain, which had always inspired me, was obscured by mist or low cloud every day. Our bedroom was at the back of the house, yet the cold seeped in there too.

I was allowed a week of sick leave by the Red Cross so I took advantage of it, sleeping late every morning, keeping Birgit close beside me. We both disliked slipping out of our warm bed into the icy room, walking on bare floorboards because we had not been able to afford carpets or rugs, then going shivering into the toilet, which was situated on the weather side of the house, or downstairs where the floors were of stone. For the first two or three days we were as happy as we had been in the first weeks we were married. The silent presence of our baby son or daughter, growing daily, at last presented us with a certain future. The prospect of becoming a father gave me a lot to think about: simple joy at the prospect of having a child, of course, with deeper fears about finding myself inadequate to the task of fatherhood. Beyond that, there were the larger worries: what right did we have, for instance, to bring a child into a world of warfare and fear? But the excitement tended to make up for everything. We would doubtless cope. For Birgit, additionally, the pregnancy felt like a new protection for her against the risk of internment. She showed me letters she had received from the Home Office while I was in London — the officials never said as much, but it seemed she was still being classed as Category 'C,' unlikely to be taken in unless she transgressed against the law in some undefined way.

The letters were not our only reminders of war. Even without the outward signs — the apparently endless list of rules and restrictions that were announced on the wireless every day, the rationing of food and clothing, the depressing news of cities being bombed and ships being sunk, the constant activity of warplanes overhead — even without them I had to live with a sense of disquiet that my weeks in London had somehow allowed the war to infiltrate me.

I felt that my pacifism paradoxically turned me into a carrier of war, in the way some people, immune from disease, become carriers and transmitters of that disease.

Wherever I went, wherever I looked, signs of the conflict sprang into existence around me. I loathed, feared and dreaded war, yet I could not escape from it even when I slept. I often dreamed of fires, explosions, collapsing buildings, high-pressure jets of water playing against crumbling walls, the sounds of sirens, whistles, shouts; in the middle of most nights I would wake up in a sweat, then lie there in the dark, trying to tell myself it was only a dream. I was repelled by the images, but at the same time I knew that I had become addicted to the dangers of war, something it was almost impossible for me to admit. I was safe at home with Birgit — or as safe as any civilian could be — but I ached to abandon the safety and throw myself into hazard once again.

I had been home only a day or two when we heard on the wireless that the city of Coventry had been completely destroyed by the Luftwaffe in a single night of bombing.

vi

In the morning of the day after we heard the news about Coventry, I was woken up by Birgit climbing out of bed and moving quietly around our bedroom, apparently trying not to wake me. It was starting to turn to daylight outside. Birgit was dimly silhouetted against the curtains as she dressed. I admired the shape of her womanly figure, her enlarging breasts, her thickening trunk.

'What are you doing?' I said, before she left the room.

She looked back in surprise, apparently unaware until then that I was awake. 'I have to go shopping. It's important to be in the queues early, before everything sells out. Tomorrow I can't, because I am teaching. So I go now.'

'I'll come with you,' I said, because already I had been at home long enough for me to start feeling trapped by the house.

'No. This I want to do on my own.'

I argued with her for a while but she continued to move purposefully about the house and soon she left, promising to return as soon as possible. I followed her to the door and watched as she walked briskly along the lane towards the bus stop on the main road. I went back to bed and read the morning newspaper, delivered after Birgit left. The news from Coventry was depressing and worrying, as the rescuers went about their necessary searches through the damage. With those hundreds of people killed and acres of property destroyed, what would Churchill order as a reprisal? I feared the retribution of a warmonger. The war was out of hand. Some people said that it could not be worse than the endless succession of night-time attacks on our cities, but I believed both sides capable of more. I dreaded to think what it might be.

When I was dressed I made myself a cup of tea, then returned to our bedroom. Standing on the chair, I reached up to the shelf at the top of the wardrobe, groping into the back for the RAF cap that had been hidden there before. Rather to my surprise, I discovered that the cap was stacked on a small pile of clothes that were neatly folded. I pulled out what I could find and laid everything on the bed.

There appeared to be a complete uniform. As well as the cap there was a shirt, a pair of stiffly pressed trousers, a belt, a tunic, a tie and a pair of brightly polished black leather shoes. The tunic bore the twin 'wings' sewn over the breast pocket, signifying that the wearer was a qualified pilot. There was also the ribbon of a decoration, but I was unable to identify it.

I closed my mind to all the implications of the uniform being in my house. Instead, I quickly removed my own clothes and put on the RAF outfit. I stood in front of the full-length mirror, clad in the coarse stiffness of the unfamiliar clothes, staring at the transformation they wrought on me. I turned away and looked back over my shoulder. I stood in profile, squaring my shoulders. I tilted my head up, as if scanning the skies. I saluted myself. Engines seemed to roar enthrallingly around me; distant explosions echoed.

I heard a movement outside the room. I froze, fearful of being caught in a guilty act, but my mood quickly turned to curiosity and irritation. Who would be in the house?

I strode to the door, feeling in those two or three paces that the crisp uniform gave my movements a quasi-military bearing, and pulled it open.

My brother Jack was standing on the landing at the top of the stairs. He was dressed in his uniform. We stood and faced each other, mirror images of each other.

I knew then what must be happening. Somehow, I had awoken that morning not to my own reality but to another lucid imagining.

Jack saluted me.

There was another noise downstairs. I went quickly towards the apparition of Jack, pushed past him, terrified of meeting his gaze, and swept by him without our touching. The house was mine; it smelled and sounded and felt as normal as ever. How was I imagining it? I was determined to get away from Jack, to escape from the house, seek the cold air outside, break out of the hallucination. I hurried down the stairs.

As I passed the door to the living-room I saw Birgit, standing with her back towards me, bending over something that was spread out on the table, apparently reading it. I stopped at the doorway.

'Birgit! You're here too?'

'Yes, of course.' She straightened and turned towards me, pressing her hands down against her sides, stretching her shoulders.

'You said you were going out. I heard you —'

'JL, what's the matter?'

'JL? Why do you call me that? I'm Joe!'

'My God! I thought —'

I glanced down at myself, the tie, the shirt, the blue unyielding cloth of the tunic. I felt the cap on my head, saw the shining toes of the black shoes. I moved away from Birgit and looked at the long bevelled mirror that hung on the wall in the hallway, next to the front door. Jack's exact likeness stared back at me, his military bearing, his fresh and slightly rakish good looks, his strong hands. I lowered my face so that I should see no more of him.

vii

It was the morning of the day after we heard about Coventry, as dawn was breaking. I was on my side of the bed, lying on my back, wide awake. The room was almost in darkness but the bright, lucid images of the hallucination still dazzled me. As I had found when I was in the ambulance, the transition from one reality to the other made me feel as if I had been kicked back in time: a few tentative steps taken along a path, then a sudden jolt and a return to the place from where I had begun.

Now Birgit was sleeping beside me, the weight of her arm thrown across my stomach and pressing down on it. She was large and warm against me. I felt isolated and frightened, taking no comfort from her closeness, the intimacy with which we slept. I groaned aloud, realizing that these imaginings were exposing my own worst fears to me. She had called me JL. Why? I felt Birgit stirring, probably woken by the noise I had made. She nuzzled her face against mine as she woke, affectionate and happy to find me there. She rolled against me, her soft breast resting on my arm, her belly pressing against my side.

A few seconds later we were both fully awake, sitting up and leaning back against the hard wooden headboard of the bed. Birgit turned on the lamp on her side of the bed and pulled her woollen cardigan around her shoulders. It was eight-fifteen. Dawn came late because of daylight saving time, extended into the winter months. Somewhere in the distance we could hear the engines of a large aircraft droning low over the mountains.

The images of my hallucination tormented me: they seemed so real, so plausible. I had *felt* the coarseness of the uniform's fabric against my skin. The house was exactly as I knew it, as I saw it then. My brother Jack was someone I knew better than almost anyone else in the world. I began to tremble, unable to understand or accept what it meant, or what was happening to me. I put my arm around Birgit, pressing her to me. She cuddled up against me, clearly unaware of what was going through my mind.

After a while I left the bed and went along the landing to use the toilet. When I returned Birgit was sitting fully upright. Her hair was untidy from sleep, her eyes looked puffy. I noticed that she was resting one of her hands across her stomach.

I turned on the overhead light, scraped a chair across to the wardrobe and climbed up to reach inside the shelf at the top.

'Joe, what is it you doing up there? Come back to bed.'

'I've got to resolve this,' I said grimly. By pushing my arm all the way in,

I made contact. I felt the cap at once, then groped around for the rest of the garments I had imagined. There was one other garment, lying underneath the cap. I pulled it out, with the cap. The cap, a stiff shirt. Not everything.

Enough, though, enough to make the point.

'Who put these in here?' I said, shirt in one hand, cap in the other. I held them up to her, almost a threat.

'Of course I did.'

'They're JL's, aren't they?'

'Yes.'

'What are they doing here in our house?'

'I'm looking after them for him.'

'What? Why should you look after clothes for my brother?'

'He . . . he brought them one day. The shirt needed washing and the cap had to be cleaned. He asked me to keep them there for him. He has others at the airfield.'

'So Jack's been at the house? While I wasn't here!'

'Yes.'

'What's been going on between you two?'

'Nothing going on! What do you think of it?' She moved in the bed, shifting her weight on to her legs, which she folded beneath her so that her body was more erect. She tensed her shoulders momentarily, then relaxed. 'JL is your brother! You have been away. Week after week after week! What do you think I do? I have no friends here. No one in the village, in England. Everyone who meets me hears my voice and thinks I am a spy for Hitler! I am the Nazi with the husband who does not fight. People whisper. They think I can't hear. Your parents don't speak to me. My mother and father are dead, so it is thought. I'm on my own here, all the hours in the day, then the night, then the day again. Perhaps there is a letter from you will come, perhaps not. If not, I can play music for no one to hear. Or catch the bus and go to the shops where there is nothing to buy. Some life I lead!'

'What about Jack?' I said. 'You know how Jack and I feel about each other. Why has he been coming here while I'm away?'

'It's always away you have been! JL is on leave only here a day or two, here another day, what they allow him. He has no choice in the matter. Once, he wrote to me and asked me if he could spend his leave with you and me, with us both, because he didn't want to go home. But you were in London. I didn't know how to contact you in time and he sounded desperate. He wanted to be away from the air base for a while, so I said yes. He came.'

'Just once?'

'No, he has been here three times. Maybe more.'

'You never told me.'

'Maybe five times. You are never here so I can tell you.'

'And he leaves his clothes in the bedroom.'

'No! What do you think? What are you accusing me of?'

Something like this can rarely be resolved properly in a marriage. The stakes are so high that pursuing it leads to areas from which you cannot retreat. So, while I could, I did retreat from the terrible consequences of what I was thinking. Birgit and I were drawn together by larger events: the dangers of the war, the coming of our new baby, the love we had felt for each other for so long. I could not bear to think of anything or anyone disrupting them, least of all my own brother. My row with Birgit caused a long silence of bitter feelings that lasted all day. Following that there was a quiet truce in the evening; that night we made love.

I spent the next two days convalescing as best I could and reported back to the Red Cross office on the following Monday morning.

12

Extract from **Germany Look East! - The Collected Speeches of Rudolf Hess,** *selected and edited by Prof. Albrecht Haushofer, University of Berlin Press, 1952; part of Hess's speech at Leipziger Triumphsportplatz to Hitlerjugend [Hitler Youth], May 1939, concerning the then Deputy Führer's wish for peaceful co-existence with Britain and its Empire:*

'[For those of us who squatted in our dug-outs with our faces in the mud, for those who listened with stilled breath while the bullets of the English enemy sang through the air above our heads, for those who suffocated in our gas-masks, for those who lay in shell craters through the freezing nights, the Great War brought one passionate conviction. I carry that belief close to my heart even now. It is carried also by the Leader, who fought valiantly for the Fatherland in the same war. That conviction is this.

'[War against the English race must not be fought by German people. Our argument is not with another Nordic race! Our argument is elsewhere!

'[We saw, in that most terrible war, the slaughter of hundreds of thousands of young German men and boys. Each of them loved the Fatherland, as you and I love the Fatherland. Yet they died! They did not shirk their duty. They did not hide. They did not even ask why they had to make the ultimate sacrifice.

'[It falls to us, this new generation of German national patriots, to give them the answer. England is not our enemy!

'[We seek space to live. We wish the development of the German race. If the English give us the free hand we need, we will have no dispute with them. If war is to come, it will be their choice, not ours. We who survived the land-mines and the shells and the gas of the Great War say again and again: we will spare the world another war.

'[But only if England allows it!

'[Heil Hitler!]'

13

Holograph notebooks of J. L. Sawyer

viii

I arrived at RAF Kenley in the early hours of the morning, with another Red Cross official called Nick Smith, after a lengthy and hazardous journey through the heavily bombed suburbs of Brixton and Streatham.

Our passes took us without delay through the security barrier at the Kenley air base. The driver deposited us beside a Nissen hut, in which we found several more civilians who were already waiting. I added my small suit-case to the pile that had been placed next to the main door, then went to stand as close as I could to the stove to warm up after the long drive. I was given a bowl of hot soup and I sipped it gratefully.

I had said nothing to Birgit about the journey I was to undertake, because a flight to Switzerland in the middle of a bitter land- and air-war with Germany was obviously hazardous. In the days before the flight I had spent a lot of time studying a map of Europe, trying to work out in advance which route was likely to be the safest, the one that would take us the shortest distance over occupied countries or Germany itself. Landlocked Switzerland did not seem to offer many safe ways in and out. I guessed that the likeliest route would be a long dogleg: down the western coast of France, followed by a sweep eastwards across the area of southern France that was under the control of the Vichy government. The direct route across Germany would be much shorter, but seemed full of dangers.

From one of the windows of the Nissen hut I could see the white-painted aircraft on the apron, waiting for us to board. I couldn't pick out much more than the plane's shape, because of the darkness, but I could see there was a great deal of activity going on around it.

'Gentlemen, may I have your attention, please?' I turned and saw that two high-ranking RAF officers were standing by the door at the end of the hut. One of them was holding up his hand expectantly. Silence fell. 'Thank you. We're going to ask you to climb aboard the aircraft in a moment. I must apologize in advance that the accommodation is a little spartan on board, but the crew have done their best to make you comfortable. Once the plane is in the air, may I ask you to move around the cabin as little as possible? The flight is going to be a long one, so the aircraft is heavily loaded with fuel and if there is too much movement inside the plane it could upset the trim. I'm sure I don't have to underline that point. In particular, on the subject of moving about during the flight, once you're on board you will notice that the front section of the cabin has been screened off with curtains. We must ask you not to go through to that part of the cabin until after the aircraft has landed and the other passengers have disembarked. Everything you require will be available in your part of the plane. I think you were also advised to bring sandwiches and drinks with you? Good. You'll be pleased to learn that there is a toilet on board, and you won't need a degree in physics to work out how to use it.'

We smiled around at one another nervously, a roomful of men who had obviously all been wondering the same thing. We were soon ushered through another door at the side of the hut and walked in the darkness across the concrete apron to the aircraft.

I was one of the first aboard and so I chose a seat at the back of the plane, next to one of the portholes. I had never been up in an aircraft before, so I was eager to see what I could of the outside world once daylight came. Of the other passengers, I knew only Nick and another Red Cross official whom Nick had introduced me to when we first entered the hut. This was a chap called Ian Maclean from the Edinburgh office. He and Nick took seats a few rows ahead of me. Everyone else on the flight was a stranger to me.

After another long delay the engines started, setting up a great racket and vibration throughout the cabin. Everything was louder and rougher than I had imagined it would be. The engines ran for ages while they warmed up. I was feeling extremely nervous as the plane finally began to move with an unpleasant wallowing sensation along the runway, rocking alarmingly from side to side. Once we left the ground, however, the motion of the aircraft became surprisingly smooth, though not much quieter.

I made myself as comfortable as possible in the canvas bucket-seat. Like everyone else I could see from where I was sitting, I kept my thick overcoat on because the cabin was unheated. I stared with interest through the tiny porthole, trying to gain some impression of the dark land below. In fact, while the darkness remained I could see little more than the steady blue-white stab of the exhaust flame from the engine on my side of the aircraft.

When the sun came up at last I saw that we were flying over the sea. I guessed it must be the English Channel, but if so the pilot was taking us across the widest part. Our aircraft droned on and on above the uninspiring sight of grey waves, seemingly immobile below. I was beginning to feel dehydrated and hungry in the chilly cabin, so I dug out my sandwiches and flask of tea.

The plane flew on, barely changing its course or attitude. The great white-painted wing spread out in front of me, partly obscuring the view ahead. I continued to watch what I could of the sky, expecting at any moment to see German fighters swooping down on us. It was impossible to relax, to put out of my mind how many risks there were in such a flight.

Three hours into the flight I finally got up from my seat and moved forward through the cramped cabin to where Ian Maclean was standing in the narrow aisle, his head bent under the low metal roof of the aircraft. I stood with him, just as uncomfortable. We spoke for a while, raising our voices over the engines' racket. Ian was less nervous about flying than I was, which helped me relax a little.

'I can't help noticing we're still over the sea,' I said. 'Shouldn't we be crossing land by now?'

'For safety they stay over the sea as long as possible,' Ian said.

'You've done this trip before?'

'Not exactly. I flew to Stockholm once. There's not much land to fly over, whichever route you take.'

'But Switzerland?'

'Is that where they told you we were going?'

'Yes. Are we going somewhere else?'

'No, I don't think so. They told me that, too. It could be a cover story, but you never know.'

I leaned down and forward, peering through the nearest window. All I could see was a patch of cloud and a glimpse of the grey neutrality of the waves far below.

Indicating the thick curtain that blocked off the cabin, a few feet from where we were standing, I said, 'Any idea what that's about?'

'Nothing official was said, was it?'

'Are they hiding something from us?'

'It's probably someone rather than something,' Ian said. 'We had a couple of VIPs on board when we flew to Sweden that time. I think they were diplomats, one of them German. The crew did the same thing with the curtain then.'

It was difficult shouting to each other over the engine noise, so Ian and I cut the conversation short and I returned to my place. I shifted around in the narrow seat, the canvas sagging beneath my backside like an old deckchair on a beach, and I tried again to position myself comfortably. I resumed staring out at the sky. I was wide awake in spite of not having had any sleep during the night. I was alert, still tense from the novelty of the long flight, interested in the whole experience despite the lack of incident it contained. I'm certain I did not drift off to sleep, nor did my thoughts wander.

Even so, I failed to notice that mountains had come into sight. When I first saw them they were distant and half concealed by the wintry haze, but within a few minutes the plane began to pass between the higher peaks. I saw them in increasing detail as they loomed up on either side of our plane. They seemed dangerously close. How had we reached them so quickly after being above the sea? Maybe the land, when you flew high enough, had the same look as the surface of the ocean? It was hazy everywhere. But now the tedium of the preceding hours was banished. The upper snow-covered slopes of the mountains were a dazzle of reflected sunlight, making them hard to look at. I pressed my forehead against the porthole and stared instead more acutely down at the ground, a valley floor, way below, heavily wooded and with a bright, silvery river snaking from side to side. The plane began moving dramatically, the wings tipping and the engine note frequently changing as the pilot adjusted the course. We were passing through rough air, which made the aircraft kick up and down in a worrying way. It felt as if we were zig-zagging through the narrow valley, at times flying perilously close to the rocky walls. We were sinking closer to the valley floor with every minute, until the nose of the aircraft lifted, the flying motion steadied, the engines throttled back. Moments later we were cruising low above the ground — there was a bump, then another, and after that we were rolling at speed along a runway, with a glimpse of concrete buildings placed behind trees on the periphery of the aerodrome, the mountains rising up beyond them.

The plane came to a halt at last, its engines coughing to silence. We stood up, stretching our backs after the long confinement in the uncomfortable seats. I was behind everyone else as we shuffled up the narrow aisle between the seats. When the man in front of me went through the door and clambered down the short flight of steps outside, I was alone in the cabin. Instead of climbing down after the others, I took hold of the curtain and swept it aside. Beyond it was the forward part of the plane's cabin, with six seats, three on each side of the aisle. There was no one there. At the front of the cabin, another curtain was drawn, presumably enclosing the cockpit. I could see movement beyond and in a moment someone on the other side opened the curtain and stepped out of the cockpit into the passenger cabin. A tall figure stood before me, dressed smartly in an RAF uniform, the peaked cap at a jaunty angle on his head.

It was my brother, Jack.

I stared at him in amazement, but his affable smile did not fade. He seemed unsurprised to see me.

Behind him another RAF officer appeared from the cockpit, pushed past Jack and, after a quick glance in my direction, went through the door and out of the aircraft. 'You coming, JL?' he called from the top of the steps outside.

'I'll be with you in a moment.'

I said to Jack, 'I had no idea it was you flying the plane!'

'Well . . . now you know.'

My heart was drumming. I looked around: daylight was glancing in through the open hatch, and beyond the broad white spread of the wing I could see the backs of the other men I had been flying with, as they walked towards the low buildings a couple of hundred yards across the apron. The co-pilot was following them. Behind me was the confined compartment of the plane: the utilitarian metal floor littered with discarded papers, cigarette ends, pieces of bread-crust dropped from sandwiches. It was plausibly real and actual, but I was gripped by the conviction that I was trapped in another lucid imagining.

'Jack, don't keep doing this to me!'

My brother stood there without responding. It was hard for me to look him in the eye, because I was terrified that if I did so I might be held there by him.

'Where are we?' I said finally.

'This is Zürich, of course. Where your meeting was planned, exactly as they told you.'

'What the hell's going on, JL? How are you involved in this? Do you know why I'm here?'

'I'm just the pilot.'

'This is a Red Cross flight!' I said. 'It's a neutral aircraft on a diplomatic mission. You're a serving officer in the RAF. You shouldn't be involved.'

'All aircraft need pilots. My Wellington's being re-equipped with new engines, so rather than hang around the airfield with nothing else to do I volunteered for the trip.'

'But you're RAF crew,' I said again.

'Not while I'm here. I'm a co-opted pilot, working for the Red Cross.'

Finally, I did look him in the eye.

I said quietly, 'Why are you doing this to me, Jack?'

'It's nothing to do with me, Joe. You know that.'

So I turned away from him, in misery.

ix

The aircraft droned on through the bright winter sky, the sea a grey-blue plain lying indistinctly far below us. I was relieved to be on my own at the rear of the cabin where there was no one to see me. I was shaking and trembling, on the point of weeping.

I was convinced that the injuries I had suffered during the Blitz were driving me mad. The visions were crippling me mentally. I was no longer able to tell truth from fiction. That was the classic definition of insanity, wasn't it? The delusions had begun that night in the ambulance, but had they ever ended? Was everything I thought of as real in fact another more subtle and extended delusion, a lucid imagining of forking alternatives, while in reality, real reality, I lay in the back of the noisy Red Cross ambulance, still being driven slowly across benighted England?

From the signs of the inactivity of everyone else in the cabin it seemed there was still a long way to go before we were due to land. Several of the passengers appeared to be asleep, their heads lolling uncomfortably, nodding with the constant movements of the plane. Others stared down through the tiny windows. One or two were reading. Ian Maclean, who for a long time had been standing in the aisle, was seated again. The thick curtains hung impassively across the front part of the cabin. It was no longer quite so cold and because several people had been smoking there was a familiar fug in the air. I lit a cigarette of my own to help me stay awake. I was beginning to feel sleepy but I shifted position in my seat and took in several deep breaths, unwilling to run the risk of falling into a second mental lapse.

When I next looked out through the porthole, I saw land far away to my left: there was a mountainous coast out there in the distance, wreathed in clouds and mist. It was so far away it was impossible to make out details or to try to work out which place it was, but I stared across at the view, glad to have something on which I could focus my eyes. Eventually the plane dipped its wing and turned in the direction of the land, but we continued to fly on without any perceptible loss of altitude. About half an hour later we were flying over a large city, the plane gradually losing height and tipping and turning as it manoeuvred towards a landing.

For the second time that day, as it seemed, I braced myself for the landing as we swooped downwards. Soon the plane was skimming at treetop height. I could see a few buildings and hangars, with a glimpse of the city in the distance.

When the plane had landed safely it taxied for a long way, finally coming to a halt close to a modern brick building. The engines fell silent and the passengers began to shift in their seats.

'Gentlemen!' One of the passengers who had been seated at the front of the compartment, close to the curtained partition, was already on his feet, holding up the palm of his hand. Like most of us on board, he could stand upright in the cabin only with some difficulty because of the low ceiling. 'It's my pleasure to welcome you to Lisbon, a beautiful city that many of us in the Red Cross already know well. Most of you were told that we were travelling to Zürich for this meeting but, as you know, in wartime deceptions are sometimes necessary. However, we are in neutral territory and are therefore free of that sort of thing for the next few days.

'So, for those of you who don't know me,' he went on, 'my name is Declan Riley and I am from the Dublin office of the Red Cross. I know we are anxious to leave the aircraft after such a long flight but I must detain you for a little longer.'

Behind him the curtain billowed slightly, like one hanging in front of a window that is suddenly opened. We could feel the plane reacting to movement, as whoever had been in the forward part of the cabin stepped through the aircraft, presumably about to disembark at the front of the cabin.

'I was going to say that I have three pressing matters to inform you of,' Mr Riley continued. He indicated the movement of the curtain beside him. 'I think the first of them has already made itself known, however. We have been honoured to share the flight with two or three people of great distinction and importance, who will be taking a leading part in the discussions over the next few days.

'The second matter is that from this moment on, whenever we speak together we should do so in German.' He paused for his words to take effect, then continued. '[Amongst other reasons you have been invited to take part in this important conference because of your ability with the German language. Even if in the next few days you meet someone from your own country, and he or she does not speak German, you must continue to speak in German and we will arrange for an interpreter to be present. We realize that this is an unnatural and possibly time-consuming process, but it was a precondition by one of the parties that everything should be conducted in German.

'[The third matter naturally follows on from the second. You do of course understand that everything that is going to take place over the next few days will be of the highest sensitivity. It must therefore be treated with the utmost confidentiality. You will be asked to sign an acceptance of this in a little while. A mere formality, of course, because I know we share the fervent wish that the meeting should succeed. I don't think there is anything else for the moment . . .]' He glanced enquiringly down at the man who had been sitting beside him throughout the fight, and who shook his head briefly. '[Well then, my best thanks, gentlemen. Let us hope the meeting brings positive results!]'

A ripple of applause followed his speech. I followed the others up the shallow incline of the cabin aisle, waiting in line as one after the other we leaned down to exit through the hatch. Just before it was my turn to go through, the dividing curtain was suddenly swept aside and a young RAF officer stepped through. He nodded politely to me, then moved on down the cabin.

I stepped through the hatch, descended the little flight of metal steps, and began to walk across the tarmac in the warm sunshine behind the other men.

x

After a perfunctory examination of our passports at the airport, we were joined by another group who had flown in by an earlier plane. Several of these people were from Germany or from German-occupied territories, although all were officials of their local Red Cross societies. After brief introductions we were ushered outside to a line of cars.

First stop was a large private house, not far from the airport, where a delicious buffet meal was awaiting us. At first, those of us who had arrived from Britain carefully took small portions, unused to seeing the lavish quantities of food that were laid out before us, but gradually the reality sank in that we had left behind the rigours of wartime rationing, if only temporarily. I shared my table with two officials I did not know, a man and a woman who had arrived from Berlin, representing the German Red Cross. They had no more idea than I what was the purpose of this meeting, but I did begin to speculate in my mind. Presumably others were doing so too. Something big was clearly afoot.

We returned to the cars and in a long cavalcade we drove through part of Lisbon itself, then headed west along the coast that forms part of the bay of the Tagus river. It was already getting late in the afternoon and the sun was moving round so that it was ahead of us. To our left lay the great expanse of the Atlantic; to our right were glimpses of wooded mountains. At every rise and turn we saw breathtaking views of coastline and sea. We drove with the car windows open so that we were assailed by the scents of the flowers and shrubs that grew thickly beside the road.

We eventually reached a small seaside town called Cascais, built with pretty, white-painted houses and adorned with hundreds of palm and deciduous trees. We were taken to a large hotel on the seafront and everyone was assigned a room. Here we were allowed a little time to refresh ourselves after the journey, before we returned to the cars. My room had a huge double bed and a balcony from which I could look out across the sea.

The main road through Cascais ran parallel to the beach, then climbed out of the town across a low headland. Once we were outside the town, the scenery changed: it became a wild coast of igneous deposits, where cliffs of black and brittle rocks jutted out into the sea. The water was so calm it was like the surface of a mirror, the sunlight glinting magically from it, but such was the swell and reach of the ocean that as the waves came into the shore they formed high, rolling breakers. They dashed against the cliffs with spectacular explosions of spray. A white mist hovered over the coastline, in spite of the warm sunshine.

Not long after we left Cascais, our cavalcade of cars turned through wide gates and moved slowly up a tree-shrouded driveway towards an immense, pink-painted villa. This beautiful castellated house, with its acres of cultivated gardens, its terraces, shrubberies, swimming pool, private cinema and many other comfortable facilities, was to be my base for the next few days. It was called *Boca di Inferno* — the Mouth of Hell.

xi

At one end of the main hall of the villa was a reception area, where visitors once would have been invited to wait. Here a number of easy chairs had been arranged around an ornate marble fireplace which to all appearances was used only rarely for open fires. Closely packed bookshelves stood on each side, as well as a number of oil paintings of important past residents of the house. In an alcove beside the fireplace was a large photographic portrait in a gilt frame, not ostentatiously placed but in view of most of the hall. It was a studio portrait of the Duke and Duchess of Windsor, the former King Edward VIII of Great Britain and his American wife, Wallis Simpson. Their signatures were inscribed at the bottom of the picture. Beside the portrait two small national flags stood close together, placed so that their poles crossed: the British Union flag and the Nazi flag of the Third Reich.

A cocktail reception was held in that long hall during the early part of our first evening in the Mouth of Hell. At first, most of those present were the various delegates from Red Cross branches of the different European countries, but as the evening wore on the principals began arriving. They joined our party without fanfare or introduction, but moved quietly through the crowd and joined in conversations. I did not recognize them all, but Nick Smith and Ian Maclean whispered to me the names of the ones they knew. In this way I learned that Dr Carl Burckhardt, president of the Swiss Red Cross, was there, as well as one of the most celebrated Red Cross officials in the world, Count Folke Bernadotte, head of the Swedish section. The British Ambassador to Spain, Sir Samuel Hoare, arrived in mid-evening, closely followed by Sir Ronald Campbell, his colleague at the British Embassy in Lisbon. Both were accompanied by teams of embassy officials, who circulated deftly around the room, speaking excellent German. Later, representatives from the German embassies to various neutral countries began to arrive.

At eight-thirty, George, Duke of Kent, the British king's younger brother, was announced from the door. He was greeted by Sir Ronald Campbell and was then introduced to the leading figures who were present. His entourage, all of who were dressed, like the Duke, in civilian suits, dispersed themselves about the room, joining conversations with great affability and courtesy. At one point, as I circulated around the party, I overheard the Duke speaking to Count Bernadotte, a relaxed, amused conversation, conducted in fluent German.

At nine o'clock everyone moved through to a large dining-room in an annexe, where dinner was served. We took our places according to the seating plan. The two senior Red Cross officials took their seats at the head table with the Duke and some senior German officials. I found myself sitting next to a military attaché from the German Embassy in Madrid, SS-Obergruppenführer Otto Schäfer. He was making an effort to be polite to me and I responded as best I could, but in truth I found him boorish. We had little in common, although this did not stop him telling me about his background. Over the years, he said in his harsh Pomeranian accent, he had been involved in many proud acts of the Nazi SS that I had never heard about before, but which I found depressing and frightening, even when humorously cast in a supposedly defensible version by one of their perpetrators.

At the end of the dinner Dr Burckhardt made a short speech, reminding us of the unique and historical importance of our meeting, of how much depended on a successful outcome and that although for the time being we must conduct ourselves in the utmost secrecy, in the years to come people would realize what we began in this unique house in such a beautiful and wild part of Portugal.

We drank a toast to the success of our own efforts.

Dr Burckhardt had sat down again when one of his aides walked swiftly across to him and leaned over to mutter something. Naturally I could not hear what was said, but Dr Burckhardt moved immediately to the Duke of Kent's side and spoke quietly. The Duke nodded and smiled. Dr Burckhardt returned to his seat.

Moments later a new entourage of delegates entered the room, as unceremoniously as most of the others. But their arrival caused an undoubted stir throughout the room; the SS general beside me suddenly stiffened. The leader of the new arrivals walked confidently across to the head table to greet

Dr Burckhardt and Count Bernadotte, who led him straight away to meet the
Duke of Kent. Both men stood together, smiling and shaking hands with
great amiability, clapping each other on the arms and shoulders. The room
had fallen into silence.

The new arrival was Deputy Führer Rudolf Hess.

xii

Next morning the first round of negotiations began. We all had a part to play.
As a junior official I was assigned to a document party in a side room, drawing up, presenting and endlessly revising a long series of detailed statements
that were used by the senior representatives as position papers.

I was one of only a few Red Cross delegates in the working group: the
rest were British and German officials from the embassies or their respective
governments, together with constitutional lawyers from Britain and
Germany, negotiation counsellors from the Quaker Society of Friends and
observers from the five main neutral European powers: Sweden, Switzerland,
Ireland, Portugal and Spain. Everything was conducted in German, fluently
and naturally by all present, although we produced the position papers in
both English and German. For the first hour or so we were stiff and formal
with one another, perhaps watchful for one side or the other to seek special
advantages, but as the hours went by we became familiar and friendly, forming ourselves into an efficient and harmonious group.

Although mine was only a small role in the proceedings, I felt I had been
allotted an important and interesting task. On our team fell the responsibility of writing down the verbal agreements made by the principals. We worked
out the form of words in which the tentative measures should be recorded,
discussed them among ourselves for the variations and nuances of language,
and finally sent them back to the principals for further negotiation and, it was
hoped, eventual agreement. In this position I was able to see not only the
details changing and growing as the talks went on, but also the larger picture
taking shape. We laboured under pressure, as the various delegates and their
advisers would hurry in with new notes and demand that everything be ren-
dered into clear language with the minimum of delay. I worked with increasing excitement and dedication, realizing that I was playing a crucial part in
bringing the terrible war to an end.

Our second-storey room was on the southern side of the villa, looking down across the wooded grounds towards the sea. There was a wide balcony outside and many of us took advantage of it, pulling our tables and chairs into the sunlight, working at our papers in the warm, wintry sunshine, breathing in the scents of the garden, hearing the great sea crashing distantly against the rocks below.

The only occasions when everyone was in the same place together were during the two main meals of the day. It was a sight whose strangeness never failed to impress me: there in one large room we had senior representatives from two opposing sides in a bitterly fought war mixing socially and congenially. Rudolf Hess and the Duke of Kent were often seen in each other's company, their attendant officials kept at a distance, as if to protect the two men's privacy. This ease was matched all through the various levels at which we worked. On my second evening, for instance, I was seated next to Generalmajor Bernhard Altschul from the tactical Luftflotte 4 based in northern France, in charge of many of the aircraft which were, at that time, attacking British cities almost every night of the week. He was a cultured and intelligent companion — it took a force of will to think of him as being responsible for the hundreds of civilian deaths and injuries that were occurring as a result of the bombing.

By the second day we were settling into a routine. It became possible to predict when there would be peaks of activity required of us and when there were likely to be quieter moments. One of these more relaxed periods came along about midway through the afternoon, so I grabbed the chance for a little solitude. I left the villa and walked through the grounds on my own, relishing the break.

It was a most beautiful spot, cool under the trees, warm in the sunshine. Beyond the thicket of trees was a short stretch of untamed land: long grasses and hardy-looking bushes growing wild, sloping down towards the top of the cliffs. Rough pathways had been worn through the vegetation, so I followed one of them and soon came to the spectacular rocky cliffs. I squatted down to watch the waves rolling in, the surf and spray exploding excitingly against the rocks. The scene had an almost hypnotic effect: the quiet sea with its glistening lights, the waves moving endlessly in towards the shore, gaining weight and height, rising and peaking before they hit the cliffs, then bursting outwards and upwards in a vast spray.

'[This coast is known as the mouth of hell,]' someone beside me said.

My reverie was instantly broken. I turned and looked up. It was Stellvertreter Rudolf Hess, who had walked up behind me unheard, the sounds of his approach muffled by the soft ground and the rush of the surf and spray.

I scrambled quickly to my feet, surprised and slightly alarmed.

'[I was taking a short break, my gentleman Deputy Leader!]' I said defensively.

'[I am doing the same. You have been before, to this part of Portugal?]'

'[No, sir.]'

'[Let me show you the Mouth of Hell itself. I was here at this house last year. Another visit in the endless quest for peace. You were not present, I think, but you no doubt know who was resident here at the time. We shall have better luck this time with our efforts for peace, I believe!]' He grinned amiably at me, a sort of uncontrived leering smile that revealed the narrow gap between his two front teeth. '[If we walk along the cliff we will find the natural feature after which the house was named.]'

Hess was alone. Unless the three SS officers who acted as his bodyguard were concealed somewhere about, he must have slipped away from them. It was unusual for any of the negotiating principals to be seen without their entourages. The previous evening, during an informal briefing by Declan Riley, the ancillary negotiators, of whom I was one, were warned not to engage in any conversation with a principal that could later be construed as a bargaining position. It had certainly never occurred to me that I might find myself having to heed that advice.

Hess indicated that we should follow one of the paths leading along the cliff top. I walked a few paces behind him. He seemed unconcerned about turning his back on me. He was solidly built but not stout, wide rather than muscular. He walked with a flat-footed gait, his back straight. Although his short bristly hair was still dark and thickly growing, the bright sunlight revealed a circle of baldness on his crown, oddly off-centre. It was, as I later learned, the result of an injury sustained in a bierkeller brawl during Hitler's years of struggle for power. If reminder was needed of the Nazis' violent background, it was there on the crown of Hess's head.

Before we had gone far we approached the lip of an immense pit, a deep cavity in the cliffs whose presence was concealed from the house by a screen of low trees and bushes. When we had gained the edge, the huge size of the roofless cavern was revealed: it was almost perfectly circular, approximately a hundred feet in diameter and about the same in depth. The sea churned and boiled at the base of the cauldron: every wave that came in exploded into the immense fissure, bursting and spraying in all directions at once.

I stared down at the sight for two or three minutes, impressed by it, but even more disconcerted by the presence of the notorious Nazi leader standing beside me. When you stand over a vertiginous drop of that sort, where a fall would lead to certain death, thoughts of stumbling accidentally are uppermost in your mind. With them, inevitably, come the parallel thoughts of jumping or of being pushed. Rudolf Hess was an arm's length away from me, leaning, like me, to stare down into the pit. If one of us were to fall? If one of us were to push the other?

I shrank away from such thoughts, physical violence being abhorrent to me, but at the same time I could not forget who was there beside me, what he stood for, how many human lives his war had already taken, what a threat his regime presented to the security of the rest of the world.

He straightened and we both moved back from the edge.

'[Did you know the cliff once was used as a prison?]' Hess said, raising his voice above the roar from the cauldron.

'[A prison?]'

'[The main jail was elsewhere but they created punishment cells in these cliffs, at the high-tide mark. Troublesome prisoners were put there for a while, so they could have a bad experience of solitary confinement.]' He gave me another leering smile. '[It was the French and German prisoners who were most often placed in the cells. Never the British, though. I wonder why not? Come, let me show you. One of them is along here somewhere.]'

He set off along the footpath once more and I followed, chilled by his oddness. He turned out not to be sure of the site of the cell, because we walked to and fro along the path for several minutes without success. I was becoming guiltily aware how long I had been away from my work. Hess eventually lost interest in the search, looking thoughtfully towards the ground as we sauntered along. We came to a halt in more or less the same place as I was sitting when he came up to me.

Then he said, in a more confidential voice, '[We have met before, I think. Do you remember that?]'

'[I have seen you before, Deputy Leader,]' I said. '[But I am certain I have not had the pleasure of meeting you in person until today.]'

'[No, you are wrong,]' he said emphatically. '[I know your name from the list of Red Cross negotiators. You are Sawyer, J. L. Why should I remember that name? Your face also is familiar.]'

'[I was a competitor in the Olympic Games. I had the honour of accepting my medal from you, but I'm sure you would not remember me from that.]'

'[In Berlin, you were? An athlete, then?]'

'[I was a rower, sir.]'

'[Maybe so. We have moved a long way from those days, have we not? So, you are English as I thought?]'

'[Yes, sir.]'

'[What do you English people think now of war? We have had a taste of war and perhaps we do not like it as much as we thought.]'

'[I have always been against war.]'

'[So you say. But it was you English who declared war on the Reich.]'

'[Herr Deputy Leader, I should not be talking to you about such matters. I am only a junior official, with no influence on the principals.]'

'[So why are you here?]'

'[Ultimately because I am a pacifist and I wish to see peace made.]'

'[Then we agree more than perhaps you think. I too have made the long journey here because my quest is for a peace between my country and yours.]'

'[Sir, I am not representing my country. I am working for the Red Cross as a neutral.]'

'[Yet you say once you competed in the Olympic Games. Were you then a neutral?]'

'[No. I was rowing for Great Britain.]'

'[So, tell me, what do the people of Great Britain have to say about the war? Do they want it to continue or do they want it to stop?]'

'[I think they are tired of war, sir,]' I said. '[But I also know they will never give up fighting so long as there is a threat to them.]'

'[Tired of it? Already? There could be much worse for them to come, I think. The Leader has many secret weapons at his disposal.]'

The way he instantly seized on the idea that the British were wearying of war made me bite my lip. I remembered the warning we had been given by Declan Riley the evening before.

'[I believe the British prefer peace to war,]' I said as carefully as I could. '[But the threat of invasion and the actions of the Luftwaffe bombers have made people angry and determined to win.]'

'[What of the party for peace in Britain? Do you ignore what they say?]'

'[I'm not aware of them, sir. I have heard no talk of peace when I have been in Britain. Who is in the peace party?]'

'[They are around you, Mr Sawyer. In this house! Do you think I am imagining them?]'

'[Mr Churchill is running the country. But in my own opinion, Churchill is a troublemaker and warmonger —]'

'[Mr Churchill has not been invited here, as you can see!]' Hess interrupted me without apparently having listened to what I was saying. '[Churchill is an impediment to peace! He is the problem I have to solve, Mr Sawyer. The Leader is prepared to sign a peace treaty with the English but he is not willing to negotiate with Mr Churchill or any of his yes-men. The Leader passionately craves peace with Great Britain, but how do we persuade Churchill? Since we are here to speak of peace, what is your opinion? Would Churchill agree to a separate peace, or should Churchill be replaced? Important changes would have to follow an agreement such as the one we seek in this house. I speak of replacements in Germany, as well as in England. Will you British play your part and replace Churchill? With Halifax, say, or one of the able gentlemen who is with us for this conference?]'

'[I can't say, Herr Deputy Leader. I am not a representative of the British government.]'

I was terrified by the sudden intensity of the man. His distinctive, deep-set eyes were staring firmly at me, challenging me for an answer. But I was already in over my head. The information or opinion Hess wanted from me was impossible.

For a moment longer he continued to stare at me, then he made an impatient gesture. '[It is as I thought! Only the Reich wants peace!]'

He turned away from me with a bad-tempered, dismissive wave of the hand, and began to stride up the rough path in the direction of the house. I walked quickly after him, sensing already that if word of our conversation reached my superiors in the Red Cross, I would be boiled in oil.

We breasted the rise and came to the stand of trees that grew between the grounds of the house and the cliff area. Two SS officers in their sharp black uniforms were waiting on the lawn, staring towards us. I sensed trouble piling up on trouble for me. Hess came to a halt and faced me as I caught up with him.

'[We have work to be doing,]' he said in a more reasonable tone of voice. '[Mr Sawyer, let me tell you that even if you do not remember our earlier meeting in Berlin, I have myself now recalled the circumstances. Perhaps you have deliberately put them from your mind. We have indeed moved a long way since then. I understand the danger you are in, of being a British neutral in time of war. You can be sure I will say nothing of it again.]'

'[Thank you, Herr Deputy Führer,]' I said.

'[Later, perhaps, you and I will have another opportunity to speak in private.]'

It was not to be. That was the only private conversation I had with Rudolf Hess during that stage of the negotiations. In fact, I scarcely saw him again before the end of the conference.

Almost from the moment when I returned to the villa the pressure of work on us greatly increased, with dozens of position papers, protocols, draft agreements, revised drafts, codicils and memoranda in need of practically instantaneous preparation and translation. None of us complained about the strain that the workload was placing on us, because of the unique importance of what we were doing, but for the next thirty-six hours we worked with hardly a break.

In the early hours of our last morning at *Boca di Inferno* Dr Burckhardt unexpectedly walked into our room and we rose to our feet in astonishment. Smilingly he signalled to us to relax. He was looking as tired as everyone else: I knew from the glimpses I had had of the main discussions that he had hardly been away from the conference hall. He was the only one of the principal negotiators who had visited us in our workmanlike domain, with its typewriters and notebooks on every working surface, the dirty glasses, cups and plates scattered everywhere, the piles of discarded papers all over the carpet, the jackets slung across the backs of chairs, the tobacco-heavy air.

Dr Burckhardt made some self-deprecating remark about being curious to see for himself where the real work had been going on: the furnace of the engine-room, as he described it. He said he was pleased to report that the talks between the British and German delegates had reached a conclusion and he thanked us for our dedication and uncomplaining labours. We gave him a polite but enthusiastic round of applause. As it sank in what the conclusion to the conference might actually mean, our applause turned quickly to loud cheering. Dr Burckhardt smiled modestly, nodding around to all of us.

At the end he caught my eye and with an inclination of his head indicated that I should follow him out of the room. I did so, with my hard-working colleagues watching me with noticeable curiosity.

Outside in the corridor, when he had closed the door to the room, Dr Burckhardt shook my hand warmly.

'[Mr Sawyer, I wish to thank you on behalf of the International Red Cross for your contribution this week.]'

I mumbled something about doing no more than what I had been asked to do, and so on.

'[Yes, indeed. We are all working for the same thing, but it has been a particularly effective meeting. You should say nothing to your colleagues at the moment, but there will be a second round of talks in a few weeks' time, when the agreement will be ratified. The date and place have not yet been set, but the conference will take place near the beginning of May. I should add that your personal presence has been especially requested by one of the principals. May we count on you to be available?]'

'[Yes, of course, Dr Burckhardt.]'

'[You have a family in Britain, I believe. Would your responsibilities there prevent you from making a second journey on our behalf?]'

'[No, sir. My wife and I are expecting our first baby. But it is not due until the end of May.]'

'[All our business should be completed by then. Indeed, you've helped make it probable that your baby will be born in peacetime. Congratulations, Mr Sawyer!]'

With that cheering news he shook my hand again and wished me well, and that was that. I stood in the corridor, thunderstruck by the idea that peace was not an abstract notion but an achievable reality in my own life. Our baby would be born to a world of peace.

I had not fully realized that before! I felt joy rising in me. Great relief consumed me. I wanted to run and shout, but instead I stood by myself in that corridor, tears in my eyes, realizing that I was privy to the greatest, most important news in the world.

I went back into our office. In a daze I helped my colleagues to finish off the few remaining tasks and then to tidy up the room. A little more than an hour later I was in my bed in my hotel room, so excited I could hardly sleep, despite the exhaustion that was drowning me.

The next day I returned to England in the same white-painted plane, and two days after that I was reunited with Birgit at home in Rainow.

xiii

Everyone who was involved in the Lisbon agreement was sworn to secrecy and was provided with a cover story of some kind, to explain our absence. I had been to North Wales, it turned out, training with new rescue equipment received from the USA.

The events of that sunny winter's week in Cascais are a matter of history, and no secrecy remains. What we drew up and agreed was a protocol for peace, terms which were required to be ratified at the highest levels for the armistice to be binding. Several weeks lay between the first and second peace conferences, a time of intense diplomatic and governmental activity, unwitnessed by anyone outside the inner circles of the two governments and the ruling council of the Red Cross. I certainly had little to do with what went on and was left in a vacuum of uncertainty.

Because I was a party to the drawing up of the agreement, I believed I knew every clause, paragraph and sentence by heart. What I did not know was what the people at the highest levels would make of the deal.

Would Hitler accept it? Would Churchill?

14

Prime Minister's Personal Minutes and Telegrams, January–June 1941; from Appendix B of The German War: Vol. II — Their Finest Hour *(1950) by Winston S. Churchill (Duke of London).*

Prime Minister to Secretary of State for Air and Chiefs of the Air Staff
January 17, 1941
Some of the German aircraft shot down on our shores must still be in repairable condition. I have seen enlightening reports on the state of their armour, engines, weapons and so on, after detailed technical examination at Farnborough. Are we able to get any of the aircraft back into a condition in which they might be flown, as for training sessions?

In particular, are we able to get one of their twin-engined Messerschmitt 110s working and flying again? One is needed urgently.

Prime Minister to Home Secretary
February 28, 1941
What sort of facilities do we have ready, should one of the people presently running Germany fall into our hands? We shall of course use the Tower of London as a salutary short-term measure (and let it be known we are doing so, as it would be a popular move in, e.g., the USA) but since we expect the war to be a long haul we must have other provisions to hand. Ordinary criminal prisons would be out of the question, as would for different reasons the PoW detention camps, so we should have as a contingency some other kind

of secure accommodation. There must be several country houses, castles, etc., which could be sealed off at short notice without too much trouble or rumours spreading.

Pray let me have a list of suitable sites in due course.

Prime Minister to Secretary of State for Foreign Affairs
March 2, 1941

I'm grateful to our security advisers, through your good offices, for the information concerning Germany's plans for Madagascar. I recollect the idea goes back to Bismarck's day and has been resurrected from time to time by those who wish only to move the Jewish 'problem' to another part of the world.

British policy in this matter should be discussed and settled in Cabinet at the most convenient upcoming meeting, but for the time being may be briefly summarized thus:

As the mandated power for Palestine we have no wish for mass and ultimately destabilizing immigration in that region. Although this is not an option under the Madagascar Plan it is as well to be certain of our own policy on such a related matter.

Madagascar itself is currently under the control of Vichy France and sits athwart our main circum-Africa sea route for the importation of oil from Persia and Iraq. However, so long as the UK controls the Suez Zone, as we intend to go on doing indefinitely, and so long as there is no effective German presence on the island, we perceive no real threat from Vichy-controlled Madagascar to our supplies.

Any attempt by Germany, as outlined in your memorandum, to set up a puppet state on Madagascar, administered by the SS and populated by disaffected exiles from European Jewry, no doubt under conditions of extreme inhumanity, would be a matter of the utmost seriousness. In such a case we would be obliged to mount prompt and effective military intervention, a duty from which we would not shrink.

Pray advise me of the numbers of the Jewish population, as best known, not only in Germany but also in the states currently controlled by the German occupiers. We should be prepared for all contingencies.

Prime Minister to Secretary of State for Air and Chiefs of the Air Staff
March 4, 1941

The bombing results against German targets for last month show no marked improvement on the previous month. The number of sorties is up but the photographic reconnaissance shows a remarkable lack of accuracy. Our new four-engined heavy bombers will be operational in the next week or two so I am looking for better results all round. I note also that losses of aircraft are increasing steadily and the numbers of our airmen posted as missing is almost twenty-five per cent up on the previous month. The war will not be won if we merely send our young men into danger and death, without prospect of result.

I enclose a copy of the final report from the Min. of Works concerning the damage caused by the Luftwaffe to the city of Coventry. Since November, when the attack occurred, it has seemed that the nightly bombing of British cities has, if anything, been stepped up. Kindly report back to me with your proposals.

Prime Minister to Secretary of State for Foreign Affairs
April 23, 1941
Red Cross representatives have been noticeably busy in recent weeks, using our airfields for their various enterprises in travelling abroad, presumably to neutral countries. Although the procedure for Red Cross use of our airspace is well regulated, I note that we are provided with little information about the known destinations of their several flights, or indeed what is intended by them. We do enjoy excellent relations with all levels of the Red Cross, their work in the Blitz has been exemplary and much official gratitude has been expressed to them. We remain tolerant in every respect of Red Cross activities, hoping for the best. We do not actually need to know what they are about, nor should we officially enquire.

Pray let me have a summary of what intelligence on the British Red Cross you have to hand and any more that arises in the foreseeable future. We do naturally have vital national interests in all parts of neutral Europe.

Prime Minister to Secretary of State for Foreign Affairs and Lord Privy Seal
April 25, 1941
In response to your several private memoranda I am content for Foreign Office staff to make yet another search for any files or written material concerning the Duke of Windsor, our former king. The papers to which I allude are the sort of papers to which I always allude in this context.

All personal and state papers, to the point of his abdication, are naturally sacrosanct and are anyway safely in the usual repositories. I am concerned with the later period in His Royal Highness's peregrinations, up to the point in August last year when he accepted Governorship of the Bahamas.

I am particularly anxious to locate material that arose during the Duke of Windsor's flight last year from the house called La Croë, now in the part of France controlled by the regime in Vichy, his time soon afterwards in Madrid and of course the weeks he spent near Lisbon. It still seems likely he received aid and comfort from agencies other than H. M. Government.

To suggest that there are likely to be no papers left from his period of flight and confusion is mistaken: no household as large as the Duke's can fail to leave a trail behind it. For instance, several telegrams passed between myself and His Royal Highness while he was in Madrid. We possess those, but there would be others of similar ilk. Sir Ronald Campbell was our Ambassador in France at the time of the fall. He is now, of course, our Ambassador in Portugal and holds a substantial archive. Information from our Spanish embassy has been slow in coming forward, for some reason.

I have never discounted rumours that leading Nazi officials have been observed in Spain. I dare say Portugal is another place they favour with their presence from time to time. The Duke resided in a villa near Lisbon for a month, during which time he was out of contact with London except on the most superficial of business. Material related to that particular period, in that particular house, is that which is most urgently required.

Prime Minister to Secretary of State for War and Home Secretary
April 30, 1941
I am enclosing a report from D Section, under the usual classification. Pray respond with a detailed analysis and proposal for action as soon as you may.

It could amount to nothing, but on the face of it we should at least be better informed about this kind of thing. D Section are maintaining observation on the young man who is the subject of the report. For various reasons the section's activities have been neither consistent nor continuous. The immense difficulty of mounting any sustained intelligence operation while the German air raids continue speaks for itself and I can only commend the sterling work they have so far achieved.

In the present matter, which I find unusual, we have as the subject a serving officer with RAF Bomber Command, one Flt Lt Sawyer, apparently a pilot who has performed his duties with great bravery and skill, already decorated for gallantry, but who is said to have been associating with one of those anglicized German nationals we have not yet rounded up. In Sawyer's case it is a young woman, to whom it is said he is married. She is a naturalized British subject who came to the UK before the war.

D Section have not been able to confirm the marriage, saying that the register office where the records might have been found was destroyed in an air raid in September last year. They maintain Sawyer is not married to the woman but is merely cohabiting with her. There is evidence from neighbours which I have disdained to read. Taken in all, though, the matter and the circumstances surrounding it give rise to disquiet.

What makes the case unusual and worthy of attention is that Sawyer was registered, at least for a time, as a conscientious objector with links to the British Red Cross, for whom he has apparently been working in some capacity. How he rationalizes this while being a serving officer in the RAF is central to the mystery. I have no rooted objections to any of such behaviour, but not all in the person of one man, all at once or at all in wartime. He cannot be allowed to continue in this multi-faceted role, especially as a substantial portion of his life appears to be usefully involved with our bombing offensive against the Nazis.

The report obscures more than it clarifies. It seems likely to me there has been some confusion of identity, but I require it to be cleared up. The German woman under suspicion should be left to her own devices, as I have an abhorrence of young people being locked up without good reason.

15

Holograph notebooks of J. L. Sawyer

xiv

After Lisbon, I returned to my life in Rainow with a sense that at last the war was about to finish. Granted leave of absence by the Red Cross, on full pay, the only memento I had of that extraordinary meeting in Portugal was a brief handwritten letter from Dr Burckhardt. He passed it to me before I boarded the aircraft for the long flight home. In it he asked me not to involve myself in the normal day-to-day work of the Red Cross, but to hold myself ready to travel at short notice.

During those days at *Boca di Inferno* I had come to think of myself as a neutral in the war. I was an intermediary, a Red Cross official, someone who composed or translated important documents that could, quite literally, change history. But within a few hours of returning to Britain I felt myself become partisan once again: English, British, not neutral at all. I found it an enlightening experience. I had assumed, before I went to Portugal, that by being a pacifist I counted myself out of partisanship, but when you are in a war you cannot help but identify with your own people. It gave me a lot to think about.

I slipped back into something that felt similar, but not identical, to my old life. Birgit was in the last weeks of her pregnancy, a situation which took on a whole extra level of meaning now there was the prospect of peace. While I was away, Birgit had become much more dependent on Mrs Gratton, the elderly woman who lived in the cottage down the lane. She seemed to be constantly in our house, often bringing her strange, middle-aged son with her. When I first returned from Portugal I felt I was almost an intruder in the house. Mrs Gratton was always fussing around, seeing to the laundry and washing up the dishes, making Birgit drinks and snacks, while Harry busied himself with odd jobs: cutting logs and bringing them in, cleaning windows, sweeping out the kitchen floor and that kind of thing.

Perhaps for these reasons my first weekend at home, after Lisbon, was not a happy one. A distance had opened up between Birgit and myself. I wanted to be a loving, dutiful husband, involving myself in the last weeks of her pregnancy, but Birgit would say little to me about how she felt, or about her hopes and fears, or indeed anything about the plans she was making for when the baby arrived.

I helped her clean out and paint the small spare room, which would eventually become the child's own bedroom, but because of her condition I ended up spending most of the time working on my own. The off-white distemper, which like all house paint was normally almost impossible to obtain because of the war, had been provided by Harry Gratton. He called round a couple of times to remind me of the fact, while I was putting the stuff on the walls.

People in Rainow were still talking about the night of the heavy bombing in Manchester, which had happened while I was away. After two big raids in December the city had been left alone, but the previous week the bombers had returned. Harry Gratton told me that at the height of the raid the fires were so intense that the people of Rainow, watching from their hill many miles from the city, could feel the heat on their faces.

Irlam Street, where the Red Cross building had been, no longer existed. While waiting for the Red Cross to find alternative premises, I hung around the house, hoping in a vague way to make amends to Birgit for my long absences, trying to forge something like our old closeness together. I still felt cut off from her, but I reasoned that once our baby was born our lives would change for the better. Of course, once the secret I was carrying became a reality, life would be different for everyone.

The prospect of that burned in me like a beacon. When I heard people complaining about the constant difficulties they were having in feeding their children, or their worries about their sons or husbands in the forces, or even the endless problems of simply travelling around, I knew I had it in me to reassure them with the greatest news of all. Another week, I could say to them — put up with it for another week or two, maybe a month, then it will be over. The broad, sunlit uplands Churchill promised last year are in sight at last.

But the weeks were starting to slip by. When I returned from Lisbon I expected to be summoned back to the next round of talks almost at once. Surely everything was in place and agreed? The terms for peace had been comprehensively negotiated: both sides had given way on several important elements of the original proposals, but in the end a realistic agreement had been reached, one that gave both Britain and Germany a way out of the war. One side could emerge with honour intact, the other with strategic freedoms in place.

Clearly there was an obstacle. Once I was back in my humdrum life, undergoing the same inconvenience and hardships as everyone else, overhearing conversations in buses and pubs, listening to small talk in shops, it was obvious where that obstacle lay. It was in Churchill himself. He had identified himself, or he had become identified, with a plucky British determination to fight on and on, whatever the odds. Churchill was the symbol of everyone's hopes. It was not only inconceivable that Churchill would step down, it was inconceivable to millions of ordinary Britons.

I could not even imagine what the parallel situation in Germany would be like, in the way Hitler himself had come to personify the German nation.

The German night-time Blitz on British cities continued. During the five weeks in which I waited for Dr Burckhardt's call, cities like Bristol, Birmingham, Plymouth, Liverpool, Exeter, Swansea, Cardiff and Belfast had their hearts blasted out of them by concerted bombing attacks. The Blitz on London continued at the same time as the attacks on the other cities, almost without a break. In the Atlantic, U-boats were sinking British ships every day of the week. In the North African desert the fight for Egypt and the Suez Canal went on, much more dangerously for the British since the arrival of Rommel's Afrika Korps. In Greece the British were being beaten back.

All those deaths. All those losses. All that destruction.

The war was being prolonged when it could have been halted at any moment.

One night, after Birgit and I had gone to bed, we heard the air-raid sirens drone out their chilling warning. We were both instantly awake, stiff with fear in the dark. I started to climb out of bed.

Birgit said, 'Don't go from me.'

'We should take shelter.'

'They will not come near us. Stay here with me.'

'No . . . it's never safe.'

I helped her out of bed, first propping her up then swinging her legs around. She stood up unsteadily and for a moment we leaned on each other and embraced in the dark. The hard ball of our unborn child pressed between us. The sirens faded away, into ominous silence.

'Are the planes coming?'

'I can't hear them,' I said. 'But we mustn't take chances.'

We pulled on woollen garments for warmth, then picked up our pre-packed emergency bags and went downstairs. We had no special shelter in which to hide, but because the house was built of stone and the staircase ran next to the chimney we had put emergency bedding, lighting and water in the triangular space beneath the steps. I suspected that while I was away Birgit must have spent many nights alone in there.

We crawled into the narrow space and made ourselves as comfortable as possible. We lay with our arms around each other. I could feel the baby moving inside Birgit's belly, as if it was picking up our feelings of fear.

The sirens started again and almost at once we heard the sound that everyone in Britain dreaded most: the droning, throbbing noise of engines overhead, a Luftwaffe bomber formation coming in, high above. I felt Birgit's arms tighten around me. The aircraft were passing directly over the village, the characteristic drumming rhythm seeming to shake the stone walls of the house. We braced ourselves for the sound of bombs, the horrifying shriek of the tail whistles, the shocking explosions; I had lived with those for so long in London.

We heard the Manchester guns first: the sharp, shattering bangs, easily distinguished from the sounds of the bombs going off. As always, it was an encouraging noise, lending the sense that the bombers would be warded off. But then, over the racket of the guns, we heard the first bombs as they fell and exploded in the streets.

I could not lie still in the dark with a raid going on so close and despite

Birgit's protests I wriggled away from her, crawled into our darkened hallway and found my coat and shoes. I let myself out of the house. In the dark I crossed the lane and moved up to a mound of earth which I knew would give me a clear view to the north and west.

The sky was rodded with white shafts of searchlights. Bright flashes of anti-aircraft shells exploded briefly in the air by the cloudbase. Trails of tracer bullets raced upwards. The city was already spotted with bright points of orange fire. A glowing static fireball rested in the centre of the city, like a small sun that had alighted there. As I watched, more bombs went off, more fires took hold.

'Manchester's getting it again,' a man's voice said beside me. 'Not as big a raid as last time, but getting it bad.'

I nodded my agreement in the darkness and turned towards the sound of the voice. He was standing behind me but there was not enough light from the fires to illuminate his features.

'Second time since Christmas, isn't it?'

'So it is.'

'I missed the others,' I said, but as I spoke I realized who the man must be. I said, 'Isn't that you, Harry?'

'That's right. You're an old hand at the raids, your missus tells me. Away down south and all that.'

'I was working.'

'In London, wasn't it? Or was it in Wales? Doing a bit of rescuing?'

'A bit of that,' I said, finding myself falling into the rhythms of his speech. 'I'm not going back for more.'

'You should be down there in Manchester tonight. Looks like they could use an expert like you.' There was a taunt in his voice, a sort of mocking challenge. He was beginning to needle me.

'Not now,' I said.

'Not your sort of place, is it? Manchester?'

'I was injured and I'm still suffering the after-effects, if you must know. I've had enough for a while. Maybe you should go and volunteer.'

'Not me. I've too much to do around the village. Birgit told me you'd been injured. Then you went off vanishing, and that. Your baby's due next month, isn't it?'

'That's right. Last week in May.'

'Glad you're back in the village, Joe,' Harry said. 'Birgit needs you with her. Husband shouldn't be away, at a time like this.'

'What did you say?'

'None of my business, I know, but —'

'That's right. It's none of your damned business.'

'I'm round the village most of the time, Joe, and you're not. I hate to see a nice young woman alone, baby on the way, and that.'

'Look, Harry —'

We both ducked reflexively as one of the larger German bombs exploded not far away. London people called them parachute mines: they threw up a distinctive white-yellow ball of explosive fire when they went off. A second or two later, the sound and the blast from the bomb came at us, banging me backwards from where I was standing. I stumbled, recovered my balance and crouched down so that I could watch the rest of the raid.

'A close one, that,' Harry said. 'Still, you must be like those Londoners, used to this kind of thing.'

'It's as bad there as it is here,' I said. 'But London is bombed most nights.'

'They'll be all right. Expect you will be too, when the war's over. You off on another trip soon, then?'

We stood there together, watching the fires spread, seeing the huge funnels of dark smoke rising, sometimes even glimpsing some of the raiding planes if they swooped low enough to be lit up by the fires on the ground. The explosions were merging into one long roar. A big raid. The second in a month.

'You want to stay out here and watch a bit longer?' Harry said. 'I could go in and see if Birgit's all right.'

'What?'

'It's no trouble to me. Quite a few times while you've been away I've been round while there's been an alert. Just to make sure she's managing OK. She's all right with me. Mum and me can take care of her. Don't you worry, Joe. If anything else happens to you while you're working, and that, and you don't come back afterwards, I'll take care of Birgit. Be my pleasure. She needs a man to look after her.'

I turned to face him, but he was already walking away from me, down the lane, losing himself in the dark.

'Just you keep away from Birgit, Harry!' I shouted after him, but there was no reply.

I turned back to watch the rest of the raid, but I found that while the last exchange with Harry had been going on the attack had come to an abrupt end. One by one the stalks of light from the searchlights were switched off, the flames died down, the smoke drifted away, the drone of the engines receded into the distance. The great urban sprawl of Manchester became dark again, blacked out in the night.

xv

We were in the narrow triangular space beneath the stairs, our arms around each other, our unborn baby fretting between us. Birgit was asleep but I snapped awake. I held tight, forcing myself to be still, not to move suddenly so that I might wake her. The baby kicked at me, a small but distinct pressure against my side.

The night was silent. What happened to the raid? There had been the sirens, sounding the alert, but because the authorities never knew exactly where the German planes were heading there were a lot of false alarms. Had there been an all-clear yet? I was testing my memory for reality. Birgit and I had left our bed when the siren sounded, so that had been real. After that, though? The raid, the conversation with Harry outside in the night?

I could hear no engines, guns, bombs, sirens.

This lucid hallucination was the first I had suffered since I went to Portugal. I had begun to believe I was over them.

For the second time, as it seemed, I disentangled myself from Birgit's arms and slid along the hard mattress on the floor. She groaned in her sleep, shifting to the side, helping me shuffle away from her. I pulled on my coat and shoes, again. I went quickly to the door, opened it and listened in the night. All was darkness and silence. I stepped out into the cold air, crossed the lane and scrambled up the mound from where I could command a view of the plain below.

Everything was in darkness, blacked out, huddling in the night, silenced by the fear of raiders. I glanced back at the bulk of the Pennine hills beyond our house: it was possible to make out the curve of the moors against the slightly less dark sky.

While I stood there, shivering, I heard the all-clear: the first single-note sound drifted in on the wind from miles away, but one by one the other sirens on their town hall roofs, their fire station gantries, their school outbuildings, their church towers, took up the eerie but comforting message. No raid after all, they said; not tonight. Maybe somewhere else is getting it, but not here, not now. It's safe to leave shelter, to return to your beds.

I went back into the house, secured the door, and returned to the space beneath the stairs. Birgit was half awake, because of the sirens. I cuddled her fondly and helped her climb the stairs, taking her first to the lavatory then back to our bed. We crawled between the cold sheets, Birgit moving around many times while she tried to make her distended belly comfortable. I pressed against her, holding her, trying to warm her with my own chilled arms and legs.

xvi

The next morning, while Birgit was taking a bath, I went to my bureau in the corner of the living room. I took Dr Burckhardt's letter from the lockable, central drawer.

I read again his expression of thanks, the request for me to stand back from normal Red Cross duties for a while, the continued payment of my wages. His plain letter, handwritten and hurried in tone, was for me a guarantee of reality. It was a link back through unreliable memories to that memorable conference in Lisbon. I was not misremembering that. I had been there and it had really happened.

I felt that a sign of my improvement was the fact that I was starting to recover from the attacks more quickly. As the day went by I was able to forget the hallucination about the air raid and I began to wonder instead what I could do to occupy my time until I heard from Dr Burckhardt.

I was idle and useless around the house, aggravating a situation I did not properly comprehend. It was not a happy period. During the week that followed my spectral vision of the air raid Birgit and I argued many times, over trivial matters and large ones. We spent time in separate parts of the house. I felt we were becoming strangers to each other and I had no idea what I could do about it. I was miserable when I thought about what she and I were becoming. All the excitement of knowing each other, all trust, all familiarity, most of the love, had been beaten out of us by the experience of war. Only the unborn child, restless in her belly, remained to link us together. But what would happen after he or she was born?

One evening, while I was listening to the BBC, I heard a report of the previous night's RAF attack on the north German port of Kiel. It was described in the usual confident terms of the propaganda issued by the Air Ministry: the raid was pressed home by the crews with great skill and determination and while under attack from intense anti-aircraft fire. The target was described, as always, as a military one. In this case, many port installations and German army supplies had been damaged or destroyed. But the BBC also said that the damage had been widespread — surely that would mean many of the bombs fell outside the port area? Then there was the admission that more of our planes than normal had been shot down. It sounded as if the German night fighters had been unusually effective.

Inevitably, my thoughts turned to Jack. It is true that I did not often think about him deliberately, but that was because it was easier not to. For many years we had been so close: inseparable, our parents used to say about us. Some identical twins were like that. We did everything together, tied by an instinctive sense of kinship, of inherent oneness. We both tended to drift in a state of abeyance if we were separated. At school the teachers made us sit in different classes, but as soon as the breaks came we were together again. Because of that constant intimacy we grew up without many friends, our closeness not only self-sustaining but excluding too. It continued into early adulthood: when we were rowing together we used to say we were one mind in two bodies. But for the last five years, since our return from the Olympics, we had been almost completely separated, first by choice then more recently by the conditions of war.

Had we been drifting in abeyance once more, without each other? Because of my idleness around the house I began to think so, at least of myself. I thought back over my year of active pacifism, going it alone, or trying to, when most of the other men of my age were in the forces. None of my beliefs had changed, but I did begin to wonder if I had been approaching the problem the right way. Then there was Jack. Since the war began I had been making assumptions about him and his motives, but I knew that deep down we had to be much the same. We were much the same in so many other things. We had the same father, came from the same family tradition of tolerance, liberal conscience, anti-warfare. What might he be going through, while he flew against the enemy?

I had pushed Jack away from my conscious thoughts. I already knew how the war encouraged the temptation to avoid important decisions, to put things off, to try to suppress feelings, to stop worrying about this or that. But how could I have done that to Jack? The news of the raid on Kiel — in itself one more attack in a war filled with such attacks — reminded me yet again of the peril that he was facing in the RAF. I assumed that as an operational pilot he would be fully engaged in the bombing campaign. Every time he went on a raid his life was at risk.

I held secret knowledge that would affect him. Peace was imminent, while warfare continued. Danger remained until the last shot was fired, the last bomb dropped.

16

Selection of entries from the diaries of Dr Paul Joseph Goebbels (Bundesarchiv, Berlin, 1957), translated into English by T. F. Henderson. During this period Dr Goebbels was Gauleiter of Berlin and Reich Minister of Public Enlightenment and Propaganda.

March 28, 1941 (Friday)

Yesterday: Overthrow of the corrupt king of Yugoslavia. New King Peter is only seventeen years old. Churchill welcomes his coup as of the arrival of a saviour.

No air incursions overnight; news from Bulgaria as excellent as expected; more good news from Libya; we have made both these triumphs public. The Italians not doing so well in Abyssinia, but we need more details.

Working madly at full stretch, before a flying trip to Wilhelmshaven to inspect bomb damage. Already we are rebuilding the city, using the damage as an excuse to get rid of many outdated buildings and to remove the undesirables who live in them. Back by plane to Hamburg, then train to Berlin.

I am asked to review the cases of Betzner and two other 'poets,' sentenced to prison for inappropriate activities. They are all swine who deserve longer sentences than the court was able to give them. Have ordered an investigation into their family backgrounds. There's always something you can find out about scum like these.

Haushofer came to my office in the evening. Says that rumours of peace are running riot all over the USA, but that they appear to stem not from us but from London. Hess's ranting about a peace party in Britain takes on a semblance of reality. At the same time, Roosevelt is thoroughly insulting. He claims the Reich's wish for peace is not sincere. This is the sort of bumpkin we have to deal with.

April 4, 1941 (Friday)

Yesterday: A great gloom has descended over England as our successes continue. Twenty thousand tons of their shipping have been sunk in one day. More advances in the desert; the British are in complete retreat and surrendering on all sides. Where will we keep the extra prisoners? No incursions by air. We continue to smash the English cities. Half the population of Plymouth is homeless, the rest are suffering abject misery and screaming for surrender.

I am so busy during the day that I do not eat; everything is too much. Visitors call on me constantly. One of them was Speer, apparently wasting time because he has nothing to do while we are in Bulgaria. Speer is a snob and poseur who thinks he is the only one in whom the Führer confides. I remind him we are too busy now to be rebuilding Berlin.

Amongst other matters Speer mentions that the Führer bitterly regrets that we are fighting England. He describes England as our natural ally. I have heard it so often I am almost ready to believe it. I tell Speer what we are doing to keep our English friends awake every night, teaching them a lesson with our bombers and undermining the possible support of the Americans. Nothing frightens Roosevelt more than the idea that we will make up with the English, so we are simultaneously smashing the British and helping the Americans stay out of the fighting.

The British Ambassador in Moscow has had a meeting with Stalin. Our sources say that it was longer than usual and appeared to be serious. They must know by now what we are planning! I wrote a note to the Führer on the subject, and signed and dated it to be on the safe side, but I will not trouble him with it just yet.

April 7, 1941 (Monday)
Yesterday: Belgrade was completely destroyed as we moved in on them. Russia pleads with us for peace; that's more like it! USA predictably grumbles at us. Forty thousand tons of shipping sunk. Another successful night over England — how long can they put up with being bombed out of their beds every night? No air incursions by the RAF. Italy not doing well in Abyssinia, but they are all brown-trousered cowards who can cook their own goose.

Hectic but enthralling day, writing the story of Belgrade for the newspapers. We are emphasizing that it's not finished yet, hard times lie ahead, but the action will be swift and decisive. Message received from the Führer: he wants to know if we are ready for the big push next month. I take it he means to ask by this: will the English have come around to our point of view by then? I tell him that it is so.

I have forbidden any more dancing in public places. Unsuitable activities in wartime have to be controlled. I called in the reporters from the American newspapers and told them that it was a public safety matter, because of the risk from the air incursions.

In the evening: Hess called in to see me. A rare visit. He is such a poof and a weakling! He is about to make another trip to Lisbon, says he has made up his mind on his own to do it, but what did I think? Of course what he means is that he is trying to find out from me what the Führer thinks. And that means he worries if the Führer will still let him go if he finds out. I gave Hess the assurances he wanted, but his stock has been lowered recently. If it goes wrong I will tell everyone he is mad, because most people think that anyway.

A glorious day for the Reich!

April 21, 1941 (Monday)

Yesterday: the Führer's birthday. Hess came back a week ago from his trip to Lisbon without saying anything about it. So I put him up to delivering the radio tribute to the Führer, as there was no one else who would do it. I expected him to deviate from the script I wrote for him, but he read every word. No originality in the man.

No incursions here, but we sent 800 aircraft to London. The British are losing their morale. Even Churchill's fine words cannot rally them after this. We shall follow it up with more. Good news on other fronts: Libya, Serbia, Greece, even the Italians have been holding their own in Abyssinia. The Führer told me last week that he does not want to have to send troops to help Mussolini again. Already our triumph in the Balkans has been delaying the main event. When we have cleared Greece of the English we can concentrate on the real war.

The public are not listening to the wireless often enough. It could be dangerous to morale. Who knows what they might do instead? I have issued new rules and incentives.

In the evening: another visit from 'Fräulein' Hess, visibly nervous because he thinks the Führer will find out what he's doing. I reassure him that he need not worry, that the Führer is completely behind him. Hess is a toady! This is the first time he has tried to act without the Führer's knowledge. A great lesson to be learned. He worries that we are hitting the British too hard, too successfully, that they won't want to discuss peace. I convince him otherwise, because it is important that he makes his trip, if not for the reasons he thinks.

May 10, 1941 (Saturday)

Yesterday: A heavy raid on Mannheim, with much damage and many deaths. In revenge we send 200 aircraft to England, so they have nothing to laugh about. We hear of appalling damage done to the port of Hull, worse than anything they have done to us. Twenty thousand tons of shipping sent to the bottom by our U-boats.

Moscow has withdrawn recognition of some of the territories we have occupied. They sound as if they are worried about something. Stalin is planning to stay out of the war as long as possible, so that England and Germany exhaust themselves. Then the move to bolshevize Europe will begin. That's what the Russians think, but by then it will be too late. Soon we will turn to the East. Two strokes at once will thwart them. Peace on one front and war on the other, both totally unexpected. It is dangerous to have so much depending on that lickspittle Hess.

This week's newsreel is one of the best we have yet produced. I authorize it at once, and order that a copy be sent direct to the Führer at the Berghof. It has given me new confidence in our cause.

Goering sought me out after dinner. He is even fatter now than before and is having trouble breathing; he did not remove his ridiculous cap the whole time he was with me. He wanted to know what information I had about Hess, so I told him some of it. He showed me a flight plan Hess has drawn up and offered to let the Luftwaffe take care of him if the Führer ordered it. So tempting. I wonder if the Führer is behind this after all? Hess is his favourite but everyone thinks he is mad. How else would the Führer close the war with England if Hess were stopped?

May 11, 1941 (Sunday)

Yesterday: This was the day the Führer planned for the next great strike. May 10 was the first anniversary of the start of the offensive in the West and his sense of opera demanded that we balance it with our move in the East. Not to be! The generals who are expected to do our work are snivellers! They say we have too many men in the Balkans, but the English have been kicked out of Greece so what do they have left to complain about? I have been trying to find out when the new date will be but no one seems to know when it is.

Huge raid on Hamburg in the early hours of this morning, but as always the British fliers were frightened away by our barrage of anti-aircraft fire. Most of their bombs fell in the river and few of the others went off. As if to make up for their failure, the English sent a paltry secondary force to scatter incendiaries on Berlin. Little damage but a great deal of pointless aggravation. Meanwhile we sent more than seven hundred aircraft to deliver the *coup de grâce* to London. It's too early for confirmation, but the pilots report that London was ablaze from one end to the other.

Our short-wave broadcasts to the USA need improving, so I shall be taking personal control. There is no point pussy-footing about. Roosevelt is a danger to our plans, because of his ignorance of the issues and receiving too much influence from Churchill. We will seize Roosevelt by the throat and shake him until he falls apart. Few Americans realize that Roosevelt is a cripple.

I have forbidden all mention of Russia in our press. Just for the time being. If nothing else it will rattle Stalin's spies.

Hess disappeared as expected. He took off from the Messerschmitt factory in Augsburg on a supposed test flight, then headed off towards the north. He refuelled in Holland before flying out over the sea. To my amazement he followed the flight plan he showed me, so everyone knew exactly where he was. The man is mad, of course, and it has been the devil's own job keeping him away from the American reporters. The Führer has been concerned about him for some time, it should be said and will now most certainly be said. With Hess gone it will be easier to convince everyone that he had become unstable. This is the line we take if everything goes wrong, as it surely must. Once I was certain Hess was on his way I alerted Reichsmarschall Goering at what I considered to be an appropriate time. The Luftwaffe will no doubt have dealt with the poor man, whose service to the Party has been without parallel. A great National Socialist hero! I shall be busy with this one as soon as we hear the reaction from the English. After that, we can get on with the war. I would like to see Roosevelt's and Stalin's faces when they hear about Hess.

If Goering fails to deal with Hess, I shall complain about him again to the Foreign Ministry. It won't have any real effect, but Goering hates Ribbentrop as much as I do and it will distract them from other things if they engage in another squabble.

To Lanke in the evening, to be with Magda and my children, and to indulge for once in an early night. Everyone around me has been in wonderful high spirits. We all sense that at last the real war is about to begin.

17

Holograph notebooks of J. L. Sawyer

xvii

I told Birgit that I had been called in to work for the Red Cross again, that I would not be gone for long. She asked no questions, offered no complaint. I needed to get away from the house for a while and we both knew it.

I travelled across the country to Lincolnshire, a journey which in peace-time, by car, would take only a few hours. Now, when members of the public were in effect banned from using their cars, public transport was the only way.

The slow train journey, calling at every station and with many unex-plained delays, took me the best part of a day and a half, including one night huddling in the dismal waiting room in Nottingham station after I missed my connection. I was exhausted by the time I reached Barnham, the town clos-est to my brother's RAF station, and I counted myself lucky to find a vacant bedroom over the bar in one of the High Street pubs and went straight to bed.

Because I was so tired I assumed I would sleep through the night with-out interruption, but I felt as if I had only just dropped off when I was woken by the sound of engines.

Aircraft were flying low over the centre of the town, their engines strain-ing and roaring. I thought I was used to the noise of aero engines, near and far, hostile and friendly, but these were entirely different. Waves of deafening sound battered against the sleeping town.

Once the brief panic of being woken by a loud noise started to recede, I realized what was happening. The planes must be taking off from a local air-field. I was fully awake in seconds. I scrambled across the room, threw the window up, then leaned out and craned upwards.

The planes, powerful twin-engined bombers I recognized as Wellingtons, were travelling low above the roofs, swift, dark shapes outlined against the faint glow of moonlit clouds. The sound of the engines was more than a loud roar: it was a physical concussion of noise, beating not only against the walls and windows of the building but creating a perceptible rhythm against my head and chest. I was exhilarated by the endless reverberations, the shattering, thrilling commotion. I soaked up the sound like a man feeling a downpour of rain after a month in the desert. It was a terrifying but enthralling experience, something so powerful and engulfing that I felt it could not be understood until it was shared with others. Yet I realized, with a sudden jolt of surprise, that I seemed to be alone. There was no traffic in the blacked-out street below, there were no pedestrians walking home, no one else standing at a darkened window to stare up at the deafening sky.

Then I thought, then I realized: this is not real.

A sense of dread sank through me, a familiar sick-feeling anxiety that I could no longer trust my senses. Once again I had woken from what I thought was sleep to what I thought was reality: to a lucid imagining.

I could shrink away from it as I had done before, let the sinking feeling of dread course through me and take me with it, waking me up properly and pulling me out of the delusion. This time, though, I chose instead to remain, to experience the illusion to the full.

I stayed at that window while wave after wave of bombers took off across the town, sweeping low over the roofs. I tried to count the planes: fifty, a hundred, two hundred, three hundred, more and more, roaring off into the vengeful night.

I rejoiced in the unreality, letting the magnificent crude cacophony of powerful engines flood around me, drowning me in their deluge of sound.

xviii

Barnham is a market town to the west of the Lincolnshire wolds, built of pale red brick and tiles, a windy place that morning, under a sky thick with low, leaden clouds. At the back of the town, beside the railway station, there were stockyards for the weekly livestock markets. In the narrow streets close to the centre of town, the houses were built in terraces, backing on to each other, but there were larger, more prosperous-looking houses where the town started to blend with the countryside. I walked past them, following the main road in the direction of Louth, but found myself in flat, uninteresting farmland, marked out with trees and hedges but with few other features to give ease to the eye. I looked in all directions as I walked, knowing that there were two RAF bases in the immediate vicinity of the town, but I could see no signs of anything that might signify the presence of an airfield: a water tower, hangars, a windsock. I turned back.

A short while later I was walking again down the High Street in the centre of the town, past the pub where I had spent the night. I glanced up at the window where I had imagined I was standing in the dark. It looked small-er from street level, as if even when fully open it would not be large enough for a man to stand by it and lean through. Familiar shops were open along both sides of the main street and people were going about their unexception-al chores of shopping and making deliveries around the town. It was a place rather like Macclesfield, without the interesting Pennine scenery.

I knew my brother was based at RAF Tealby Moor, close to a village of that name, but the direction signs had been taken down all over Britain the previous year. I didn't want to ask the way: ever since the war began in earnest most people were wary of strangers.

I found a café and drank tea and nibbled at some sweet biscuits, not sure what to do next. While I was still sitting there I noticed a number of airmen were walking down the High Street, some of them in small groups or pairs, others singly. Thinking that Jack might be among them I finished my cup of tea and went outside.

Jack was not there. The RAF men were a mixture of officers and men, apparently unconcerned with differences in rank while they were off duty. I was impressed by their casual manner, the fragments of flippant RAF slang I overheard as I passed. One or two of them looked at me strangely.

At the western end of the High Street was a wide, flattened area, partly a car park and bus depot. A cream-painted single decker bus was standing next to the public lavatories. A young man in a blue RAF uniform and cap was sitting behind the wheel, reading a morning newspaper.

I sauntered over, trying to look as casual as possible. The airman folded his newspaper and looked at me incuriously.

''Morning,' I said. 'You're the Tealby bus, aren't you?'

'Yes.'

'Thanks a lot.'

I retreated, walking across the road to where there was a small park. The heavy clouds were thinning away to the east and soon I was able to enjoy the spring sunshine. As I wandered around I kept my eye on the waiting bus. At about a quarter to eleven the airmen began drifting back to the bus, climbing aboard noisily and waiting inside for the others. A group of six kicked a ball around in the dusty area. When the bus was full the driver started the engine, turned out of the parking area and set off towards the west.

I went quickly to the side of the road and watched the bus as it drove away into the distance. After about half a mile it slowed suddenly, making a left turn.

xix

RAF Tealby Moor was about two miles from Barnham, a long but not an impossible walk. I arrived soon after midday, discovering that the road along which I had seen the bus heading brought me directly to the guardhouse at the main gate. The airfield was laid out in farmland away from the village from which it took its name, with no other houses in the vicinity. It was clear that any civilian seen hanging around outside the entrance to the base would be challenged. I kept my head down and my hands stuffed into my pockets. I walked on past the gate.

The road followed a long stretch of the perimeter fence. Once I was away from the main cluster of admin buildings and hangars, the fence became a double strand of barbed wire, presenting only a token barrier against the outside world. As I walked along I saw many of the aircraft at dispersal: they had been moved out to positions around the perimeter so as to present a more scattered target should enemy intruder aircraft appear. The planes were Wellingtons, with their round, snub-nosed fuselages, twin engines, gun turrets at front and rear. Most of the aircraft were being serviced or repaired by technical ground crew, with auxiliary power supplies wheeled up to the aircraft, ladders propped against the sides of the planes, men standing or squatting on the wings next to the opened nacelles of the engines.

As I walked past them, no one inside the base took any notice of me.

Eventually the road and the fence took different routes, the road swinging left and dropping down a shallow incline towards a bridge across a narrow river. I could see the church spire of a village in the near distance. The perimeter fence turned sharply to the right, heading out across the fields. From where I was standing I could see that it was where the main runway ended in a wide apron, allowing the aircraft to turn before or after using the runway. I saw a few signalling installations, a couple of huts, a caravan, the long straight road of the concrete runway.

While I was standing there, I heard the sound of an engine and I saw a small RAF truck running along the inside of the perimeter wire towards me. An officer was sitting in the front seat, next to the driver. More men stood precariously on the open platform at the back. I thrust my hands into the pockets of my coat and walked along the road in the direction of the main gate, trying to seem immersed in my own thoughts. The occupants of the truck did not look interested in me, but the officer gazed long enough to acknowledge me.

After the vehicle moved on out of sight I retraced my steps and found a narrow, unmade path that followed the outside of the perimeter fence. On the far side of the main runway and its apron, where the fence doubled back towards the main part of the base, there was a thicket of trees. I climbed over an old stile and moved among the trees. After a short walk I came to a place from which I could gain a clear view of the end of the runway, yet where I would not be easily spotted from the airfield.

I stood there for an hour or more, rewarded in mid-afternoon by the sight of several of the bombers being flown on test circuits low around the field. When the pilots opened the throttles and the propellers turned at full speed for take-off, the sound was exhilarating. I was close enough to be able to see the man at the controls, but because of the thick jackets and helmets it was impossible to tell if any of the pilots was Jack.

By about four in the afternoon I was feeling cold, hungry and thirsty. I had intended to stay on at the side of the airfield as long as possible, but I had not planned properly. I left my position in the trees and started the long walk back to town.

The next day I killed time in the town during the morning and most of the afternoon. After lunch I telephoned the airfield and asked to speak to Jack. He was not available, so I left a message that I was staying at the White Hart in Barnham and would like him to contact me there. When I said that I was Jack's brother, the officer who had answered the phone unbent a little and said he would pass on the message but added that Flight Lieutenant Sawyer would be on operational standby for a few more days.

I made suitable preparations for the second expedition, buying some sandwiches and a large bottle of lemonade from the pub. I dressed as warmly as I could.

It was already evening as I passed the main gate. In the west the clouds were clearing to reveal a golden sunset. It took me another twenty minutes to walk round the far end of the airfield to the thicket of trees. It was still just about light, a calm, silvery twilight. I stumbled through the small wood, making my way to the position I had found the day before.

As soon as I was there I realized that a raid of some kind was about to be launched. Low lights glinted from within one of the small buildings near the end of the runway. Several vehicles stood about, including a fire tender.

I waited, sitting with my back against the bole of a tree. I ate my sandwiches and drank the lemonade, keeping a watchful eye open for activity. When my back became sore I stood up, flexed my legs and arms, trying to ease the growing stiffness. Eventually things began to happen. Two people wobbled slowly down the side runway on bicycles, leaned them against the hut and went inside. A few minutes later, somewhere down in the main part of the airfield, I heard a plane starting its engines. Soon it was joined by another, then another, then more. Red and green signal lights fluttered along the runway, shone briefly and went out. I heard a telephone bell ringing.

The engine noise grew louder and in a few moments I saw the first of the bombers taxiing slowly down the side runway towards the turning point. It came slowly on, the wings rocking up and down as the plane lurched along the uneven surface. It passed only a short distance from me, turning towards the main runway but coming to a halt. The stream of air thrown back by the propellers blustered against me, tainted with the rich smell of gasoline.

Already a second bomber was lumbering down the side runway, with another following. On the far side of the airfield I could see others moving along too. The noise of the engines was swelling. The plane closest to me suddenly roared more loudly, the blast of air against me stiffening. The plane rolled to the end of the runway, turned smoothly, headed down the long concrete strip. At first it was travelling so slowly I was convinced a running man could easily overhaul it, but gradually the heavily loaded machine began to pick up speed. Green signal lights glared ahead of it.

A second Wellington was already moving from the far side to the end of the runway. The signal briefly turned red, then green again. The plane rumbled forward slowly, in a great commotion of power.

Behind it, the next plane was already taking up position.

I counted twenty-two aircraft in all. From the first plane to the last the whole procedure of launching them into the air lasted less than fifteen minutes. Silence fell on the airfield as the last plane climbed away into the gathering night.

Stumbling through the trees, I set off on the long walk back to the inn.

xx

For the next three days I took the walk along the country roads to the airfield, trying to see what was going on, making myself feel that in some way I was

participating. I never failed to thrill to the spectacle of the heavy planes claw-
ing their way into the air.

Early in the morning of the fourth day I was woken by the landlord of
the White Hart, telling me in an aggrieved voice that I was wanted on the
telephone. Dull with sleep, I followed him downstairs to the small phone
cubicle at the back of the public bar. It was Jack.

He said he was surprised that I was there in Barnham, in the neighbour-
hood of the airfield, but he did not ask any questions over the telephone and
suggested that we should meet straight away. He told me he was about to go
on leave for forty-eight hours and was anxious to be on his way.

Once more I trudged along the road through flat Lincolnshire fields,
arriving at the gate a little before ten in the morning. Jack was waiting for me.
He was in the road outside the main entrance, smoking a cigarette and with
a newspaper folded under his arm. He looked the picture of the romanticized
RAF pilot that you sometimes saw in the newspapers and on the newsreels:
young, dashing, carefree, taking on the Hun with bravery, good humour and
an unwavering sense of British fair play. I couldn't remember how long it was
since we had last been together, but as soon as I saw him I felt a familiar surge
of many of the old feelings about him: love, envy, resentment, admiration,
irritation. He was still my brother.

Jack was in no good humour as I walked towards him.

'What in blazes are you doing around here?' he said at once, with no
greetings, no expression of warmth, no hint that it must have been more than
a year since our last meeting. 'This is no place for civilians. Several of the
patrols have seen you out there, hanging about on the perimeter fence. That
makes people nervous. It was only because I was able to intervene that you
haven't been arrested.'

'JL,' I said. 'It's me. Can't you even say hello?'

'Why didn't you let me know you were coming?'

'I'm not doing any harm,' I said. 'I've been trying to get hold of you.'

'Lurking around in the woods at the end of the runway isn't the way. Why
didn't you drop me a line first?'

'It was something I did on an impulse. I have to talk to you face to face.'

'Couldn't you have put it in a letter?'

'No, it's too . . . sensitive. If it was opened by someone else —'

I saw something change in Jack's expression: a fleeting evasiveness, a
guilty look. He fiddled with the cigarette he was holding.

'Would this be something to do with Birgit, by any chance?' he said.

His question surprised me. 'Birgit?'

'The baby must be due soon. There isn't anything going wrong, is there?'

'No, it's not about Birgit. Why should you think that?'

'*Are* there any problems?'

'Everything's fine. We aren't expecting the baby for at least another five weeks. At the end of next month.'

'You've come away and left Birgit alone at home? In the last weeks of her pregnancy? How could you do that?'

I suppose that I too might have allowed a look of guilt to cross my face.

'Look, JL, Birgit's doing fine,' I said. I could not rid my voice of a defensive note. 'She's a healthy girl and a neighbour's keeping an eye on her while I'm away. I wouldn't have left her if there was any risk. Anyway, I'm going home tomorrow.'

'So if it isn't Birgit, what's the important news that can't wait?'

'Can we find somewhere a bit less public to talk?' We were a few yards away from the guardhouse at the airfield entrance, with several airmen in view. At least two or three of them were within hearing distance. With an inclination of my head I tried to make a wordless signal to Jack that I wanted to move away a little, but stubbornly he would not shift.

I moved closer to him, sensing his resistance to me. Speaking softly, I said, 'I'm sticking my neck out to tell you this, JL. It's as secret as anything can be. But I have information that the war is about to come to an end. Maybe in a week, two weeks. There's going to be a cease-fire.'

Jack laughed sardonically, drew on the last of his cigarette, inhaled, and tossed the glowing end into a puddle.

'You've come all the way here to tell me that?'

'It's absolutely true.'

'So are the other rumours that go around a place like this every week.'

'JL, this one isn't a rumour. I know what I'm talking about.'

'I don't believe it.'

'It's true!'

'A cease-fire is never going to happen,' he said. 'Even if it's not a rumour. Even if there are some people who want one. Wars don't suddenly end because somebody decides it's time to stop. They go on being fought until one side or the other comes out on top.'

'The last war ended with an armistice.'

'That was different. In effect the Germans surrendered. No one's going to start negotiating for peace now, on our side or theirs. The war has at last begun to go our way and we're in too deep. We've gone beyond the point of no return and we have to see it through to the end.'

'You sound like Churchill.'

'Maybe I do. Is he suing for peace?'

'No, of course not,' I said, realizing how much I was blurting out from the store of confidential information with which I had been entrusted. 'But it's the real thing, I swear it. I've already said too much, but for various reasons Hitler wants to negotiate a cease-fire with Britain. Obviously something inside Germany is about to change, although I don't know what. Whatever the reason, Hitler wants to make a separate peace with Britain.'

'Since you mention Churchill, he would never stand for it.'

'Churchill's already talking.'

'Talking? Churchill is talking to Hitler?'

'Not directly. There are secret peace negotiations going on through inter-mediaries. This is why it's dangerous for me to tell you. I've already let out more than I should.'

'Your secret's safe with me, Joe. Even if Churchill went mad and said he wanted to negotiate, the country wouldn't let him. Not now, not after Dunkirk, not after the Blitz, not after the other sacrifices.'

'It's about to happen, whatever you say.'

'How do you happen to know this, anyway?'

'I obviously can't tell you that. I'm only peripherally involved, but I do know what I'm talking about. It's the real thing. There's going to be an armistice and it's going to be agreed soon. Perhaps even by next week.'

We had by this time, with unspoken consent, turned our backs on the air-field gate and were walking slowly along the grassy verge. JL offered me one of his cigarettes and we both lit up. I felt a quiet, unexpected surge of senti-ment about being a twin again, if only in small things, walking together with my brother, smoking with him.

'All right, let me suppose for one minute it's true,' Jack said. 'What on earth is the point of me knowing it?'

'You've got to come off operations, JL. Straight away. Couldn't you apply for some kind of ground job? Every time you go out on a raid you're in dan-ger. There's no point getting yourself killed now.'

'A lot of us tend to think there's not much point being killed at any time.'

'Why won't you take me seriously?'

Jack shook his head. 'Maybe you mean what you say because you have some special knowledge. Maybe you mean what you say anyway. Maybe you only think you mean it.' I felt a stirring of resentment, a feeling that probably showed in my face. Jack, apparently reacting to it, went on, 'All right, Joe, perhaps I even *wish* you meant it. But I can't wander into my station commander's office and tell him I don't feel like flying any more. He'd take me down to the bar, buy me a beer and tell me not to go around with such bloody silly ideas. Anyway, there's no point even discussing it. I don't want to stop flying. What about my crew? Can I tell them too? What about the other crews? I can't walk away from the squadron because my brother tells me a rumour — all right, passes me some information about the war coming to an end. Do I keep it a secret from the others? Then watch them go on putting themselves in danger? Or do you want us all to walk out?'

I heard the sound of aero engines in the background, caught by the wind and carried across the flat landscape, a growling reminder of war.

'JL, I simply want you out of danger for a few days. I've been sworn to secrecy about the cease-fire, but I have to tell you about it because you're my brother! I didn't go so far as thinking about how you might work it out with the air force.'

It was the longest conversation Jack and I had had in years. We were standing still again, a few feet away from each other, side by side on the grassy verge of the country road. We kept drawing on our cigarettes, using them like punctuation, for emphasis. We weren't exactly looking each other in the eye, but we were as close as we had ever been since we grew up. I was trying to take his measure, trying to cut through and eliminate the complicated network of memories, childhood, obsessive sports training, falling out, my marriage to Birgit, all the events that lay unfathomably between us, the subjects we were still touchy about, the arguments we never resolved, a maze of alert responses from which we could bounce off irretrievably in the wrong direction, separating us once again. I felt for a moment it might at last be possible to leave that behind us, simply become brothers once again, adult brothers, joined by our resemblance to each other rather than driven apart by it.

But then he said, 'You don't know what the hell the war's about, do you?'

The moment of possible healing was lost. We both looked up as a black-painted Wellington bomber roared away from the runway behind us, climbing heavily into the air, drowning us with its ferocious noise.

I was shaken into wakefulness. A plane was passing low over the pub, the centre of the town, out there in the night. The engine noise vibrated the window glass and shook the floorboards.

I was not in bed. I had left the bed.

I was standing in my room at the White Hart, wearing my pyjamas, halfway between the bed and the window, one hand resting on the wall for support. I was blinded by the jolt from bright daylight to night-time darkness, the real world, the illogical reality of my life. Lucidity lay only in the mind.

I shook my head in frustration and disappointment, still feeling the daylight presence of my brother. I could taste the tobacco in my mouth and throat, felt I should exhale the cigarette smoke I had sucked in as the plane took off behind us. All that smoking, all that talking, somewhere out there in the mind, somewhere in nowhere at all.

I sat on the edge of the bed, thinking about Jack and what he and I had seemed to be discussing. It was a recapitulation of my own preoccupations, of course.

From time to time more planes flew low across the town.

Finally, feeling cold and isolated in the blacked-out night, aware of the silent town out there beyond the small window, I crawled back under the thin blankets, lay still, tried to feel warm again. I was wide awake, replete with unwelcome thoughts. I tried again and again to calm my mind, turned over in the narrow bed, seeking comfort. Time went by — eventually I must have drifted back to sleep.

I was woken by the landlord, hammering on the door of my bedroom and telling me in an aggrieved voice that I was wanted on the telephone. I rolled out of bed, dull with sleep. I followed him downstairs to the small cubicle at the back of the public bar. I picked up the phone. It was Jack.

As he spoke I was looking around at the empty bar room, remembering. I could hardly concentrate on what Jack was saying. I was thinking, *This must be another lucid imagining!*

Jack fell silent, apparently waiting for my reply. Then he asked me again: what had I wanted when I left the message at the adjutant's office? I stumbled out with the words: I need to meet you, it won't take long, can it be today? Now?

He sounded surprised but quickly agreed that we should meet straight away. He told me he was about to go on leave for forty-eight hours and was anxious to be on his way.

Once again, therefore, I walked the long road that lay between the flat Lincolnshire fields. I had plenty of time to think, to test the authenticity of what was happening. I made a deliberate attempt to observe what was around me, almost to measure it. I looked at the sheep as they grazed in the fields, saw the hedgerows that lined the road, felt the texture of the road surface itself, the sound of the light wind in the trees, testing these mundane impressions as if to find flaws in their reality. I was aware of myself: the feeling of the air temperature around me, a minor discomfort in one of my shoes, the aftermath of the greasy, undercooked breakfast grudgingly provided by the pub landlord, a growing impatience to resolve everything with Jack.

I continued to walk along, but instead of being impelled by the urgent need to see Jack, I was now more concerned with the nature of the world around me, the essential quality of its reality. I was certain I had entered another lucid imagining, but if so it was the first time I understood that fact almost from the start. Although I had experienced lucidly, I had never before *thought* lucidly too.

Was it a sign that the problem was coming to an end?

I carried on walking, the road between hedgerows, the fields, the unilluminating sky, the distant sound of aero engines.

I arrived at the airfield shortly before ten in the morning. I checked my wristwatch to make sure. Jack was already waiting for me outside the main gate. He was smoking a cigarette and had a newspaper folded under his arm. As soon as I saw him I felt a familiar surge of many of my old feelings about him: love, admiration, envy, resentment, irritation. He was still my brother.

He was looking the other way as I was walking towards him. Finally he glanced across and saw me, then looked away again immediately, with a guilty hunching of his shoulder. He took a drag on his cigarette and tossed it on the ground and crushed it beneath his foot. It looked to me unmistakably like a self-conscious signal of rejection. Months of frustration suddenly boiled up in me without warning.

As soon as we were close enough to speak, I said, 'Look, JL, what's been going on between you and my wife?'

I winced inside to hear myself say the words. Even to myself I sounded hectoring, weak, irritable, negligible. My voice trembled on the brink of falsetto.

Jack looked startled. 'Is that what you've come all this way to say?'

'Answer the question. Are you up to something with Birgit?'

'Hello, Joe,' JL said calmly. 'It's good to see you again after all this time, brother of mine. Couldn't you even say hello before starting in on me?'

'You always were a sarcastic bastard.'

'Joe, for heaven's sake, calm down!'

I was about to shout something in rage at him, but at the last moment I realized how close we were to the guardhouse by the gate. Several airmen were in view.

'You've got to tell me,' I said, suddenly finding myself out of breath. 'What's been happening at home while I wasn't there?'

'Let's take a walk,' JL said, inclining his head to indicate we should move away a little, but stubbornly I would not shift. JL turned to face me directly and spoke softly. 'Birgit's your wife, Joe. Why do you think I would get involved with her?'

'Do you deny it?'

'The way you mean it, of course I deny it.'

'Do you deny you've been to my house while I was away?'

'Joe, it's not what you think.'

'Don't tell me what I'm thinking!'

'You kept going away and Birgit hardly ever knew where you were.' Jack was keeping the sound of his voice level. It made me listen to what he was saying, even though anger and resentment were still clamouring within me. 'OK, Joe, some of that time you were missing and that wasn't your fault, but until the police located you Birgit thought you had been killed. She has no phone at the house, the people at the Red Cross either didn't know where you were or wouldn't tell her. And surely I don't have to tell you what she's been going through since the war began? Half the people in the village think she's a German fifth columnist. The government keeps threatening to lock her up. She's pregnant. She's convinced her parents have been murdered. You were away somewhere. What she wanted — I'll tell you what she wanted, though I'm certain that in this mood you won't believe me. She was lonely, needed a friend and above all else she wanted to speak German for a while.'

'You went all the way over there and spoke German to her!'

'She was desperate for company, someone she knew and could relax with. You know that Birgit and I have always been close friends. From all the way back, in Berlin.'

'You never made much of a secret of it.'

'Why should I? I'm extremely fond of her. It's even true I was once madly in love with her, but that was years ago and you put an end to it. She's been your wife for all this time. Joe, she loves you so much! Can't you believe I respect that?'

When had Jack been madly in love with Birgit? I hadn't known that.

'So what did you two talk about in German?' I said jealously, wanting to know but also sounding sarcastic. Jack and I were so much alike.

'I can't remember. It wasn't important. Whatever it is that friends talk about.'

'Important enough for you to travel all that way across to visit her.'

'Joe, I told you why.'

We had by this time, with unspoken consent, turned our backs on the air-field gate and were walking slowly along the grassy verge. JL offered me one of his cigarettes and we both lit up. I felt a quiet, unexpected surge of sentiment about being a twin brother again, if only in small things, walking together, smoking together. The sound of aero engines struck up again, much closer and louder, caught by the wind and carried across the flat countryside, a growling reminder of war.

'JL, at least tell me this. Was it you who made Birgit pregnant?'

A gust of wind made the engines seem louder. The cigarette I had taken from Jack had been in its packet too long, or it had been crushed while it was carried around. It was flattened and loose-packed. When I sucked on it, tiny fragments of glowing tobacco flared up from the end. How long had Jack been smoking? It was the longest conversation I had had with my brother in years. We were standing still again, a few feet away from each other, side by side on the grassy verge of the country road. We kept drawing on our cigarettes, using them like punctuation, for emphasis. We weren't exactly looking each other in the eye but we were as close as we had ever been since we had grown up. I was angrily trying to take his measure, whether he was lying to me or telling me a simple truth.

'Come on, JL! Was it you?'

'You don't know what the hell Birgit wants or needs, do you?' he said, in an almost despairing voice.

We both turned in surprise as a black-painted Wellington bomber lifted away from the runway behind us, climbing heavily into the air, deafening us with the ferocious noise of its engines. I waved my fist in frustration, knowing what was about to happen.

As the darkness of the night fell around me a plane was passing low over the roof of the pub, flying across the centre of the sleeping town, out there in the night. The reverberations from the engine noise shook the window glass.

I was not in bed. I had left the bed. I was standing next to it, wearing my pyjamas, in the narrow gap that ran alongside, halfway between the bed and the window, one of my hands resting on the wall for support.

I felt stray tobacco strands sticking to my lips. I picked them away with my fingertips, licking my lips to clear them.

I sagged with depression. I did not try to go back to sleep again but crouched uncomfortably on the floor of the room beneath that small and inadequate window, watching the dawn light slowly spreading across the low grey clouds.

In the morning, as soon as I heard the landlord moving around downstairs and before there was any risk of the telephone in the bar ringing, I paid my bill at the inn and began the long journey home, following the interminable and indirect train-route across England. It took me another day and a half of tedious travelling and waiting for connections. We were in the first week of May, the month our baby was due to arrive.

Mrs Gratton and Harry were both in the house when I walked in and they made me a cup of tea. They told me Birgit was asleep upstairs. Everything was going well, Mrs Gratton said, no cause for concern, the baby was due to arrive on time, but they were waiting for a visit from the doctor. Birgit had spent an uncomfortable night.

I went upstairs as soon as she woke and we spent an hour or more together until the doctor came to visit her. I heard Birgit tell him she was suffering worse back pains than before and that her legs were swollen and were losing sensation. The doctor reassured her it would not be long before her troubles were at an end.

When everyone had left the house, Birgit gave me the small pile of letters that had arrived for me while I was away. Prominent among them was a letter in a typewritten envelope, posted in London two days earlier. It was from Dr Carl Burckhardt and it requested me to meet him in London in two days' time.

18

Extract from Chapter 6 of The Last Day of War *by Stuart Gratton, published by Faber & Faber, London, 1981:*

. . . some theatres of Luftwaffe operations were quieter than others. All the occupied territories required air cover, although once Operation Barbarossa was confirmed for June 22 and aircraft were needed on the Eastern Front, cover was progressively reduced in certain areas to the minimum operational level.

One such was Luftflotte 5, which was responsible for the whole north-western German coast from Emden in the west to the northern tip of occupied Denmark. Although bomber *Geschwaders* of Luftflotte 5 were deployed against British shipping in the North Sea and had attacked British targets such as Hull, Grimsby and Newcastle, the Luftwaffe presence in Denmark was mainly as a defence against RAF minelaying operations in the Kattegat Strait.

On May 10, 1941, the process of partial withdrawal to Germany had already begun, leaving the night-fighter *Gruppen* seriously reduced in man-power and machines. That day, Oberleutnant **Manfred Losen** was a pilot of IV./NJG 35, flying the Messerschmitt Me-109E fighter from Grove airfield on the west coast of Denmark. In the afternoon he and the other members of his *Staffel* had flown over the sea for a short gunnery calibration and test. They returned to the airfield before 6 p.m. local time for a meal and a rest, before the duties of the night began. He tells the rest of his story:

'I was called in to the battle room by my superior, Major Limmer. His first question was to ask me how long I thought it would take me to get into the air if an *Alarmstart* was called. I said that I thought the aircraft were already refuelled and the weapons reloaded, so that we could scramble in a matter of minutes. He said that was good and asked me to stay on the alert.

'About half an hour later he called me in again, this time looking frantic. He said, "Something urgent has come up. It's an unusual job and you must start straight away. There will be no radio ground control, so take all the aircraft you can and report back to me in person when you land." He went on to explain what we should do. He said that the British had apparently repaired a Messerschmitt Me-110 that had been shot down over England and were flying it in German markings on a special spy mission in our sector. It was due to pass within our range at low altitude in the next thirty minutes. Our orders were to shoot it down. No warnings were to be given.

'I asked how we could be sure that if we saw a Me-110 it would be the one we were looking for. Major Limmer told me not to ask questions and ordered me to leave at once. We scrambled straight away and took off into the sunset, heading due west across the sea. I had managed to find only three other aircraft ready to leave, so that was the greatest strength we could muster for the flight. The pilots who scrambled with me were naturally curious and as soon as we were away from the base they came on the radio. I told them that their orders were to stay with me at all times and to follow my lead. I also told them that strict radio silence must be observed until we after we landed.

'We carried enough fuel to patrol for about one hour at low altitude. After about half that time one of my *Staffel* overhauled my aircraft and flew close beside me. I recognized the pilot as a good friend of mine, Unteroffizier Helmut Köberich. He pointed upwards with his hand. When I looked up I could see that at about two or three thousand metres above us there were scores of British two-engined bombers heading on a south-easterly bearing towards Germany. It was a beautiful evening, still with much pale light in the sky. It wouldn't last long and the conditions were almost perfect for an attack. Helmut obviously wanted to go after the bombers, since that was what we were trained to do. I managed to restrain him.

'Not long after that I saw a tiny shape in the distance, flying on a northerly bearing, at about the same altitude as us. I immediately turned in that direction, with the rest of the *Staffel* following. At this time we had only a few minutes' fuel left before we would have to return to base, otherwise we would be forced to ditch before we reached land. In five minutes we overhauled the plane and easily identified it as an Me-110D, bearing what looked like normal Luftwaffe markings. According to my orders from Major Limmer I manoeuvred my plane into a suitable position and launched a diving attack. The other planes followed me. I attacked at once, letting off a long burst of cannon fire. Because I was using tracer I'm certain that at least some of my shells struck the other aircraft. The pilot of the Me-110 was alert and took immediate evasive action, diving into the cloud layer below him. The rest of my *Staffel* followed him, firing their machine-guns, while I circled round, gaining a little altitude, ready for a second pass.

'I dived again, picking up a great deal of speed. I passed through the layer of cloud, but there was no sign of the Me-110 where I thought it should be. I searched around in all directions, but I could only conclude that either he had escaped or he had already crashed into the sea. I resumed our former altitude and soon joined up with the others. We flew directly back to base.

'Although I had been ordered to report to Major Limmer, as soon as we parked our aircraft we were immediately told to board a truck, where two armed *Gefreiters* were in charge of us. We were driven to one of the hangars on the far side of the airfield and there interrogated closely about what we had done and what we had seen. Our versions of the event were all more or less in agreement with each other, but even so we were questioned until after midnight. It was accepted that we had damaged the other aircraft but that we could not claim it as a definite kill. At the end we were allowed to return to our quarters, but we were warned in the most serious terms possible that we must never reveal what we had been doing that night.

'Later, after the war, I met men from other *Nachtjagdgeschwaders* (night-fighter units) and learned from them that they too had been scrambled on the same night for the same reason: a British-operated Me-110 on a secret mission. One of them, from our base at Aalborg in Denmark, claimed to have seen the Me-110 shot down. Another, who had been based at Wittmundhafen on the Ostfriesland coast in the north of Germany, said that they had not been able to find, let alone engage with, the Me-110, but he said that their orders had come direct from Generalmajor Adolf Galland, whose orders in turn had come from no less a person than Reichsmarschall Hermann Goering. They were told that the Messerschmitt was being flown by Rudolf Hess and that Hitler had had a last-minute change of mind about making peace.'

Manfred Losen was later posted to the Russian front, where he served for two years in most appalling conditions. In 1943 his plane was shot down by a Mustang of the USAAF and he was taken prisoner. He spent three years in a PoW camp in Texas. He now lives in Houston, where he has recently retired from the Dell Computer Corporation.

19

Holograph notebooks of J. L. Sawyer

xxi

In normal times I suppose it would probably take ten or fifteen minutes to stroll from the YMCA near Holborn to Admiralty House in Trafalgar Square, but on the morning of May 7, in the immediate aftermath of a raid, it turned out to be an arduous expedition. Many of the streets were blocked by fallen buildings and detours were necessary. Fire engines and ambulances were moving around constantly and at several of the worst places of bomb or fire damage the rescue workers were still digging and pulling at the fallen masonry in search of anyone trapped inside. Flood water from broken mains was in every street. Bulldozers were attempting to remove the worst of the wreckage from the streets. My walk, which began in the spirit of curiosity and discovery, ended with my hurrying along, concerned not to get in the way of the emergency services, trying not to notice the many pathetic and touching scenes of damage and loss.

I was shocked to realize how quickly I had forgotten what hell the bombing brought.

In common with many of the official buildings in the area Admiralty House looked like a fortress: at ground level every inch of the perimeter was protected by walls of sandbags about twelve feet high. Above, the windows were sealed with metal shutters. Clearly, it would be no more able to withstand a direct hit from a high-explosive bomb than any other building, but it was certainly intended to survive almost everything else.

Dr Burckhardt, together with two other officials, was waiting for me in a small anteroom along the main hallway. He greeted me effusively, speaking in excellent English with what I discerned to be a cultivated accent.

'Our meeting is to be delayed somewhat,' he said, after we had reassured each other that we were well and in good order. 'Because of the raid last night, the Prime Minister felt he should go on a short personal tour of some of the worst-hit areas. He says it is the best morale-raiser he knows. There is some tea here, if you would like a drink.'

For the next hour we waited, usually in silence, engaging only in small talk. Throughout our wait, the door to the room was open. From my seat I could see along most of the hallway outside. When Mr Churchill arrived he did so without fuss or ceremony. I saw the shadows of movement beside the main entrance as people passed through the narrow corridor created by the high banks of sandbags, then a man in a civilian suit walked in. He was closely followed by the familiar figure of the Prime Minister, who was dressed in a brown overcoat and tall-crowned hat and carrying a cane. He wore a gas-mask case on a strap hung across his shoulder. As he began to divest himself of all this, more of his entourage came into the hallway behind him: two or three more civilians, uniformed senior members of the navy, army and air force, and a superintendent of police. Churchill nodded to these people briefly and shook hands with them, then walked down the hallway towards us. He was accompanied by one other man.

We stood up quickly as he came in. He was not as short as I had imagined him to be. He was slimmer about the waist too. He was also much more spry and youthful in his movements than I had anticipated. To see his famous face so close up was, in spite of my many hostile feelings about him in the past, a considerable experience.

Finally, he spoke. 'Let me apologize for keeping you waiting, gentlemen. I realize how important your mission to see me is, but as you no doubt know we suffered a serious raid last night. I like to get about to see the people if I can. However, I am ready to proceed.'

We followed him out of the room, Dr Burckhardt walking alongside the Prime Minister as we ascended a wide, curving staircase. The interior of the building was gloomy, because the windows were shuttered and the electric light bulbs which were in use were low-powered, but it was still possible to glimpse the grandeur of the famous building, from which Britain's naval operations were directed. I glanced at my wristwatch — it was eleven fifteen.

20

UK Government; Cabinet papers protected under indefinite rule (Order in Council 1941); released under EU Public Interest Directive 1997, Public Records Office (www.open.gov.uk/cab_off/pro/)

> *Minutes of Prime Ministerial meeting, commencing 11.18 a.m., Wednesday May 7, 1941, Cabinet Room, Admiralty House. Present:*

P.M. (Prime Minister, Mr Churchill)

C.O.S. (for Chiefs of Staff Committee, General Ismay)

For. Sec. (Foreign Secretary, Mr Eden)

War. Sec. (Secretary of State for War, Capt. Margesson)

Air. Prod. (Minister of Aircraft Production, Lt. Col. Moore-Brabazon)

Air Min. (Air Minister, Sir Archibald Sinclair)

Pr. Sec. Air Min. (Private Secretary to Air Minister, Grp. Capt. Sir Louis Greig)

H.M. Ambassador — Spain (Sir Samuel Hoare)

H.M. Ambassador — Portugal (Sir Ronald Campbell)

Intn'l. Red Cross (Dr Carl Burckhardt)

Br. Red Cross (Mr J. L. Sawyer)

R.S.O.F. (Religious Society of Friends [Quakers], Mr Thomas A. Benbow)

Note-taker (Self, J. Colville)

[Minutes remain in handwritten note form, as agreed by all parties. File to remain exempt from 30-year rule for Cabinet papers. File closed indefinitely by Order in Council.]

PRIME MINISTER:

[Introduction]: Welcome to all. Introductions all round. Compliments to Dr Burckhardt — P.M. is a great admirer of Red Cross. Apologies received from Count Folke Bernadotte (Swedish Red Cross), Mr Attlee (Lord Privy Seal).

C.O.S. to represent all armed forces' interests; agreed *nem con*.

[Meeting commences]: I have read your paper and commend you for it. It is an ingenious work of great historical interest. Will enter annals of magnanimous achievements. Undoubted skill and diplomacy. Great congratulations. However, it is unacceptable in theory as well as in practice. It will not hold. I will have none of it. The War Cabinet will have none of it. The Br. people will have none of it. We have no intention of making a deal with Germany.

DR BURCKHARDT:

It is not a deal with Germany, but a restitution of peace and order in Europe. Not one-sided. A separation of Britain and Germany from the state of war. Our best information is that Hitler himself is probably behind it.

H.M. Ambassador — Spain:
The former king has endorsed it.

P.M.:
The endorsement of our former king is not relevant to affairs of state. That is not to be discussed today. Where have I seen you before?

J. L. Sawyer:
I don't know.

P.M.:
Why aren't you wearing your RAF uniform?

J. L. Sawyer:
I am not a member of the armed forces. I am an unconditionally registered conscientious objector.

P.M.:
I can't talk to Hitler. He won't talk to me. We cannot pursue that line of approach. It would bring Japan into the war and keep the USA permanently out. Stalin will have none of it. The USA will have none of it. The Polish, Free French and Commonwealth powers will have none of it.

C.O.S.:
Intelligence reports from Poland confirm German troop concentrations are continuing to build up on Soviet border.

For. Sec.:
Stalin has been informed about German build-up but he is suspicious of our motives.

C.O.S.:
We can't stop Hitler if he moves eastwards. We should not even try.

P.M.:
[Sums up Br. approaches to Soviet Union on this.]

[Continues]: Hitler always said he never wanted a war on two fronts. If he is about to start something in Russia, nothing could be more to our advantage. Gentlemen, thank you again for your magnificent contribution to the cause of peace, but H.M. Gov't has no position to make to or defend against Hitler. We are at war and shall see it through. That is the final word on the matter. Good day to you all.

P.M. indicates the meeting has ended.

Dr Burckhardt:
[Appeals for further discussion.]

[Continues]: We have a genuine opportunity for peace with prospects for stability within Europe thereafter. The war could end this month. Neither side would make concessions to the other. A cease-fire and withdrawal. Britain's prewar position apropos Europe restored. Commonwealth secured. Sovereignty of France restored.

P.M.:
What about Poland? We went to war in her cause.

Dr Burckhardt:
Poland is unsolved problem for time being. The Red Cross is proposing that German withdrawal be in two phases. In the first, the occupied countries of Western Europe will be relieved. In the second, the occupied territories of Middle and Eastern Europe, including Poland, will be up for discussion. We are proposing a second round of negotiations after the first phase has been concluded successfully.

P.M.:
H.M. Gov't has nothing we wish to offer in negotiation for that or any other cause.

Dr Burckhardt:
Our preliminary contacts suggest that German Gov't see this

differently. They want a free hand in the East above all other priorities.

P.M.:
We are not interested in helping Germany have what they want.

FOR. SEC.:
Vital British interests at stake. Empire at risk in Far East. India under threat if Japan enters war. Suez Canal in jeopardy. Still only a remote possibility of involvement by U.S. Gov't in European war. There are serious and growing concerns about persecution of minorities in Germany and occupied territories. Continuation of war is inevitable.

P.M.:
We have intelligence reports concerning Hitler's intentions in Eastern Europe. This is to our total advantage. No further action is necessary. The meeting may stand down. Thanks to all present for time and attention to a matter of such importance.

P.M. again indicates the meeting has ended.

FOR. SEC.:
[Requests permission to seek information. P.M. concurs.]
       [Continues]: Could we first hear summary of German peace proposals?

P.M.:
Summary only. I do not have time for details to be minuted.

DR BURCKHARDT:
[Summarizes conditions under which negotiations took place. Describes members of negotiating teams of both sides. Describes role played by Mr Sawyer.]
       [Continues]: It is necessary to address the most important detailed proposal first. A sensitive matter, but declared non-negotiable by the German Gov't. Present speaker has the

unwelcome duty of presenting this matter frankly. They propose that the present Prime Minister of UK stand down.

P.M.:
[Summarizes his negative reaction at some length and in candid language.]
   [Continues]: What is the second most important proposal?

Dr Burckhardt:
The abdication of the present king in favour of the restoration of Edward VIII.

P.M. proposes adjournment to the meeting. All parties retire and convene in separate adjacent rooms. P.M. requests Privy Councillors to accompany him.
Meeting resumes at 11.57 a.m.

P.M.:
[Declares he has consulted attending members of Privy Council.]
[Continues]: A loyal subject of the present king. Summarizes great bravery of present king and queen in face of the Blitz. Pays tribute to their morale-raising activities during bombing. Describes immense and abiding affection held by Br. people for present king and queen. Parliament is sovereign and the present constitutional arrangement cannot be altered by P.M. Abdication of present king in favour of restoration to be non-negotiable. Constitutional hazards await. That is end of it.

For. Sec.:
Could we hear the remaining proposals from German Gov't?

Dr Burckhardt:
Immediate cessation of hostilities by both sides, including naval and air actions. Return of prisoners. Exchange of diplomats. Treaty of Versailles to be set aside. No reparations to be paid by either side. Release of currency and gold reserves. Art treasures to be restored to prewar holders.

Phased German withdrawal from Norway, Denmark, Netherlands, Belgium, Luxembourg, France, Channel Islands, Yugoslavia and Greece. Withdrawal to commence immediately. All to be completed by end of August 1941.

UK to assume responsibility for the Jewish question (to be funded by uncontested UK access to oilfields of Middle East, including but not confined to Iraq and Persia).

Germany to be given free hand in Eastern Europe. State of benevolent neutrality to exist between both countries thereafter. *[Lays documents before the meeting.]*

P.M.:

I studied your proposals in advance of today's meeting. Your deal presupposes Bolshevism to be a greater threat to Europe than Nazism and that Hitler is our best guarantor against it. UK Gov't might accept that. US Gov't would certainly accept that. Stalin would not accept it at all.

Furthermore, what responsibility for the Jews are we supposed to assume? I'm not prepared to move them all to Palestine.

Dr Burckhardt:

The Madagascar Plan is already in place.

[Outlines plan]: UK Gov't to move all European Jewry to Madagascar. Germany to assist but not to participate in or benefit by removal. No time limit to the process, but five years expected to see the process complete. UK to supervise the transfer of present Madagascan territory to independent nationhood under British Mandate, with first devolved administration before end of 1948, full independence before end of 1950.

P.M.:

What arrangements are proposed for the present Malagasy inhabitants?

Dr Burckhardt:

The island is under-populated at present. Poverty, lack of modern facilities. We propose a referendum on their wishes after 1950.

P.M.:
The Malagasy are another people who will have none of it.

FOR. SEC.:
When and where is your next meeting to take place?

DR BURCKHARDT:
Next scheduled meeting three days from now. Suggested
locations include Stavanger, Geneva, Lisbon, Stockholm and
Scotland. We prefer Lisbon or Stockholm because difficulties exist
for the other sites. Scotland ruled out as it is on combatant
territory.

FOR. SEC.:
Who suggested Scotland?

DR BURCKHARDT:
German Gov't.

P.M.:
Did Hitler want to fly to Scotland?

DR BURCKHARDT:
It was proposed by his deputy, Herr Hess.

P.M.:
I have no intention of going to Scotland, Norway or Sweden. Or
anywhere else.

DR BURCKHARDT:
[Offers sincere compliments and courtesies to P.M.]
[Continues]: The Prime Minister of UK is not invited to
the talks.

P.M.:
*[Makes forthright response at length, then requests his response not be
minuted.]*
    [Continues]: We must adjourn for consultations.

Meeting adjourns. Parties reconvene elsewhere. Privy Councillors with P.M.
Meeting resumes at 12.43 p.m.

P.M.:
An emergency meeting of the War Cabinet will be called this afternoon. If it is the wish of the War Cabinet that these exploratory
talks be pursued then I shall issue my authority for the Red Cross
to negotiate in good faith. The vital interests of the UK shall be
represented by His Excellency the British Ambassador to Spain (Sir
Samuel Hoare), accompanied by officials from the Foreign Office.
Everything ultimately dependent on the approval of Parliament.

DR BURCKHARDT:
Correction: they are not exploratory talks. Those were concluded
last month. The next talks are intended to draw up and sign the
first-phase armistice documents.

P.M.:
I knew nothing of the earlier talks and would not have acquiesced
in them if I had. The British Gov't's policy is unconditional warfare
against Germany in pursuit of military victory. I see nothing in your
negotiations to release us from that duty.

DR BURCKHARDT:
The Red Cross believes peace is not only possible but imperative.
The German wish for a cease-fire will not remain open for long.
This is an historical opportunity which should be seized by UK.

P.M.:
History is made by brave and imaginative decisions, not by tactical
surrenders. I will not accept anything from your proposal. History
this time demands we deal effectively with Hitler.

J. L. SAWYER:
On the contrary, history shows that war always defeats its own
object. No war in recorded history has produced a result that is in
accordance with the stated aims of the victor. This is because stated

aims are either disingenuous, or if sincerely meant they are undermined by the violence inherent in war.

Democracies say they fight wars with the stated intention of righting wrongs or of establishing peaceful relationships between peoples, but in reality their motives are the protection of vested interests, financial investment and the pursuit of political power. Wars are fought by tyrants ostensibly to settle a dispute or to recapture lost territory, but in practice they wish to maintain illegal control over their own people.

History also shows that whatever the apparent military outcome, violence opposed by violence always sows the seeds of future violence. It is the violence itself that distorts the result. The present war against Germany, if fought to a conclusion, might well produce the conquest of one side or the other by military means, but in the longer term the state of war will inevitably destroy many of the qualities said to be at issue.

Destruction of UK would set back the cause of enlightenment, social justice, political tolerance and liberalism by many decades. Destruction of Germany would lead to the dominance of Bolshevism throughout a large part of Europe, with the consequence that there would be greater intervention in European affairs by the USA.

Peace grasped at this moment offers the only hope for stability and harmony in the world.

DR BURCKHARDT:
[Requests that these minutes record Mr Sawyer's contribution verbatim. Note-taker records them, as above. Mr Sawyer agrees and initials the wording.] JLS.

P.M.:
[Thanks Mr Sawyer for his valuable insight.]
[Continues]: I am forced to consider the well-being of the country as a whole. H.M. Ambassador to Spain will negotiate and protect our interests. Officials will be in attendance. Only the Prime Minister may sign an armistice on behalf of the sovereign. Sir Samuel Hoare can bring it back and if appropriate I will sign it here.

P.M./DR BURCKHARDT:
[Frank, prolonged and disputatious exchange of views. With the concurrence of all present, notes of this exchange have been removed from the minutes.]

DR BURCKHARDT:
[Summary of his position]: The armistice accord is to be signed in the presence of all parties.

P.M.:
[Summary of his position]: If it is to be signed it will be signed by me in London.

DR BURCKHARDT:
I wish these minutes to record my protest, but in the interests of peace I shall endeavour to ensure that the Prime Minister's wish is observed.

P.M.:
I also reserve the right not to sign it at all.

Prime Minister leaves meeting at 1.41 p.m. Others attend briefly to details.
Meeting concludes at 1.45 p.m.

21

Document from Bibliothek für Zeitgeschichte, Stuttgart — Burckhardt Archiv (www.biblio_zeit.stuttgart.de/burckhardt)

Dr C. Burckhardt, International Red Cross Society, Geneva
May 8, 1941
(delivered by hand to Suite Boudicca, Dorchester Hotel, Park Lane, London W.)

My dear friend Carl,
   J. L. Sawyer - PRIVATE AND CONFIDENTIAL
At your personal request, and with the full cooperation of Mr

Sawyer, I have made an enquiry into Mr Sawyer's psychological outlook, which he says has been causing him great concern. You no doubt recognize that in view of the extremely short notice with which the consultation was arranged, I had no access to Mr Sawyer's medical or psychological records, nor did he come to me after a medical referral. Any examination under such conditions can only be informal. In view of my long relationship with you, both personal and professional, enjoyed for many years, I know that you will view this letter and the opinions it contains as a personal communication. I understand that Mr Sawyer approached you for help with the same problems, so I can spare you much background detail.

Our informal consultation took place at my clinic in Harley Street, London, in the morning of the above date.

Mr Sawyer presents as a prepossessing young man, with a neat and tidy appearance. He is well dressed, articulate in speech and thoughtful in demeanour. He is educated to a high level and well read. He is informed on current affairs, even those with which he has no sympathy.

His personality struck me as intriguing and complex. As a registered conscientious objector he is obviously a man of principle. I found his company interesting, but at the same time he does not have much sense of humour, he becomes irritated with minor matters and, although I was with him for too short a time to gain any firm evidence, I came to the opinion that he would be morose, obsessive and unwavering about matters on which he forms a view.

However, he is at present preoccupied with more personal concerns and it was on these that we concentrated.

Mr Sawyer is a married man and his wife is expecting their first baby. He has many anxieties about this. Firstly, he tells me that for a long time he doubted that he was the child's actual father, but he said also that in the recent past he has resolved his worries. His wife, whose pregnancy proceeded fairly normally at first, has recently shown symptoms of toxaemia, with worrying consequences. (She is apparently under regular medical supervision, so I was able to reassure him on that score.) Mr Sawyer, who I gather is about to make a trip abroad, is worried that the baby might be born while he is away. Again, I offered reassurances about modern healthcare.

Mr Sawyer is an identical twin. His brother is on active duty with the RAF, and hence is constantly in danger from enemy action. Mr Sawyer tried to explain to me that he and his brother have an extra 'bond' of affection and understanding, which can have unpredictable effects when they are separated by such events as wartime duties, family disputes, travel abroad and so on. He was not to know that I have made a special study of the psychology of identical twins, so I listened with particular interest to what he had to say. In my view, Mr Sawyer displays normal or familiar concerns about being a monozygotic twin, so once again I was able to reassure him. Complicating their difficult relationship is that Mr Sawyer and his brother fell out with each other after Mr Sawyer married. He harbours suspicions that his brother might be the real father of the unborn child. Mr Sawyer says he has evidence of this, but would not go into details. I felt I could not and should not pursue this.

Last year, Mr Sawyer suffered a serious traumatic physical event, which caused concussion together with related memory loss. Mr Sawyer says his physical recovery has been good.

Of his psychological state, though, he says that he has been suffering recurring episodes similar to the 'déjà vu' phenomenon, a form of lucid paramnesia in which he feels he is predicting events that do not in the event turn out to be true. I told Mr Sawyer that delusional incidents often occur as a result of concussion, and he accepted this. I also explained that it was common for such delusional incidents to be plausible and easily confused with real life, at least for a while.

Mr Sawyer told me that his real concern is that whenever he suffers an attack it ends with him returning abruptly to the moment the delusion began, forcing him to question whether or not it has really ended.

He also mentioned in particular that he has frequently wondered whether the life he is leading now — i.e. the work he is doing with the Red Cross, the interview he has had with me, and so on — is also one long delusion from which he will suddenly awaken, instantly invalidating everything he is now experiencing.

I assured him that it was not and suggested that my writing this letter for him to give to you would be further evidence that it was not, but of course from his point of view it settles nothing in what might be described as his proto-delusional state.

Mr Sawyer seems to be coping well with the condition and tells me that it is a lot better. He believes he has it under control. I can assure you and him that he does not appear to be suffering any deep-rooted psychosis, that he can function well in the normal world and that with time the problem should go away altogether. My only concern would be if, in the short term, Mr Sawyer were to undergo some other kind of shock — of a physical nature, or a psychological one, perhaps related to his expected child or the well-being of his twin brother — then he might suffer a setback in this regard.

> *Yours very sincerely,*
> *Frank*
> *[Franklin K. Clark MSc; Clinical Psychologist]*

22

Holograph notebooks of J. L. Sawyer

xxii

Our plane flew low over the rooftops of Stockholm, a grey-and-silver city whose outlines were delineated by sparkling channels of sunlit water. We landed on the lake called Stora Värten, to the north-east of the centre of the city, in a great plume of white spray that splashed against the cabin portholes like a cascade of pebbles. The flying-boat swooped sharply down and up while we still travelled at speed on the surface of the water, but when the pilot held down the aircraft's nose the noise briefly increased as the plane was slowed by the friction of the water. My own seat was fairly close to the front of the cabin, looking out through the porthole beneath the starboard wing.

The forward part of the cabin was curtained off not far in front of my seat. Once again, we in the rear part of the aircraft had to wait while the dignitaries at the front disembarked. This time it was not as straightforward a matter as it had been on land. I watched as a motor-boat came out from the shore and tied up beneath the wing. The Duke of Kent and his entourage boarded the boat in my full view, but by this time the secrecy surrounding the Duke's presence was a formality for most of us on the aircraft.

By the time the rest of us had disembarked and been taken at high speed to the centre of the city, it was getting dark. Most of the delegates stayed in a large hotel in the city. In the morning we were driven out into the country-side, to a beautiful mansion set in a secluded position, surrounded by forest and overlooking a wide lake. As before, I was assigned to the document team, a job I relished. The important difference on this occasion was that I was placed in overall charge of the team, something I thought a great honour.

However, it was soon apparent that it was not to be a rerun of the earlier meeting.

Deputy Führer Rudolf Hess was expected to arrive in Stockholm during the night, but clearly something had gone wrong while he was en route. He did not appear at the first session, which naturally enough meant the talks were not able to start.

While we were settling down in the palatial rooms of the mansion, his absence noted by all, rumours began to spread. At first they were sensational stories: Hess had been sidelined by Goering, Hess's plane had been shot down, Hitler had ordered Hess not to attend, and so on. From Count Bernadotte's team of assistants — it turned out that the estate belonged to the count, although he was not present in person — we learned that none of the rumours was true and that the talks were merely delayed for a few hours for unavoidable reasons.

With no facts we could rely on, all we could do was wait until the position became clearer. Dr Burckhardt, who obviously knew no more than any of us, counselled patience. We remained in a state of suspension through the morning, took an early lunch, then returned to our various places.

Midway through the afternoon, without prior warning, three black Daimler limousines approached the house at some speed. Attracted by the sound and the movement, several members of our translation team moved to the window to see what was happening. Hess was travelling in the first car. As soon as it halted he climbed down, briefly scanned the façade of the house then strode into the building.

xxiii

Within fifteen minutes of Hess's arrival a plenary session of the conference was called. All the various auxiliaries, like myself, were allowed into the main negotiating hall, the first time I had seen inside. It was set out so that the main tables formed a large equilateral triangle: the British representatives were placed on one side, the Germans on another and the representatives of the neutral governments, the Red Cross and the Quaker negotiators were seated along the third. A huge spray of flowers had been placed in the floor space between the tables.

As we assembled, the auxiliary workers being requested to sit in three rows of chairs placed behind the Red Cross, it was noticeable that all the seats at the German table were occupied but for the one in the centre.

We settled into silence, an air of great expectancy hovering in the room.

After we had waited about a minute, Rudolf Hess appeared from a side door and walked briskly into the hall, his face a mask of impassivity, looking to neither side. He was dressed in the uniform of a Luftwaffe officer. We rose to our feet. Hess, taking up his central place at the German table, nodded imperiously and we resumed our seats.

Speaking without the aid of notes, Hess then addressed the delegates.

'[My good gentlemen, I apologize for my late appearance at this most important meeting,]' he began. '[I fully intended to be here on time and, as our hosts in such a splendid house already know, we representatives from the Reich had already requested that our negotiations should adhere to a strict timetable. My lateness has ruined those plans. I regret if this fact has made it seem, even temporarily, that the German government has lost its enthusiasm for peace with honour to both sides. I can assure you that is not so.

'[I was, however, delayed in a way that everyone here, when they learn the facts, will agree was unavoidable. Yesterday evening, while I was flying to this country, as dark was falling over the sea, the plane, which I was piloting myself, was attacked by an unknown number of fighter aircraft. Although I did manage to escape unharmed, as you can see, it was not without serious damage to my aircraft. I regret to say that my fellow crewman, Hauptmann Alfred Horn, was killed during the incident. The plane was also damaged to such an extent that I was forced to make an unscheduled landing in Denmark. I have reached here today by other means.

'[It was not possible for me to identify the nationality of my attackers' aircraft. They came at me suddenly and from behind and broke off to the side when they thought they had mortally damaged my plane. However, certain suspicions do arise. It could have been that the fighter aircraft were British, patrolling above the sea in search of aircraft like mine. There were in fact

British incursions against Germany last night, so bombers were in the vicinity. But British fighters do not normally patrol so far out to sea, unless in this case there was a special reason. Could it be that subversive elements within the British cadres somehow knew that I was planning to be flying last night and that being in opposition to peace they sent out the fighters to ambush me? If so, it would mean there was a breach of security and confidentiality concerning my plans, which could place our talks in jeopardy.]'

Here the Deputy Führer paused, folding his arms across his chest with a theatrical gesture. He deliberately stared around the room, looking slowly at all of us who were there. It was a dreadful moment, because the man's anger was plain to see. His deep-set eyes beneath the distinctive bushy eyebrows gave out a challenge to everyone. His gaze lingered on the British contingent. Of course, no one acknowledged that they knew of the ambush, because it was inconceivable that anyone there would wish to sabotage the talks.

'[The other possibility,]' Hess continued, '[would be that the aircraft were sent by a dissident faction from my own side. Under normal circumstances that would constitute high treason. In comparison with it, an attack by the RAF would seem a relatively minor matter, an intelligible act of war. At this moment, though, circumstances within Germany are far from normal. Everyone here today knows that. We all face problems of acceptance of these plans within our caucuses at home. Let us not pretend otherwise. In such a way, and if it is behind what happened to me last night, I am inclined to treat it as a minor matter.

'[I can assure you once again that I am here with the full authority and agreement of the Leader and that he and I are determined to forge peace with our present enemies, the British. The events of last night have only concentrated my mind more closely on the need for a rapid agreement. I emphasize that the German government does not urge peace from a position of weakness. We seek peace with honour for both sides, based on parity.

'[I therefore announce unilaterally that I and my negotiators are prepared to reach final agreement in the swiftest way possible, and that the many small problems that arose as we tried earlier to frame our armistice will be treated, at least by us, as minor or insignificant. At the worst we can adjourn areas of small disagreement until a later meeting, in the spirit of reaching a concord about the main issue between us.]'

Hess sat down suddenly. After a moment or two of silence, several members of the neutral representatives uttered growls of agreement and approval. One or two of the British rapped their knuckles on the table. It was a half-hearted response, one that evidently did not please the Deputy Führer. He scowled around for a moment, then looked to his own entourage. They stood up hastily, raised their arms high and began clapping loudly. At this, Hess once again rose to his feet and applause broke out all round the hall. It sounded to me polite rather than enthusiastic, but Hess seemed satisfied with it.

We returned to the document room, to find that while we had been in the plenary session Hess's aides had delivered pre-prepared draft documents for translation and incorporation into the texts from the earlier meeting. I took charge, swiftly allocating tasks to the team, making sure that the non-executive observers from the Red Cross and the Quakers had full access to each worker. I settled down to work on the section of the wording I set aside for myself. The room was soon filled with the purposeful sounds of typewriters. Smoke rose from cigarettes; jackets came off.

Not long afterwards, the familiar sequence of negotiating procedures began to unfold: completed texts were checked, proofread, identified as to context, copied. Once I had approved the translation or précis, it was taken through to the teams of secondary negotiators for their consideration and revision. In the meantime, more texts were being drafted in conference, and they in turn were brought to the document room for our minor revisions and editorial insertions.

Gradually we saw the revamped armistice document taking shape, an absorbing and satisfying process.

What soon became noticeable was the amount of energy emanating from the German side of the room. It had not been like that in Cascais: the German proposals and responses then were full of feints and diversions, a series of attempts to achieve small advantages over the other side. Now it was different: it was the British who were on the defensive, objecting, compromising, quibbling, trying to nullify offers with counter-proposals.

Although I was technically a neutral in the negotiations, I was of course British-born and had spent nearly the whole war inside Britain. I was used to the subtle British propaganda put out by the various government ministries. It routinely portrayed the Germans as the sole aggressors, the wrongdoers, the invaders, the killers of innocents, and much else besides. Truth resides somewhere deep inside propaganda, but in a war neither side has a monopoly on it. In Stockholm I began to understand the Germans' position: many of the British responses were inflexible, stubborn, pettifogging, often contradictory and tinged with a moralistic tone.

At ten in the evening Dr Burckhardt sent word to our team that we should stand down for the night. The main conference was being adjourned for twelve hours. As we raised our heads, we realized that we had been working without a break more or less since the end of Hess's speech. I was not only exhausted, I was famished too. I knew everyone else must be the same, so we broke off from our tasks with relief, leaving unfinished whatever we were doing. It was not long before we were being driven back to the hotel in Stockholm, where a late supper was waiting for us.

In the morning, refreshed a little, we returned to Count Bernadotte's country house.

xxiv

The page on which I had been working the evening before was still in the roller of the typewriter. I sat down, loosened my tie and took off my jacket. Someone opened the window shutters to let in the morning sunlight. I read through the last few lines of the translation, thinking myself back into what I needed to do. I had been working on a position paper drawn up by the British negotiators, who were concerned with the German idea of parity. It was seen by both sides as central to the peace accord.

Hess, the day before, had used the German word *Gleichheit*, which in English translated as 'parity' with the meaning of 'equality of interest.' To the British team, equality of interest was neither quite what they wanted it to mean nor what they thought (or hoped) Hess had meant to convey. They preferred to substitute 'equality of rights' (*Parität*), or 'equality of status' (*gleiche Stellung*), phrases loaded with significance when it was remembered that Churchill insisted on signing the armistice himself. It was obvious he would have nothing to do with a deal which implied that the British were losing the war and had sued for peace, which might be the interpretation if the only equality that was admitted with Germany was one of vested interests. I had been trying to decide what to do about the problem — was it a question of interests, rights or status? — when we closed down for the night.

I stared at the sentence, trying to concentrate.

I was still sleepy, a condition that ever since my episodes of lucid imaginings made me apprehensive. I was somewhat reassured by my hurried consultation with the psychologist, Mr Clark, who seemed to think the problem was at an end, but to me nothing was certain. Most of those episodes had occurred when I was sleeping or sleepy. I was concerned that I had hardly slept during the night and that I had started the morning feeling unrested.

I found myself thinking about the different meanings of 'parity,' in English as well as in German.

It was a concept I grew up with: parity in all things is a concern of identical twins, often in a contradictory way. We wanted to be equal in the eyes of our parents but to be favoured by them, to become individuals with independent lives while remaining twins, to develop separately while retaining a special bond.

Perhaps this was what Hess was trying to suggest: introductory material to the draft agreement spoke sentimentally of a tradition of brotherhood between Britain and Germany, twin countries, forever joined, forever separate, benevolent neutrals. The Germans described what they saw as common cultural purpose, innate likeness between the two peoples, a shared sense of civilized responsibility. Fine words, so long as you did not consider the war. That was what they sought: to remove the war, to strengthen the natural bond.

Was it a coincidental clue about me and my brother Jack?

Through over-concentration I was becoming blind to the subtleties of meaning that existed between the various translations, so I called over one of the constitutional lawyers and asked his advice. One of the Quaker advisers who was from Germany sat with us while we discussed it. Semantic nuances were a concern of us all. Our work with the documents took place in a situation where diplomacy, language and national interests intersected. The lawyer considered for a moment, then said he thought that *gleiche Stellung*, parity of status, would be the correct way to express the concept. The German Quaker agreed. We consulted an official from the German embassy in Stockholm, a member of the document group, and he also thought that was right. Gradually we crept to agreement. It went into the next version of the draft, submitted to our principals in the main conference hall.

Not wanting to work everyone to exhaustion again, I used my discretion as leader of the team and called a thirty-minute break in the middle of the morning. Several of us walked downstairs and out into the grounds, admiring the cold peacefulness of the pine forest and the large, calm lake. Birds flew noisily and freely in the neutral air. I remembered many of the other document workers from the days in Cascais; our mood was different here. In Portugal there had been the exhilaration of possibilities — an armistice was an enthralling prospect. Now that peace was in sight we simply wanted to

conclude the process and the work was more of a grind. Most of the transla-
tors drifted back to their desks long before the end of the break period.

We had resumed work when I was summoned to Dr Burckhardt's office,
a small room next to the main conference chamber.

'[It has been agreed by the principals that the talks will end by 6 p.m.
today,]' he said brusquely. '[There will not be an extension beyond that time.
Anything that has not been settled by then will have to remain unsettled. Do
you think you and your team can complete all documents?]'

'[Yes, sir, if we have the texts to work with. There have been no obstacles
so far. Everything seems to be working smoothly.]'

'[Good. No one is expecting any real problems at this late stage, but you
never know.]'

He said nothing about the reason for the decision, so I assumed it had
been adopted as an artificial but agreed deadline, to make sure that the negotiations would not drag on for ever.

We therefore entered the last and hardest period of translating and edit-
ing, reacting to the increased amount of discussion that was taking place
between the principals. We did not stop for lunch but were provided with a
cold buffet from which we took what we needed. There was a burst of extra
activity soon afterwards, but then the pressure began to ease. By mid-afternoon I was able to delegate the actual drafting work that I would have done
myself and by four o'clock at least half the team had no more work piled up
on their desks. Half an hour later, the last document was sent through to the
principal negotiators and their advisers.

Everyone in the document team had seen sections of the draft armistice,
sometimes many times over. A few of us had been able to see the whole thing.
I knew to my own satisfaction that it was as nearly complete as it was possible to be. It was an intriguing, complex document, almost shocking in the way
it confronted what a few weeks before would have been unthinkable. For all
the complexity of the ideas and principles the armistice addressed, and the
difficulties we had sometimes found in writing them down, we finished the
work an hour and a half before the deadline.

In the period of calm that followed, an unreal sense of euphoria mixed
with apprehension settled on me. The impossible seemed to be about to happen: the war would end. At the same time, the thought of the armistice going
wrong at the last minute was terrible, with the USA, the Soviet Union and
Japan being drawn into a global conflagration.

All international treaties are as significant for what they don't say as for what they do. Every page I had worked on was heavy with unstated fears about a wider war.

I was pacing about on the lawn beneath our window, feeling chilled by the easterly wind but needing a few minutes of solitude, when I was approached by a man I recognized as one of Dr Burckhardt's staff.

'[Mr Sawyer, if you would be so kind. Your presence is requested.]'

The formal courtesy of the man's words and manner indicated the call was something special. On the way back into the house I grabbed my jacket from my desk and quickly combed my hair. At that moment I had no idea what to expect, but assumed it must be connected with the document work.

Dr Burckhardt was waiting in his office and as soon as I appeared he stood up. We shook hands.

'[Mr Sawyer, I am as grateful as ever for your contribution to the agreement. Like everyone else here, you will see shortly the fruits of everyone's efforts, against which my own thanks will be nothing. In the meantime, though, I have received an unusual request. I wonder if you would be good enough to speak privately to Herr Hess?]'

'[In some kind of official capacity, Dr Burckhardt? On behalf of the Red Cross?]'

'[He has asked for you by name and requested that no note-taker or interpreter should be present.]'

'[But what is it about?]'

'[I don't know, Mr Sawyer.]'

He indicated that I should follow him. We walked along a short corridor that led away from his office. At the end was a wide hall that opened at the bottom of a grand staircase and beyond it was a double door, decorated with gilt inlays and rococo decals.

xxv

Dr Burckhardt closed the doors behind me as I went through. I was immediately aware of the vast size of the room — a long lounge, with several clusters of easy chairs and settees arranged around low tables — but had no time to take in the rest. Rudolf Hess was standing by himself a short distance from the door, waiting for me. His hands were clasped behind his back and his broad figure was silhouetted against the daylight from the large window behind him.

'[Good afternoon, Mr Sawyer,]' he said at once, in his curiously tenor voice.

'[Good afternoon, Herr Deputy Führer.]'

He shook my hand in an odd way, vigorously but with his fingers gripping weakly, then led me through the room to where two large armchairs faced each other across a wide table. A tall, glass-fronted bookcase, stacked neatly with uniformly bound editions, loomed over us. A jug of coffee had been placed on the table, together with a selection of cakes. Neither of us sat down but stood self-consciously near the window. Because it was on the other side of the building from where we had been working, the room faced across a part of the estate I had not seen before: a short distance away from the main house was a long row of single-storey buildings, stables perhaps, which fronted a paved yard. Many large cars were parked there.

'[We have much to celebrate, do we not?]' said Hess.

'[Yes . . . it is a great achievement.]'

'[And with time left over. We hoped to be finished by six, but we find we have slightly more than an hour to spare. I have seized the chance to speak to you alone. We have a great deal to look forward to. At last the way is paved for change in the world. England and Germany will be friends once more. An important alliance with consequences that will be felt around the world, the foundation of a new Europe.]'

'[Yes, sir.]'

I glanced around the room, feeling nervous of the man. As Dr Burckhardt had said, there were no aides present and the long room was empty.

'[The last time we spoke together you were not certain we had met before. I assume that you do remember our conversation at the Mouth of Hell?]'

'[Of course, sir.]'

'[You said you were unsure of your neutral status. An Englishman who competed as a sportsman for his country, yet one who claimed to be a neutral in all other things. An interesting position. Let us enjoy coffee and cakes.]'

Hess indicated the refreshments on the table, but I was suddenly gripped with fear of the man. Two rooms away from us, no doubt under close guard by several groups, there existed an immense document of several dozen pages, written in the two main languages of English and German, with summaries prepared in French and Swedish, which ordained that peace had been forged between Hess's country and mine. But it was as yet unratified, unsigned by

either government. Until then, this man was a prominent member of the
regime that was enemy to the country where I had been born. The conflict he
detected in me, that of nationality against neutrality, was largely the result of
Germany's aggressive actions against other countries. He spoke of restoring
friendship between our two countries, yet throughout my life Germany had
been synonymous with threats to peace, persecution of its own people and
military invasions of other countries. I was neutral not because of uncertain
loyalties between countries, but because I loathed war.

Hess bent over the table, pouring himself a black coffee and selecting for
himself two small cakes covered with a thick layer of dark chocolate. I had
not seen such delicacies for nearly two years, because of the rigorous food
rationing at home. Hess popped one of the cakes, whole, into his mouth,
scattering crumbs as he worked it around.

'[So how do you feel, my friend Sawyer, now that we have peace at last?]'
Hess said, chewing on the cake. Dark crumbs were sticking to his protruding
teeth.

'[I am relieved, of course. I suppose it is what I have been hoping and
working for.]'

'[To you English, peace will mean the end of fighting. No doubt you will
be thankful for that. But for Germany it will be different. The peace will
bring the dawning of a new age. Much will change. You must come to
Germany and see what I mean.]'

'[Thank you, sir. I should like to do that, at some time in the future.]'

'[No, I do not mean to make polite conversation. I have a purpose in
wanting to meet you. I have spoken to Dr Burckhardt and he speaks highly
of you, as well he should. I can see with my own eyes that you are a fine young
man. I would wish to explain to you in detail what is about to happen within Germany, but for the time being I cannot. All I can say is that after today,
once our peace has been signed, many changes will take place. They will occur
at the highest levels of our country. Do I make myself clear to you?]'

'[I'm sure you're right, Herr Hess, but my place is in England —]'

'[At the highest levels, you must understand. Within one week from now
— I can say no more than I already have. Events will have to take their
course. There is likely to be a period of upheaval in Berlin, and for the sake
of continuity I shall need around me trusted people whose grasp on
Germany's international role is beyond question. The appointment I am suggesting would be an administrative one, technically as a junior diplomatic
officer attached to the civil service, but it would in reality have wide-ranging

executive powers. The title would be Group Leader of Schooling and Morality. *Schule und Moral* is the department I have myself been administering in Berlin for several years and through its networks to the regions I have been able to keep control of all intelligence matters. The position I created will soon be vacant. We would work in close personal propinquity, you and I. The office is a pleasant one, situated in Unter den Linden, on the corner of Neue Wilhelmstrasse. In fact it is immediately opposite the building that was until recently the British Embassy. I dare say that the embassy will soon resume its former function, a proximity I expect you will find not only amusing but useful, as I have done in the past.]'

I could only stare uncomprehendingly at him. He put the second cake in his mouth, worked it around, then slurped at his coffee to wash some of it down.

'[So what do you say, Mr Sawyer?]'

'[Are you offering me a job in Berlin, Herr Hess?]'

'[I could give the job to any one of a thousand, ten thousand, young people in Germany and each of them would be loyal to the great cause. But I am looking ahead to the days when the cease-fire will have taken permanent effect. Not long from now Britain and Germany will be instrumental in building a strong Europe, a coming together of the two dominant nations of the modern age. Imagine a joining of the cultures that between them have given the world Goethe and Shakespeare, Wagner and Gershwin. The challenges ahead will require the best young people from both countries to take up positions in the capital cities of their former enemies. I simply suggest that you might like to be among the first. What do you say?]'

If he had asked me what I thought, rather than what I was going to say, I could have told him the answer was no, then and there. But thinking and saying were not at all the same.

I found his company intimidating, intrusive and coarse, making me dissemble. All through these high-flown ideas he was chewing and swallowing the sticky cake, using a fingernail to dislodge the crumbs from between his front teeth. He also had a disconcerting habit of approaching and standing too close when he spoke. I could smell his breath and a scent of some kind of oil he used on his hair. He was not wearing the Luftwaffe uniform on this day, but was in dark-grey trousers and a beige shirt, with a tie clipped neatly to the front. He had a way of turning his head slightly to one side, then rolling his eyes back to gaze at me, which each time briefly gave him a frantic, somewhat deranged appearance.

'[I think I really need time to consider, Herr Hess.]'

'[Yes, indeed. I expected you to say that. What exactly do you need to think about and for how long?]'

'[I love working for the Red Cross and I have not given a thought to leaving.]'

'[All that sort of work will of course end when the war finishes. In the new Europe we will have no need of the Red Cross. One month from now you will be without a job. That must surely decide the matter for you.]'

'[There would be other considerations, too.]'

'[Name them.]'

'[Well, for one thing, sir, I am married. My wife is expecting our first baby —]'

'[She may come to Berlin too. Bring the child. There is no problem with that.]'

If until that moment a tiny particle of me might have been tempted, I knew that what he was proposing was out of the question. With the Nazi regime still in power, no matter what the 'changes' would turn out to be, Birgit would never return to Berlin. It crossed my mind to wonder if Hess might, perhaps, know something about Birgit's background. After all, he claimed to have kept control of what he described as intelligence. It was a disquieting thought to have in the company of this powerful man.

Hess took a third cake, a rectangular piece of yellow sponge, coated with what looked like marzipan. He bit it in half, apparently disliked the taste and threw the second piece aside. It landed on the floor, close to the base of the large bookcase. He looked around for somewhere to dispose of the piece he already had in his mouth but finally spat it out on the carpet. He drained his coffee, swirling it noisily around his teeth, then refilled his cup.

'[Whatever your objections,]' Hess went on, '[you will come to Berlin shortly. All things will be possible soon. You need not decide until then. But let me tell you I have made up my mind. I think you are greatly suited to work with me.]'

'[Thank you, Herr Deputy Führer.]'

I was hoping that would signal the end of the meeting, but Hess suddenly turned away from me and returned to the large window overlooking the stables.

'[Ah!]' he said expressively. '[We have important company. So soon. They were not due to arrive for another hour or so. Your Royal Air Force is reliable in some matters, I think.]'

I too looked through the window and in a moment saw what Hess was talking about. A short height above the pine forest, about half a mile away towards the west, a four-engined flying-boat, painted white all over, was passing right to left from our point of view. It was so low that for much of the time it was out of sight behind some of the hills in the near distance.

'[I can't see any markings,]' I said. '[Why do you say it is the RAF?]'

'[We should go down to the lake to be a welcoming party!]' Hess said abruptly. '[I shall be there too, in good time, but I was not expecting the arrival so soon.]'

He indicated that I should leave the room. I opened the door and held it for him. He stepped through, leaving a hazy smell of body odour and hair-oil in his wake. There was no one else in the hall. Hess turned back to me and shook my hand again, with the same finger limpness as before.

'[You must be there when the plane disembarks its passengers,]' he said. '[I think you will find that on board there is a great surprise for you, Mr Sawyer!]'

He raised one hand, then hurried up the wide staircase, taking the steps two at a time.

Thinking that I should immediately report what Hess had been saying to me, I went quickly to Dr Burckhardt's office and knocked on his door. When there was no answer I eased the door open and peered inside — the room was empty.

I went back to the wide hall, remembering that on the far side, beyond the staircase, there were doors leading to the outside. I hurried through, coming out at the top of a double flight of stone steps that descended to the perfectly laid driveway circling round in front of them.

Before me was an astonishing sight. Most of the people I had been working with in the house, plus many others, were hurrying down the sloping ground in the direction of the lake. Nearly all of them were on foot, scurrying across the grass towards the wooden landing stage that stretched out into the lake. Clearly the plane had turned up before it was expected. Two black limousines were driving along one of the parkways, vanishing in and out of the trees as they too made towards the wooden pier. The white plane was in view now, the sound of its engines droning across the silent forests. The aircraft was heading away from us but flying low alongside the huge lake that was part of the mansion's estate.

I walked quickly down the steps and began to cross the long sloping lawn towards the lake. In the far distance, the white aircraft was starting to turn, heading back to us.

As I watched it, I was stricken with a thought that almost paralysed me. I came to a halt, feeling completely isolated.

I had been fighting off a feeling of unreality all day, assuming that over-work and the late night were taking their toll. I had lost a great deal of sleep in the weeks leading up to the conference. There was anyway a sense of the fantastic about the whole day's proceedings: the rapid progress towards completing the treaty, the huge house and its isolated grounds, the interview with Rudolf Hess. And on top of it all there was something Hess had said: his unusual emphasis on the RAF, his prediction that there was a surprise for me on board the plane.

I believed I knew what that surprise might be. I dreaded that I would be right.

Almost all my episodes of lucid imaginings directly or indirectly involved my brother and led to a confrontation, which in turn led to an abrupt return to my real life. I was certain as I stood there in the cool northern sunlight, watching the white plane skimming low above the tops of the trees, that when the aircraft landed I would discover that the pilot was my brother.

I glanced around at the placid Swedish scenery, the forest, the lake, the grand house, the scattered group of my colleagues hurrying down to greet the aircraft. How could I be imagining anything so subtle, complex, apparently unpredictable? Should I let the hallucination continue around me, or should I back away from it? Once before, ultimately to my regret, I had decided to let it run, but also, in the past, I had foreshortened the experience when I realized what it was. Both events had traumatizing effects on me.

Two of the Quaker negotiators from the document team had left the house behind me. Now they passed me on their way down the long lawn.

'[Mr Sawyer, are you not happy to be at the lake?]'

'[Yes, I am going there now,]' I said, forced to push my despair into the background.

I fell into step beside them. I knew neither of them well, although I had worked with them both in Cascais and here. Their names were Martin Zane and Michael Brennan, former construction workers from Pittsburgh who had moved to Britain at the outbreak of war. Until they became involved with the Red Cross peace moves they were working in London with the air-raid rescue squads. They had both undertaken crash courses in German at the beginning of the year so that they could work with Dr Burckhardt, but the language was still difficult for them. It would have been easier if we spoke in English while we were together, but the German-only rule was invariable. As a result, we said little to one another as we walked down to the lake.

We could see the flying-boat in the last moments of its landing manoeuvre, gliding towards us low above the trees then dipping its nose towards the still waters of the lake. It looked to me as if it was flying slowly, but as soon as the hydrodynamic underside of the aircraft touched the water an immense spray shot up on either side, to be thrown back by the propellers in long cylindrical vortices. After much bouncing and splashing the aircraft finally slowed until it was able to sail like a cumbersome boat.

I could see the two pilots, unidentifiable in their helmets, peering forward from their seats across the nose of the aircraft so as to guide it accurately. The plane, engines roaring, jinked from left to right as it manoeuvred closer to the long jetty. Two men on the side of the pier were standing by with boat-hooks, but they weren't needed. The captain expertly brought the plane to a halt so that its hatch was against the end of the landing stage, the starboard wing shading the wooden walkway like a canopy. The hatch opened smartly from within. Two ropes were thrown out and the men quickly secured the fuselage.

As the engines fell silent and the propellers ceased we pressed forward for a better look at whoever the passengers might be. From the roof of the fuselage, immediately behind the cockpit, a tiny flagpole was pushed up, with the Union Jack fluttering. There was a delay while steps down from the aircraft were pushed into place and secured on the none too steady pier. While this was going on I heard the sound of a motor-car engine: an open-top Daimler drove quickly along the lakeside parkway and halted in a scattering of gravel close to the end of the pier. Rudolf Hess stepped out, resplendent in his Luftwaffe uniform, the Iron Cross at his throat glinting in the thin evening sunlight.

Two men from his entourage, dressed in black SS uniforms, flanked him.

Both pilots of the flying-boat had removed their helmets. They too were leaning towards the canopy on the landward side of the cockpit, so that they could watch the arrival of their passengers. I could clearly see both their faces. Neither of the pilots was my brother Jack.

A few moments later, preceded by a senior staff officer from each of the three armed forces and followed by a group of civilians, Winston Churchill stepped down on to the pier. He walked slowly along it, looking to neither right nor left, until he was met by the Duke of Kent. Churchill removed his hat, bowed deeply to the Duke and they chatted privately for a few seconds.

xxvi

Rudolf Hess and Winston Churchill sat side by side in the conference room. They both stared straight ahead at the photographers, neither of them acknowledging the presence of the other. The table where they were sitting was the one that had earlier been occupied by the negotiators from the Red Cross and the neutral states. The other two tables had been removed, but the spray of flowers remained. Both men were sitting with bound copies of the treaty in front of them, open at the first page of protocols. They looked as if they were about to sign the treaty, holding brand-new fountain pens, supplied for the occasion by the Red Cross.

The two photographers leaned towards them — flashes dazzled everyone in the room. The photographers moved back to the side table with their equipment, ejected the burnt-out bulbs and squeezed in new ones. They returned to the table where Hess and Churchill were waiting. They took similar shots, but this time from different positions. After the bulbs had been replaced again the negotiators and the auxiliaries posed in a group behind Hess and Churchill, while more photographs were taken. I, being tall, stood in the back row, towards the left end, between Martin Zane and Michael Brennan, about seven places away from Dr Burckhardt. The picture shows that I am smiling, like everyone else in the photograph; everyone, that is, apart from Churchill and Hess. The flashlight has bounced off Churchill's spectacles, concealing his eyes behind two disks of reflected light.

When the cameramen left, we remained standing behind the two statesmen to act as official observers of the signing of the Treaty of Stockholm. Churchill first signed the version drafted in German; Hess signed the English version. After the signatures had been dried with blotting-paper rollers, the two versions of the treaty were exchanged and each statesman signed the copy that was in his own language.

Hess laid his pen on the table. Churchill twisted the cap on his own pen, then carefully placed it inside the breast pocket of his jacket and patted it with his fingers.

Both men continued to sit side by side, staring straight ahead. A Red Cross man went over to the table and turned the two versions of the treaty round, opening them at the witness page. One by one the rest of us moved forward, standing briefly in front of the two statesmen to lean over the bound copies and attest to the signing. I wrote my name at the end of the list, added my signature and wrote in the date: May 12, 1941. I was trembling as I did so, almost overcome with the emotion brought on by the immense importance of the occasion.

As the last witness signature was added, Dr Burckhardt indicated to the two statesmen that the ceremony was completed. Both stood. Hess was at least six inches taller than Churchill.

He turned to Churchill, clicked his heels together at attention, extended his hand, and said, '[Prime Minister Churchill, it is the greatest of honours to sign such an historical treaty with you. Let us pray that we are living in the first moment in a new destiny for our great European nations!]'

Churchill said nothing and kept his hand resolutely tucked into the flap of his waistcoat. I happened to be standing a short distance away from him. Realizing that he spoke no German — or was affecting not to — I said, 'Sir, would you wish me to interpret for you?'

'If you would be so kind,' Churchill replied, not looking away from Hess. I translated what Hess had said.

Churchill replied at once.

'Herr Hess,' he said, 'let us pray instead that our accord has more substance to it than the one you have made with Russia.'

'[What is it you say?]'

'He claims not to understand, sir,' I said to Churchill. 'Should I interpret for him too?'

'I happen to know that the Deputy Führer speaks English perfectly well.'

'The Third Reich is seeking peace in good faith,' Hess said, contriving to look genuinely surprised and confused.

'I know your game, Herr Deputy Führer. In a few weeks, when you have shifted your aggression to the east, everyone in the world will also know what you are up to.'

'There is no need for that!' Hess shouted, in English.

'There is a need for an end to the war between us and that is what we have each obtained. What you decide to do next is a matter for you. I may add that after this hour, should one stick or stone of yours fall anywhere upon Britain, or upon our Commonwealth, or upon any of our allies liberated by the armistice, we will turn back on you with a simple fury that will never be surpassed.' Churchill turned on his heel with a sprightly movement and spoke in an entirely different manner to Dr Burckhardt. 'Thank you for what you have done, sir. I'm sure I can speak for the Duke when I say how much we are looking forward to dinner with you.'

They moved towards the exit, leaving Hess behind them. The peace was sealed, but not with a handshake.

xxvii

Dinner was served in the banqueting hall of the mansion, with everyone who was involved in the negotiations seated along the sides of one immense table that ran the entire length of the room. By contrast with the relaxed mood of the two previous days, Churchill's arrival appeared to have split the conference into its three constituent groups. He had succeeded in creating a frosty, almost hostile atmosphere between the two main groups when all delegates had mixed convivially with everyone else until his arrival. He and the Duke of Kent, together with the ambassadors, the chiefs of staff and the secretaries from the Foreign Office, sat at one end. Hess and his similarly sized retinue were at the other. The representatives from the neutral states, the auxiliary negotiators and the document team occupied the middle ground.

Churchill was sitting on the opposite side of the table to me, about fifteen seats away. In spite of everything I still felt about his warlike nature I was dazzled by his presence. Although I had been closely involved with the preparations for the treaty, I suppose that I had never really believed Churchill would bring himself to sign it. Yet here we were with the process complete. Even as we were dining, the teams of constitutional lawyers from Germany and Britain were elsewhere in the building, engrossing the text, making it ready for release to the public record. Churchill appeared to be deep in conversation with the Duke, but I could not help noticing that from time to time he gave me a direct and unblinking stare, which I found disconcerting.

Hess and his group left without warning in the middle of the meal. During the first two courses he and his officials were deep in conversation, conducted with much intensity. They did not wait to finish their venison course. Without a word to anyone else at the table they suddenly rose to their feet, scraping back their chairs. They strode quickly to the exit.

At the door, Hess turned back, stamped his feet together and raised his right arm in the Nazi salute. The room fell silent. Hess held the pose for a moment.

'*Heil Hitler!*' he shouted and marched out of the room.

Churchill said into the silence, 'Good Lord.'

He turned back to the Duke and continued his affable conversation as before. The mood in the room lightened noticeably.

Now that our negotiations were complete I was starting to think anxiously about returning home. I could not see what more work I would be called on to do for the Red Cross, but the inescapable fact was that I could not return to England on my own. I tried to find out from some of the people I was sitting close to what the arrangements for flying home were going to be, but everyone else was in the dark too.

At the end of the dinner, Winston Churchill rose to his feet and made a brief speech. For me, it was a moment of high anticipation, the thought of being present when he might have something to say of historic significance. As soon as he began speaking, though, it was clear that he saw this as no opportunity for high oratory. In plain language he merely congratulated us on our work and said that despite the apparent bad faith of the Nazi leadership he believed the treaty would hold and that the peace would be genuine and lasting. He also explained that he was obliged to return to London as soon as possible. After his few words he sat down to warm applause. Somehow, imperceptibly, he had turned the meeting round: it was no longer an international forum for peace, but was now a Churchill occasion.

Not long after, we began to collect our personal property together as cars arrived to take us back to our hotel in Stockholm. When I passed through the main conference room for the last time, I saw Winston Churchill there. He broke off his conversation and came across to me, his cigar smoke trailing behind him. He was cradling a brandy balloon, with a generous quantity of the liquor swilling around inside.

'I remember you from our meeting at Admiralty House last week,' he said, without preamble. 'Your name is J. L. Sawyer, is it not?'

'Yes, sir.'

'Let me ask you a question, Mr Sawyer. Your name had already come up before I met you. There was some confusion about you which I think Dr Burckhardt might finally have resolved for me, but I should like to hear it from you too. He tells me you have a brother or a close relative with the same name as you.'

'I have a brother, Mr Churchill. We are twins, identical twins.' I briefly explained about the similarity of our initials.

'I see. Your brother is the one serving in the air force, I take it?'

'Yes, sir.'

'And he is the married one of you?'

'No, sir. I believe he is still single.'

'But then you are married. To a German?'

'My wife is a naturalized British citizen, Mr Churchill.' I added quickly, 'She came to England before the war began and we were married five years ago.'

Churchill nodded with some sympathy. 'I understand your concerns perhaps. There is no need for you to worry any longer about your wife's position. But let me say that I have been amused by the confusion your name was creating, because something of the sort once happened to me. When I was younger I discovered that there was another Winston Churchill loose in the world, this one an American. A novelist he was and rather a good one too. We were both writing books and before anyone realized what was happening we innocently caused a muddle. Ever since I have used the S for Spencer as a middle initial, but only on my books.'

He seemed to be in an expansive, talkative mood and in spite of his warning at dinner that he had to hurry back to London he did not appear to be in any great haste to leave me. Because of that, I raised the subject that was on my mind.

'Sir, do you suppose the Germans really intend to observe the peace?'

'I do, Mr Sawyer. As you know, most of the impetus for peace came first from their side. Hess clearly intended that he and I should fall into each other's arms like long-lost brothers. That is not my way in any event. Although I will parley with Nazis I do not expect to have to hug them afterwards.'

'He seemed furiously angry as he left.'

'Indeed he did. But if it is any consolation to you, I can tell you that the peace has already broken out. Because you have been here in Sweden, you will not know that on Saturday night London suffered the worst air raid of the war. Terrible damage was done and many people died. Since then, though, not a single German plane has crossed the Channel. We too launched massive air raids against Germany on the same night, but they were the last we will be flying. U-boat activity in the Atlantic has entirely ceased. The desert war has halted. Our navy is still on patrol, the air force is flying constantly and the army remains vigilant everywhere, but there hasn't been a single hostile incident from either side since Sunday afternoon. Because we have not yet had the opportunity to announce our armistice, the war will continue in theory for the time being, but in every practical way there has been a cease-fire for more than twenty-four hours.'

Mr Churchill swirled his brandy one more time and tipped the balloon against his lips.

'Then why did Hess act the way he did?' I said.

'I do not know. Maybe because I refused to shake his bloodstained hand.' Churchill made a chortling sound. 'I suspect darker deeds will soon be afoot, and his departure in that fashion was a little play-acting for our benefit. Most people are afraid of the Nazis, but I find them tiresome, as everyone else will too, once their threat to our safety has passed. This reminds me, though. Now that we have entered the post-war period you'll have to find a new job. I have one I can offer you. We are going to need an organizer with special skills to act on behalf of British interests in Berlin. It would be an administrative job, concerned with moving all those people to Madagascar. It'll be a huge responsibility, but Dr Burckhardt says that no less a man than you should be the one.'

I heard what he said with an extraordinary sense of déjà vu.

'I really don't know, sir,' I said, the arguments against such a move fresh in my mind. 'I would like to have time to think about it. There's my wife, and the upheaval —'

'The government can take care of problems like that. You would be attached to the Foreign Office, working from the British Embassy, but it would not be a diplomatic appointment. You'd be responsible directly to the prime minister's office.'

'To you, sir?' I said.

'To the office I presently hold. As you should remember, I shall not be holding the office much beyond the end of this week.' I felt myself starting to blush at my gaffe. Mr Churchill paid no heed. 'Of course you may have time to think about it. We won't need to make the appointment until next month and work will not have to start until August.'

Churchill stuck his cigar into his mouth and walked away from me.

23

Extract from Prime Ministerial broadcast, BBC Home Service, 6 p.m., Tuesday May 13, 1941. Full version in Hansard, May 13, 1941.

Mr Winston Churchill:
'This afternoon at two o'clock I had the honour and privilege of informing Parliament that the war between Britain and Germany is

at an end. I have just returned from Stockholm where I have signed a full armistice with the German government. There can be no greater or better news than word of peace. Everything for which we fought over the last year and a half has been achieved, in spite of terrible difficulties. Our country has endured the greatest onslaught of arms it has ever known. We have seen our cities burned, our cathedrals gutted, our homes shattered. We have lived of necessity in darkness, in fear, under the drone of enemy planes.

'For the last twelve months, after the fall of our allies in Europe, we in Great Britain, together with our friends from the Empire who came to our aid, have stood alone against the scourge of Hitlerism. We have not shrunk from the duty that history thrust upon us. It fell to us, to our generation of ordinary men and women, to resist the Nazis with unbending resolve. We did it because we had to. We did it without question, we did it bravely and with unrelenting vigour. We did it with thoughts of freedom, and hope, and a wish for a better world. We did it because there was no one else to do it.

'Herr Hitler and his legions have marched across Europe. They were a terrible enemy: harsh, ruthless, mightily armed and seemingly devoid of human feelings. But we finally stopped Hitler at the Channel coast of France. Last summer, thinking it was only a pause in his great progress, he went to France to see for himself. He stood on the Pas de Calais and looked across the narrow waters towards our white cliffs, so near and yet so far. He reached out for them, intending to take them. It was then that he found his match at last. The indomitable spirit of the English, the Welsh, the Scottish, rose up without question or pause for thought, prepared to lose everything, determined to lose nothing, ready for sacrifice, eager for victory. In truth, we had little more at first than a fist to shake at Hitler. The courage of the British race was never better shown, never admired more widely. Our finest hour followed, our most splendid year, our saving grace. Our tiny island, battered though it has become, bombarded though it was, and besieged as it has been, remained free. It is free now. And it will remain for ever free.

'Hitler's war has been fought in vain. He has not prevailed. We have not yielded to his threats, dodged his bombs or run away from his shells. We are still here, as united as ever in our resistance to him. Our reward is that an honourable peace has been achieved.

'We British are slow to anger, quick to forgive. We are cheerful, optimistic and generous, we love our homes and our families, we cherish our countryside. We are sometimes puzzling to our friends, eccentric even to each other. We are an island race who have taken our culture out to the world. But as Herr Hitler and his friends have discovered, we are also tough, brave and resourceful. We do not yield to threats. We do not panic. We do not give up. We cannot be bullied into submission. When knocked to the floor we spring back at once to our feet, our defiance redoubled, our anger the more keen, our determination to fight for what we believe in more deadly than before.

'A year ago I promised you that if we should come through this struggle, the life of the world would move into broad, sunlit uplands. That prospect is before us at last.

'We did not seek or want this war. We had nothing to gain for ourselves by fighting it. We had no territorial gains in mind. We did not even have a quarrel with the ordinary German people. We fought only for the principle of freedom. We were not prepared to be pushed around by the Nazis, and did not see why anyone else should be. So the moment did arise and we therefore braced ourselves to the necessary duty. We dared to resist, we dared to stand firm, we dared to fight to whatever end it would take. The sacrifice has been made and now it is at an end. We have come through the darkest hours this country has ever known, and we are the greater for it.

'I said as I began that there could be no better news than the news of peace. I have, though, one extra tiding for you, that I believe you will consider to be an improvement even on peace itself. Just before I went into the House this afternoon word came to me that there have been great and important and permanent changes inside Germany. In a sudden access of good sense, the German people have removed Adolf Hitler from office, and not a moment too soon. We do not yet know the fate of Herr Hitler, nor are we going to expend any energy in trying to find out. Good riddance, I say, and here I know I speak for us all. The man who has replaced him as German Chancellor, Rudolf Hess, is the co-signatory to the cease-fire we have arranged. We may safely assume that our peace accord remains in place. Herr Hess, in my experience, will not be any easier to deal with than his predecessor, but at least we shall not have to fight him.

'We therefore have a rare opportunity to celebrate our country's glory and for that reason I have declared tomorrow a public holiday. Tomorrow, celebrate with deserved and unashamed joy, in reward for what you have earned. Tonight, though, as a preliminary, we can turn our backs on the recent past with a simple gesture of freedom. Celebrate tonight by switching on the lights in your house and opening your curtains, throwing wide your windows. All danger is past. Let the world find out where we live, see us again for what we are.

'Long live the cause of freedom. Advance, Britannia! God save the King!'

24

Holograph notebooks of J. L. Sawyer

xxviii

Our negotiating team flew back to England the day after Churchill departed. After a long run across the lake, the great white seaplane lifted away from the smooth waters of Stora Värten. It climbed slowly in a wide, shallow turn above the trees of the countryside and the steep roofs of Stockholm. The mood of everyone in the cabin of the aircraft was one of great elation. None of us stayed in our seats for long during the flight, but for most of the time we clustered excitedly in the narrow spaces and aisle, talking eagerly about what we had achieved, how we had done it, what our hopes were for the bright future that we had helped create.

When the pilot announced some three hours later that the plane was flying along the British coast I moved to one of the seats next to a window, staring out with feelings of rejoicing at the green countryside, the line of white breakers, the smooth blue sea. We were somewhere above the Channel, following the English south coast, not high above the waves nor far from the land. I could see small seaside resorts, tall white cliffs, distant downs. On this day of bright sunshine the country looked remarkably whole from the plane, undamaged by the war. I knew that close up the reality was different, but from this passing eminence it was possible to glimpse England as she had been, as she would be again.

When we were not far from Southampton a flight of RAF Spitfires appeared from high in the blue, streaking down past us, cavorting and rolling, repeatedly circling us as we growled slowly along above the waves. They stayed with us all the way to the Solent, a joyful escort. As we were preparing to make our landing they moved away, formated in the distance into the shape of a long vee, then made one last pass above us, the roar of their engines clearly audible inside our cabin. Then they disappeared towards the land and our slow, cumbersome flying-boat made its crashing, bouncing arrival on the choppy surface of Southampton Water.

Half an hour later, as we stepped ashore from a naval launch, a small crowd applauded us politely. We went through the formalities of arrival in a slight daze, hardly daring to believe that the radical lifting of the mood of the country which we could already sense was real, permanent.

I craved to go home, to see Birgit, to be there with her in the last days before our baby was born, but the problems of travelling around in wartime Britain were not yet a thing of the past. The government had at short notice declared the day a public holiday — PE Day, Peace in Europe Day — and there were no trains, buses, or indeed any easy or affordable way of leaving Southampton until the next morning.

So there was one more night I had to spend away. The Red Cross found us rooms in a small hotel away from the town centre. The dock area and much of the business quarter of the city had been destroyed during the Blitz and choices were few. I decided to make the best of it. As soon as I had put my bag in my bedroom I went to find the others downstairs.

At the bottom of the main staircase I saw a tall figure standing by the window, staring out. He was in military uniform and was holding his cap beneath his left elbow. When he heard my footsteps on the stairs, he turned to look at me and quietly intercepted me as I went to pass him.

He said, 'Are you Mr Joseph Sawyer?'

'I am.' I felt the first tremor of concern.

'I'm Group Captain Piggott, sir, attached to 1 Group, Royal Air Force, in Lincolnshire. I'd like to speak to you privately. I hope it won't take more than a few moments.'

'It's Jack, isn't it?' I said at once, responding to the man's grave tone of voice. 'You've brought bad news about my brother.'

The officer indicated a door leading to a small lounge at one side. He held it open, so that I could walk through ahead of him. He closed the door behind us. Everything about his manner indicated that the news about to be broken to me was the worst.

'I'm afraid it is about your brother, sir.'

'Has he been killed?'

'No, I'm relieved to tell you that he has not. But he has been badly wounded.'

'How serious is it?'

'His wounds are extensive but his life is not thought to be in danger. I haven't seen him myself, but I was able to speak to the doctor in charge before I came here to contact you. Your brother is in hospital and he's under sedation. He's young and strong and they believe that in time he will make a full recovery.'

'Can you tell me how bad his injuries are?'

'I don't know the full details, Mr Sawyer, but I was told that among other injuries he has a fractured leg, cracked ribs, a blow to the skull, many cuts and bruises. He was injured when his plane was shot down. He spent about eighteen hours in an emergency dinghy before he was rescued. This is often the fate of our airmen. If we could only find them and transfer them to hospital before they are exposed to the elements for too long, they would be able to recover more quickly. However, we do what we can.'

'When did it happen?'

'His plane was shot down on Saturday night, early Sunday morning. Your brother had taken part in a successful raid against Hamburg when his Wellington was hit by flak. There was only one other survivor from his plane. The navigator, I believe.'

We stood there in silence for a little while, the air force man standing courteously beside me while I tried to take in the import of his news.

The last raid of the war, Churchill had told me. The last we will be flying, he had said.

xxix

From the time of my accident during the London Blitz, six months earlier, I

had not touched a drop of alcohol. There was a deliberate reason for it: I had
no idea what triggered my lucid imaginings but they often occurred when I was
drowsy or when my attention wandered. Some instinct told me that drinking
might increase the likelihood of an attack. It had been reasonably easy to stay
away from alcohol since then. At certain times — such as in Stockholm, when
many toasts to the peace treaty had been drunk in champagne — it was possible for me to find a non-alcoholic alternative without making a fuss about it.

But that first night of peace was a special one for everyone: Peace in
Europe Day, a time to let your hair down if ever there was one.

After Group Captain Piggott had taken his leave, I tried to decide
whether I should make a telephone call to my parents (who had no idea
where I was or what I had been doing for the last week) or give up my plans
for the evening and find some way to travel across the country to see JL in
hospital. I saw a public telephone booth in the lobby of the hotel, so I dialled
my parents' number. There was no answer. I assumed they must have gone to
visit Jack in hospital. I was lurking indecisively in the hallway next to the
reception area, wondering what to do next, when Mike Brennan, the Quaker
adviser from Pittsburgh, saw me. After that, there was no more doubt and no
more argument.

In the company of five other members of the Stockholm team, Mike and
I set out for a long evening's celebration on the town. We started in the pub
next to the hotel, then followed huge crowds of people as they began to con-
verge on the bomb-damaged city centre. The whole population, it seemed,
was out on a night of revelry like no other they had known for months or
years. At midnight we were in East Street, outside the looming, dark shape
of the art gallery, pressed in a shouting, waving, dancing, sweating crowd. A
church clock somewhere struck the hour; we cheered and yelled as lights
blazed from every building, the defensive searchlights came on for the last
time, criss-crossing the sky above us, and a final defiant cannonade of anti-
aircraft shells exploded in the air.

xxx

The next morning was predictably run through with remorse, a groaning discomfort and a renewed determination to get back on the wagon. Rather to
my amazement, I woke up in my own bed in the hotel, having found my way
back to it somehow, or having been taken to it.

I leaned over the tiny hand-basin set against one wall to rinse my hair with clean water, then towelled it dry. I washed my face and arms, dried myself briskly. I put on my clothes slowly and carefully.

By mid-morning I was aboard a train heading north out of Southampton, fragile but recovering. I was feeling mildly nauseated all morning, but by midday I was a little better. It was a long time since I had experienced a hangover. I felt detached from reality, wrapped in a shroud of numbed feelings. When I looked at some of the other passengers in the compartment with me, I knew I was not the only one. It had been a memorable evening, what I could remember of it.

The train arrived in Manchester in the late afternoon. I walked across the concourse of London Road Station to where the suburban trains terminated. I was extremely hungry, having skipped breakfast at the hotel and discovered that there was no food available on the train. The snack bar was closed. It was warm in the huge station concourse, the air rich with the steam and coal smell of trains. I had time to step outside to the station approach for a few minutes, breathing the cleaner air, but looking out across the desolate landscape of ruined and burned-out buildings.

Eventually, I caught a local train to Macclesfield.

xxxi

Now comes the final part of my story, almost impossible to write down.

I was in an unsteady emotional state, because of the heavy drinking of the night before, because of the long train journey, because of the lack of food, because of general exhaustion. Perhaps, most of all, because of the stupendous peace treaty that had been attained and the fact that I had played a part in it. I was not ready for what was to happen.

At first, however, I was reassured. Macclesfield's appearance remained much as I remembered it when I last saw it: no more bomb damage had occurred in the final few days of the war. A place of large factories and silk mills, overlooked by the wild hills of the Pennines, Macclesfield possessed that unique northern English feeling of industry and moorland, a town with a wide bright sky and narrow dark streets. Familiarity wrapped itself around me comfortingly.

I left the station, walked through the foot tunnel where I had been jostled one night, long ago, and emerged into the Silk Road. Immediately opposite was the long straight hill of Moor Road, climbing up towards Rainow.

I walked briskly up the slope, enjoying the sensation of putting my muscles to use once again. I began to make small plans for the future. I saw everything in positive terms of healing and recovery. My cares, my fear and hatred of the war, had slipped away with the coming of peace. The baby would be born soon, with all the unpredictable changes that he or she would bring to our daily lives. Birgit and I could have more children, move to a larger house. Jack would recover from his injuries, after which there was the hope of an eventual reconciliation with him. With the war out of the way I could seek a real job, perhaps even accept the proposition from Churchill for a government job in Berlin. Anything was possible again.

I came to the place in the road where I had a choice of ways. I could continue along the main road, climbing the hill, then turn off after about a quarter of a mile into the country road that led to the lane past our house — or I could cut across a couple of fields, saving a few minutes and part of the long climb. I remembered the last time I had walked across the fields: it was in one of my lucid imaginings, the first of them in fact. I paused there at the iron gate. The associations were still so strong. I dreaded repeating what had happened before. I went on up the road, seeking normality. This was the way I had always ridden my bicycle, during the time when I was working in Manchester. It was a stiff climb, but after the smoke-filled rooms and forced inactivity of the last few days, as well as the night of heavy drinking, I was sucking in the fresh air as if it was an elixir. I could feel my blood pumping through me, my senses opening out.

Soon I reached the top of the climb and was walking past the village houses of Rainow. I slowed my pace a little, because now that the road was shallowly slanting downhill there was no longer the need to push myself so hard. I glanced at each of the houses I passed, thinking that Rainow — which Birgit and I had originally discovered by chance — was in fact an attractive place to live. Every time I saw the expansive view across to the west I fell in love with the place again. Maybe we should wait for one of the larger houses to fall vacant, then try to buy it or rent it? Or again, because most of the disadvantages of our own house were to do with its leaks and draughts, and most of those were caused by the neglect of the landlord, maybe we could buy the house for ourselves? It was large enough, comfortable enough, or could easily be made to be.

Forming such harmless plans, I turned off the village road on to our lane, passing the house on the corner where Harry Gratton and his elderly mother lived. There was no sign of them there, although windows were open.

I came to Cliffe End, the familiar old house in which we had lived since we married, looking the same as always. I walked up the sloping path to the door, pressed my hand to it and found it closed. I fumbled for my keyring, then tried to get the key into the lock.

A new lock, shiny in the sunlight, forbade my key from entry. I tried the handle again, pushed against the door with my shoulder.

I hammered the flat of my hand on the door. I was trying not to think about why the lock had been changed, why I had to call for entry to my own home. I heard footsteps behind the door, a shape glimpsed through the frosted glass. The door was opened by Harry, looking round at me, blinking against the low evening sunlight. He looked grey and tired, unshaven, like someone who had not slept properly. As soon as he saw that it was me he held the door wide open, making a show of being welcoming, friendly. My house.

'What are you doing here?' I said churlishly.

'It's good to see you again, Joe,' he replied. 'Quite a surprise, I'd say, after your being away and that.'

'Where's Birgit?' I said, trying to push past him, because he was blocking the narrow hall. I threw my bag on the floor, where it knocked against our low table in the hallway, the one where I stacked up newspapers after I had read them. No newspapers were there now. The table tottered, moved along and its feet scraped across the bare floorboards.

'No need for that.'

'Get out of my way!' I shouted at him. 'I don't want you in my house all the time. Whenever I go away I always come back to find you round here, busying yourself with my wife!'

'Listen, Joe, you watch what you're saying to me!'

'Harry, what's going on?' It was Birgit's voice, sounding to me as if it came from the direction of the kitchen. I shouldered past him, collided with the side of the table I had dislodged, and staggered against the door post. The room was empty. I turned back, finding that Harry had moved behind me with his arms outstretched, as if to restrain me. I swung my arm against him, pushing him aside.

I heard Birgit's voice again, raised anxiously. This time it seemed to me to come from above, so I thrust myself past Harry, took the stairs two at a time and ran along the landing. She was not upstairs. I knew that I was not hearing, registering properly. There was a faint buzzing in my ears and I felt dizzy, unable to focus. I had gone too long without food and I was still tired after the excesses of the previous day.

Harry positioned himself halfway up the stairs, watching me. He had a fearful look on his face, as if he expected my next move to hurt him.

I said, 'Where's Birgit, Harry?'

'If you'd stop running around like that, you'd find her. We were in the living-room when you burst in.'

'Is she all right?' I began walking down the stairs. He retreated below me, taking the steps backwards.

'Birgit's fine. So is your baby boy. Where have you been? We've been trying to find you, but nobody knew where you were.'

'A boy? I have a baby boy?'

Harry was suddenly grinning. 'He's asleep at the moment. Come and see him.'

I hurried down the stairs, Harry stepping to one side to make room for me. I pushed open the door to our living-room. Birgit was standing, facing the door as I blundered in. I took in an impression of chaos, of a huge pile of clothes, an ironing board, Mrs Gratton standing at the board with the flat-iron in her hand, a scatter of knitted toys, small garments, squares of white cloth draped over the fireguard, a smell of boiled milk, steam, porridge, urine, talcum powder. In a wicker basket on a metal stand by the window, I could see the tiny shape of a baby.

'Joe, he's so beautiful!' Birgit was radiant — she looked plump and well, her cheeks were pink, her face was round, her dark hair glistened on her shoulders.

'Let me see him!' I went to the cot and leaned over it. I gently pulled back the light blanket that was shrouding his head. Down there was the tiny, screwed-up face of my new son, his lips compressed, his eyes tight shut, wrinkles of pink flesh. I knew I shouldn't wake him but I couldn't resist. I reached in, picked up the tiny body with both hands, cradled him as well as I could, touched back the folds of the blanket with my fingertips so that I could see his face.

He opened his eyes: a truculent frown, a myopic stare past me, a tiny wet mouth opening and closing. I put my face closer to his, trying to make him see me. I moved my head back to take a better look.

There, in his face, I saw myself, the resemblance, the knowledge of my family. All my own impressions and sensations of the day, everything that I had done and gone through in the past few hours, faded away. I felt something like a pause in the progress of the world beyond me, a halting. Silence briefly surrounded me and my son, emotions rising theatrically. There he was, alive in my arms, surprisingly solid and heavy. He had my father's colouring, my shape of head, a look in his eyes that I recognized as a family look which was detectable even through the corrugations of a baby frown in a loosely fleshed face.

I could see myself in his face, see Birgit's familiar looks, all indefinable yet exact. I could see me and therefore I could see my brother. Everything of my life was contained there in that tiny fragment of new life.

Birgit had moved so that she was standing beside me. She rested a hand on the arm that I was using to support the little boy's weight and I felt her squeeze my muscles.

'Joe, he's such a lovely baby!'

'What's his name? Have you named him yet?'

'I wanted to wait for you, but everyone has been pressing me to call him something.'

'I'd no idea he was coming now. I thought he wasn't due for another three weeks!' I stared down blissfully at my son, trying to think of a good name to call him.

'It happened at the weekend, while you were away,' Birgit said. 'It started on Saturday afternoon. He was early, but he's almost up to normal weight. He's going to be OK, Joe!'

We stood together, beaming down at the tiny child, waves of happiness radiating from us.

'We decided to call him after my dad, Joe.' I turned in surprise. It was Harry Gratton, standing behind me. I could feel his weight on my arm as he too leaned forward to peer down at the baby. 'His name is Stuart.'

'You named my baby?' I said incredulously. '*You* called him Stuart! How the hell —?'

'It was my decision, Joe,' Birgit said. 'My idea to call him Stuart. It is what I wanted also. Stuart is a good British name, I think.'

Beyond Mrs Gratton, who had paused in her ironing to watch me cuddle the baby, I saw a movement. A man had been sitting in the armchair behind her, facing away from me. He stood up now and turned towards me, smiling and beaming, joining in my difficult moment of paternity.

Happiness swung full circle to tragedy in that moment. It was Jack, standing there in his RAF uniform, standing in my house, already there with Birgit and the baby when I arrived. Jack, who I had been told was unconscious in hospital somewhere, Jack who haunted my lucid imaginings, who thrust me back to reality.

I stared at him in amazement, knowing that it could not be him. Not really.

I glanced once more at the little child, who looked so like me, so like Jack, but then I thrust him away.

Birgit took the baby from me, cradling her arm around him protectively, pressing him closely to her soft body. I was losing control as exhaustion and emotions overtook me at last. I moved back, one halting step, then another. My heel caught on something behind me and I tripped at once. I fell backwards, crashing to the floor, my arm colliding with the wicker cradle, pushing it to the side. I hit the back of my head hard on the floor and for a moment I thought I was going to lose consciousness.

The others rushed towards me, Birgit reaching me first, kneeling down with the baby clutched against her chest, a hand reaching out to me. Jack moved to stand behind her, over her, towering above me. They were both speaking but I was deaf to their words. I looked away from them both, up at the ceiling immediately above me. It was cream-painted, made of metal, held in place by a line of tiny painted-over rivets. The vehicle was lurching as we bumped along, but my legs and waist were held in place by straps. I was finding it difficult to breathe, as if other straps had been tightened across my chest. Panic rose in me. I could raise my upper body, twist to look around, but in the cold and dimly lit interior of the ambulance there was little to see.

On the stretcher shelf across from me was a young woman, sleeping. I remembered her name was Phyllida. Phyllida managed to look at ease in spite of the swaying of the vehicle, the endless racket from the engine and transmission. Her eyelids lay quietly at rest. Her lips were slightly parted and one of her arms dangled over the side. The stiff, utilitarian cut of her Red Cross jacket took on softer lines as she slept. Even as I was struggling for breath I was captivated by the unexpected intimacy of finding her there with me.

I gripped the side of the shelf as the ambulance ran across a pothole in the road's surface. The jolt expelled breath from me. I knew where I was, what had happened. Everything I feared about my lucid imaginings had come to be. Six months of my life had reversed, slipped away from me.

The vehicle rumbled on through the night. All that I thought I had gained and put solidly and unarguably behind me, the flying journeys abroad, the meetings in great houses, the deal between Hess and Churchill, the outbreak of a final peace, once again lay ahead in that delusional future.

All of it would be lost if I gave way at the end.

Yet also ahead of me lay that life which was obscurely rejecting me: my alienated brother, the marriage that was failing, the son who had been born and named in my absence, the intrusion of others, all of it the product of my own neglect.

I lay on my back, staring up at the neutral ceiling, watching helplessly as my vision slowly dimmed. Desperation for life rose in me. I wanted to hold on so that I could re-awake in that post-war world. I dared not lose what I had gained, whatever the personal price, but each breath was becoming harder to take in and use. Darkness spread within me, bringing a feeling of stillness, an end to turbulence, to the struggles. The close of my life, the loss of that peace.

Surely it had not all been an illusion, the noble peace we had struck, the separation of the two great countries away from the horrors of war?

The pitching motion of the ambulance stabilized, the harsh sound of the engine died away, the dim lights faded. I struggled against it for a while, but gradually a sense of calm began to flow meekly through me, offering me peace — not the kind I had always sought, but an alternative to it. I felt the encroachment of final darkness, its cold and endless embrace.

The terror of it made me resist, however, through that night.

I clung to my life, forcing myself to breathe evenly, without anxiety, watching Phyllida sleep and dreaming of waking to a better future.

Christopher Priest

Christopher Priest was born in Cheshire, England. He began writing soon after leaving school and has been a full-time freelance writer since 1968.

He has published eleven novels, three short story collections and a number of other books, including critical works, biographies, novelizations and children's non-fiction.

The Separation won both the Arthur C. Clarke Award and the BSFA Award. In 1996 Priest won the James Tait Black Memorial Prize for his novel *The Prestige*. He has been nominated four times for the Hugo award. He has won several awards abroad, including the Kurd Lasswitz Award (Germany), the Eurocon Award (Yugoslavia), the Ditmar Award (Australia), and Le Grand Prix de L'Imaginaire (France). In 2001 he was awarded the Prix Utopia (France) for lifetime achievement.

He has written drama for radio (BBC Radio 4) and television (Thames TV and HTV). Two of his novels are currently under contract for film adaptation.

As a journalist he has written features and reviews for *The Times*, *the Guardian*, *the Independent*, *the New Statesman*, *the Scotsman*, *the Washington Post* and many different magazines.

He is married to the writer Leigh Kennedy. They live in Hastings, England, with their twin children, Elizabeth and Simon.

Website:
www.christopher-priest.co.uk